- Ann[illegible] Book One

"An irresistible page turner. With a splash of international adventure and plenty of surprises, Stolen Obsession is an entertaining read and a great beginning to the Annalisse Series."
— Self-Publishing Review, ★★★★½

"…Bell delivers a great, slow-building romance, gently examining her characters' painful pasts."
— Kirkus Reviews

"The villains are devilishly evil and diabolical. A highly entertaining read." InD'tale Magazine Review

"…Bell makes your heart beat faster at the same time fall in-love with the two main characters. You will witness adventures of a lifetime but danger still follows them. Saving the love of his life and this guy will do everything. Prepare and the author will blow your mind." — Goodreads Review – 5 stars

"Marlene Bell creates a spine-chilling Annalisse Series debut steeped in mysticism and vengeance. The narrative combines vivid descriptions and misleading dialog that set the flow of Bell's fast-paced thriller. Plenty of twists, turns, red herrings, and chapter cliffhangers. An international tale of mystery steeped in ancient Middle Eastern charms."
— Amazon Review by A. Lock – 5 stars

"...Stolen Obsession is a beautifully written novel and hard to put down with a curse, antiquities, and murder. A mystery that will stay with you long after reading." —Goodreads 5 stars

"Numerous times Marlene M. Bell takes me to the brink of suspenseful tragedy, only to keep them safe and let me know there is more danger to come. She leads me to the edge of a cliff. I feel I'll fall off, but she yanks me back from the precipice saying...not yet... but soon." —Fundinmental Review

SPENT IDENTITY

A NOVEL BY

MARLENE M. BELL

This is a work of fiction. Names, characters, dialog, places, and incidents are products of the author's imagination. None of the events depicted in this book are real. Any similarities to actual events, locales or real persons, living or dead, are entirely coincidental and not intended by the author.

Cover design by Isabel Robalo – IsaDesign.net
Book design by Kevin G. Summers

ISBN: 978-0-9995394-2-2
ISBN: 978-0-9995394-3-9 (eBook)

For my sister Cheryl, with love

Walker Barn

"The decomposing corpse churned with insect larvae. Inspector Stewart calculated that in a few short hours, most of the girl's flesh would be eaten by—" He stumbled in the dirt; his nose buried deep inside the latest copy of *NZ Inspector*. The farm chores could wait. He had to know how the murder mystery ended. Leaning against a fence post, he thumbed to the last page and glanced down. A pink lump shaped like a horseshoe rested out of place near his wellie boots. "Gum, here?" Miss Walker hated chewing gum. He folded the detective magazine in half and shoved it in a back pocket. "That's not gum. What the…?"

A row of dirty teeth embedded the object.

In disbelief, he bent over and examined the dentures. Miss Walker had all her teeth. The real ones. "Whose are these?"

His eyes followed gouges in the dirt that led to the barn. He left the teeth behind for the moment and cautiously tread outside the marks. Something or someone had left the trail along the ground. He stopped midstride. Should he stay and investigate or warn his boss?

Check on Miss Walker.

He broke into a dead run for the farmhouse, but as he sped up near the barn, a piss-awful smell hosed him. Pulling out his magazine, he covered his nose and mouth. Decay thickened the hot air. He opened the barn doors, gasped, and dropped to his knees.

"Bugger! Miss Walker's horse is dead!" He checked the mare's stall, but she was inside, alive, with her ears pinned back. "If it's not Maggie, what—" He spun a quarter turn and stared at two human legs sticking out of the first stall.

CHAPTER ONE

Annalisse Drury's brownstone gave her claustrophobia—and Boris a bad case of hairballs. Manhattan living wasn't her thing anymore. The country was far safer for them anyway. She came to that conclusion by the time she'd accelerated her BMW toward the family farm in Goshen.

As she drove past stands of poplars alongside New York Highway 17, her thoughts took her deeper into the woods. A whitetail buck in his summertime rust coat darted out from a thicket of downed cedars. Annalisse swerved, giving the deer a chance to escape her grill. She slowed and recovered to the shade of shaggy maples, dirt raining on her new paint job.

Annalisse slammed the gearshift into park and leaned against the headrest, sweaty and agitated. She lowered the air conditioning and readjusted the rear-view mirror, checking for traffic, wishing she'd hit the pillow earlier the night before. Her brown hair stuck to her head like an ill-fitting cap, lifeless. Swollen lids shaped her green eyes into bloodshot pools of uncertainty. A telltale sign of crying herself to a fitful sleep.

Over her home.

Over pressures at work.

Over Alec Zavos.

In record time, Annalisse arrived in her aunt's driveway at Walker Farm, parked, then flexed tired muscles, setting aside her loneliness. She rolled down the window, releasing the stale air from her cramped quarters, and admired the farmhouse with its shed dormers and wraparound covered porch. The redwood swing Uncle Ted built for her aunt hung motionless in the overheated air. She and her aunt read historical novels there by the hour beneath hummingbird feeders with bright little birds buzzing about. Their favorite place to wait out a thundershower or enjoy a cool autumn day. As always, the memories of her uncle brought a tinge of sadness.

Country living held the promise of something better than skyscrapers and cold streets crowded with absentminded New Yorkers fascinated by their phones. The farm held her together. That, and Aunt Kate. This weekend would be an escape from Zombieland. With her aunt's help, by the time she headed back to the City tomorrow, her teetering doubts about Alec would be resolved.

Her aunt influenced every major decision Annalisse had made since she arrived on Walker Farm at age thirteen. Kate would know if she should give Alec the shove.

Annalisse lifted her nose to the south wind just as it brought over a smell of decay. That kind of odor always unnerved her.

She shook it off and tugged her overnight bag out of the car and down the gravel path, reflecting on her life-changing trip to Greece last October. The week across the ocean brought Annalisse closer to Alec's mom and gallery partner, Gen Zavos. Prior to the Zavos Art Gallery's grand opening, their relationship was cordial but not close.

The terrifying event on the Zavos yacht and its aftermath brought Annalisse into his small family and Alec into a future she wanted with him. The undeniable connection between them made it easy to ignore the rumors and the tabloids—his escapades, his women, and his lavish lifestyle. The guy in Greece was the man she'd fallen hard for. She knew the real Alec, now drifting from her, and she desperately missed him.

Near the porch steps she pivoted toward the largest barn for the source of the stench. Movement at the fence line caught her eye, possibly a summer calf on the neighbor's property—a rookie disaster to be sure. No self-respecting cattleman in upstate New York would calve in July with its bugs and humidity.

"May as well call the vultures with the breakfast bell," she grumbled. The scent of honeysuckle from pots on the porch quickly replaced her concern for something dead nearby.

Annalisse batted away a swirl of stock flies near the threshold, stomped dust from her boots, and opened the farmhouse door. The kitchen embraced Annalisse in bright yellow and a gingham-curtain hug. Country comfort missing from her Manhattan two-story brownstone. She found her aunt at the gas range, wearing her checked apron.

Kate hunched over the stove in a stony trance, mesmerized by the flames licking at the bottom of her cast-iron skillet.

"Mornin', lambie. Breakfast's started—didn't expect you this weekend." She turned the bacon, not bothering to address Annalisse with her eyes. "I made waffles. Take them. I'll make more."

Annalisse breathed in heaven and sunshine through the bacon pops and smoky aromas while she waited for Kate's usual cheerful banter.

"I left the City at seven. I should've called, but I had to get out of there. Have you seen Ethan today?" Annalisse dropped her suitcase by the door and gave her aunt a one-armed squeeze and a kiss on the cheek. A habit from living at Walker Farm as a teenager. Simpler times. A loving dose of reality Annalisse had longed for since moving to the Village.

"Ethan's long gone. He's out before dawn doin' chores."

Ethan Fawdray, fresh from New Zealand, had shown up on Kate's doorstep looking for work the week before Christmas like a gift, when Annalisse's desperation to find reliable, local ranch hands hadn't turned up any prospects. Since he'd arrived in this country without family, Annalisse watched over him like a big sister. Ethan's quirky, down-under speech and playful innocence lifted her spirits when she visited. Having Ethan help Kate with the livestock chores and tractor work put Annalisse's mind at ease.

Light speared the crisscrossed windowpanes, temporarily blinding her. She cupped a palm at the glare and studied Kate's movements and skin tone, wondering if her aunt had experienced another heart episode and was trying to hide it.

"Remember the time you left a raw pork roast in the car?" Annalisse pulled a chair at the family table and leaned around a vase of lilacs that propped an envelope. The return address belonged to a man she despised.

"Good heavens. Why bring that up?" Kate shoved bacon around the pan, the strips slapped mercilessly against the edges.

"The breeze outside. At first I thought something died."

"Probably an old coon. Caught one stealing the barn cat's food the other night. That pork shoulder scooted out of one of those slippery grocery bags. I always ask for paper, and that young man—"

"Auntie, you left meat in your SUV for two weeks. Totally wiped out the new-car smell. It took months for the stink to wear off." Annalisse tapped the table end. "I could've sworn I caught a whiff of decomp outside. Tons of flies attacked me at the door. Does Ethan have sheep in the big barn?"

"Maggie's in there." The metal spatula pinged in the spoon rest as Kate spun around. "I didn't leave it in the car. Moved through the meat aisle like a speed demon that day—in such a hurry I wasn't sure I'd even bought the damned roast. What difference does it make now?"

"Is the mare all right?"

“We found her lame yesterday in that darn rocky pasture. Ethan says it’s a stone bruise.” Her sharpness sliced like a razor blade. “If you’re implying the mare’s dead in her stall, forget it. She’s fine.”

Her aunt’s hostility felt wrong and out of character even for one of her worst bad days. She couldn’t explain Kate’s crankiness unless health was a factor, or maybe Ethan had given his notice, and they’d be on the hunt for more ranch help? Annalisse hoped neither were to blame. Kate graciously found strength after Uncle Ted’s suicide. Annalisse admired how she rose above her resentment at being abandoned on a big farm, earning the respect of the community.

At seventy, Kate had survived a second heart attack, but the event had sapped her strength. With the farm in Orange County, an hour and a half from Annalisse’s brownstone, Kate’s heart was a constant source of worry. Her cardiac doctor made her give up the heavy chores and look for a ranch manager or face another shot at the Reaper. Aunt Kate gave in when she found Ethan, someone she could trust.

The passing of time had tamped down the heartache of losing so many in Annalisse’s family but was also a wake-up call to cherish loved ones.

“Let me help you get breakfast together. Sit, and I’ll finish. I’m numb from sitting so long.” Annalisse stood and rubbed her denim butt cheek.

Kate lifted her palm. “Stay put.” She checked the ceiling, moving her lips in a silent prayer before stripping her apron and tossing it over the back of a chair. “Not myself today, and I’m taking it out on you.” Kate reached her gnarled fingers across the hardwood table and patted Annalisse's hand. "How's that handsome Alec? Catch me up on the juicy details. I could use a good thrill." Kate's overplayed smile deepened the crags at the corners of her mouth.

"Thrilling would be a fun change."

Annalisse hadn't spent an entire day with Alec in weeks. Her Mondays through Fridays at the gallery consisted of working alongside his mother, Gen, as her antiquities appraiser. Annalisse's work, although rewarding, played a poor second to hanging out with Alec at Brookehaven, his estate near the Catskill Mountains.

Before Alec, Annalisse appraised historical objects at her gallery with joy. Although every day was a new adventure to places she wanted to visit and cultures she found fascinating, Alec's estate, his racehorses, and compassion for animals triggered Annalisse's longing to be part of something bigger than artifacts and paintings.

To be with nature on a ranch.

A place like Walker Farm or Brookehaven.

"You have vacation coming soon, lambie. Don't tell me he's run off again."

"Since Greece, he's abroad three weeks a month. We're more like casual roomies than a couple. I see more of his horses. At this rate, Alec can forget being a practicing vet." Annalisse forced a laugh. "There are days when I ache to be near him and hear his laughter."

"What's stopping you?"

"His mother was spitting mad when he canceled our plans for next week. Gen closed Zavos Gallery for *us*. I wish I hadn't been there to see them argue. Ugly stuff." Annalisse met her aunt's obsidian stare. "Am I better off without him?" She picked at a worn spot on the table, fighting tears. "Alec has the entire corporation on his shoulders. With his dad gone, he can't let Gen down."

"What are you going to do about it? I see how Gen dotes on you like a daughter-in-law. Alec's existence is impressive, but is he the right one?" Kate tugged at the bobby pin securing her braid and snugly repositioned it. "You look like hell, by the way. How long since the two of you humped in the sack?"

Annalisse coughed on a gulp of too-hot coffee, burning the roof of her mouth. To Annalisse's recollection, the last time Alec had initiated sex or been an eager participant escaped memory. Was it four months? Five? Looking back, Alec might have been trying to tell her he wanted an open relationship. Annalisse had assumed they were exclusive.

She looked down into her cup so Kate couldn't read her eyes, but it was too late.

"It's worse than I thought." Kate huffed. "My girl, you're pushing thirty. A man who leaves his gorgeous girlfriend alone, waiting for a glimpse of him, doesn't deserve her. I had high hopes for you and Alec. Look at your ol' aunt. Don't wait around until my age. I'm way past catching the eye of a younger man." A sigh escaped her lips.

Annalisse withheld a knowing smile. On Sundays, she'd hang back and watch distinguished widowers from Kate's church, polished in their shiny ties and gelled hair, give her aunt the yearning once-over. When Kate took her hair out of braids, the silvery gray framed her cheekbones in the most attractive way.

The townspeople of Goshen had envied Kate and Ted's idyllic marriage. Behind closed doors, things weren't so perfect. When they were alone, the tension between them was a tightrope. The expert facade concealed the rift in their marriage.

Her uncle was the town's go-to masonry guy—everyone's friend—until he abandoned them six years ago. Had her uncle sought freedom or self-destruction when he jumped into the East River? Annalisse didn't have the answer, but Kate might know. Her aunt had mentioned a suicide note.

Annalisse poked at the unsealed letter and slid it over to Kate. "Your son mails from the office these days instead of phoning?" Jeremy Walker's attorney logo filled the upper quarter, matching his oversized ego perfectly.

Kate's earlier stone face returned, but she made no movement toward the envelope.

"Auntie? What is it?"

In one jerk, Kate swept the envelope to the floor. "The little bastard's selling the farm."

"What?" Jeremy may as well have reached into Annalisse's chest, wrenched her heart out, and mashed it in his fist. "In his dreams." The chair scraped as Annalisse stood, pointing to the letter. "May I?"

She pored over the text, her hand trembling. His words were clipped and formal, as if written to a new client. Jeremy intended to put his mother out and sell the homestead, including the acreage.

"It's not his to sell. Is it?" Annalisse verified the company header and Jeremy's unusual choice for ink—his signature penned in light green flourishes, the color of dollar bills.

"My kids couldn't give a rat's ass about this farm. Jillian in her fancy glass house in Seattle. Grandkids I don't see. Jeremy, so obsessed with making money he never broke a sweat on this place." Kate's wrist grazed her forehead. "You and me—we worked this farm. Lambed out the flock, worked the cattle on horseback, planted crops..." Her palm slammed the table with a crack. "Selfish little shit. Just like his dad."

Annalisse put the letter aside. The earlier thorn in her aunt's rear made sense now. She had to calm Kate before she had her third heart attack.

"Uncle Ted said he paid off the farm years ago. You're the deeded owner of Walker Farm. Jeremy can't sell it."

"I wanted the farm for you. We love this place the same."

Annalisse allowed Kate's words to sink in. She'd daydreamed about taking over the farm after her aunt. "Jeremy has no legal rights here. Even if he could, why do this to his own mother?"

"He has the right. When Ted died, I almost lost the farm. I quitclaimed it to Jeremy. He insisted. It was the only way he'd loan me the money. Wish I hadn't now, but it's done. Remember those two horrible drought years? When you went away to college? Crop failure put the farm into serious debt. I went through my savings for tractor payments, feed, fertilizer—you name it. Banks weren't making many farm loans after the crash. A single woman without a husband's support was shit out of luck, so I went to my kid to bail me out."

She and Kate had argued over admission to SUNY Community College versus a university. A commute from the farm to Middletown, twenty minutes away, was practical on many levels, but Kate had insisted Annalisse attend New York University for her art history degree. Walker money had covered four expensive years of NYU tuition. Money sacrificed when it was badly needed on the farm.

Annalisse crossed her arms, and her voice cracked. "I offered to use my inheritance to pay for college, but you wouldn't let me." She paced the linoleum, absently counting the squares. "I could've helped you."

"Don't be silly. That was *your* money left to you by your parents, God rest their souls." Kate eyed the ceiling and made the sign of the cross. "Consider it a rainy day fund for when you start a family. You'll need it, believe me."

Annalisse shook her head. "Starting a family feels light-years away. When my parents' house literally blew up, and I had nowhere to go, you and Unc took me in. I don't deserve your farm. I'm an orphaned brat who's burdened the Walker household for sixteen years."

"That's stupid talk! My sister's daughter belonged with us. We would've taken Ariel, too, if—" Kate choked on the words she was about to say. "I've never regretted it. Not one single day."

"Say that to Jeremy. He hates me. When I went from visiting cousin to permanent resident, he couldn't wait to leave home. I'm the reason he's turned on you." Standing behind her chair, Annalisse massaged the knots in Kate's shoulders to busy her hands. "It's time I repay a debt. I have a little set aside over and above the inheritance. Everything's yours. I don't know how much you owe, but we'll find a way to pay it and keep the farm. Jeremy can't take it from you."

She wrapped her aunt in an awkward embrace, catching the clean scent of Ivory soap. Annalisse couldn't recall a single moment she'd hugged her own mother in the same way that came so easy with Kate.

Small shudders swept through Kate's shoulders and skittered cold against Annalisse's skin, raising chill bumps.

Her aunt existed for the farm and its animals. She'd wither and die if she were forced to live in town. Kate had suffered while Annalisse partied it up at college, oblivious.

"Jeremy owns everything?" Annalisse asked.

Kate gently tugged Annalisse out from behind her and motioned to the ladder-back chair across the table. "Until I pay him back. All legal and tidy, you know. He promised I could stay here, dammit. Ted's gotta be shifting in his watery grave right about now. I'll talk it over with Jillian. She's gracing us with her presence this weekend."

"Jillian's here… in New York?"

"I doubt it's a social call," Kate said.

"We can fix this. You aren't leaving."

Family farms survive calamity all the time. They would too.

Kate leaned over to touch Annalisse's fingertips. "However this turns out, I want you to know—your being here was a blessing, not a hardship. Don't ever forget it. I love you like no one else can." Kate straightened for a moment. "Now's a good time to tell you something so you'll—"

A figure raced by the window and clomped onto the porch, rattling the boards.

"Miss Walker!" Ethan's voice and fist resonated off the screen door like a mallet pounding the house. "Are you inside?"

Kate darted for the door, slinging it open.

"What in hellfire's the matter?" Kate pulled him by the arm over the threshold. "Get your wits together and tell me what's wrong."

Gasping and wheezing, Ethan bent over at the waist, his spiked hair dripping with sweat onto a dirty T-shirt. His skin had a gray-green hue to it.

"I'm feeling crook." He crossed both hands over his stomach.

Annalisse brought a glass of water over to him. "Drink this. Slowly."

He threw the water back in a few swallows, wiped his mouth, and nodded his thanks.

"Tell us what this fuss is about." Kate folded her arms. "Calm yourself."

"You need to see the barn. At first, I thought he was pissed or buggered, but the pong—"

"English, Ethan. Catch your breath." Small cracks formed above Kate's upper lip as she spoke.

"Something's wrong with Maggie. I knew it." Annalisse's pulse ratcheted up along with her blood pressure.

Kate grabbed Ethan by the elbow. "Look at me. Tell us what happened."

He opened his eyes wide and stammered, "There's a… a dead bloke in the stall."

CHAPTER TWO

Split rail fencing whizzed past Annalisse in a blur. Hundreds of stained boards melted into each other in her sprint to catch up to Ethan. He ran yards ahead in the long breezeway leading from the house to the big barn. Kate was breathing heavily behind Annalisse.

Closer to the barn, the air was heavy with the undeniable odor of advanced decomposition, a ripe chemical cocktail so powerful she had to stop to cough and cover her nose.

Who died in the barn?

She stumbled in the dirt tracks left by farming equipment and twisted her ankle in a hole. Reaching for the nearest post, she held on, closing her eyes, unable to take another step.

Ethan trotted back to her. "Annalisse, did you hurt yourself?" His words heated her neck.

"Need a minute." Her forehead rested against the grooves where she welcomed the rough edges and oily scent of treated wood. "Sprinting on a cup of Kate's coffee wasn't too swift."

"Got a case of the colly-wobbles myself."

Ethan's tight-lipped smile offered little sympathy.

"Colly-wobbles?" Annalisse smiled back, guessing his slang meant he felt as horrible as she did.

Kate appeared behind her, out of breath. "No time to dally. Don't like tracing my steps twice. It's supposed to be over ninety today. That person isn't going to smell any fresher by noon. Step it up."

"Remember what the doc said. I don't keep the AED in the barn." Annalisse backed against the post, rubbing the soreness out of her ankle.

"I don't plan to use one, and the guy over there's too dead to need one." Kate pointed toward the barn, then she asked Ethan, "Anyone we know?"

"Shouldn't we call the coppers?" He lifted his phone from a pocket.

Just like Ethan—straight out of a *Dick Tracy* flick. Ethan's little house was a museum of action heroes and crusaders. Pristine comic books—American, Japanese, and nineteenth-century penny dreadfuls from the UK—were in clear protective sleeves on every tabletop and free counter space. The mark of a true collector.

When Ethan wasn't trimming feet, feeding the stock, or sitting on a tractor, he lounged on his futon with a detective thriller or mystery, keeping up with his book club's newest releases. Instead of typical items like canned goods and dishes, paperbacks lined his kitchen cabinets. Annalisse worried about his terrible eating habits and brought him meals. Especially on summer days when he sweated off his weight. He rarely accepted Kate's food because he found her cooking too rich.

The fact that they were on their way to view a corpse wouldn't faze Ethan or her aunt. People with livestock have a pragmatic attitude toward death. The countless lambing seasons where Kate lost ewes from uterine prolapses and multiple births put death on a list of the expected for Walker Farm. One winter, a pair of domestic dogs jumped into the pasture and slaughtered twenty-eight head of sheep in a matter of minutes—the loss of life in volume toughens a person's psyche. That 2:00 a.m. predator attack cemented how Annalisse dealt with the dying and dead. She frequently heard Kate explain it best: "When you have livestock, you have dead stock."

Kate reached out, her eyes mournful. "I haven't forgotten what you went through with the Freeman girl. A look-see and we skedaddle. I promise."

"Do you want me to call?" Ethan waggled his phone toward Kate.

"Not yet. We'll check it out first. I don't tolerate trespassers, especially those who drop dead on my property."

Annalisse's limited enthusiasm for an impromptu viewing had faded. She walked past the stall, barely acknowledging the pair of legs in the doorway. "We're contaminating a homicide or suicide scene. Aren't you worried about stepping on clues?"

"I didn't say we'd manhandle the guy. Stay there if you want." Kate shrugged and spun a one-eighty.

"Who's the Freeman girl?" Ethan arched his brows.

"Never mind, young man." Kate cut him off.

"Annalisse has a point—we should stay here. Our footprints in the dirt could implicate us."

Kate shrugged. "What's a few more? You work here, and I live here. We'll be careful."

Annalisse knew changing Kate's mind was an exercise in futility. A stranger had died on Kate's property. Auntie was damned sure going to find out who and why. But for Annalisse, the memory of finding Samantha Freeman's buried body last fall didn't help in the motivation department.

"No one touches him without gloves."

From the vet chest inside the barn's entry, Annalisse jiggled disposable obstetric gloves over her hands and arms to the shoulder. Gloves they used when a ewe or cow needed help during delivery. What they were doing was wrong on so many levels, but she never said no to Kate. She'd learned that from a young age. Annalisse intentionally turned her back on the pair of legs sticking out of the first stall, praying they'd miraculously disappear like they had for the Wicked Witch of the East in Munchkin land.

"Don't fuss with the gloves. Covering the hands is good enough." Kate erupted into a smoker's cough and staggered back. "His smell's about to knock me over. Did he crap his pants?"

"Maybe. Carbon dioxide from ruptured membranes—fluids leak from every opening."

Annalisse burped. Her mouth tasted like she'd fought the sheep for their cud and won. "Can't stay here long."

"It's called autolysis. I can take over if you want."

Ethan's statement rang with the authority of a bookish sleuth. As if he'd actually investigated crimes before, which, of course, he hadn't.

In the distance, a driver skidded its car's tires, raising the urgency of the task at hand. *Focus and move.* Annalisse jumped into the next stall covered in fresh pine shavings and grabbed a breath, then another. *Do this. It's not Sam.*

She joined Kate next to the open stall. The man was facedown and shoeless, in unmatched socks—athletic on one foot, a dark dress sock on the other. Both with holes in the material. He could've arrived at the farm alive—committed suicide or murdered or was dropped off after death with outside help. Common sense made the latter more likely from rigor's grip on the body and his wet clothes.

Annalisse knelt, grabbed an ankle with two fingers, and shook.

"Whew, ripe." She waved the air and held her nose with the clean glove. She glided a hand lightly along the slick fabric. The body looked frail, and his stained T-shirt and floral pants could've belonged to a woman. "Where are his shoes, and why is he soaked through?" Annalisse held up her palm smeared with moisture.

"Check pockets for ID." Kate gave Annalisse a gentle prod. "Hurry."

Instinct warned her to leave and let the authorities handle the corpse, but the tone in Kate's voice pushed Annalisse on. Careful not to rumple the fabric too much, she searched the man's torso.

"Something here." Annalisse hardly recognized her strained voice.

Behind her, Kate rolled the stall door wider. "Grab it."

Annalisse slid a glove inside the back pocket and came up with a billfold. Turning from the body, she flipped through the compartments of the chintzy wallet.

"No money or driver's license, just this." She extracted a damp, faded card and showed it to Kate.

Kate drew Annalisse's wrist closer. "City of New York. Thomas Taylor." She gasped and withdrew. "Thomas? God no! I need to see his face. Ethan, get a glove on and show me his face." Her chartreuse complexion left Annalisse with more questions.

"I'm already down here. Who's Thomas?"

Kate turned away speechless, making it impossible to read her.

A creep of unease gripped Annalisse's muscles. "Auntie?"

"Huh. I have an Uncle Tom Taylor, but he's a journo in Europe somewhere." Ethan tossed the remark out matter-of-factly, and Annalisse caught Kate passing him a dirty look.

"Annalisse, put that card back and stick it in his pocket like you found it. Get away. You're done with this unfortunate gentleman." Kate's sharp tone and movements loosened a wisp of hair from her bun. "We're wasting time. Glove up now, Ethan."

Annalisse mused how Kate had changed the body from an intruder into a gentleman. The dead man, *Thomas,* had triggered her sympathy or perhaps a happier memory. Kate drenched the name in intimacy. Annalisse sensed that her aunt had tucked away an earlier trauma much deeper than selling the farm or finding a body on the premises.

The formal letter from Jeremy nagged her. And in the mix, a dead man inside the barn—on the same day. Coincidence? Jeremy connived, but murder to prove a point wasn't his style. Subtle trickery was more like him. And anyway, he had the legal right to liquidate an asset instead of frighten his mother from the farm.

Struggling against her gag reflex, she returned the wallet and made room for Ethan.

He slowly lifted the corpse by the shoulder, turning it over so Kate could see his face.

The first signs of bloat disfigured the body but not enough to obscure his features. Annalisse didn't recognize him, but she couldn't be sure about her aunt. Thomas Taylor meant something to Kate.

Ethan bent over the man's neck. "Purplish lines. Maybe ligature strangulation. Check out his eyes. See those dots on the white part? Petechial hemorrhage. The bloke's been strangled all right." He exposed the dead man's gums. "Yeah. Missing teeth. I found dentures not far from the barn. They're probably his. Let's gap it."

A satisfied hum passed Kate's throat. "Agreed. Set him the way he was. Everyone out. Gloves off and in the garbage. We'll have to tell the police we touched the body; they'll find our gloves anyway. I'll mention the teeth you found. I'm calling them now. Meet me at the house."

Kate and Ethan left, and the barn fell silent. In fact, the only sounds inside since they'd arrived were human noises. Annalisse jogged near the end stall where pine shavings freshened the air, and she stripped the crackling gloves from her arms. She'd forgotten about Maggie.

"Maggie girl?" She peered into the dim stall for the old farm horse.

The buckskin mare moved deeper into the corner; her ears pinned back.

"Mag, don't worry. I know it smells bad in here."

The horse smelled death. Most animals shied from it, but predators were drawn to it. On kill days when the slaughter truck arrived, every sheep downwind moved to another part of the pasture. Blood and death couldn't be scoured from the traveling slaughter van, no matter the effort.

"You heard Miss Walker. Gap it." Ethan approached from out of nowhere and took her gloves. He placed them in an empty feed sack along with his own and shoved the bag down the side of the garbage barrel. "Come on." He gently nudged Annalisse's shoulder. "I'll move the mare when the bloke's gone."

When Annalisse walked outside the barn, humidity and heat waves clouded her vision. Down the long breezeway, Kate's silhouette stood alone, rigid as a granite statue and just as gray in the shade of the farmhouse roof. Annalisse could only imagine what memories stirred in her aunt's head. Seeing this man with a familiar name was an added thorn in an already bad day.

In less than twenty minutes, crunching road base heralded the arrival of multiple vehicles. Annalisse swallowed the nausea creeping northward from her gut. She quickened her pace and made it to Kate's side by the time the ambulance driver shut off the engine. A sheriff's white cruiser with a huge bumper guard rolled in and stopped in the shade of a cluster of birches.

"Where's the victim?" The driver stuck an arm outside the ambulance.

"You're too late to do anything now except cart him off." Kate shaded her eyes and pointed. "He's in the first stall on the left."

"Didn't take long for the turkey vultures to circle." Annalisse shuddered. Buzzards were nature's cruel joke for cleaning and renewal. But their hairless, wrinkled, prehistoric red heads tearing at roadkill were hard to watch in action. "I hope they bring the man out soon."

"Ethan will have to dig that stall out a foot. Death sticks to the ground for days." Kate glanced around. "Didn't see him go by. Where is he?"

Annoyed by the onslaught of officials, Annalisse wanted to blurt that it wasn't her turn to watch him but thought it best to keep the sass to a minimum. "We have to take the mare out of there. Ethan's getting another stall ready in the lower barn."

"Once everyone leaves, we'll be back to normal," Kate insisted.

Nothing was normal. Soon there may not be any stalls to clean if Jeremy got his way.

Following a flamboyant wave of arms to the ambulance driver, a uniformed cop with bottlebrush brows sprang to the farmhouse in Godzilla steps. He offered no smile as he flipped open a tiny notebook that almost disappeared in his pudgy hand. Pressed seams ran from the deputy's short-sleeved shirt and breast pockets and completed their journey down his brown slacks.

"Did you place the emergency call, miss?"

Annalisse checked the name tag above his badge. "Officer McDonaugh, that *person* in the barn has never been here before today—alive or otherwise."

"I called." Kate hit her with the "shut up" look. "My hired man found him."

"Alive or dead, Ms—"

"Walker. Katharine Walker. Annalisse, please find Ethan. I'll go to the barn with the deputy and tell him what we know."

"Ma'am, I'll take your statements here. The scene's off limits to everyone but investigators."

"Then let's go inside where it's cooler." Kate went up a step.

"Under the circumstances, we'll stay outside. I'm sorry for the inconvenience."

"Are detectives going to scavenge through the house too? Without a warrant? You've got to be kidding. It's hot out here, officer, and my aunt has health issues. At least let me bring a fan out for her."

Two more cream-colored sedans barreled down the drive, pulling in behind the patrol car.

"You may not have to wait long." He tilted his head. "Detectives. We're closing the scene at the roadway."

"I can't stay here." Kate turned to Annalisse, clasping her hands to control the noticeable shakes. "Would Alec mind if we spent the rest of the weekend at his place?"

"What about Jillian? Isn't she coming here?"

"Hell with Jillian. We'll leave her a note."

The stinging snub caught Annalisse off guard. She touched Kate's wrist to calm her. "Alec won't mind.

We'll bring Ethan with us. He can water everyone and let 'em out to pasture until tomorrow." She turned to the officer. "My… friend has an estate in Monticello—half an hour north in the next county. We'd like to stay there while you investigate."

The officer analyzed her with a creepy stare, moving his lips at odd angles. "Now I remember. You're that Drury girl with Alec Zavos."

"Have we met?"

His smile was a simple show of teeth. "Recognized you from the papers. The Zavos family, well… let's just say they're big news upstate. Tragic what happened to Pearce. He was a friend to the department." McDonaugh removed his hat and swiped at a trickle of sweat. "I don't see a problem with you folks staying at the Zavos place after statements. As long as you make yourselves available in case we have more questions. We need to talk to your hired man and anyone else who's had access to your farm recently."

Annalisse had plenty of questions of her own. On the ride to Brookehaven, she intended to ask Kate about the man named Thomas Taylor.

CHAPTER THREE

Barely two sentences were spoken between Annalisse and her aunt after the officer's interrogation. They showered and changed clothes to rid themselves of the dead-guy smell that clung to skin and fabric, and she rushed to pack a small bag for Kate.

Annalisse cringed when Kate asked her for the keys to the BMW and dropped her bottom into the driver's seat. Annalisse didn't have the heart or energy to argue over who'd drive to Alec's. Kate insisted she needed the highway practice and wanted to give her rheumatoid hands something to do.

Annalisse pitched forward against her seat belt for the umpteenth time, sloshing acid coffee dangerously close to the back of her throat. She'd flown forward and back so many times with Kate stabbing at the pedals, it felt more like a bad carnival ride.

A blunt sadness dumped on top of her coffee.

It was hard to get jazzed about going to Brookehaven when Alec wouldn't be there this weekend or next week. She could use some consoling—in light of her aunt's troubles, compounded by the scene they'd left behind.

At Rock Hill, Annalisse's thoughts darkened to match the low band of cumulus clouds hanging over Holiday Mountain slope. They'd passed through a stray shower with just enough water to spot their windows and further dirty Annalisse's new marina-blue paint job, but she didn't mind. She had a thing for the ozone smell of raindrops on hot pavement. The aroma signaled a cleansing and renewal and a way to take her mind from the sickening odor pasted inside her nostrils.

Annalisse was eager to ask Kate about the man in the barn but at the same time afraid of her answer. Eventually they'd find out who the mysterious man in the stall was. If she didn't press Kate too hard, she might learn something about this Thomas Taylor as well.

Kate remained quiet and broody, settled deep into the bucket seat. The same stone iciness of the morning stained her face as her eyes burned a hole in the spot where the dash met the windshield.

"I hated leaving Ethan to the wolf pack back there. Did you see how he looked at us when they asked him to go back to the station?" Annalisse asked.

"The dicks weren't happy with his answers. That kid thinks he's some kind of CSI guy. Volunteers too much information."

"Dicks?"

Kate side swatted Annalisse's leg without a glance her direction.

"Mind out of the gutter, lambie. I didn't mean that. Dicks—you know, detectives."

"Ethan's rubbed off on you. He spends too many paychecks on forensics books. We should have gone with him to the sheriff's office. You know he'll accidentally say something stupid and act guilty." Annalisse picked at a hangnail. "How's he getting home?"

"I told him to call if he needed to make bail," Kate replied with a hint of a smile.

Kate's half-assed joke didn't make Annalisse feel better.

"Take the next exit. Are you as hungry as I am? Helga isn't expecting anyone at the estate today. I hate to drop in for lunch." Annalisse rolled her window down and watched the pizza place whiz by, then the last deli disappeared, along with the exit. "I guess that's a no."

"How can you eat? Doesn't anything faze you?" Kate popped the steering wheel cover with a palm. "I'm not sure I'll be eating for a week," she huffed. "You and Ethan are a fine pair, I swear."

"We've seen worse, Auntie. What happened was horrible, but the dead guy's not our main problem. Losing the farm is."

Kate nodded. "You don't think Jeremy did that to that… person, do you?"

"Not his style."

Kate turned to gape at her. "As opposed to what?"

"He's a white-collar professional. You have written notice he intends to sell the farm. I can't see his motive for that man in the stall. He doesn't need your permission. Do *you* think your son's capable of murder?"

Kate shifted beneath her seat belt.

Annalisse studied her aunt's deadpan expression. "You do?"

"No. Don't put words in my mouth."

"Driveway's coming up." Annalisse pointed out her window, stabbing the air. "Slow down, you're going to miss it."

Kate applied the brakes in the same jerky motion she used on the gas pedal. "Know what? I'll drop myself off at the stables first." She looked in the rearview mirror and cut across the next lane.

"Not before you eat or drink something. I won't have you keel over."

"Tell Helga not to fuss. I need to be around the horses… to think. I'll grab a drink from Alec's little fridge."

Kate turned the BMW into the bricked drive in front of Alec's huge showplace horse barn with the silver horse jumping out of a big *B* on the header. Hardly a barn, but he liked to call it that. The magnificent thirty-stall breeding headquarters with office and tack area *and* an arena, all under one roof. The facility was opulent, full of hot-walkers, wash racks, birthing stalls, and the finest saddles money could buy. The dream to live with Alec and work beside him in his veterinary clinic had slipped from her grasp.

A flash of heat stung Annalisse's cheeks. The time when she and Alec "had to talk" was almost there, and she dreaded it. She closed her eyes, hoping to relax.

The BMW's engine shut off, and something rough lightly grazed her cheek. Annalisse knew Kate's callused hands, and she opened her eyes.

"Lambie, this has been a hard day for you. I'm sorry. Bet you wish you'd stayed in that comfortable little brownstone today, eh?"

Annalisse ran her tongue over the film on her teeth, tasting the bottom of an old pot of coffee. She unclicked her belt so she could face her aunt.

"Before you go for your walk, would you please be kind enough to tell me who *your* Thomas Taylor is?" Annalisse steadied her gaze, memorizing the solemn brown eyes staring back. "Or was? Don't deny you know that name."

Her aunt blew a haggard breath. "It's just someone I haven't thought of in a very long time. A story I'm not ready to tell yet." Kate patted Annalisse's thigh. "Don't worry. When I do, you'll be the first to hear it." She slid out of the driver's seat and closed the door, looking up as the first few drops of rain dotted the hood. "Looks like that ass soaker is here. You'd better get inside with Helga." Kate smiled. "Go on."

"How long are you going to be with the horses? The storm could be a bad one."

"I'll be in after a while."

"Say hi to Harriet for me. She's in the stall next to Kris."

Kate was almost to the barn when she turned to wave and yell over the breeze, "I know."

Annalisse watched her aunt's silvery braid disappear into the murky space of the long concrete breezeway. Kate hadn't bothered to turn on the bank lights inside. Knowing Kate, she wouldn't want to spook the horses.

Climbing over the console, Annalisse adjusted the car seat and clicked her seat belt. *Kate shouldn't be alone.* She unclicked the belt. Slowly she reached for the door handle. But sometimes she needed the quiet time to sort problems out and cool off ticklish situations. "What the heck." Annalisse cinched the belt again, then checked the rearview mirror.

Arguing with Kate was like arguing with a mountain. Neither would budge. But unlike the mountain, Kate got angry. Because Kate's last heart attack was due to stress, Annalisse thought better of confronting her. Something in her aunt's eyes gave their current situation an uncomfortable edge. She remembered the feeling. The same dread she had when Alec left the Turkish hotel to rescue his mother, telling her to stay behind. Then didn't come back.

***

Alec's house felt unusually damp and gloomy when Annalisse let herself in. A hint of cologne she'd given him for his birthday still lingered in the space, and her heart jumped a beat. She liked the sweet heat and cedar notes and the fact he'd changed his scent for her. For just a little while. Because the gift came from her, he'd said.

Rain spatters tapped the tall windows in earnest, and her thoughts went to Kate alone in the stables. Annalisse admired her aunt's sense of purpose, but she never got used to it. She gazed through the water-streaked windows beginning to fog from the temperature drop. She had a muddled view of the stable doorway, dark and empty. Annalisse stepped closer to the estate house's massive doors and considered again how mad Kate would get if pulled away before she was ready, then stifled a shiver.

The only sound in the room was the whoosh through the gutters and downspouts outdoors and the tink of metal contracting. Had Helga gone out? The house was unlocked, so she had to be nearby.

"Helga? Are you upstairs?"

Her question was met by heavy cracks and scrapes on the staircase reminiscent of a building collapse. Helga's wooden clogs accentuated the steps of a woman built like a Sumo wrestler.

"Child, did I forget you would be here?" Helga patted her tight bun. "The mind fades these days. Forgive me. Have you eaten?"

"Please don't go to trouble, unless you have easy… leftovers?"

Helga never threw out food and endlessly replaced the assortment of leftovers. Annalisse figured it was due to her upbringing and a grandmother who'd endured years of war where food was a luxury. Alec's housekeeper came from southeastern Germany near Austria in Bavaria. Her everyday cooking included traditional dumplings with tons of beets and potatoes in most of her dishes and Annalisse's favorite. Bratwursts. She could eat her weight in Helga's pork sausages with nutmeg and caraway. Although her food was heavy in starches, Helga's home-cooked meals were comforting and rich. Having her oversee the house for Alec was a blessing that his mother offered him when he bought the estate. Helga Rissman used to cook for the Zavos family on Crete, but Gen felt that a bachelor with a three-story Tudor mansion needed a full-time cook more than she and her husband did.

"My aunt is with me. We're here unannounced, so you haven't forgotten the visit." Annalisse headed to the kitchen. "We can help ourselves. I'll heat up something from your stash."

"My job. Schnitzel or meat loaf and potato salad? I should have enough for a couple of plates. Alec hardly touched his before his driver took him to the airport." Helga bustled past Annalisse, giving her shoulders a tweak and a rub as she rounded the counter. "Where's your aunt?" She glanced into the living room, out the kitchen window, and to the ceiling. "It's raining sheets. Is that hail?"

Pounding ice hit the tile roof, reminding Annalisse of muffled applause.

"Auntie's out with the horses."

"Horses? Now?"

"She's in the barn. Helps her de-stress. We've had one crappy morning. By the way, you should lock the front door when Alec's not home. Even with security outside, you never know."

Helga nodded. "I know. Don't tell Alec; he worries so. Forgot to do it when I went out for the paper. I just can't get used to locking doors. I told him I'd be careful, but I'm glad we have a guard."

"I won't mention it, but please, something as simple as a delivery can be deadly."

"Of course, you're right. I've tried to blot out that business about the brownies."

Bad business for everyone—before, during, and after their trip to Crete last fall. Poisoned brownies nearly took Helga and Boris, her rescue kitty, from them. She couldn't blame Helga for trying to forget the stomach pump ride to the hospital. Not a week passed where a reminder of Sam's death and the Zavos family ordeal didn't negatively affect Annalisse.

Helga pulled a few platters from the refrigerator shelves and set them on the granite in a clatter. "Did that man ever catch up with you?"

"What man?"

"Yesterday, I think. Friday, yes. A middle-aged fellow came to the door, asking for you."

"What did he say?"

"Nothing. When I told him you weren't here, he turned and left."

An uneasiness rolled over Annalisse. Few if anyone would come all the way to Alec's estate during the week to look for her. The public knew she and Alec were an item, but her friends would call or check the gallery or brownstone first. She bit her lower lip.

"Did he give a name?"

"He left in a hurry when I told him you weren't here. I've never seen him before, but he's a handsome man." Helga clicked her tongue—something she did when she wanted to underscore a statement.

"Gen could've sent him here for some kooky reason." Annalisse passed off the stranger as not worth worrying about. "That has to be it. She must have forgotten to tell me. He's probably a buyer who came by the gallery to buy one of the pieces, and Gen couldn't be bothered."

A two-hour drive from the City one way was a lame excuse even for her to believe. Annalisse traced her steps the previous day. She and Chase Miller, her longtime friend from NYU, closed the gallery yesterday once Gen had left them alone at lunchtime. Chase brought a pizza by the brownstone and stayed until around nine. No older man had contacted her.

"I wouldn't give it another thought." Helga sprayed a head of lettuce and pulled the leaves apart. "Who's in that white car?" She brushed at the blinds and leaned over the sink.

Annalisse joined her and looked out. She kept a breath in her lungs until she recognized Alec in business attire emerge from the driver's side. She wondered why he'd returned so soon and hadn't called the driver for his Bentley.

"It's Alec. He told me he'd be gone until the strike threat was over. There's no way he had enough time to get to the plant. Maybe they settled with the union, and he called his trip off."

Alec jogged to the house, splashing puddles beneath his Cucinelli moccasins with the tassels she'd poked fun at when he'd modeled them for her.

Helga elbowed Annalisse. "Hurry. Lock the door. We don't want him to find the door unlocked." Her cheeks plumped when she winked.

Annalisse sprang to the door and set the dead bolt.

Seconds later, Alec jiggled the knob, and his knuckle tapped the solid wood. "Forgot my key. Helga?"

Annalisse opened the door, and his eyes rounded in utter delight. When his killer smile appeared, she fought the urge to jump into his arms. Stoic and composed would better remind him that he'd abandoned her and the vacation.

"I missed your car out front." He tossed the umbrella on its side, shedding off the water, and dropped his briefcase on the doormat. Alec stretched out his arms, with the smoldering look of a man who'd been without a woman for much too long.

Unless Annalisse was imagining him through her eyes—hoping he'd missed her as badly as she'd missed him.

In one graceful movement, Alec stepped through the threshold and drove her against him, just like the early days when they couldn't keep their hands off each other. She'd forgotten how good his muscular thighs felt mashed into hers.

Alec explored her with clear gray eyes. "On such a lousy day too. Having you here is the best gift ever."

He glanced into the kitchen and wrinkled his nose. "Least I could do was bring you a present… like room freshener. Helga, what's that smell?"

"Must be a guilty conscience messing with you," Annalisse injected before Helga could respond.

He raised a brow. "Mine or yours?"

"Seriously? You forgot about our bed and breakfast trip?"

He pressed his lips to hers—a throbbing, toe-curling kiss. The kind she loved. When he tasted her with such abandon, it left her weak-kneed and deliriously hot. Alec drenched her in a sea of sweet cedar while he cradled her face delicately in his hands, sinking, searching her mouth deeper, and drawing her closer.

Annalisse floated outside herself but came back sharply when she realized Helga couldn't miss their steamy show. She was mad at Alec, after all. Sidestepping from him, she wiped the corner of her mouth, somewhat embarrassed.

"It's crazy outside. I've been driving in sunshine for hours, and a few miles down the road, Stormageddon dumped felines and canines and maybe even a few equines on me." Alec grinned, waiting for her reaction to his animal metaphors.

"Only a vet would use those terms. You must be starved. Helga's heating something for us."

"Not what I'm hungry for." His dimples accentuated his aristocratic jawline.

She pulled her hand from his. "What's happened? Where's this sexy Mr. Zavos been? I've given you up for lost."

"Helga, we'll take a rain check. We have a long overdue date."

He pulled Annalisse down the hall to the drawing room. The stretch of dark paneling opened into Alec's eighteenth-century world of ball-and-claw, Chippendale-footed legs, and Colonial-period mahogany with roughhewn wood on the ceiling. The huge room with the rock wall fireplace the length of it was her favorite part of the house. She could hole up forever in that beautiful room he'd designed for comfort and ambiance.

Once he'd pulled the french doors behind them, and they clicked shut, he guided Annalisse to the fainting couch.

Helga's giggles erupted from the kitchen.

"We shouldn't do that to her. Did you see Helga's mouth drop? We'll give that poor woman the vapors." Annalisse drawled out the last few words, fanning her cheeks, imitating a proper Southern lady. "It's great seeing you so… unscripted. How'd you get away from the union bosses?"

Alec slid his belt from the loops and slipped off his tie, liberating the first few buttons of his simple dress shirt. Tall, in white broadcloth and thigh-hugging slacks, he was one of those guys who made everything he wore look good.

She admired the brawny biceps and strong shoulders. Not surprising that he worked too much for an occasional workout, but the illusion remained in his thick, athletic neck and small waist.

He began unbuttoning at his collar, exposing a tiny bit of hair, then stopped and checked to make sure she was paying attention.

"Are you going to undress? Here? With Helga on the other side of that wall, painting pictures in her mind? This is so unlike you."

Alec leaned back on his loafers and continued to observe her without answering her. He dropped his gaze from her to the floor and kicked off his shoes.

"Sweetness, I'm such an idiot." A clap of thunder shook the room. "Chief Thundercloud agrees." He chuckled and sat on the edge of the couch, leaning over to take off her boots. When her feet were bare, he tickled the bottom of her foot.

Her legs jerked reflexively, and she sucked air between her teeth. "You know that drives me nuts." Annalisse reached out. "I like it. It's good to have you this close and happy for a change." Her hand dropped to bare skin, and she savored how it leaped under her fingers when she stroked his chest.

Alec towered from above, covering her with light kisses, tracing a line from the corner of her mouth and down her jaw, making her shiver with anticipation.

She moaned, holding him against her neck, arching into his caresses. "Alec, I've missed you." He responded by turning his attention to more sensitive areas, her skin tingling with each pass of his lips. She wriggled against his weight to allow the expanse of his body to mold into hers.

He tongued a patch of skin near the collar of her blouse, then abruptly pulled back.

"Do I taste that bad?"

He laughed. "Promise not to hit me. I don't know what shampoo you've changed over to, but your hair smells like Mom's leftover cioppino that sat out too long."

"Fish stew?" She pulled a lock of hair beneath her nose, and a pungent stench hit her nostrils. She'd taken a shower at the farm but hadn't washed her hair after finding the body. "It's not the shampoo." She scooted upright in the lounge. "I didn't think. Shoot." She wasn't in the mood to discuss what happened at the farm or any misgivings about their relationship. "What did you mean about being an idiot?" She switched the subject to give herself time to reorganize the dreaded "we have to talk" conversation weighing on everything else.

"I'm thinking about making a lifestyle change. I doubt Mom's gonna like it."

"You're scaring me. Isn't taking over for your dad lifestyle change enough?"

"On the road, it hit me. If Dad were alive, he'd rake me over a bonfire for what I've done to *us*. Mom used to warn him about long hours and missing family time until he finally got the picture. I'm falling into the same rut. I've got to let something go." He slid next to her on the silk fabric and propped himself on an elbow. "I hope you haven't made other plans. We're going to that bed-and-breakfast next week. I don't need to mess with Signorile's day-to-day stuff. I have good managers in Pennsylvania—and Italy. They can handle union issues." He held her hand and gave her a pleading look. "Have I lost you?"

Tears prickled at the heartfelt admission. Alec's veterinarian career had been on indefinite hiatus since Pearce's death. He wanted the family business to thrive and not disappoint Gen. The only way for that to happen was to shove his practice aside. The move had changed him.

And her.

"Is the part about leaving the car business to your managers your lifestyle change?"

"Not exactly."

Her heart deflated, but she couldn't bring herself to pry further. When he was ready to tell her, he would. Annalisse's throat tightened on the possibility the relationship was truly over. This could be Alec's way to lessen the blow.

"It's hard to be in a place when your heart lies somewhere else." She clarified herself in the steadiest voice she could muster. "I'd rather be with someone I love more than the job too."

"I'm surprised you've put up with me this long. Who do you love?" Alec asked bluntly.

She swept back his damp molasses-colored hair, admiring his thick waves. She chose her words cautiously. "I had made a decision—well, more like came to a conclusion. When you canceled our vacation, putting the union strike first… I thought you didn't care about us. If you didn't, how could I? If your lifestyle change doesn't include me, I understand." She tapped the end of his nose to keep it light, even though she was falling to pieces inside.

"Marry me."

Annalisse couldn't reply. Suspended in time, her pulse quickened. She must have imagined his words.

Alec's body went rigid next to hers. "I have lost you." He jerked upward.

As he turned, she caught him by the arm. "That's not it…"

The Louis XVI clock on the mantle chimed twice. Aunt Kate had dropped herself at the barn about an hour ago.

"Then what is it?"

"Is it two o'clock? Kate should be in by now. I left her—"

"She's here? Where? Taking a nap?" Alec's voice was sharp, no doubt because she'd dismissed his marriage proposal, but she couldn't help herself.

Annalisse pointed toward the stables. "Horses."

"In this storm?" His fingers flew over the shirt buttons. "How could you let her stay out there?"

"She insisted, and it wasn't raining then." Annalisse reached for her boots and slid one foot inside. A hot flush crept up her throat. "Don't blame this on me. You know how stubborn Auntie gets. She goes to the animals when something bothers her, just like I do. We've had an awful scare. Two, actually." She yanked on her second boot. "You weren't the only one with stuff going on today."

His mini tantrum and all that went with it would have to wait. Annalisse replayed their past few moments on the lounge in case she'd missed a gesture—any signal from him that a proposal was imminent. She wondered how long he'd thought about proposing or if he'd thrown the words out there as a test for broader discussion.

As soon as they could spare some private time together, she'd get Alec to open up and tell her his plans. How did he come up with marriage, today of all days? She wasn't ready to marry anyone.

"I'll fill you in on what happened at the farm while you change." She caught up to him at the doors.

As fast as humanly possible, Annalisse recited the day's events to Alec on the way to the master suite. He changed and slid his Glock beneath his belt and offered her one of his jackets.

"Too bad I forgot my wellies." Ethan's term for rain boots slipped out of her mouth. She fidgeted with a zipper tab, wanting to kick herself.

Maybe Alec wouldn't notice.

"Really?" The word flattened against the bedroom walls.

He'd noticed.

She'd manage fine with her leather boots.

They stopped at the door to gauge the storm's intensity. A mix of broken sunshine and white thunderheads drifted over the mountain range. The worst of the storm had passed, and Aunt Kate was indoors, after all.

CHAPTER FOUR

Annalisse tightened her grip on Alec's hand when they found the slider door closed at the barn entrance. She was sure the door was open when she drove the BMW across the street. Maybe Kate had closed it to keep the wind and rain out. Talking herself out of being worried, she shuddered as the door squeaked its way along the rails. The noise always grated on her nerves.

"Kate?" Alec called out into the dead air.

Annalisse hurried past him. "Auntie!" she yelled. "Alec, check the office and tack rooms. I'll peek inside the arena." The barn was eerily quiet. Too quiet. She pushed dread aside, along with the dull headache behind her eye sockets.

"No." He snatched her hand back and pulled her next to him. The look that passed over his face was one of deep concern. "We stay together. Walk with me."

She hated to admit her stubborn streak was similar to Kate's. Alec could attest to that. She'd left their Turkish hotel on her own to save his mother from the Russian mafia after she was told to stay put. Almost twenty years living with and around her aunt had made Annalisse more independent and less afraid in dangerous situations. It was hard to know if that was a good trait to have.

Not a single horse snickered or whinnied, and the barn's air hung heavily in clean bedding. Annalisse's blouse stuck to her arms underneath the jacket from fear or mugginess, or both. Alec must have moved the mares into the lower barns or pastures. She glanced into Kristol Magic's and Harriet's vacant stalls.

"Harriet's running with the mares? Are any of the thoroughbreds here?"

Alec shook his head. "If Kate planned to spend time with the horses, she won't find 'em here."

"Damn. I should've taken her to the house." The flutter of regret couldn't rewrite what Annalisse had done. "Is it hot in here?"

She shucked her jacket and whispered under her breath, "Aunt Kate, why didn't you come back to the house?" She ran to the end of the aisle where brick and concrete stopped and arena started, searching for her.

"Slow down, art lady." He stopped her from going deeper into the covered arena that was groomed and perfect, without a single shoe or hoof print marring the soil.

"She must have walked down to the broodmare barns. Where else would she be? In that soaking rain, she wouldn't stand at the fences." Annalisse wrapped an arm around Alec's waist. "It's logical she'd go to the horses."

"Hard to believe she'd walk there in that muck. Let's go back and get the ATV."

"Isn't your breeder manager working today?" Annalisse planted her feet on the bricks. "Can't you call him to check down there?"

"I told him to take the weekend off."

"You go. I'll stay here in case Aunt Kate shows up."

"We go together. We've checked this building already. She's not here."

Annalisse stomped her boot, feeling like a spoiled little kid. "I'm not moving from here. I dropped her here. I'm staying here." She folded her arms and glared at him.

Alec softened. "Fine. Here." He reached around and extracted his pistol, handing it to her. "Don't give me that look. Take it. You don't have your phone on you, and neither do I. One of us needs a cell phone with our contacts. Promise me you'll stay in the office." He showed her again how to use the Glock. "If Kate returns—keep her here."

The hair stood up on the nape of her neck. Alec was being dramatic. After all, they were alone in the barn. Why would they need a gun out here?

"I'm not taking your gun, Alec. When you come back, bring my purse, then we'll both have a weapon."

He had cleared the end of the barn before she'd finished her sentence.

"Stay in my office," he hollered over his shoulder in the strengthening wind.

"Great. Just great."

Annalisse slid the Glock into the jacket she carried and wandered the length of the barn, taking more time inside each stall. Heaven forbid, Kate had collapsed in one of them. She found nothing but fresh shavings and a halter left behind by someone too hasty or lazy to put it back with the rest. She checked the office in case Alec returned and found she hadn't listened to his instructions again.

The heat inside his sanctuary was stifling. Laying the jacket over the chair back, she fluffed her blouse, sending air between skin and sticky polyester. She plopped down in the chair, skidding backward on the plastic desk mat. Her stomach roiled with acid, which hardly helped her headache.

The refrigerator was fully stocked with water, and she helped herself to a bottle, spending a few extra moments in front of the open fridge door. The cold air recharged her. Annalisse helped herself to ibuprofen from Alec's desk drawer and sat down again, spinning a three-sixty in her chair. She admired the tall crystal trophies with golden horses frozen in time. Multicolored rosettes scattered about attested to Brookehaven's successes on the racetrack. Glass cases with Alec's achievements in the world of horseracing lined two walls. He'd surrounded himself with the things that were important to him, but not a single tchotchke or photograph of his dad, his stock car days, or the sports cars that kept Alec on corporate planes so much.

Memories of Alec's statesmanlike father, a charismatic man she'd met briefly in Greece, were still too painful for everyone who'd lived through the attack on the *Gen Amore*. Time couldn't wipe away those hateful men and the devastation they'd caused to the Zavos family on the Aegean Sea.

Annalisse's first time in the ocean on the most beautiful yacht—Gen, forced to witness her husband's murder, and Alec mercifully knocked out where he'd missed the gruesome display. Annalisse had seen it all, and she wished she hadn't. There were disturbing details of Pearce's battle with the mafia that she still kept from Alec to this day. She hoped by keeping them tucked away, the images would eventually fade from her nightmares.

At least being with Aunt Kate on the farm had spared Annalisse the firsthand knowledge of her own family's final moments. Kate had saved Annalisse from her parents' and sister's fate, albeit by accident.

Annalisse's heart warmed at the framed picture on the corner of the desk. She and Alec riding Kristol Magic and Harriet through Mimosa trees blooming in pink splendor. Annalisse smiled, remembering Gen directing them that day like a Broadway production to get the perfect shot. Gen was just as meticulous about the artistry she kept in her gallery. A trait she'd passed on to Alec. Another thing about him Annalisse loved.

"He's proposed just now. Why?" she asked the empty room. If she married him, how long before Alec's duty to family left her alone and unfulfilled? What would change? Annalisse doubted he'd leave Signorile to the managers because he felt a strong sense of responsibility, even though she'd selfishly wished she could have Alec all to herself. She and Alec were at cross-purposes with obligation and happiness.

Thoughts of Kate brought her back. "Auntie, you'd better have a good excuse for worrying us." She searched the walls and desktop for a clock. The one on the desk had stopped at ten o'clock at some point. She checked her wrist out of habit, having forgotten her watch when she left the brownstone—on a day she could sure use one.

Stepping into the breezeway, she picked up the loose halter she'd laid on the floor and headed to the tack room. Annalisse hung the halter on a hook in the dark room, enjoying the mixture of horsehide and leather treatment in the air. Alec would smell great in that scent, she decided, and flipped on the light switch. A rough, handmade table made of burled wood butted against one corner, with two small chairs tossed unnaturally on their sides. The sight stopped her midstep. Alec was too much the neat freak to leave a room flipped upside down.

She thought maybe the grooms were messing around inside and left the halter behind. She picked up the chairs and stood them near the wall when it struck her. Kate might have come here out of the rain.

Only one item lay on the table. A black ballpoint pen. She picked it up and searched furniture for signs her aunt had been there. Annalisse closed her eyes, forcing herself to relax. The room was rocking, playing tricks on her vision. Her fingers strayed over the length of the ballpoint from sharp end to flat top. Everyday ballpoints were lightweight plastic, but this one had weight and a militaristic look and feel to it.

The pen's gun maker's logo sparked a memory.

"You were here, weren't you?" She studied the pen and checked the table for a note, wondering why Kate would take out her self-defense pen. Annalisse dropped it on the table and frantically shoved saddles from their racks and stands, checking every niche a person could hide.

Aunt Kate never used the tactical pen for writing. She'd promised Annalisse to keep it with her all the time. The steel tip was hard enough to use as a weapon, but its appearance was innocent to an attacker.

Annalisse couldn't recall if her aunt had a purse or fanny pack when she left the car. The pen could easily fit into either. She ran from the room toward the arena, yelling Kate's name until her throat was raw. Finally, she leaned against a stall and gave in to the tears she'd held back.

Kate must have fought off an assailant. Why else would she have taken out the pen? What jerk would mess with a frail old woman? No one knew she and Kate were on their way to Brookehaven, other than a few law enforcement officers and Ethan.

Jogging to the barn entrance for some sign of Alec, she mulled over the day's events for answers, all the way to leaving her brownstone that morning.

She came to the same conclusion each time. Jeremy.

"So help me, asshole, if you've hurt her...," Annalisse muttered, clenching her fist. But Kate's son at Alec's made no sense. She shook her head, sure that even Jeremy wasn't stupid enough to pull off a stunt like kidnapping his own mother. Annalisse was too close to the situation and not thinking clearly. He couldn't be behind this.

Annalisse paced the curved drive at the stable, deciding whether to find Alec on foot or wait for him in the unbearable humidity. She walked beyond the building and scanned the acres of vinyl fences and pastures. Nothing moved out there. Down deep, she believed

Kate was no longer on the estate, but only Alec could confirm that. She unbuttoned her blouse halfway and tugged it away from her wet skin. A ghostly gray had moved in from the west; distant rumbles pounded a steady drumbeat of more storms to come.

"C'mon Alec, while it's dry. I hate this waiting." She hugged herself against a sudden gust that made her shiver in the muggy air. "Where could she be?"

As long as there was the tiniest smidgeon of hope, she wouldn't give in to the scenario that played out in her mind. Surely Alec had found Kate at the other barns and had her with him in the ATV.

Her heels were sore from the jarring they took inside her boots. She wandered back inside, shoulders slouched, headache chipping away at what strength she had left. A dull engine noise hummed from behind the arena.

"Please be with Alec," she said, darting outside.

Alec's four-wheeler zigzagged down the path, slinging mud and puddles beneath the tires. Annalisse strained to glimpse a passenger. He was alone and in a hurry.

The lump grew in her throat.

Annalisse grabbed the nearest post to steady her shaky legs, allowing the slick metal to bear most of her weight.

Alec parked alongside the building and hopped out into the mud. "Annalisse, are you all right?" His boots slurped in the muck.

He couldn't meet her gaze. His use of her given name told her everything.

"Any sign of her?" Her voice cracked.

Alec gently pried her from the post, supporting her with a strong arm around her waist. Ignoring her was answer enough.

"The storm washed away all signs of footprints or tire tracks." Alec's sorrowful eyes met hers. "Just because she's not here, doesn't mean we won't find her."

"We have to find her. She's all I have." Her arms encircled his neck, clinging to him while wracked with sobs. "I don't want to be here… without her." Tears stung her cheeks, and she pulled back, mad at herself for losing it in front of him. Crying showed weakness. Her aunt taught her that a lady couldn't afford to show anything but strength. "What I found inside…" Her sentence trailed off into another round of weeping.

"Tell me."

Relaying her suspicions and what she'd found in the tack room, Annalisse fell again into Alec's arms. She would bask in his comfort for as long as he allowed. She felt less afraid, drawing strength in good times as well as their worst disasters. Alec eased her anxiety almost as much as sitting in a pen of lambs at Walker Farm. Her jaw clenched, and sorrow overwhelmed her picture of the lambs. How could she allow the farm to be sold? If something happened to her aunt, what would the future look like?

Annalisse kissed Alec's neck, sniffed, then stepped back. "I thank heaven for you. What's with the bucket on the seat?"

"Your purse is on the floorboard. Let me get your pistol and phone."

He turned, but she caught his wrist.

"And your Glock's in the office. That's not what I asked."

"Let's go inside." Alec picked up the feed bucket in one hand and her leather tote in the other. "Rain's back. We'd better move fast." He glanced upward as thunder echoed much closer than before.

"Why leave the ATV behind?"

"I've left enough tire trenches. A little rain won't hurt ol' Betsy. Bill needs to do the rest."

"Who's Bill?" Annalisse asked, having a hard time staying in step with Alec.

Inside the office, Alec drew up the leather accent chair, placing the green bucket near his feet.

Annalisse took the guest chair with one eye on the container. "What did you find at the other barns? Shouldn't we keep looking for Kate?"

"I've called my PI friend, Bill Drake. He owes me a favor. I know he'll help us even if he's busy."

She processed his lack of information, expecting more details.

"Why do I feel you're talking past me?" she asked. "Who is he, and how can he help?"

Alec raised his hand. "Okay. This won't be easy to hear. If you're sure you're ready." He hung his head and muttered something inaudible.

"Let's have it." Gooseflesh crawled over her arms. Alec rarely used that voice with her. She dropped slowly into the seat, clasped her hands, and fixated on the crown of his head. "Go ahead." A white flash and a loud crack filled the office, and she flinched. "That was close. We're in for a gully washer."

“Considering your day at the farm and Kate’s disappearance, I called Drake while I was at the lower barns. I found this.” Alec lifted the bucket and tipped it so the bottom was visible.

Annalisse found nothing unusual about a needle and syringe near a barn. Alec was a vet, after all.

“The needle probably fell out of a garbage bin. Call your manager. I’ll bet he knows where it came from,” she said.

“This is a thirty-gauge needle. See the yellow hub?” He tipped the bucket again. “Horse hide is thick. Eighteen or twenty gauge is what we typically use on the horses. This needle is too small and thin.”

“Don’t you ever use that size needle?” Annalisse shifted uncomfortably in her chair.

“It’s the kind for heroin addicts. Small needles work well in the vein.” Alec set the pail aside and scooted his chair to the front of the desk. “Here’s the tough part. I’m asking Bill to take the syringe down to a lab and test it for substances. I was careful not to handle it directly. I think it might have been thrown there since it was just a toss away from the horse path.”

Annalisse sat in a stupor. “What’s heroin got to do with Kate’s disappearance? So some rider on a horse tossed it?”

Alec cleared his throat. “We can’t turn in your aunt as a missing person yet. It’s only been a couple of hours. That’s where Bill comes in. You and I know this situation is all wrong. Kate should be here, but she’s not. I used heroin as an example of the kind of drug that could be used in a syringe with that fine a needle. The larger the gauge number the smaller the needle.”

"Yeah, I know. Finish your thought."

"I think... Kate might have been drugged. Until we know what's in that syringe, we can't be sure. I have lots of meds on the premises, but everything is locked. I've checked, and my vet truck is still secure. No one has tampered with the truck."

Alec's ideas were entirely possible, but the question of why still lingered.

"How soon will your friend get here?"

"He's working in Connecticut, but he told me he'll be here first thing tomorrow. He's driving down."

"Did you check with your security guy monitoring Brookehaven? Maybe he saw something."

Alec shook his head. "No dice. According to him, he saw when you pulled up in the BMW and watched Kate get out but never saw her again once she went into the barn. Nothing suspicious when he made his rounds, but he admitted he didn't notice much in the heavy rain."

"Then we have nothing. Dammit." Annalisse sighed, picturing the tack room and pen on the table. "If Kate was nabbed in the tack area, how does the syringe between barns fit into this? She would've been going to or coming back from the horse barns if that were the case."

"Your aunt wouldn't go willingly. She'd fight. We don't know if she was taken by one or more people, but I doubt she left the ranch alone."

"You're saying she was dragged down the breezeway, outside the front of the barn, and around the side to the path? Security would've seen that," she added.

"The tack room has an exterior door. Kate could've been surprised by someone coming in from the outside. This person might have pretended to be a groom or groundskeeper. No reason for her to be alarmed."

"True."

"If she fought back with the tactical pen, the kidnapper could've stripped it from her. When she resisted, he drugged her and tossed the syringe later. I'll run the theory past Bill." Alec pointed to the bucket. "I need to know what residue is in that syringe."

Her aunt's medications mixed with other drugs might trigger another heart attack. If Alec's premise was correct, Annalisse would never forgive herself for leaving Kate alone. But someone waiting at Brookehaven didn't seem right, unless it was the older man who'd asked Helga about her at the estate. Perhaps Kate wasn't the target, but *she* was? Was it possible for a kidnapper to watch and wait at Walker Farm for her or Kate to leave?

"Alec, some old guy came to your house yesterday asking for me. Any idea who it was?"

He gave her a blank look. "Did you tell anyone you were coming here this weekend?"

"I called Chase this morning to check on Boris overnight while I went to Kate's for the weekend. You were supposed to be out of town, and I don't like to bother Helga when you're gone. No one knew I'd end up here, not even Chase." She drew a cat face on the blotter and doodled in whiskers. "I should call him. I doubt that we'll be doing anything remotely like a vacation next week, but I'd like Chase and Boris here. Do you mind if he hangs out at the estate and brings my cat? He could be a huge help to us."

Alec nodded. "Good idea. Do you think you could've been the target?"

"Maybe. But that corpse lying in Kate's barn makes me think otherwise. The way Auntie reacted to his ID card, I sense he was placed there to spook her." Annalisse shuddered at the recollection of the man's body. "You coming home and us being at your estate was organic—" Her phone muffled a tone inside her purse.

Swiping the screen, she groaned and turned it around for Alec to read the name before answering.

"Ethan, hey."

"Where's Miss Walker? She's not answering her phone. I need a ride to the farm."

"Are you still at the sheriff's office?"

"Yeah."

She nodded at Alec. "We… uh… have a situation."

"She told me to call. She there?"

"Hang tight. I'll call right back. Promise."

Annalisse ended the call and dropped her phone on the desk. "Now what? He needs a ride. How can I leave?"

"Tell him to call somebody else." Alec's voice had a hard edge.

"Who? Ethan doesn't know many people. Doubtful he has the money to call a cab. I told Kate we'd bring him to Brookehaven when he was done with detectives. The farm is taped off at the road. We figured with you away we could get our bearings here."

Alec swept his hair and added, “Bill may show up early.”

“Stay here. I’ll get Ethan.”

“I don’t like the way he looks at you.”

Annalisse smiled. “Your green horns are showing.” She reached over and pinched his arm playfully. “He’s as harmless as my own brother if I had one. Until Bill arrives, playing taxi driver will give me something else to do and give me a chance to ask Ethan my own set of questions.”

Her phone played a Mancini orchestra ringtone, and Kate’s name popped up.

“Ah!” She snatched the phone. “It’s her!” Annalisse swiped the screen. “Auntie, where are you?” She waited a few seconds for Kate’s voice. “Aunt Kate? Hello?” Nothing. Annalisse called back, but the call went to Kate’s voice mail.

“Was that her?”

“Her number. Someone may be jerking us around. Why?” Annalisse sank deep into her chair and stared into her phone. “I’m too antsy.” She got up and hugged him. “I’m sorry you came home to this. I won’t be long.” She kissed his temple quickly and glanced into the open breezeway from his office. The maples near the barn entrance shook in a loud hiss, shedding the first round of sprinkles from the foliage. She took a breath, longing for Kate to walk through Alec’s door. “Gotta go. Please report her disappearance to the locals. I don’t care if they give you a hard time for reporting too soon. Tell them what happened at Walker Farm this morning. We need an official missing person’s alert in this county.”

CHAPTER
FIVE

How Annalisse wished she could snap her fingers and Kate would pop next to her in Alec's rental car. What if her aunt had been alone this morning at Walker Farm? Would she have been abducted there? Was the person who planted the body in the stall watching from a distance? Did Ethan know more than he'd told them? Questions crowded Annalisse's thoughts as she watched the door of the Orange County Sheriff's Office.

"Geez, Ethan. We've got things to do." She tapped the steering wheel. A man in a white T-shirt stepped out of the brick building. Annalisse recognized his slow saunter. "'Bout damn time."

She unlocked the passenger side and motioned him to hurry.

"Reckon you've been waiting for me? They called me back inside to sign something." Ethan shrugged.

"I'm not *even* going to ask what you signed. Tell me later."

"Didn't recognize this white car. I was expecting the blue bomb."

"Alec's rental car. When I got back into the BMW to pick you up, the engine kept dying. Alec didn't want me stranded. It came out of the paint shop running just fine until I parked at Brookehaven."

"Where's Miss Walker?" Ethan strained over his headrest for a peek at the back seat. His suntanned complexion darkened in the shaded interior of the car.

"Did Kate call? Did investigators give you the third degree?" She glanced sideways at him periodically as she drove.

"Spent more time asking about my Kiwi heritage than anything else. Bloody tall poppies."

"You're a frustration and a half. What does that mean?" She shook her head. "Never mind. I can guess. I'm ordering an American-to-New Zealand dictionary." She pulled the Chevy Malibu away from the parking slot.

Ethan laughed. "I've got one I'll loan you. Two English-speaking countries separated by the English language." He tipped his head toward the building. "The coppers were a cheeky bunch. They sure love themselves."

"This is serious. We have a situation with Kate, and Alec came home unexpectedly. Do you have a friend you could stay with for the weekend?" Annalisse hoped he did.

"Naw. Why can't I stay at the farm?"

"You want to? I thought you might feel… We'll do that if we can. It's better for the animals to have you there. Did the sheriff say anything about the dead guy?"

"Not to me."

"Have you heard from Kate?" She rapped the steering wheel column with the base of her freshwater pearl ring.

He shook his head, and his smile disappeared. "She doesn't ignore me unless she's mad."

Ethan was notorious for rubbing Kate thin at times. Ethan could be on the lazy side, preferring to read a novel, even if it meant shoving the job to the back burner. When Kate gave him chores to do, she lost her cool when she found them not done.

Ethan received the abridged version of what had happened when Kate left for the barn. The light in his wide-set eyes melted away.

"Someone's got her?"

"We think so." She'd kept the part about the syringe to herself.

Annalisse checked the console for the clock. Almost four. They had a little daylight left to do some searching. Time enough to cover a few places on the farm before getting back on the road.

Alec's ringtone played from her phone in the cup holder.

"Hi. Any news?" she asked.

"No. You?"

"We're almost to the farm. Ethan wants to stay if we can still get in. He hasn't heard from Kate either. I'm worried, Alec. If she's been taken, why haven't we heard something by now? It's like Gen and her kidnappers all over again." She waited a while for his voice. "Alec?"

"Thinking. Bill's still in Connecticut, so I'll meet you at the farm. In case you guys might have missed something."

"If investigators are still there, I doubt they'll let us poke around."

Ethan spoke in a whisper. "Not even."

"What about my BMW?"

"I had it towed, but it's Saturday. Mechanics won't look at it until Monday." Alec's tone had sharpened.

"What about Kate? Someone might contact you there. I don't think you should leave." *No, no, no.* They needed all stations covered: Alec's estate and Walker Farm.

"Is Ethan there with you?"

"You know he is."

Ethan swiveled around with a mischievous smile, taking more interest in the conversation.

"Annalisse looks good today, huh, Alec?" he bellowed.

She swatted Ethan's knee and shook her head at him in the most animated way she could manage while navigating the road.

"Damn you," she mouthed at her passenger, getting a snicker in return.

"Don't leave your aunt's place. I'm on my way," Alec said.

By the time she thought of another objection, he'd hung up.

"What the hell was that?" Annalisse slammed her phone onto the console and sent Ethan a dirty look.

"You don't fancy compliments?"

"That… was a cannonball hitting Alec's foxhole when he wasn't expecting it. We're at war with enough forces already. Don't blow up the allies. I draw the line at smart-asses mucking up my personal business."

"I'll slag off."

"Try it for once or *have a go*, as you like to say." She stared at the dash and drew a few calming breaths. "We've all had a shitty day." She turned the Chevy into the Walker Farm entrance, past the weeping willow farm sign, anticipating yellow crime tape or a closed gate. She found neither and relaxed the tension in her shoulders. "That's a relief." She slowed and scanned the property, motoring the driveway at idle. "See any vehicles?"

"Don't see anyone walking around either."

"Hopefully, they took the man out of the barn by now. You tend to the livestock, and I'll check the farmhouse again." She continued toward the house and almost stopped out front but instead wove them behind the farmhouse and parked with the engine running.

"Where are you going? Alec wants you to stay here."

"I don't always do what Alec says." A confrontation between Alec and Ethan was a good thing to avoid. She'd tell Alec not to bother coming when she drove out.

Gravel crunched in the distance, getting louder.

"Move it, Ethan! Head for the bunkhouse. Haven't you answered enough questions today?" Annalisse switched off the ignition. She scrunched down in the seat in case the visitor drove around back. "Damn, damn, damn," she said under her breath. It was too soon to be Alec. More likely, an officer had returned to the crime scene. Even though the Malibu stayed hidden from the road, she'd be seen leaving.

Weighing her choices, she opted for making their presence known to law enforcement. She could only hope for the sheriff or detective they'd met earlier in the day since Alec had some pull in the community.

Annalisse stepped out of the car and closed her door quietly. She walked around the house, openly rounding the bend to the breezeway, acting as normal as possible. So far, she found no sign of people or vehicles nearby. She held her breath for as long as she could against the cadaver odor that lingered on the air.

Crime-scene tape crisscrossed the barn entrance from top to bottom, crackling in a light breeze. The closed stall door blocked any prying eyes from seeing where the man had lain.

Footsteps scuffed from behind her.

"Ethan?"

Annalisse turned and recognized one of the detectives who'd arrived in the first wave of investigators. He stood with his feet wide apart and arms crossed. His heavily padded shoulders gave him a weightlifter stance.

"I'm Annalisse Drury." She reached out and took his hand. "I'm glad you're here. I came back because my Aunt Kate's missing." She tilted her head to the north. "From the next county. We think she's been abducted."

He nodded. "McDonaugh thought you might show up. We'd like another day here to look around."

Annalisse said, "Will you let Officer McDonaugh know about my aunt? She's only been gone a few hours, but she didn't vanish without help. I'd like to file a missing person report."

"Why check the crime scene?" The detective scratched his head. "It's more likely she'd be in the house if she came back here."

"I wanted to check the hired hand's work. Do you know if the mare's been moved?"

"Nothing living or dead in the barn to my knowledge." The detective without a name puckered his lips, then returned them to normal.

What a jerk for reminding her about the corpse.

"About my aunt…" She tossed hair over her shoulder to show her distaste for his flip attitude. "Never mind. You probably aren't interested unless you've got a homicide." Annalisse spotted Ethan and waved him over.

"I watered everyone up. What did I forget to sign?" Ethan asked, staring down the detective.

"Sorry for earlier, miss. Long day." He took a pen from his jacket. "Tell me about Mrs. Walker. Didn't she leave with you?" He pushed his sunglasses lower on his nose, peering over the top of them.

"We left together." Annalisse let his earlier remark go. Having Orange County officials involved would put manpower on the disappearance. The more entities who knew about Kate, the better. "I'll fill you in on what happened."

Minutes later, the detective was out of questions. He'd busily scribbled in his black notebook but stopped writing when she casually mentioned the needle and syringe.

"Can you and the sheriff's office search for Kate?" she asked.

"That's Thompson limits in Sullivan County, miss. Not our jurisdiction. But I'll put the word out. If you'd like to file that missing person's report, drop by the Sullivan County Sheriff's Office."

Ethan scratched his head, and his expression softened. "I just thought of something. May not be important, but I forgot about Miss Walker's son showing up yesterday."

"Jeremy was here? Yeah, that's kinda important." Annalisse held the comment she was about to add. She doubted Ethan knew Jeremy planned to sell the farm. Aunt Kate wouldn't take him into confidence like that. Moving next to Ethan, she touched his arm. "Was Jeremy acting weirder than usual?"

"I didn't hang around long enough to hear. He came with a briefcase and had a stone face like the men on your Mount Rushmore."

"What time was that?" The detective flipped open the notebook, pen at the ready.

"'Round two, I think. Yesterday. When he left the house, I heard Miss Walker yell something at him. Couldn't make it out."

"A happy yell or mad yell?" Annalisse asked, knowing full well what his answer would be.

"She's never happy when her son comes calling."

"I think Jeremy knows where his mother is. He may even know about the man in the stall. Hell, he might have put him there." Annalisse had no proof, but to her knowledge, investigators didn't know about the sale of the farm. Her heart rejoiced at the thought of Jeremy holding on to the bars in a jail cell where he couldn't hurt Kate.

"Why would you say that?" The detective turned a fresh page in his little book.

"They were feuding about selling this farm," she said quietly.

"Miss Walker's selling out?" Ethan asked, and dropped his jaw.

"Is that right?" He scribbled a few words and handed her his card. "If you hear anything new on Mrs. Walker, call me. It could help with this investigation." He smiled half-heartedly. "I wouldn't worry. It's only been a few hours. She'll turn up."

Annalisse read the name on the simple white card. Martin Trask.

"Detective Trask, have they identified the man in the stall yet?" She wondered if the stranger was actually who the identification card said he was. Not that the man's name would tell her anything more, unless he wasn't Thomas Taylor.

"They're checking against the print database." Trask's official-speak brushed off any chance of hearing details.

"When you have something conclusive, please let me know. Bad enough he dropped out of nowhere dead, but why did his clothes feel wet?" She turned up her nose. Annalisse's curiosity had ways of raising more questions with authorities. She instantly regretted the mention of his clothes.

Trask raised his glasses high on his head and looked at her quizzically. "I heard it might be sea water. If *you* didn't touch the body, how did you feel his wet clothing?"

So much for a quick departure.

CHAPTER

Damned if he'd stay at the estate while the ranch help hung around with Annalisse at Walker Farm. Alec didn't trust Ethan to stay clear of her. Especially after her cool reception to his marriage proposal in the drawing room. He'd picked the wrong time to bring it up. As usual, his timing sucked.

"Nice job, idiot," Alec grumbled under his breath. "You couldn't wait."

He grabbed a light jacket while recalling his mother's order to fix it with Annalisse and cancel his Pennsylvania trip—their argument at the gallery still fresh in his mind. Whatever it took, he had to make things right or lose her. Alec tasted bile, imagining Ethan's intentions beyond being a farmhand. With his chick-magnet accent.

"Probably turns it on more just for her."

"Did you say something?" Helga untied the apron from her wide waist, laying it over a barstool.

Alec grabbed the car keys. "Helga, I'm taking off. If you hear from Annalisse or a Detective Drake, have them call my cell."

"Should I expect you for dinner?"

"For now, plan on Annalisse and me. Chase and Boris won't be here till Monday."

She clasped her hands. "How lovely to see Chase again. And he's bringing little Boris too." Helga put the apron on she'd just removed. "Better get busy."

***

Alec stepped comfortably on the throttle, shifted, and then held the brake, spinning the tires. He glanced into the wing mirror at the twin lines of rubber and smoke billowing behind. The burnout helped transfer some weight from his chest to the gas pedal. Beneath his fingers, the steering wheel shuddered as the Michelins found traction under the chassis.

The oily top road had dried since he'd arrived but was still tacky from the storms. In his haste, he'd taken off with the Signorile's top down and storm clouds were still in the area. Small puddles glistened along the route near the edges of the road. He applied pressure to the accelerator.

His phone rang, and he checked the screen as his heart flipped to a dark place. Tina. He hadn't spoken to his ex-wife since she'd asked for a larger divorce settlement. He'd agreed to her ridiculous demand only because she'd taken alimony off the table. She planned to marry her drug-dealer boyfriend, Karl. The man who'd pressured Tina into an affair and hooked her on a little white powder and a lot of sex after she miscarried Alec's child. Often, Alec questioned his true feelings for Tina. If he'd ever loved her or if pressure from his mom for grandkids had pushed him into marriage before he was ready.

He rarely made any decision without weighing how it affected his mother in the long run. She ruled the family dynasty with her overbearing, always-right attitude. Dad had tolerated Mom's hands on the reins, and Alec let it slide because it was easier, but he had to stop making mistakes with Annalisse as he had with Tina.

Throughout college, Mom endlessly prodded him to find a "nice, old-fashioned girl," as she put it, and stop dating Ivy League gold diggers because they couldn't be trusted to look beyond his looks and money. Alec blamed himself for not seeing the warning signs with Tina. He'd hoped that her restlessness and depression would go away once she got pregnant again. He should've recognized that playing with baby clothes and filling their crib with new toys each week wasn't a good reality for her. When she dropped out of school, they'd moved on to different planes of existence—and Karl moved in to fill the void Alec left by tuning out his wife's mental crisis.

The phone rang for the sixth time, and Alec debated whether to ignore it, but curiosity won out.

He pressed the Bluetooth. "Zavos."

"How cool are we?" A watery voice that sounded like it came from under the ocean rolled out of the speaker. "Fooled ya." Not Tina. Tina's husband.

Alec instinctively curled his hand into a fist, recalling the time he'd used it as a battering ram on Karl's jaw when he'd found them together, naked, in their bed.

"Who let you out, Brooks? Last I heard, you were somebody's bitch from a cell in Attica."

"You always were an asshole."

"Is Tina all right?"

"You care?"

Alec ended the call, shaking his head. "Not enough to talk to a felon home wrecker."

Tina's number rang back, and Alec said, "Brooks, I haven't got time for this. What's up? Where's Tina?"

"She doesn't know I'm calling."

"So?"

"You'd better listen this time. How's that long-legged chickie-poo of yours? Does she know about you?"

"Is there a point to this?"

"When we hit the tabloids with what we have, you'll be glad we had this talk."

"Prick." Alec downshifted. He should've blocked the call.

"Say that now. When your chickie sees you all over Monica on the Italian Riviera—"

"I don't know what you're sniffing dude, but this talk is over." Alec played with the Bluetooth button.

"Your hand planted on the ass of an Italian actress when everyone knows you're with Anna-babe might make some news." Karl's joy from the Signorile's speakers sounded like a bad dream.

Alec hadn't been around any Italian actresses since he was twenty-two and single, before he and Tina were married. His dad's business took him to Palermo, capital city of Sicily, the large island that sat off the toe of Italy's boot. There were tons of pictures on the internet of Alec in places all over Europe. On the yacht, at parties with corporate heads, in casino ballrooms. It was possible that Tina took photos of him before they were married but never of him touching another woman. He never did that in public, opting for discretion. Paparazzi had the habit of showing up everywhere.

"Old pics from spider-webbed archives won't get you much." Alec shrugged off a future where a startled and hurt Annalisse found a tabloid newspaper with a picture of him cheating. Unfounded dirt in the tabloids would devastate their fragile relationship.

"If you won't pay, plenty of rags will." Karl broke in on Alec's thoughts. "*Reveal Reality* is holding their Monday edition cover for me."

"That salacious rag?"

"It's only a rag if you're in it." Karl's bellicose laughter shook the interior.

"I'll take you to court."

"Yeah, once the damage is done with Anna-babe? You wanna take that chance?"

"Does Tina know what you're doing?"

"We need the money, and you've got enough to splurge a little on your buddy Karl."

"How much?" Alec clenched his teeth. Karl must have blown through Tina's generous settlement, or she did. At this point, it made sense to give them a check to go away, even though he'd never been unfaithful to Annalisse. They were fighting on enough fronts at the moment.

"Ten K a month," Karl said.

Alec laughed. "You wish!" he yelled over the sound of his shirt snapping in the wind. He knew once they got used to spending a monthly stipend, they'd up the ante and he'd never be done with them. "Blackmail somebody else. Your parole officer might like to hear about this. I'll put my investigator on it. You've met him."

"Arrogance ain't a virtue. See ya in the funny papers. Oh, one more thing. If I don't get enough dough, I'm telling the world your other secret."

Alec felt the fumes of anger spread through his chest. "Yeah?"

"You know the one. A biggie. You had a private eye on it a few years back."

"What are you smoking? I'm hanging up."

"Your dad's not around, so he can't go to jail for it, but what I know will kill your little empire without firing a shot. It's better for everyone if you cooperate."

Shit. Tina had sworn herself to secrecy.

The call ended on Karl's grunt.

Alec considered the strength of his position. Threatening to reach out to Karl's parole officer might scare him enough to cool his jets, but he doubted it. He had to count on the real possibility Tina and Karl might be hard up, and he'd have to plan what to do if Karl went to that tabloid with a lewd picture from the past. *Reveal Reality* wouldn't stop with one photo. If Tina had more, he'd see his face splashed all over the media. How would he sell the corporation?

Karl's going to the media with his second threat was unthinkable.

Karl used his wife's phone, but Alec wasn't certain he was actually out of prison. The call might have come from inside, but it wasn't likely he'd be allowed to use Tina's phone. One more thing he'd have Bill Drake check into. If Tina's husband was loose, he would cause trouble.

Alec passed out of Goshen's city limits, where the drive had switched from tight curves to a long straightaway. The thought of being with Annalisse once again urged him to increase his speed. Alec rounded a sharp corner and hit a low spot, invisible until water hit the undercarriage. It splashed the passenger side, wetting his right shoulder and soaking him to the skin.

"Whoa!" He glanced right for half a second at his doused leather seat and carpet, then applied mushy brakes, pumping them harder to match the strength of his gritted teeth.

The Signorile shimmied at the rear and broke into a spin.

The car floated out of his control as he turned into the slide.

"Come on, dig in." His mind raced through his options.

Alec tightened his left-handed grip on the wheel, madly downshifting and then pulling the emergency brake. The Signorile had a mind of its own, centrifugal force pushing him deeper into his bucket seat. He grabbed the shoulder harness, digging his nails into the fabric, unable to stop the violent spin and his nausea that followed. The smell of burnt rubber and damp dirt filled his nose while the sports car made its third revolution close to a marshy stand of maples in feet of water.

The car careened into slippery grass.

Alec closed his eyes and clutched the wheel with both hands.

He opened them just in time to brace for the tree trunks charging at the Signorile.

***

It sickened Annalisse to come back to Walker Farm with Kate missing. She squirmed to find a more comfortable spot on the porch swing beneath her. The slats, rigid and unbending, pinched her sweaty thighs. When the swing was new, it used to be comfy enough to curl up and nap to the bird chirps and wisteria wafting the air. She couldn't help but smile when the swing creaked like a tiny frog on each upstroke. The sound took her back to the tales her aunt had told her about living in rural East Texas and listening to the Texas sheep frogs. How their croaking near the water's edge mimicked a flock of bleating sheep. Someday, Annalisse would go to the South and listen to them for herself.

Kate wasn't on this farm, and from the sun sinking in the west, she and Ethan were wasting precious daylight. Detective Trask was more interested in picking apart their dead-guy stories than finding her aunt. Trask's voice floated in and out on the light breeze. From Annalisse's vantage on the porch, she could see poor Ethan nervously touch his face, dancing around like he needed to find a bathroom soon.

Annalisse wouldn't allow herself to believe Kate would leave her like the Drurys had sixteen years ago. The afternoon the gas main exploded, taking out almost a city block, wiping away the family home in Kensington with her sister and parents inside. Annalisse relived the terrible event from television so many times. But there was nothing a young girl could've done to prevent what happened that day.

Annalisse's mother, Amy, had favorite homilies she used to spout while Annalisse and Ariel did their homework. *Wealth is fleeting, love lasts. Live each day close to God, and you'll be fine.* Annalisse remembered rolling her eyes at her sister, barely ten years old, as they erupted into giggles.

"You'll understand when you're older" was Mom's most frequent reply. In a child's mind, days were long, and people lived forever. She'd ask for the explanation tomorrow. A tomorrow that never came, followed by days of sadness too numerous to count.

Annalisse drifted back from her reverie as Martin Trask finished the interrogation with Ethan. Trask had grilled her about what they'd done to the body in the barn before the sheriff arrived. Simply put, she'd added the Walkers, Ethan, and herself to the suspect list with her foolish but innocent line about wet clothing. Holding back how they'd rummaged over the man for identification had made them all look guilty.

Less one.

Someone had Aunt Kate.

A chicken flapped its wings near the porch and strutted away before she could tell which one it was. Annalisse thought of her aunt's savory chicken and dumplings on cold Sunday evenings after church. Uncle Ted's Rhode Island Reds pecked around the barns, scratching morsels from the dirt, oblivious to one of their own in the stew pot on the stove. Fresh bacon from their hand-raised hogs fried next to the family recipe of eastern crab cakes only Kate could make. Fond memories Annalisse struggled to lock away so they wouldn't escape her mind—in case Kate didn't return.

Her chest heaved, and she immediately lost her appetite. So many things were left unsaid between them. So many questions. Thomas Taylor. How to keep the farm from Jeremy. Kate's doctor's warnings. Annalisse squeezed the wooden armrest, wincing at the splinter she picked up in her thumb.

"Damn." She pulled it out with her teeth, spitting the splinter to the porch. The swing was a Walker monument on the farm. Her uncle had built it for Kate's birthday one year, and smaller versions hung from strong branches for her and Ariel when they visited. She glanced at the trees where their swings used to hang—taken down long ago by her uncle in a fit of rage over something she couldn't recall.

"C'mon, Ethan." Annalisse hopped out of the swing and strolled toward them. "We don't have time for this, people," she muttered.

The engine noise from the road distracted her, and she stopped. A light-colored vehicle turned in to the farm entrance, too far away for Annalisse to recognize—until she did.

Jeremy's car.

Bitterness roiled in the back of her throat. She had plenty to say to him.

Running hard to make it to Detective Trask before Jeremy could park, she pointed at the car, huffing for breath, stopping next to Ethan.

"That's Kate's son. Pick his brain for a while." Annalisse gulped for air. "He knows something. I can feel it."

Trask motioned for them to stay behind.

Annalisse turned to Ethan and said, "Screw that. Wait for me. This won't take long."

"And miss the fireworks?" He scrunched his nose. "Bollocks."

She intended to slam Jeremy for selling the farm. If Annalisse couldn't stop him, she needed to explain things to Ethan in her own way. Line up another job for him if possible. If he didn't have his place on Walker Farm, Annalisse wasn't sure where he'd land. She couldn't leave him behind today with investigators still poking around. Ethan had to come with her to Brookehaven.

"Please, wait." She rested a hand on Ethan's shoulder. "A few minutes."

With head down, Ethan walked to the porch in a shuffle, looking back once over his shoulder.

Annalisse had no idea where Alec was or how much time had passed since she and Ethan arrived, but she had to sink her claws into Jeremy. She walked up to Detective Trask as if Jeremy were invisible.

"Detective, we need to go, if there's nothing else?" From the corner of her eye, she witnessed Jeremy's mouth twitch. A dress shirt tucked neatly into his weekend chinos held the wrinkles from a long drive. Without missing a beat, she whipped around to face Jeremy. “Saw your letter today, weasel. You’re not selling the farm from under your mother. How dare you try to put Kate out of her home.” She raised her voice along with her hand. “I should slap you where you stand!”

“Miss Drury.” Trask stepped between her and Jeremy.

“I’m not afraid of her.” Jeremy sidestepped defiantly. “For your information, the farm belongs to me, not Mom.”

“I couldn’t care less how you swindled the farm to cover a loan. We can pay you back. There’s no reason to sell. Don’t you understand? Your mother needs this place.”

Detective Trask retreated and drew his notebook out of his jacket.

“Mom doesn’t have the money to pay me back, Anna…lisse. If she did, I’d have it.”

“I do.” She smiled demurely.

Jeremy tipped his head to the side in curiosity. His beady eyes reminded her of Ted. “I doubt it.”

He didn’t know a thing about her finances, and she had no idea what Kate owed, but she’d given him something to think about.

“This place is dead weight. I’m tired of losing money. Mom can’t handle the work. How many more heart attacks do you want her to have? Three? Five? Two’s not enough?”

Annalisse hated the sneer and curl of his lips when Jeremy felt that he had the upper hand in an argument.

Oh the pleasure she'd feel from punching him in the mouth until his teeth fell out. She balled her fist against her thigh.

Trask put his book away and stepped next to her.

"What. Did. You. Do. With. Her?" Annalisse reached out and grabbed Jeremy's arm, shaking hard, sinking her nails into his soft flesh.

Jeremy jerked away from her death grip.

"I'd be careful, Orphan Anna. Assault charges are a bitch." Jeremy wiped at his shirt for good measure.

Orphan?

"I'm no orphan, unless you've done something with your mother. You know where she is!" Annalisse turned to the detective. "See, this creep is behind everything. Ask him what he knows."

"What are you raving about?" Jeremy tucked his shirt deeper into his trousers but kept his focus on her. "You're certifiable." He turned and faced Trask. "Who are you, and what's going on?"

"You know damn well what's going on. What have you done with Kate?" Her patience hung by a thread.

"Where's Mom? You mean she's not here?" Jeremy looked at the house, then to her.

Annalisse observed him for signs of lying. A glance down or away from her. Neither happened.

"Mr. Walker, is it?" Trask held out his hand to Jeremy. "I'm one of the detectives working this case." He handed Jeremy his business card.

Jeremy glanced at it and pocketed it just as quickly. "What case? Will someone explain what's happened?" He scratched his head, his eyes straying to the farmhouse.

"Does Jillian know what you're doing?" Annalisse asked, barely able to contain her outrage. "Where are you keeping Kate?" A tear escaped down her cheek, and Jeremy did a double take, his mouth agape.

Trask pulled her aside and whispered, "Let me talk to Mr. Walker. If I learn anything about Mrs. Walker, I'll call. We have your number."

She nodded and waved at Ethan to follow her.

Meeting Jeremy face to face made her skin crawl. Did he know more than he said? Her aunt didn't have any enemies, and her disagreements were limited to her children. Who else could be terrorizing her?

But Jeremy lied so much, it was as if he ate falsehoods for breakfast.

Annalisse rounded the house and swiped at her tears as she approached the car. She opened the door, hit a button on the fob, and turned the air conditioner to full blast.

Ethan dropped into the passenger seat, staring at her. "I'm not staying here?"

"Unfortunately, no." Annalisse rested her forehead on the steering wheel, allowing the rush of air to dry her cheeks.

"I'm sorry."

"For what?" She turned his way.

"He hurt you."

Annalisse buckled her seat belt. "It goes deeper than that. I thought I could leave you here, but Trask isn't ready to release the scene. We'll come back tomorrow. I wonder what happened to Alec?"

"Got over his jealous streak maybe."

"Or he heard from his detective friend about Kate. Let's head back."

Ten minutes into the drive, the road changed from wide sweeping turns to a tight corner. The earlier rains had left large puddles pooled here and there.

"Better slow down, Annalisse. Lots of water ahead."

"What's that on the right?" Annalisse lowered the passenger window and pointed at the orange cones marking off a section of the shoulder. "Is that a car in the trees? It must have just happened. Wonder if anyone's inside."

She slowed to a crawl. When she recognized Alec's sports car, she screamed and whipped out of the lane. A blaze of red hugged the stand of old maples, twisted and flattened on the passenger side.

"God, please be okay." She couldn't see Alec.

"What are you doing?" Ethan grabbed the dashboard.

She halted the Malibu half-on, half-off the road and flung open her door. "Call somebody!"

CHAPTER SEVEN

Annalisse picked up the acrid smell of sulfur and burnt rubber as she ran to the crumpled car.

"Alec!" She leaned on the driver's door, checking the interior and underneath the carriage, finding no sign of him. Annalisse reached across the hood and touched the metal. Still warm. Unable to focus on the Signorile's details, her empty stomach lurched, and she took a step backward. Alec's sports car was a broken shell, but how was he?

She studied the driver's side for any signs of blood. Debris filled the floorboard, and the clutch pedal had twisted. Scouting a three-sixty path around the car, she scanned the grass in case he'd been ejected from his seat, then she spotted the safety cones once more.

"Crikey," Ethan whispered. "Think he's all right?"

"He's bad about seat belts. I hope he wore his. No blood anywhere. Has anyone reported the accident? Cones are out, so someone must have seen this. Where are the damn cops? I can't believe they'd leave the scene with the car here."

"Tow truck dispatched." Ethan shoved his phone into his pocket.

"Where was he taken?" Annalisse chewed on her lip. *Please be in the hospital and not the morgue.*

"Ask him." He pointed at the interstate and the squad car crossing the opposing lane.

Annalisse broke from Ethan and waved down the black-and-white.

The patrolman turned on the car's light bar and drove his vehicle to the shoulder so that it faced the Malibu head-on. He spoke into his radio and stepped outside, leaving the driver's side door open and garbled voices spilling from the interior.

"Can you help us, please? My… Alec Zavos was driving that car." She motioned to what was left of the Signorile. "He was on his way to meet me. Do you know where they took him?"

"You're parked dangerously close to traffic, miss. Please move your vehicle from the roadway." A young cop clad in a black shirt and slacks spouted the next few rehearsed words. "On the other side of these cones, please." He gestured where she should move the Malibu.

"Yes, sir. Please don't leave."

Annalisse gave Ethan her best "stay there" look, got into her car, and backed deeper into the grass, careful not to get her tires stuck in the mud.

"Do you know the driver's condition?" she asked the patrolman.

"Are you a family member?"

Annalisse nodded slowly, considering whether to elaborate on the lie. If it got her more information.

"Fiancée."

Saying that with Ethan overhearing made Annalisse wince. Without looking, she sensed his jaw drop. If he told Kate her fake engagement news before she had a chance to explain—she brushed off the idea. Technically, she *could* be engaged to Alec, if she'd agreed in the drawing room. But Kate's disappearance trumped all else.

Why did he ask if she was family? The patrolman's question came back to her, along with the urge to throw up.

"He's alive?" Annalisse stared the man down, her heart doing the cha-cha against her ribs.

"I'm sorry, I'm here to direct traffic away from the scene. Another officer reported this before he got called away." The officer waved her and Ethan farther from the road and got back into his patrol car.

"Annalisse," Ethan said carefully. "The car's mashed on the passenger side. Hardly a mark on Alec's side. I wouldn't fret. If he's in hospital, I'm sure it's just a niggle. No worries."

"I hope Alec comes out of this with only sore muscles." She squeezed his arm reassuringly. "I can't think the worst."

The officer shut the squad car door and approached Annalisse. "The driver's been taken to Cedar Ridge Hospital."

"How serious?" she asked on wobbly legs.

"Minor injuries."

She unclenched her jaw. They still had a chance.

"Thank God. Thank you so much for the information. C'mon, Ethan."

"If you know the driver's insurer, I'd notify them."

She nodded and started for the Malibu when another question came to mind. "How long ago was he taken by ambulance?"

The patrolman shrugged. "Sorry, miss."

***

Annalisse's throat iced over when the arctic blast struck her at the automatic doors of the hospital entrance. She looked behind her for Ethan, who'd hung back a few paces, halfway wishing she'd told him to wait in the car. Leaving him in the parking lot with the car running wasn't an option. He'd had a rough day too.

Annalisse went to the front desk and asked for Alec.

A plump brunette in pink scrubs ticked the keyboard with her long, acrylic nails and checked the computer screen.

"Are you family?"

Annalisse nodded without hesitation. "Fiancée." Lying came much easier with strangers.

"Alec Zavos was admitted to the triage room thirty minutes ago."

"May I see him?"

"Hang on." The receptionist went back to her screen. "He's been moved." She clicked her mouse. "And admitted to a private room."

"How bad is he?"

"I don't have that information."

"What room?" Annalisse hated the nauseating odors of bedsores and bowel movements floating around hospital corridors and how frigid the personnel behind the counters were, but hospitals were a necessary evil.

"Can't you give me his room number?" Annalisse croaked through her dry mouth.

Ethan tapped Annalisse on the shoulder. "It's gonna be okay."

She twisted around, finding Ethan's concern quite charming beyond his cool accent.

"Room 344."

"Great, thanks. Is there a waiting room on that floor?"

"Yes. At the end of the hall on the east corridor."

Annalisse pushed Ethan toward the elevators, weighing Alec's possible reactions to her bringing Ethan along. From Alec's unknown condition to time lost in the search to find Kate, she worried about it all. There were so many issues unresolved, with no good answers.

Annalisse pointed to the door numbered 344 and exhaled quietly. She peered through the small window in the door at Alec propped against a stack of pillows, his ankle elevated, his neck in a brace. The injuries looked worse than minor.

She whispered to Ethan, "Please be kind. No smart remarks about his driving skills or screwball things like that. I'll tell him about Jeremy and the rest." When Ethan didn't reply, she glared at him. "Got it?"

"Yeah, yeah. I'm not a kid."

Annalisse knocked on the door and waved through the tiny window.

"Art lady!" Alec sat straighter against the pillows, flashing his smile that warmed her like hot cocoa.

Annalisse dropped her tote and flew to his bed.

"I've been crazy worried about you. When we saw your car—"

"Shh." He pulled her down to his mouth, searching hers with urgency and finally let her go. "I screwed up." Alec lifted his ankle. "Good thing Dad builds a solid car."

She smiled at the mention of Pearce, Alec's handsome father. It brought to her mind the last sweet memory of the Zavos family patriarch, in his Bermudas, sitting on the deck of their yacht, the *Gen Amore.* Before he was brutally murdered in front of her.

"Pearce is definitely keeping an eye on you." She kissed his forehead. "Anything broken?" She touched the neck brace. "What did the doctor say?"

Ethan stirred from behind. "Hey, Alec."

Alec narrowed his eyes. "The kid."

"Ethan, would you mind waiting down the hall. I won't be long."

He grumbled, "Feel better," then gave them a flat-handed wave and closed the door behind him.

Annalisse observed Alec's face. Not a single scratch or bruise marred his handsome jaw and chiseled features.

"Looks like the Signorile took the brunt of it. All things considered, you look great. Did you swerve to miss another car?"

"I was driving too fast with too much on my mind," he said sheepishly. "Hit some water at the hairpin where I landed."

"I saw the spot." She touched the bandage on his ankle. "Broken?"

"Sprained." He fiddled with the brace below his chin. "And they think whiplash. Told me to wear this." Alec lifted his shoulders. "I'm ready to rip it off. Now I know how pets feel in the cone of shame. Sucks."

"How's your ribs?" She zeroed in on his arm shielding his rib cage. It took Alec many weeks to heal from his last ordeal with broken ribs.

"They took a pretty good whack from the airbag and seat belt." He grunted softly and reached for her hand. "When you think you're gonna die, it's… While the car spun, I thought of Dad, Mom… you." He uttered a wistful sigh.

Someone knocked on the door, then it opened.

"We have an appointment with imaging." An orderly addressed Annalisse instead of Alec.

"Sure." Annalisse pulled her hand from Alec's. "I'll wait on the verdict and drive you home if they'll let you escape." She smiled at the orderly. "How much longer?"

"We're backed up down there. Couldn't say."

Alec's phone trilled next to the bed.

"I'll give you a few minutes." She nodded to Alec and left the room.

He picked up the phone, and his mouth opened. "Look." He turned the screen toward Annalisse.

She grabbed his wrist. "A text from Aunt Kate? She never texts. Does she text you?"

"No." He tapped the screen, wrinkling his nose. "What the hell?"

Annalisse sat on the edge of the bed, imagining the worst, and took his cell. A two-word text glared back at her.

Love her.

“Huh?” They’d discussed Alec that morning, but would Kate reach out to him? Why not call and let them know where she was?

“Is there another meaning other than the obvious?” He took his phone back, studying the message again.

“It can’t be her. Auntie would call. She has to know we’re looking for her by now. Is that the kind of message she would send? Knowing her?”

“I’ve wondered if your aunt saw me drive into the estate and wanted to give us a little privacy. Like Mom’s famous for doing.”

“Kate would think like that too. We weren’t expecting you back so soon.” She shook her head. “She wouldn’t leave without telling me.”

“Maybe a friend picked her up at the barn?” Alec asked.

“And took her where? Auntie doesn’t make snap decisions. She would never just leave.”

“How do you explain this?” He flipped the phone around once more.

“I can’t.”

CHAPTER EIGHT

Annalisse's stomach growled mercilessly on the way to the third-floor waiting area inside Cedar Ridge Hospital. At the vending machine, she bought chips and two Snickers bars. Who knew when she'd get anything better? She chuckled, rubbing her arms for warmth in the chilly hallway. Having spent more time with Alec than she'd originally intended, she hurried to give Ethan the snacks as a peace offering.

"Thought we could use these. Sorry I took so long."

Ethan took the foil pouches, tossing aside the women's magazine in his hand. He sat alone in the waiting area, with soft jazz lilting the corner space filled with padded chairs, two sofas, and a love seat. All of which looked comfortable enough to nap on.

"Nothing to read in this place. Learned some cool makeup tips though." He grinned her way and tore the wrapper off a candy bar. "Are we going now?"

"They're checking him out for internal bleeding. I told Alec I'd stay to hear what the doctor says. Do you mind?"

"Naw. Thanks for the nibbles." He raised his candy bar.

Annalisse collapsed on the sofa next to him, shoving her tote in the crack between cushion and arm. The sofa had given way beneath her, and she shifted closer to the armrest.

"Are you certain there weren't any farm visitors? Like a salesman or someone from the church?" she asked. "Anyone besides Jeremy that you might've forgotten? An older man with gray hair maybe?"

"Just regular people. Miss Walker has lots of friends."

"I know, but think hard, Ethan. Any strangers or unusual behavior may give us clues."

"Miss Walker clues or clues about the dead bloke?"

"Take your pick. Don't leave out anything, even the little stuff." Annalisse caught a shift in his gaze. "Tell me."

"I forgot about Monday. I was busy moving the sheep to another pasture." He rubbed his temple. "Crikey dick! You're looking at me like I did something to Miss Walker and the wrinklie in the stall. It wasn't me."

It was a wonder her aunt hadn't clobbered him for his New Zealand slang. She tried to parse his figures of speech and ran into mixed messages.

"I didn't mean to offend you. What happened Monday?"

"Nothing." He took a big bite of his Snickers.

"Don't be like that." She hesitated, then decided to fill him in. "Detective Drake comes in from Connecticut tomorrow." Annalisse explained Alec's friend and followed up with Kate's recent text to Alec's phone.

"Miss Walker doesn't know how to text. Tried to show her once, but she didn't get it."

"I'm convinced wherever Aunt Kate is, someone has her phone—making her play around with us—or *they* are. Lord knows why. Alec's friend Drake can't get here soon enough for me."

Before her mind had a chance to drift into full-blown worry mode over Kate's whereabouts, Annalisse opened her bag of nacho chips, savoring the salty spices. "Heavenly." She ate until the bag was empty, licking the seasoning off her fingers, then wiping them with a napkin from her tote.

"Made short work out of that." Ethan laughed, sifting through the pile of magazines on the side table. "Too bad they don't have any crime magazines."

"Hospital reading caters to warm and fuzzy. Do you like novels? I brought one of my favorites with me for the weekend. I've read it so many times, the cover's ready to fall off." She pulled the book out with a sly smile. "Forget it. You wouldn't like a chick book."

Ethan peered at the book. "*The Thornbirds*. A good flick. Reminds me of home."

She sprang against the cushion. "Tell me about home. Take my mind somewhere I've always wanted to visit."

Delight twinkled in his eyes. "You know I'm from En Zed."

"Is that some island next to the mainland?"

"Naw. It's what *we* call New Zealand. A short version."

"What's it like?" She leaned her head back and took a deep breath.

"My mum and da are runholders on the South Island."

"Now?"

"Yeah."

"And a runholder is…"

"Owns a sheep station. Like—a sheep farm?"

"If you have sheep back home, why come to the States? Who's running the station?" She perked up at the chance to learn something new.

"My da. Mum told me to find Miss Walker."

Annalisse hadn't heard the Fawdray name before Ethan arrived. She wondered if Kate knew the family, and if so, how well.

"Then your mother knows Auntie?"

Ethan shrugged. "I guess. Don't know. Times got hard on Woolcombe Station. That's the name. Da paid my way here. Said I should find Miss Walker. She'd get work for me."

"Interesting. They both must know her. What's your dad's first name?"

"Robert. Robert Fawdray. Three generations of Fawdrays, starting when my great nana and nandy came over from England in the 1880s."

"Never heard of him. How many sheep do you run?"

"We had around fifty thousand."

"Head?" She raised her brows. "That's intense."

"Yeah. Don't know the last count. The drought wiped out the range where the woolies graze. Wool quality suffered, and we had to cut back. Sheep numbers have dropped in En Zed. I think it's down to six or seven sheep per person living on the islands. Used to be something like twenty-two sheep to every person. Our place is in the Canterbury region where there's still a fair sum of woolies."

"Bet it's beautiful there."

"Temuka has anything you want. Ocean, fishing, mountains, and pastures so green they sting your eyes in the spring." His face went blank, and he hinted at a smile. "I miss it. You'd like it. You should go sometime."

"I wish."

Ethan swiveled in her direction. "Seems to me you have enough to get there. I mean, it's expensive to fly down, but you could stay with us."

Not a chance. Alec would hate that. Not without him.

If the farm sold, Ethan would be back in New Zealand sooner than he expected. She twisted uncomfortably, afraid to imagine a future without Walker Farm as her sanctuary. She thought she heard a voice call "lambie" and gripped the armrest, searching the hall for Kate's wispy figure that wasn't there.

"You could stay at Woolcombe." Ethan touched her hand. "Mum would like you. You're a pretty one."

She laughed away his compliment and used the excuse to sweep her hair aside to slide her hand from his. Alec said Ethan had the hots for her, but until now, she hadn't noticed it.

"When I go back, I'll take you if you want. You're a natural around the sheep, Annalisse. I know they're your favorite."

A man in blue scrubs rounded the corner nurses' station, took off his skullcap, and approached the waiting area.

"Ms. Drury?"

"Yes."

"Your fiancé checked out just fine. No internal bleeding. One fractured rib and a badly twisted ankle, but he'll heal quickly. Mr. Zavos will have to stay off that foot for a few days, but he's well enough to go home." The doctor with more white hair than dark smiled with friendly eyes, nodded, and left.

"He *is* your fiancé?"

Ethan wasn't about to let the doctor's comment go since she'd already said that word twice today.

"I had to say that for information," she said quietly.

"He's not your fiancé then?" He looked down at her ring finger.

Having Ethan and Alec together in the confines of the Malibu wouldn't work. She couldn't trust Ethan not to seize an opportunity to compete for her. The way her luck was going, he'd mention traveling to New Zealand with him. As nice as a visit to his sheep station might be, that wasn't going to happen. She needed to figure out where at the estate to put him so that he wouldn't provoke Alec and disturb their plans.

Alec had offered to call his chauffeur when he was released. The Bentley was roomier than the Malibu, and she'd be saner there. Annalisse pulled the rental car keys from her tote and handed them to Ethan.

"I'm going to be a while with Alec, getting him checked out and all. It's better for him to have more room in the back seat for his ankle. I'll call Alec's chauffeur and have him bring the town car for us. Can you find your way to Brookehaven?"

"If the car has a GPS on board, I'll find it. If not, I'll use my phone." He scratched his head. "I can drive the Malibu if you want to stay with Alec in the back seat. No need to call the chauffeur."

"I appreciate that, but he'll be more comfortable in the Bentley's big back seat. Helga is a great cook, and you've got to be starving. I'll give her a buzz and tell her you're coming. She'll make up one of the guest rooms for you. Hand me your phone." She tapped in the estate's address. "You're all set. Start dinner without us. I don't know how long we'll be."

Ethan hesitated. "Seems a waste to call another car when I'm here and can drive you."

"When you get to the estate, take a walk across the street. Alec's stables are gorgeous. There's still time before it gets dark." Annalisse smiled, pushing his phone into his palm. "I have to go. We'll strategize on Aunt Kate in the morning when Alec's friend gets here."

Ethan asked another question, but she pretended not to hear him. Having Ethan underfoot undermined her plan to discuss her complicated relationship with Alec privately. From missing in action to a marriage proposal, Alec had thrown Annalisse into uncertain territory.

CHAPTER NINE

Annalisse opened her eyes to rat-a-tat echoes assaulting the master suite. Expecting to find Alec asleep next to her, she slid a hand over his side of the coverlet, chilling her fingertips along the satin fabric.

She checked the clock on the nightstand. "You shouldn't be up walking around without help, Zavos," Annalisse mumbled, catching a glimpse of a huge red-capped woodpecker sinking his beak into a nearby cedar. "You're the noisy critter." She flipped on her side and flicked her hand. "Shoo." The bird flew off, but it gave her little comfort from the throb at her temples.

She rolled out of bed, still clothed with what she'd worn yesterday. They'd returned late from the hospital, and after she'd situated Alec in bed, she was too tired to change. The day's activities kept sleep at bay till deep into the night.

Alec, on the other hand, had no trouble with sleep. If it weren't for Helga and the chauffeur's strong arms, Alec would still be in the town car. Extra good drugs from the hospital had him so drowsy, he couldn't walk without assistance. His bad ankle added another level of difficulty to the task of getting him from vehicle to bedroom. Annalisse seriously doubted Alec would recall much beyond the wheelchair ride out of the hospital building.

From nowhere, a stab of loss made her gasp, knocking her to the edge of the bed. Eighteen hours had passed since Aunt Kate disappeared, and they were no closer to finding her. Annalisse hoped that Bill Drake arrived early enough to get a good start on the morning, even though it was Sunday.

She snatched one of her travel robes from Alec's walk-in closet, stripped down, and tucked herself inside the terrycloth. Although sunshine filled the suite, goose bumps paraded down her arms, migrating to her legs. She cinched the belt at her waist. Helga's coffee would take the edge off her case of the chills and rejuvenate her mind.

Annalisse opened the massive bedroom door and slipped into the long corridor, tiptoeing on the hardwood in case Alec had fallen asleep in one of the guest rooms. On the way, she was greeted by the aromas of coffee, cinnamon, and sausage. Helga hummed as she worked her wooden spoon in a dance with the sides of a bowl.

"Good morning! Sleep well?" Helga stirred the bowl once more and set it aside.

"Where's Alec?"

"Here and there." Helga made a terrible attempt to twitch a smile away, and when she couldn't, the housekeeper opened the refrigerator and buried her head inside.

"What's going on? How long has he been up?"

"Since before that silly rooster crowed. Wakes the dead, he does. Four o'clock every day. I can set my watch by the noisy rascal." She rolled the *R* in "rascal" and wiped her hands on her apron. "I'll get your coffee. Re…lax." Helga pointed to a stool at the counter and poured Annalisse a big mug full.

"Is Ethan still asleep?"

"Heavens no. He's out with Mr. Reardon. Alec thought he could help with the horses today."

Annalisse relaxed, picturing Hank Reardon in his worn cowboy hat, stomping around the stables with a cigarette hanging out of his mouth. He'd managed Brookehaven for many years. Hank was a wonder around the horses—in skilled hands when Alec traveled so much. He'd keep Ethan busy and a good distance from Alec's watchful eyes.

"Did you add rosewater to your pancake batter? It smells different in here." Annalisse sniffed the air, taking the mug from Helga. "I'm out-of-my-mind worried for Kate. I hope Alec's guy finds her fast."

"Kate is a strong one. She reminds me of Gen. She'll turn up, don't worry." Helga reached for a platter of German pastries and slid it across the granite to Annalisse. "Eat. Starving yourself won't bring Kate back sooner."

Annalisse took a buttery roll Helga called *Franzbrotchen* and downed it in a few bites.

"Did you make 'em?" she said with her mouth full, then took another. "I shouldn't, but these are sinful, Helga."

Someone squeezed Annalisse at her waist.

She swiveled into the chest of a startlingly handsome man in an ankle boot.

"Where have you—?"

Alec carefully plucked the roll from her fingers and placed it on the counter, kissing her fingertips, seductively licking her index finger. "My compliments, Helga. Damn that tastes good."

Helga blushed.

"I don't know how you deal with him." Annalisse intended to break the awkward silence. There was plenty of blushing to go around.

Alec took her by the hand and grazed the underside of her palm. "I'm worried about you."

Annalisse dropped her eyes and gave his hand a little squeeze. "Please don't. I'm surviving. Should you be walking?" She guided him to her chair. "Sit."

"You woke me up several times talking in your sleep," Alec said, mildly amused.

"No way. You were zonked out—dead to the world. And I don't talk."

"Yeah, you do."

"Have you heard from your detective friend?"

"He texted me last night. He'll be here at ten."

"Shoot. I'd better get cleaned up." Annalisse took a big swallow of coffee. "I'll take one to go, Helga."

Alec pulled her into his arms and nibbled the base of her neck. "We've got lots of time. Come on." He entwined his hand with hers. "I have something to show you."

"I'll put a plate together for you, dear. You go with Alec. Go on." Helga motioned toward the hallway, her eyes sparkling.

The french doors to the drawing room were closed. They were usually left open since Alec read and relaxed in there so often. Annalisse caught a hint of sweet spice as they approached the entrance.

He pulled her into a long, sensual kiss.

She wallowed in the taste of cinnamon and his intoxicating sandalwood scent, filling her head with sex. Pure. Perfect. Sex. Annalisse had no idea what had come over Alec, but this part of him she'd missed terribly. Her legs weakened beneath her, and she came up for a breath.

"Don't start something you can't finish," she whispered. "Standing here in the dark holding you is killing me." Annalisse drew her fingertips along his cheeks, feeling whiskers poke her skin. "What a time to be incapacitated."

"I don't necessarily need my feet." He nipped her ear.

Her nerves tingled and shook in anticipation. "What are you up to?"

Alec stepped aside, opening one of the doors for her.

Her hand flew over her mouth at the sight of hundreds of long-stemmed roses. Stunned in place, she let her eyes follow the length of a hearth lined with huge crystal vases. Deep red rosebuds, at least two dozen in each vase, lovingly tied with silver bows.

She stepped into a fantasy—crystal and roses spilled from every flat surface wide enough to hold a vase. Each bouquet supported a single white envelope with a giant *A* penned on the front.

Annalisse leaned into the closest vase on the Chippendale lowboy table, one of her favorite pieces from Alec's collection. The rich musk from the rose centers seeped into her as a million notions swirled in her head.

"All this for me?" Annalisse wandered the furniture, touching silky blooms and marveling at how magnificent each arrangement was prepared. "Alec." She grabbed the arm of a chair for support. "How did you accomplish this? On a Sunday, no less. When did you have time? Who works Sundays?" She slid an envelope from the holder on the nearest bouquet.

"I have connections."

"Is that the Brookehaven logo on the ribbons? You've done this before." Her heart sank just a little.

Alec ushered her carefully to a period camelback sofa and sat down next to her. "I have a great florist. Yes, I've been a good customer." He held the hand in her lap. "I've never done this for another woman."

She gave him a peck on the cheek and recited from the card, "I love you more than watching a filly win her first race." She smiled. "That much, huh?"

He reached into the next floral bunch and extracted its card, reading aloud, "I love you more than looking at the supermoon over the Aegean with the surf washing over our toes."

Annalisse remembered that evening well. Their torrid sex on the villa floor. Their first time together. The night before they rescued his mother from Bodrum Castle.

He handed her another.

She read, "I love you more than drinking champagne alone in Kristol Magic's stall." She snickered at the picture that flashed in her mind. "Aw." He'd used that line on her on opening night at Gen's gallery party, after Sam's death and before Alec lost his father. So much had happened to them in such a short time.

Annalisse studied the handwriting and recognized Alec's hand. "You wrote these yourself? In the middle of the night?" Her eyes glazed, counting dozens of white envelopes in the room. He'd gone to extraordinary lengths for her. "Why spend so much money?"

Alec shook his head. "All the money in the world is meaningless without you." He readjusted his boot so he could face her squarely and brought her hand to his lips. "I left you behind. I let you down. I promised never to do that to another person I loved. That smackdown with Mom you overheard made me realize how easily I'd fallen into the same trap as I did with…"

"Your ex-wife."

Alec grunted, softly holding his ribs as he reached into his back pocket.

"Alec." Her mouth went dry. "Don't hurt yourself."

He held out a blue velvet drawstring bag. "It's not what you think."

She took it from him, unsure what to do with the weightless bag the size of her palm.

"Go ahead. You can look."

Annalisse pulled the strings open on an empty bag and scrunched the bottom. "I don't feel anything inside. Is this a joke?"

"The only joke was my lame marriage proposal that fell flat. I don't blame you for ignoring it." He took what she had assumed to be a jewelry pouch from her hand and shook it upside down. "It's empty now, but after we find Kate, we'll fill this bag and more with fantastic memories so intense they'll take your breath away. I'm desperately in love with you." Alec's wide gray eyes were anxious. "Can you forgive a fool?" He fondly ran his hand through her hair.

Her eyes filled with happy tears. She closed them tightly, allowing trails of relief to trickle down her cheeks. She'd fretted over her and Alec for nothing. Except he still felt the need to keep secrets from her.

Annalisse hugged him around the neck, taking care not to crush his ribs or add more pain to his whiplash injury.

Alec roamed her back with his hand. "You okay?"

She wiped her eyes and sniffed. "Better. I've carried around a dark cloud so long, I wasn't sure there was an us left." Annalisse sank down on the sofa beside him. She pulled her knees into her chest and rested her head on Alec's thigh, playing with the strings of the velvet bag.

Alec's phone chimed with a text message. He leaned over the screen. "Drake. He's in Harriman. Forty-five minutes out."

"Where could Kate be? Someone sure as hell knows." She picked up one of Alec's enclosure cards. "Can we read a few more of these first before I hit the shower?"

"As many as you want."

CHAPTER TEN

An hour later, a surfer-type character descended upon Brookehaven Estate. All but his board and swimsuit were missing. The investigator's casual attire brought a smile to Annalisse's face.

Inside the stable breezeway with Alec and Bill Drake, she marveled at Drake's long, sun-bleached hair and cocoa butter-induced tan. Ditching the usual detective garb, Drake sported a palm tree Hawaiian-style shirt and faded chinos. His clothes were rumpled; she assumed he'd slept in them at a rest stop between here and Connecticut. Annalisse hadn't visited the West Coast, but she imagined Drake might fit as a Malibu beach bum or maybe an island hopper.

She wondered how Drake and Alec had crossed paths, then it dawned on her. *The ex.* Alec might have hired him to follow Tina and her lover. Recalling their sad mistake of a marriage made her wince.

"Mr. Drake, how long have you known Alec?"

"College." Alec's curt interruption had a sharpness to it. "Can I get you something to drink? Coffee?"

He gestured toward his office, offering Drake a kinder look.

"I'm good. Coffee'd out. Man, you haven't changed. I can't get over it."

"Must be my new moisturizer." Alec framed his face with his hands, preening a bit and flashing a bright smile.

"Like I said, haven't changed a bit." Drake turned. "Annalisse. If it's okay, I like dealing on a first-name basis."

"Sure."

"Other than what you've told me already, can you think of any reason your aunt might leave this barn on purpose? Like to meet someone or maybe called away by a friend?"

"No way. Especially after you consider the syringe we found and my aunt's self-defense pen." She pointed to the tack room.

Drake raised his hand. "I know. Just humor me."

"I'll get the baggies from the refrigerator with the stuff Annalisse mentioned." Alec navigated his boot carefully along the bricked area.

"Bill, I know my aunt. She wouldn't leave without telling me. She was taken from the barn. There's no doubt."

"May I look around?" Drake pointed to the tack room door.

"Feel free."

"One other question. Could your aunt have staged this to look like an abduction?"

Annalisse pondered that possibility but couldn't come up with a reason for such a scheme. Kate couldn't have known she'd land at Alec's.

"Auntie wasn't expecting me at the farm yesterday. She wasn't expecting to find a dead man either. Why go to the trouble to stage an abduction at Brookehaven when she could've done it at Walker Farm?"

Annalisse swept into Alec's office, leaving Bill to check out the tack room. Deep lines furrowed Alec's forehead, and he bit his lower lip, holding the plastic bags in a death grip.

"What's wrong?" she whispered.

"I'm wondering if we missed something obvious."

"Because Bill thinks Auntie might have left on purpose?"

"Partly." He lifted the zip bag and studied it. "Who would use a drug on that sweet old woman?"

Annalisse leaned against the fridge door. "I had the exact thought. Kate doesn't deserve this. Dammit." She let out an audible sigh that surprised herself with its resonance. "I sure hope your guy is good. I hate to think what's in that syringe."

"May I?" Drake entered the office with his latex-gloved hand out, taking the bag from Alec. He unzipped the top and rolled the tube in his fingers. "You found it intact like this? Outside?"

Alec nodded. "Yeah, between this building and the brood mare barn."

Drake slowly pulled out the plunger and sniffed, then set the syringe beneath Alec's nose.

"Shit. Ketavet. I was afraid of that." Alec pursed his lips.

"Surprised you didn't smell it yourself, you being a vet." Drake depressed the plunger into the syringe and deposited it in the bag. "I'll overnight it to my guy in the morning for confirmation."

"Confirmation of what? What's in the syringe?" Annalisse stepped closer to Alec and grabbed his shirt.

"Ketamine. Special K." Alec covered her hand with his. "I'm sorry, sweetness."

Annalisse pulled her hand away and backed into his desk. "Isn't that a date-rape drug?"

Alec opened his mouth, but she cut him off.

"Why didn't you tell me what you *thought* was in that syringe? You're the doctor. What will that drug do to a heart patient on ACE inhibitors?"

"I didn't want to alarm you. Baby, we don't know for sure—"

"What? If Kate was injected with it? Your truck meds were locked. What else would the drug be used for?" She asked Bill, "In your experience, what does Ketamine do to the heart?"

He made eye contact with Alec over her shoulder.

"Don't look at him. I don't want it sugarcoated."

"It depends on the person."

"It speeds up the heart, doesn't it?"

"It's known to cause heart palpitations, but that doesn't mean…"

Annalisse sat on the corner of Alec's desk, bent over, palms shielding her hot breath. She tasted Helga's pastry again as she swallowed. She slid her hands down her face. "Kate's meds increase blood flow and that… that *poison* makes her heart pound faster." She wound a lock of hair behind her ears and waited a few moments before asking both men, "Could Kate be dead because of that shot?"

"Stop." Alec reached for her hand. "This isn't helpful. Bill, what's our next move?"

"I need access to Kate's home."

"Of course you do. Join the club," Annalisse murmured. She glanced at the clock. "Ethan should check on the stock pretty soon. They need water for sure, possibly hay. Where is he? Still with Hank?"

"Who?" Drake asked.

"The nuisance who works for Kate." Alec steadied himself on his boot. "I'm riding with Annalisse."

"You're a walking casualty who can't be on his feet for long." She caught Alec by the arm. "I'll admit, going back to the farm and running into more detectives doesn't thrill me. I'm sure they don't want to see me either. I'll ride with Bill."

"Why would investigators have a problem with you?" Drake asked.

"The farm is a crime scene. Auntie couldn't stay there anyway."

"Hell with that. CSIs can't keep you out of your house. They've questioned you. The corpse was dropped in the barn, wasn't he? For now, I'm not interested in that crime scene." Drake wrapped the plastic bags with syringe and pen together and slid them into a breast pocket. "That's why the farmhand's here?"

"Unfortunately." Alec looked at Annalisse.

"How does Ethan fit into Kate's disappearance? Is he a person of interest in the homicide?" Drake asked.

"He was interrogated at the sheriff's office after they talked to him at the farm. He doesn't know anything about the vagrant or Kate's whereabouts," Annalisse said.

"I have a theory." Alec hobbled to his desk chair and sat. "He's the only one who lives with your aunt on the ranch premises, isn't he?"

"So?" Annalisse clenched her jaw. Leave it to Alec to drum up a conviction scenario starring Ethan.

"How much do you know about that kid? He shows up one day looking for work after you and Kate end an exhaustive search. That felt too convenient to me."

Drake pulled out a notebook for the first time.

"You're really going there? I know you don't like him, but he'd never conspire to hurt Auntie. That's ridiculous. As a matter of fact, Ethan said his parents sent him to the farm."

"Never heard that one. A one-way trip from New Zealand to New York. Pricey, wouldn't ya say for someone to work for minimum wage. Why not stay in his own country?" Alec tapped the desk with a ballpoint.

"He explained that. Drought brought him here. No grass, no sheep. No sheep, no jobs."

He threw the pen into a wastebasket. "The kid's at Walker Farm full time, and somehow missed the dumping of a corpse in the same barn as Kate's bay?"

"Maggie's a buckskin. A retired member of the family."

"New Zealand." Drake scribbled large letters in his book. "Annalisse, I'd like Ethan to ride with me to the farm. Do you mind?"

"He'll love a chance to quiz you about being a detective, but he'll clam up if you treat him like a suspect.

He fancies himself a bit of a sleuth." She lifted her brows. "Can you dig without coming on too strong?"

"Why are you sticking up for that egotistical...," Alec searched for his next word, "jerk."

"Detective, we'll gather our things. You take Ethan. I need some alone time anyway." Annalisse gave Alec a weak smile and walked to the side of his chair.

"If you'll excuse me, I'll take a few pictures and check in with my assistant." Drake nodded to her, and with a slight bow, he left the office.

She kissed Alec's temple. "Let's get you to the house. It's time for one of those awesommazing pain pills. It wasn't nice of me to go off on you earlier."

Alec eased her into his lap, stretching out his bad ankle. "Just do me a huge favor. Leave Ethan at the farm this time. Don't stay in the farmhouse alone. I can't protect you there."

"As long as Kate's missing, I can't stay there." Annalisse snuggled against him, feeling his neck muscles tense then relax. "I'm glad you came back."

In three hours, Kate would've been gone an entire day. Officially a missing person. Without her meds and possibly headed for another heart attack.

CHAPTER ELEVEN

The curved road to Walker Farm hadn't changed since yesterday—with one exception. Alec's mangled sports car no longer rested against the trees on the straight-away. Virginia creeper and sumac vines crawled through the four-rail fence as before, but the farm's entrance felt foreign to her, as if the road Annalisse had known since childhood was a route to somewhere she wouldn't want to go. Would she ever feel the same about Walker Farm again after this weekend?

She approached the driveway and focused on the entrance. "What the…? Damn you, Jeremy." She studied the sign put up overnight.

Detective Drake's blacked-out sedan pulled in behind her and stopped. Annalisse watched in her side mirror for his car door to open. She waited only a few seconds.

"Is there a problem?" He indicated the closed gate. "Do we need a key?"

She shook her head and depressed the window button. "I doubt it's locked. But if it is, I keep a pair of bolt cutters in the trunk."

"I like a woman who comes prepared." He flashed a bright set of horse teeth at her.

Annalisse pulled back, startled. This guy was all about the look of a television show private eye. His bleached smile was made for Hollywood.

"Good thing it's Sunday. A closed gate should mean anyone official is off duty." Small blessings. Annalisse was tired of investigators swarming the farm.

"So what's the problem?"

"That." She pointed to the four-foot square PROPERTY FOR SALE sign attached to the rails. "The sign's new. I can't believe he'd be so brazen to do this with his mother missing and an active crime on the premises."

"The farm's for sale?"

"Like the sign says—ranch house and thirty acres with the six hundred and fifty surrounding acreage if someone wants the whole parcel. Jeremy makes me sick." Annalisse examined the telephone number on the sign. "I don't know that number." She pursed her lips. "Surprised he'd use a realtor. I'd expect him to do it himself to save the six percent commission like the cheap bastard he is." Annalisse wrote the phone number down on a napkin.

Drake knocked on the hood. "Explain Jeremy inside. Shall we?" He nodded toward the house.

"I know a back entrance into the farm, just in case *you* run into anyone guarding Kate's house or Ethan's. I still have a way inside."

"Any security cameras?"

"No." Annalisse folded the napkin and put it in her tote. "Follow me to the main entrance. If the gate's unlocked, go through but close it behind you. No need to make it obvious someone's here. I'll pull up a little and check for a padlock."

She put the Malibu in gear and craned her neck through the open window. When she saw the simple latch without an added lock, she gave him an all clear.

"Go ahead. Meet me at the farmhouse. I'll pull around back." Annalisse rolled up the window and drove the fence line until it made a sharp turn to the left. Following the neighbor's access road to the south, she eventually came to a T-junction dirt road behind Walker Farm. Three clustered dogwoods fifty yards up marked the place that allowed Annalisse access through a well-disguised section of fence. At the age of sixteen, she'd convinced her aunt that they needed another way into the property. One that no one else knew about. Kate, being open to most of Annalisse's suggestions, had agreed. The times she'd used that area as a means of escape from Jeremy's harassment were too numerous to count. Jeremy had inherited his dad's quick temper and used it on her every chance he got.

"He's not selling this place without a fight."

She approached the weathered horse fence and parked, surveying on foot where the two end pieces were held together with baling wire. Rusted. Just like she'd left it years ago, the last time she'd had enough of Jeremy's torment and made a quick getaway.

Pitch pines nearby rustled their needles, and the hair on her arms stood straight. She glanced around, checking the woodsy scent for any other smell that didn't belong. Annalisse had mistakenly taken the whispering pines for the signal of a cool breeze. Hardly. The late morning heat seared her shoulders through her blouse, and residual exhaust fumes from the engine worsened her breathing in the noxious air.

Ahead, the detective and Ethan had parked next to the farmhouse built in the 1940s. Built from old timbers and little steel—a leaner time when construction materials were scarce during World War II. Annalisse loved that historical aspect of the farm, but Kate found the creaky floors and clanging pipes a pain in the backside.

Annalisse carefully pried the baling wire from the fence and peeled a large portion of the non-climb back, securing it to a post with a larger piece of wire she kept folded and buried nearby. She could easily drive the rental car through the gap.

Other than Drake and Ethan, she appeared to be alone on the farm. Beads of sweat trickled down the middle of her back, hastening her retreat to the car.

"This quiet gives me the willies." She checked for strangers again and pulled through the recently mowed timothy hay, then parked in a secluded corner near a forsythia hedge Kate had to have for its brilliant yellow color in the spring.

Drake was waiting outside his vehicle when she walked around the porch. She spotted Ethan jogging toward his bunkhouse.

"I didn't notice anyone around back. You?" she asked.

"Is that the barn in question?" He tilted his head in the right direction.

"Yeah, but let's not go there first. Start with the house."

Road noise took her attention from Drake. Sunlight glinted off the windshield of a truck slowing in front of the farm.

"Every time I walk on this porch, someone shows up. So much for doing things on the sly." Annalisse stood next to Drake as the rumble got louder in the drive. "I have no idea who that is. Better see what they want."

The vintage Ford with big tires stopped alongside the porch, its engine still running. An elderly man with a handlebar mustache smiled politely at Annalisse. His signature mustache gave him away as one of Kate's wannabe suitors from the Episcopal church. Paul.

"Good afternoon, Annalisse. Didn't see Kate in church this mornin'. Checkin' on her."

"Kind of you. We're good. Thanks." Annalisse hoped her smile put him at ease.

Paul glanced toward the barn and replied, "She never misses worship. Tied up, is she?" His eyes shifted to the detective and rested on him a few beats as if he'd sized up Drake as a rival. "Okay then. Under the weather, is she?" He swiped his mustache. "Church ain't the same without Kate."

Annalisse prickled at his nosiness. "It's my fault we skipped church. I showed up unannounced, and we lost track of time. I'll let her know you stopped by. Thanks for thinking of her." She backed away and waved, hoping he'd get the message.

He did and promptly made a U-turn in the drive.

Drake took out a notebook and wrote down a few lines. "You lie quite well." His voice mocked her.

"I did show up unannounced. I was close enough." She reminded herself he was Alec's friend there to find Kate, and she should be polite. "Is he interesting?"

"Caught him scoping out the barn."

"He knows she hangs there a lot."

"I'll get the name of the church from you later. What can you tell me about him?"

"Paul's sweet on Kate. But she has a ton of admirers. If you'd met her, you'd understand."

"Does he visit with your aunt often?"

"Mostly in church. He comes with flowers sometimes."

"They go out?"

"No. Kate doesn't date." Annalisse was distracted by the truck's dust trail. He hadn't bothered to close the gate. "Darn guy left the gate open."

"Leave it. Shall we?" Drake ushered her up the steps.

Inside the house, the humid kitchen smelled of stale bacon and fermented lilacs. Annalisse scanned the table for Jeremy's letter.

"I want you to see something." She checked the floor under the table and the chair seats for the envelope. "Huh. I'm sure it was here when we left." She continued her search in the living room, checking the coffee and end tables. The letter had vanished.

Jeremy must have taken it yesterday.

"What are you looking for?" He'd followed her into the living area, appraising Kate's numerous tchotchkes. "She collects lots of stuff."

"A letter. Actually, a letter from her son, Jeremy. He's the one selling the farm. Have a look around. What's mundane to me may be clues to you."

Annalisse searched all rooms in the house for the envelope, ending up in Kate's bedroom on her bed. She pulled Kate's presence in. Sinking her nose into the bedspread, she inhaled lavender sachets and the Plumeria perfume from her daughter's Hawaiian vacations. Kate was everywhere in this room she'd occupied with—and without—a husband for nearly fifty years.

A wide doily crocheted long ago stretched across the dresser, faded to an antique yellow from the white thread used to fashion it. Annalisse walked over to the dovetailed jewelry box she'd made as a Girl Scout for her aunt. She handled the sharp corners, recalling the proud day she gave it to Kate. Annalisse took the box back to the bed and bit her quivering lip, tasting salty tears.

She hugged the box to her breast. "Dear God, watch over her wherever she is. Please don't take her from me."

Annalisse raised the lid and set the box on the mattress. She found multicolored, clip-on earrings and the single strand of freshwater pearls Auntie always wore to church. Kate loved pearls. Uncle Ted had given her the necklace for an anniversary gift sometime back, and she'd cherished them as her most favorite piece of jewelry. The only thing missing was a locket—the one she wore the last time Annalisse saw her. The silver locket Annalisse had never opened for a look inside. Until now, she hadn't given the locket any regard.

Lifting the top tray, she sifted through miscellaneous ball points with her uncle's advertising on them and piles upon piles of bobby pins. A tightly rolled tube lay to the back of the box, secured by a scratched gold band. Her breath caught as she imagined who the ring belonged to. By its size, it was a man's ring, and from her recollection of her uncle's ring, it was his.

"What's it doing here?" She slid the ring from the paper roll and placed it inside the jewelry box then unfurled a torn corner. It looked like a print sketch, the kind used by building contractors. She held the drawing up to the light cascading through the blinds. Handwritten script filtered through from the back.

Flipping over the paper, she read, "I've often wondered what it felt like to bungee jump. The Williamsburg Bridge seems like a good place to try it. When you find this, I've escaped you for good. I couldn't live with your secrets. I hope you can. Ted."

Annalisse's throat felt like sandpaper as she clutched the note in sweaty fingers.

Her uncle's words held so much pain.

Bungee jump? What a sick joke but so typical of her uncle's dry humor.

She dropped the page to the bedspread and flattened it to quell her shaking hands. What did he mean by *secrets*?

"Annalisse?"

She folded the paper in half and slid it into her boot.

"In here."

Drake entered the room. "Another car out front." He tilted his head toward the driveway.

"Who now?" Annalisse scooped up her uncle's ring and shoved it into a jean pocket, putting the jewelry box together and depositing it on the dresser.

The screen door squealed, and footsteps thumped into the kitchen.

"Knock knock… Momma?"

The woman's shrill voice was a spear into Annalisse's chest. Jillian picked a bad weekend to come.

"Jillian. You're a long way from home."

"Mom and I have plans. Where is she?"

Kate's daughter had gained an easy thirty pounds since Annalisse's last visit with her prior to leaving for NYU. The added weight had aged Jillian beyond her forty years into an apple shape with a face too small for the rest of her. Life on the West Coast was either Shangri-La, or she ate as a substitution for something missing in her life. In her college days, pretty Jillian lugged around an entourage of boyfriends, but sadly, she lacked Jeremy's brains. Kate was ecstatic when her daughter found a smart IT manager with a new job waiting in Washington once Jillian graduated. A high-maintenance girl required a good paycheck to be happy. Kate knew the husband wouldn't let her starve.

Jillian dropped her designer bag on the table, the little metal feet clicking on the wood. "Where's Momma?" She put her hands on her hips.

"Did you have a good flight?" Annalisse hoped to avoid confrontation and leave as quickly as possible.

"My God, Annalisse. That extra baggage in the caboose isn't very becoming."

Drake coughed and widened his eyes at Annalisse.

Jillian sneered at her and fluffed out the tent peasant blouse she wore, shaking upper arm flab in the process. The sickly scent of gardenia spread throughout the kitchen, a reminder of when Jillian would douse herself in White Shoulders and pretend to be Elizabeth Arden herself, messing with every new skin product that hit the market.

"Who *are* you anyway?" Jillian gazed longingly at Drake, then squeezed into one of the ladder-back chairs with the grace of an elephant.

"Excuse me, ladies. I'll be outside."

Annalisse hadn't seen a man move that fast in a long time and wished she were right behind his palm leaves that were doing the hula on his back. Her day had shaped up nicely.

The kitchen table groaned when Jillian leaned on her breasts and planted her elbows on the hardwood. Annalisse had no desire to chat with her malicious cousin but decided it was in her best interest to find out what she could and get the encounter over with.

"Didn't Jeremy mention your mom's missing?" Annalisse dragged a chair out from the table.

"I thought she'd turn up by now. Who put that sign on the road? You?"

"Is your family here too?" Annalisse asked.

"My husband can't take vacation anytime he wants. He's watching the girls. I asked for a few days off from the shop. So, what's the scoop on Mom? She knew I was coming in this weekend."

"What shop? You have a job?"

"Part time at a gift shop. The girls have school, and I was bored to tears staying at home." She pulled out a mirrored compact and dabbed foundation on the end of her nose.

"Jillian, I'm worried about her. Your mom wouldn't leave Alec's barn and not tell me." She slid a hand inside her boot and pushed the note from Ted farther down her pant leg.

"No one gave you the right to put up a sign. This isn't your place to sell." Jillian snarled.

"Your brother's handiwork."

"I called him from the driveway. It wasn't him."

"The hell it wasn't. I read his letter myself."

"What letter?"

"The one—forget it. He's taken it. Since when does Jeremy use a toll-free number?"

"Since never. What are you talking about?" Jillian slapped the table. "Don't change the subject."

"I need to go."

Jillian couldn't care less about her mother's whereabouts and showed no concern for her either. Nothing had changed. Jillian always put herself first. Annalisse gathered her tote and slung it over a shoulder.

"Wait. How did Mom disappear?" Jillian fiddled with the compact, looked at herself again, and slipped it into her purse.

Annalisse detailed briefly the search for Kate at Alec's stables. "If you can think of anyone who might want to hurt your mother, give me their name. If Kate calls you, you have my cell."

"Maybe I should tell the boyfriend outside? He's a cutie, in a hippie sort of way." Jillian grinned broadly.

"Hippies went out with the sixties." Annalisse considered saying more about Drake's identity, then trashed the idea.

"You can't leave. I want a complete explanation of everything that happened the moment you arrived on this farm." Jillian pushed herself from the table, grating the chair legs into a high-pitched frenzy. "You were the last person to see Momma. I deserve to know the whole story." The nose in the air was a nice touch.

She deserved. All Jillian's hissy fits began with those words. Kate might have been unhappy about the daughter's move to the West Coast, but Annalisse didn't miss her one bit.

Scanning the kitchen one last time for Jeremy's note, Annalisse slipped out onto the hot porch. Detective Drake waited in the sun near the driveway.

Annalisse contemplated how to get to her car without Jillian's knowledge.

"I haven't given you permission to leave yet." Jillian slammed the screen door behind her and dug into her purse. "Darn it. I forgot to write that phone number down."

"What number?" Annalisse asked.

"The one on the sign."

Thumbing between wallet and keys, Annalisse came up with the napkin where she'd scrawled the number. "Grab your phone and call it. I'm curious about that toll-free number myself." She recited it to Jillian and waited for her thick fingers to plug in the numbers.

Jillian held the phone to her ear for a time, looking a little like a lion with her overdone mane radiating from her head. "No message."

"Who would put a number on a commercial sign without having a message? What did you hear?" Annalisse asked.

"It rang. A click, then dead air."

"I'll call it." Annalisse drew out her phone.

"Never mind. I'll try it later."

Detective Drake wandered to the porch like a lost boy or maybe to save her.

Annalisse smiled at his aloofness in Jillian's presence. She completely understood. First impressions of Jillian's holier-than-thou personality had that effect on people.

"Do you have a minute?" Drake motioned her with his eyes, indicating he wanted to talk away from other ears.

"We aren't finished yet. I'll just get my things from the car and unpack. Come back inside when you're done." Jillian plodded past Drake, eyeing him on the way.

"I'll be up in a minute." Annalisse hated the browbeating by her cousin. Daddy's girl always got her way with Uncle Ted, and it drove a wedge into the family. Kate was constantly arguing with her husband about his preferential treatment of Jillian over Jeremy. During those moments, Annalisse felt happy knowing it was better to be a cousin than a sibling of those two brats.

She stopped in the shade of a big maple, Drake behind her. She wiped sweat from her brow, praying for a slight breeze, and dropped her tote on the ground.

"That's Jeremy's sister."

"Uh-huh."

"She planned to stay at the farm. Let her fight it out with investigators. They can boot her out."

"I didn't find anything useful in the house. But Ethan's a curiosity. I can't put my finger on him yet. When we talked in the car, he recalled a group of men with your aunt several days ago."

"I think he makes up stuff just to be relevant. What about the men?"

"Ethan recognized one of them. He thought. But with the distance, he couldn't be sure. They were talking to Kate, raising their voices."

"Who'd he recognize? How many men? Ethan brought up a visit from Jeremy after the fact. He suffers from selective recall syndrome." Her gaze followed the path to his bunkhouse. "It's hard to know what to believe."

A shadow crossed behind the PI's eyes, as if he were calculating Ethan's place in recent events like Alec had.

"Aunt Kate plays bridge, bunco, and board games with ladies from the church. They gossip and drink coffee and lemonade. She doesn't entertain groups of men."

"What about the guy in the truck earlier? Could he have been here?"

She rubbed thumb and forefinger along her chin. "Kate's popular. I've never seen anyone cross the line with Auntie, but I'm not here during the week." Annalisse watched the farmhouse window for signs of Jillian. "Let's move to the side of the house. I've gotta vamoose before she changes her mind and comes back."

"Alec has a grudge against Ethan?" he asked as his shoes crunched fallen leaves.

"If jealousy is a grudge." She chuckled half-heartedly.

"Around a sexy woman like you, I don't blame him." His light eyes met hers. "Don't tell him I said that," he added with an embarrassed smile.

"I'll keep it between us." She batted her lashes and immediately regretted it. Annalisse wasn't accustomed to open flattery from other men, and flirting felt wrong but nice. "Is Ethan covering for someone? Like himself?" she asked.

"Too soon to tell. He likes your aunt a lot, and he has a thing for you."

"Please."

Annalisse's phone rang Kate's ringtone, and she jumped.

"Kate!" She crouched and extracted her phone.

"Can you record it?" he asked.

"No." She verified the number, swiped her phone, and drums pounded a rickety beat in her chest. "Auntie?"

The same open air as the last time a call came in from her aunt's phone. "I don't know who this is, but let me speak to Kate. Please give the phone to her."

Nothing.

"What do you want? Money? Tell me how much, and we'll pay."

Drake shook his head strongly and mouthed the word "No."

Synthesized music and electric guitars filled the earpiece.

Annalisse knew the tune.

"What do you want?" Lyrics from the late 1970s drifted from the phone. "Hello?" She placed the phone into Drake's outstretched hand.

He quickly punched an autodial number in his own cell, holding out Annalisse's phone as far away as his arm would allow. He whispered, "It's me. I need a tower dump on this number." Drake recited Kate's phone number to the caller. "The line's still open." He paused. "Yeah, you got it right. 'Who Are You' by the Who. Theme song to a crime TV series. Tell me when you've got something. I'll be in touch." He gave Annalisse's phone back to her while the song played. "Don't hang up," he whispered.

The music finished, and the call ended.

"Gone. The song ran over six minutes. Can you trace it?"

Drake pocketed his phone. "Not that simple. The law protects private citizens. No tracking without a warrant. Unless…"

"What?"

"Do you and your aunt have tracking apps on your phones?"

She didn't need to answer. Annalisse was sure that he read the frustration on her face.

"Is Kate on your phone plan?"

"Scratch that one too. What's with the tune? I don't get it."

"We'll have to work on that. It's easy enough to find without a recording from your phone. My assistant's good at that kind of stuff. This song isn't one of your aunt's favorites, is it?"

"Hardly. She turned the channel when that show came on. Too explicit. You said tower dump. What's that?"

"It's possible to find a cell location by dissecting out all other phone numbers on that tower. We follow the number from tower to tower and drop out the numbers that don't follow Kate's phone until we capture only Kate's phone and others who may be in close proximity. It's likely whoever has Kate also has a phone of their own. Chasing towers works well when a suspect is on the move."

"What if she's not moving? How long does that take?"

"The tactic isn't foolproof. Wireless carriers are a hassle. This may be all for naught if the caller is spoofing us by using your aunt's telephone number, but the call isn't actually coming from her phone. A location could take a while."

"Bill, we don't have a while." She fiddled with her purse. "I have to scoot. Jillian doesn't know about my escape route. Please don't mention it. Can we meet at Brookehaven in the morning to discuss Ethan and what your assistant finds? That will give you enough time to track down some people from church. I won't leave Alec longer than I have to. It's killing him to stay behind." She looked at her watch. "Almost twenty-four hours. We've got to find her."

"Can I get Jeremy's number? I'll need to speak to him in person."

"Lucky for you, he's not far. He was here at the farm yesterday. I doubt that he would drive to his New Jersey office with Kate missing. But then again, with him, you never know. If you think Jillian has an attitude, wait till you talk to *him.*" She frowned at the memory of Jeremy's smirk. "When I get to the car, I'll text you Jeremy's contact info and what I know about Kate's church friends." She studied his shirt again. "Dying to know—are you a West Coaster?"

"Florida Keys."

"Wrong coast." She laughed and turned for her dreaded jog through the pasture.

"Hey, you want me to tell the lady inside anything?"

Annalisse stopped and offered him a sly smile. "Don't mention that you're investigating her mother's case. She thinks you're my boyfriend. Play it up." She turned back and ran. *Forgive me, Kate. I couldn't help myself.*

What began as a sprint through an acre of four-inch mowed hay slowed to a fast walk to the rental car. Annalisse's shirt was drenched and her throat parched from panting like a dog. Her heart thundered, banging to the Who song playing over and over in her head, complete with Pete Townsend standing on stage, smashing his guitar to smithereens.

She sped up into an easy jog, reaching the car and finding the door she'd stupidly left unlocked. Sliding in, she started the engine and punched the button for air, sticking her face into the vent. She closed her eyes, allowing the cold to penetrate her skin and dry the perspiration.

Then she opened her eyes… and saw yellow ducks on a blue background on the passenger seat.

With a big yellow bow.

She almost jumped out of her skin. "What the hell? Ethan?" Then logic took over. She doubted the package came from him.

The paper was juvenile, made for a baby shower or a birthday. She reached for the box, then jerked her hand back, choosing instead to lean over and listen for noise inside.

Silence.

She fought the urge to leap out of the car in case the box was a bomb. What was it, and who'd left it there?

When the CIA was looking for Alec's mother, she'd learned to trust nothing and no one. She wanted badly to open the box, but people ended up dead that way. Walker Farm was filled with secrets and now another mystery. She could swipe it off the seat and drive away, but that was a stupid idea.

Call Bill.

She dug around until she found her phone.

"Hey. Wherever you are, stop what you're doing. Call me ASAP." She left the message while driving to the main road.

CHAPTER TWELVE

At the crest of the hill, Alec parked the ATV. A dozen greenish tombstones dotted the Brookehaven graveyard in a peace that calmed his uneasy mind. He wiggled the toes on his bad foot and winced when the loafer connected with the puffy tissue over his ankle bone. He dropped the shoe to the floorboard and wiggled some more. The walking boot had caused a deep-in-the-marrow ache, and the swelling had worsened overnight. He'd ditched his bandage and boot for the drive, and it felt freeing. In a long breath, he drew the centuries into his lungs while a breeze of the departed cooled his purple skin.

He recalled how he'd left Annalisse asleep in the master suite, snoring so loudly, he made himself get up or wake her with laughter he couldn't contain. The jaunt outside in solitude with chirping chipmunks and the call of Cooper's hawks gave him time to reflect on where they were going. As a couple. Had his past neglect altered her feelings for him? What would it do to

Annalisse if they didn't find Kate? What would it do to *them*?

What his mother told him privately after the vacation argument convinced him how vulnerable Annalisse was. How important an occasional romantic adventure was to their relationship and that she craved being swept away. Annalisse expected a fairy tale once in a while.

"No." He shook his head. That wasn't fair to her. A little fairy dust sprinkled over his sausage and eggs breakfast would do him wonders too.

Endless travel meetings weren't cutting it for either of them. He must set his priorities right for the sake of saving what was left of the Alec and Annalisse from Greece.

Last night and the drawing room filled with roses played out as a darn good beginning. He smiled, envisioning her lithe body lying next to him in the pink flush of afterglow. The predatory gleam in her eyes that made him hard just thinking about the intensity of her turquoise eyes—craving him. Man, she did things to him. Annalisse lit up his very existence. *How could I have ignored her, and why did it take me so long to realize it?*

He could devote more time to her if he sold the corporation. That new option came up on the ride to the airport. He'd had a conversation with a big-three car manufacturer who'd pitched the proposition prior to his flight to the union bosses' powwow in Pennsylvania. The CEO called to set up a meeting in Naples to discuss the acquisition of Signorile. A burden slowly eating away at his true career—his veterinarian practice. The empty hospital building a stone's throw from the estate was a constant reminder of what he couldn't have as long as the family business continued its current track.

He wished she was with him now. He'd promised to show her the estate cemetery so long ago. With his head resting against the wire mesh, it dawned on him—they'd never made it up here. By now, she'd probably forgotten that promise.

"Yeah, right." His laughter echoed through the forest. "She never forgets anything."

He gazed over the monuments, eaten away at the corners by storms or deer looking for minerals in their diet. Centuries-old juniper enclosed the area with their wide trunks, shading the resting places of ordinary people, brave people, valiant warriors who'd saved the nation from an English king and themselves.

"Man, if we can't find Kate… or if we do and…" Alec cringed at the thought. The loss of his father had broken him. If he'd lost his mother too, left alone to carry on for the family—Annalisse would be changed if she lost her Aunt Kate.

"I'll find her for you. Bill's one of the best." Alec's throat tightened. A promise he might not be able to keep. The dead man in the Walker barn had something to do with Kate's disappearance. Like Annalisse, he too was certain.

He twisted his Rolex around and stared at the dial. Bill said he had information for them at nine. Anything would be a start. He reached for the key in the ignition.

The rumble of a small engine approached. He craned his neck for a look.

A smokin'-hot brunette behind the wheel of a matching ATV waved.

The burden on his shoulders lightened.

In her presence, it always did.

Annalisse pulled up beside him, and he waited for her explosion when she noticed he'd driven without his boot.

"A long way from home, aren't ya?" Annalisse's smile disappeared when she glanced at his invisible footwear. "Alec." She sighed. "Look at the color of that ankle. And you drove with it?"

"Used my left foot, babe. It's okay to give it a breather once in a while. It hasn't throbbed once since I unwrapped it." He lifted his leg slightly, then grimaced when a twinge ran up his calf.

She jumped down and folded her arms. "You're right. Who am I to keep you from relapsing into a hospital bed?" She laughed. "It's cool. Helga already told me you ditched the boot." She planted a soft kiss on his lips. "Good morning. I don't remember when I fell asleep. *Someone* kept me up most of the night." The twinkle in her eyes roused him just thinking about their night of hot sex. It had been long overdue.

"New look?" He touched her longer-than-usual choice for tops.

"I'm such a boob. I put this shirt on because of this." She lifted the hem above her stomach and exposed the band of her bra. "I saw these advertised and decided I needed an option from my holster."

"Whoa. A flashbang?"

"Can't get used to the weight of my .38 between the girls. It feels like a barbell hanging there." She smiled while he reached up to feel the suede loop holding her pistol, then ran his fingers over the top of her breast. "Okay, Zavos." Annalisse swiped his hand away.

A flash of blue behind her caught his attention. "What's that?" He pointed. "Somebody's birthday?"

She reached for the gift-wrapped box. "I didn't mention this yesterday. I wanted time to think about it. Bill told me to leave it in the car and wait until he arrived. But I can't stand it. It's… calling to me."

He studied the cartoon ducks, then watched her face for clues.

"You're gonna have to let me in on the joke. What's with the ducks?"

"Move over."

Alec carefully scooted his leg aside to make room for Annalisse and a gift the size of a shoebox. When she dropped the box on her thighs, something rattled inside.

"What's in it, maracas?" He snatched the box and shook it.

"Don't!" She wrenched the package from his hands and set it down gingerly, listening near the bow.

"It talks too?" Alec stretched against his seat, dumbfounded. "You've been acting scary since you got back yesterday. Care to tell me what went on with you and Bill at the farm?"

"Nothing went on between *us*. Oh hell, here's the scoop."

Annalisse recounted the day's events at Walker Farm, including the strange call from Kate's phone.

"Why didn't you at least tell me about that call?" He squeezed her knee. "What did Bill say?"

"He had his assistant try some kind of a tower dump. They use cell towers to find people. Ask Drake. He says it's hard to trace phones."

"Okay. What about this?" Alec tapped the box. "It just showed up inside your car?"

"Pretty much. This was a bad idea. I should've left it in the rental car." She turned to get out.

"Wait." He pulled her back. "You brought it up here for a reason."

Annalisse slowly settled back in the seat. "I wanted a witness," she said, barely audible.

He scrunched his brows together, unsure of what he'd heard.

"I figured at least one of us would survive if it blew up," she added.

He ventured a chuckle, then said, "You're serious."

"I told Helga where I was going, so if we didn't return, they'd know where to look for the bodies." She dropped her head against his shoulder and joined him in nervous laughter. "I need a getaway. Do you happen to know a sweet guy who'd like to go with?" She fluttered her lashes at him.

He put an arm around her shoulder and tucked her close. "How about a walk through time instead?"

She sent him a look filled with wonder.

"Over there." He tipped his head toward the cemetery.

"Are those—grave markers? Your old cemetery's *here*?" She laid the package on the seat and took off up the hill without as much as a glance back.

Alec moved slower, careful where he placed his feet.

"Hallowed ground." Annalisse whipped her arms wide. "It's magnificent. I'll bet entire families are buried here." She crouched and wiped at moss smudging a stone on the ground. "This one has a big brick as a marker."

He couldn't keep up, so he leaned against a tree, watching her.

"This one is like a broken tablet. It's from the early 1800s. Says: DIED IN THE SERVICE OF HIS COUNTRY, 1835. Texas revolution, I think. His name is missing." She moved to the next. "Some date back to the Revolutionary War!" She turned toward him. "The research I could do here. So awesome, and in your backyard."

"I wish we could stay longer, but we can come back. It's not going anywhere." Alec shifted his weight to his good leg, his ankle throbbing with a vengeance after removing his boot.

Annalisse got on her knees and began digging with her hands. "You should see this. There's a brick the size of a lunchbox with the name LAURA SEELEY, 1851–1871. Beside it are too smaller bricks. Both say SEELEY INFANT, 1871. Oh, Alec. This woman must have died in childbirth. That name's familiar, but I can't recall why."

He smiled at the historian in her. She loved puzzles from the past. Admiration mixed with desire washed over him as he followed her tour through the centuries.

A few minutes later, she stood by his side, wiping the dirt from her hands on her shapely behind.

"What?" She swatted at imaginary debris on her butt. "Is it gone? I can't wait to come back here." She hugged him and gave him a quick peck on the lips. "Let's go. You look like you're about to keel over."

"The ankle doesn't hurt that badly."

"Don't lie. C'mon. I'll help you to your steed."

When they got to the ATVs, she picked up the package, and he caught her wrist.

"We open this now. You stand over there." He pointed to a juniper bush several yards away and waited for Annalisse to get behind it. Alec closed his eyes and drew a breath, then stripped off the ribbon and bow, taking care with the tape. A shoebox. "Nothing weird yet," he yelled. Through clenched teeth, he gently lifted the lid on a folded sheet of white tissue. When he peeled the paper back, he found a pink plastic baby rattle with a tag attached to the middle. He held up the rattle and gently shook, motioning for Annalisse to come back.

"Is that what I think it is?" She leaned in. "Who would send a rattle?"

"Take a look at what's written on it." Alec turned the card over.

"*I know who you are.*" Annalisse reread the card. "The song 'Who Are You' is played in my ear, and now we get this? She pinched the bridge of her nose. "Who's screwing with us?" She tossed the rattle into the box. "Dammit! Do you think this has anything to do with Kate?"

Alec pulled out his phone and looked at a text. "Bill's at the house." He slid the phone into his pocket. "Leave your ATV. One of the grooms can retrieve it. Ride back with me."

***

Annalisse recognized Bill Drake's sedan parked in the estate drive but shrunk into her seat when she saw the second vehicle with slanted silver letters emblazoned on the door.

"What's an Orange County sheriff doing in Sullivan County?" She tugged on Alec's polo with a sick feeling in her gut. She wanted to believe they'd found Kate, but their private detective showing up with the sheriff… she didn't know what that meant. "Did you know a sheriff was coming?"

"No." Alec wasn't smiling when he reached for her hand. "Stay positive."

The furry-browed Officer McDonaugh stepped out of his vehicle when they pulled up. She eyed Drake, who'd dressed in a more conservative short-sleeved button-down, leaning against his car, his face expressionless. Annalisse couldn't read their body language, which heightened her anxiety.

"Morning." Alec shook the officer's hand. "Alec Zavos." He nodded to Drake.

"Captain McDonaugh. I knew your dad well. He was a fine man. I'm sorry for your loss." The officer offered Alec his business card.

"Would you like to come inside?" Alec directed the men to the front door, acknowledging Annalisse with his eyes.

She stayed a short distance behind, holding the shoebox. Maybe McDonaugh's presence meant good news.

"Sorry. for the early intrusion." McDonaugh scooted the stool at the breakfast bar and sat down. He looked at the detective as if to give him the floor.

Drake asked Annalisse, "Is that the box?" He cleared his throat when she averted his gaze. "Captain McDonaugh and I had a meeting this morning. When I told him Mrs. Walker disappeared on Saturday, he asked to follow me out here. He has some news on the man found at Walker Farm."

"Do you know who he is?" she asked eagerly.

"Yes. He was a Vietnam vet, easily found in the fingerprint database. Keith Albers. Seventy years old. Lived on Long Island."

"Long Island?" She checked Alec for a reaction, but he was staring at the officer. "Was he killed on the farm or somewhere else?"

McDonaugh shook his head. "He was dumped on your aunt's property. The cause of death was ligature strangulation, but they also found marks on his neck from someone's hands and plenty of salt water in his lungs. He was riddled with cancer. Terminal. Maybe a couple of months left to live."

"Why did he pack around a Thomas Taylor ID?" When she realized what she'd said, she called herself an idiot. The shocked look on McDonaugh's face sent her into cover-her-ass mode. "I assumed Detective Trask had explained what we did. Can you blame us for being curious?"

"Your aunt told me his head was turned." The officer glared at her. "What else?"

"We looked in his wallet. That's it. Then we put everything back like we found him. I promise you."

Her tongue had twisted the words into unconvincing knots. "Curiosity." She clung to Alec's hand and squeezed so her own would stop trembling.

"Did you know Keith Albers?" McDonaugh addressed both of them.

"No. How did he get from Long Island to Auntie's barn?" she asked.

"We recovered some other DNA. Not Albers's. We're still running it down. Have you had any contact with Mrs. Walker since Saturday?" the officer asked.

"As I said this morning, Annalisse and Alec both received calls from her cell phone." Drake looked at her. "I told him about the music and that box. That you've already opened."

"At my request. I opened it. Take a look." He gave the box to Drake.

The detective took the rattle out of the tissue, raising it for the officer. "*I know who you are*. Huh." He laid it onto the paper. "Now that we've all left our prints on it. Shit."

"The sender probably used gloves. Is that little rattle about Mrs. Walker or you?" McDonaugh asked.

"What do you mean?" Alec sniped at the officer.

The captain took the box from Drake and sat in the armchair, rolling the rattle and reading the note. "I don't think the Albers case is unrelated to your aunt's disappearance. When I spoke to Mr. Drake earlier, I thought the two might be connected." He shook the rattle and laid it into the box. "Orange County has a killer, and you have a kook." He set the box on the chair and stood, shifting his gun belt and pistol. "Pleasure to meet you, Mr. Zavos. Miss." He tipped his head to her slightly. "I hope you find your aunt."

"Wait." Annalisse jumped to her feet and followed him to the door. "How can you tell the cases aren't related? My aunt disappeared a few hours after finding the Albers man. You've made a mistake. The man and my aunt *are* related. They have to be."

"Captain, when you find out who dumped the Albers guy, please let us know." Alec closed the door behind the officer.

"That was fun." Annalisse's chest was still pounding from McDonaugh's comment. She picked up the box and calmly returned the lid. "If the missing person was *his* aunt, I wonder if the good captain would be so flip. Do you agree these two events are a coincidence?" she asked Drake.

"No, I don't and neither does he. I heard the wheels working in his head while he shook the rattle. McDonaugh doesn't want me or you two poking around his homicide case. I believe Albers was dumped in the barn to trigger Kate. Partly to get her to leave the farm. Whoever put him there knew Kate would either want to leave or would be asked to leave the farm. Albers was personal. He was a message to your aunt as blatant as that fake ID card. The person who left Albers couldn't know where Kate would go but could've followed her here." Drake rubbed the bags under his eyes. "That brings me to Jeremy."

"Alec, where's Helga?"

He gave her a simple shrug.

She fought the need to look for the housekeeper and swung back to Drake. "Did you talk to Jeremy in person yet?"

"Yep. He doesn't have a clue who put up the sale sign. According to him, neither of them hung the sign on the fence."

"That's a lie. Who else did it? If we'd found Jeremy's letter in the house, you'd know he intended to sell it. How about the eight hundred number?" she asked.

"He never denied wanting to sell the farm and was authentically angry about the sign. In fact, he's probably taken it down. When I called the number, it rang three times and went right to a mailbox that hasn't been set up."

"A commercial real estate number has no way to get a message?" Alec scrunched his nose. "No way. It's a red herring, just like dumping a man in the barn with the wrong identification. Why go to the trouble to change his identity?"

"Because a Thomas Taylor shook the hell out of Kate. She calmed down when she saw the dead man's face. She didn't know him, but someone wanted Kate to *think* he was Thomas Taylor. The person who dumped the body *knew* my aunt would find that card in his wallet. I agree with Bill. The killer made it personal."

"Why?" Bill asked. "Why the messages meant for you, Annalisse? *Who are you* and *I know who you are…* isn't random."

"Don't forget Kate's text to Alec in the hospital. It's not just about me."

"There may be more to the song once we check out the lyrics," Alec added, patting her hand.

Bill waited through a few seconds of silence. "Does Mrs. Walker have early onset dementia?"

Annalisse's jaw dropped. "What?"

"Jeremy said—"

"He told you that?" She turned to Alec. "I swear I'm going to strangle him. He's going to land in hell for his lies." Fury heated her face.

Alec covered her hand, then laced his fingers with hers. "Easy there, babe," he whispered. "Kate is as clear-headed as any of us, Bill."

"His story was convincing."

"Jeremy's an expert liar. I forget more things than she does. Auntie is razor sharp in mind and wit. Damn that manipulative creep. It's an excuse to sell the farm. I think he wanted her gone so badly that he's set this up. Including following us here on Saturday and kidnapping his mother."

"I don't know Jeremy, but his denial sounded credible. Genuinely worried for his mother. It's a stretch that he'd have a man killed as a ruse to sell a property." Drake crossed his legs at his ankles. "That aside, my assistant's been working the cell location from the time the song came in." He nonchalantly drew a notebook from his pocket.

Annalisse dropped Alec's hand and jumped to the edge of the cushion. "You know where she is? Why didn't you tell us?"

"We have one cell tower and thousands of cell numbers. That's all. Unless the subject is moving, it's nearly impossible to narrow down the phone's location in a dump. If we've been spoofed, we can forget it. Annalisse, is there any reason your aunt would be in Massachusetts?"

"No."

"No relatives or friends there?"

"None that I know of." She looked at Alec. "What do you think? Auntie in Massachusetts?"

"Nothing comes to mind."

"It's a shot in the dark, but we have to start someplace. I've taken my assistant off the Connecticut case and put him on Kate full time. I recommend we check out facilities like retirement homes, nursing homes, and places similar to see if she's been admitted— since Jeremy dropped her mental state into the equation. I expect we'll find hundreds of possibilities in the state."

"What if she's not in Massachusetts but passed through into another state? Or under an assumed name? What then?" Alec asked.

He'd said what she was thinking. Kate could be anywhere. An abandoned farmhouse, a motel room— the trunk of a car. She shuddered at the image her thoughts conjured. When they were hunting for Alec's mother last fall, they'd had similar worries. There were as many options as gravel stones in Alec's driveway.

"Do you recall if your aunt took a purse?" Drake asked.

Annalisse sat against the back of the sofa to think. "Maybe. I'll check my car."

"You can't. It's at the shop." Alec tugged her down and said to his friend, "Annalisse's car wouldn't start, and it was fine when she arrived. Tampered with?"

"Entirely possible. I ask about the purse because of her medication. When I spoke to Jillian, she said something peculiar. Kate squirreled away pills in her pockets?"

Annalisse nodded and smiled. "Kate must have told her. Since Auntie's second heart attack, she's complained of mild angina. Her doctor prescribed nitroglycerin if she felt chest pain. She knows to lay off any lifting or straining. That's why we hired Ethan."

She put herself back into the Beamer the morning Kate went into the stables but couldn't visualize a handbag. "Sometimes she uses a fanny pack. It might have been under her shirt that day. I can't remember. We were in such a hurry to leave." Noticing the weight of her pistol between her breasts, Annalisse rolled her shoulders and plucked at her shirt.

"We know she has her phone," Alec said matter-of-factly.

"Jillian was helpful?" Annalisse asked, imagining her sour expression when she found out Annalisse had escaped the farm the day before.

"Totally wiggy." He coughed a frog from his throat. "Sorry. I don't usually use that term around family members. She danced around my questions as nervous as a cat. I can't be sure if she was trying to throw me off with her loony answers, or she's a space cadet."

"All she's missing is the space suit. That Seattle rain washed away what sense she had left." Annalisse laughed. She was certain Jillian's behavior around Drake was attraction. "I doubt that Jillian can help. Kate never got around to telling me why Perfect Child decided to visit the farm. We haven't seen her and the husband since her dad died."

"I'm going back for a second round with Jillian and Ethan after I meet the priest at the Episcopal church and talk to the parishioners I can find. Especially Paul." Drake glanced at his watch. "Speaking of which, I'd better roll. On my way to Goshen, I'll check in with Sullivan County and make sure that Monticello proper has the missing persons report. They're more laid-back than I'm used to." He stood and straightened a pant leg over his tennies, whisking wavy blond locks from his neck.

"Would you like us to make calls?" Alec asked.

"Sure. Start with hotels, motels in the vicinity of I-90 north of us. We'll hit the care facilities."

Alec whistled as he brushed a hand through his hair. "That's quite a spread."

"None of it's easy. We're casting a large net. Call me if you have any leads. I'll do the same." Drake dug into one of his pants pockets. "Here."

Alec caught the small object. "Flash drive?" Alec asked. "What's this for?"

"A very sensitive voice recorder. Hooks easily to a pocket or inside the button band on a dress shirt. There's a switch on the side. It has hours of capacity; plugs into a USB. The clarity beats the hell out of cell phone recordings. I give 'em to all my clients. Never know when it might come in handy. I'll see myself out." Drake waved and left.

Annalisse rose. "Where is Helga? Is she dusting the upstairs?" She walked to the base of the stairs and grabbed the banister's rounded corner. "I'm used to hearing those clunky shoes of hers."

"She's fine. Must be at the market."

Annalisse studied the empty landing uneasily. Helga wouldn't leave the estate without a note—and she always made noise. If not from her shoes, her incessant humming could be heard from wherever she worked in the house. The silence upstairs almost hurt Annalisse's ears. She hurried to the kitchen, checking for any sign that Helga went to the store. The magnetic grocery pad with a few items written down glared back at her.

"Her grocery list is still here."

Alec met her at the refrigerator. "She takes her shower in the morning. Why so jumpy?" He tugged her close. "You're a sheet of ice. After I get the laptop from my office, I'll find Helga."

"Thank you." Annalisse nestled her head on his shoulder.

Footsteps scuffed the hallway.

"See there, she's been down here all the time." Alec kissed the top of her head.

The footsteps stopped.

"Those aren't Helga's shoes," she whispered.

She wanted to run, but her feet wouldn't move.

"Alec."

Metal sliding on metal shattered the silence.

CHAPTER THIRTEEN

"Paste your noses to the fridge! Don't turn around."

Annalisse's heart climbed into her throat as she spun toward the stainless doors and pressed her forehead against the metal. She closed her eyes against the cool on her skin and the rage in a driven man's voice.

She'd encountered that violence before.

On the yacht nine months ago.

Alec covered her hand on the door, pressing his warmth into her. "Shh," he whispered.

Boot heels hit the floor hard and came at them from behind, tearing through the entry and into the kitchen. The smell of old corn chips and onions passed over her, then something hard and pointed bumped the back of her head and retreated.

"Cool it, man," Alec muttered, exerting more pressure on her fingers.

From the edge of her vision, skinny, hairy knuckles pushed the barrel of what she thought was a Glock to Alec's spine.

A hand body searched his hips and legs; she took shallow gulps of air, afraid of moving too much. Moments later, the pistol dug into her back, and she bit her lip to keep from crying out. The intruder checked her waist and hips, one side at a time, sliding to her thighs.

"Spread 'em."

Something stopped her.

The voice had a faraway undertone as if it came from the bottom of a pit.

Annalisse turned her head slightly for a look at the man, then winced against the icy metal boring into her neck.

"Kiss the fridge and spread 'em!"

She prayed that he didn't hear the quiet thump of her pistol hidden between her breasts as it hit the refrigerator. If she did what he said, maybe he wouldn't frisk her again from the front. If she fought back now, he would surely shoot Alec or her. She doubted she had time to draw her pistol and turn. They'd struggle, and someone would get hurt. Alec was already hurt. Before she used her .38, she'd choose a time when the element of surprise would work to her advantage.

She tensed her trembling body against his hand trailing the inner seam of her jeans—starting between her knees, slowly rising to her crotch. He rubbed the inside of her thighs for what felt like an eternity.

Annalisse bit her lip from the shame of his finger fondling until she couldn't stand it any longer.

"Stop it! I don't hide weapons up my ass," she yelled.

In a split second, Alec slid his body over hers and the assaulting hand disappeared.

"Get back! Tell. Us. What. You. Want," Alec said, in short bursts so close to her ear his breath tickled. "We aren't armed."

Muffled laughter.

The man's soles scuffed backward. "Get off her and go to the couch. Both of you. Now!"

Alec's weight lifted from her back, and he took her hand, tugging her along.

Annalisse whipped around and gasped at their intruder's head, then looked away. She and Alec hit the sofa cushions fast and hard.

The man holding them at gunpoint wore a huge garish mask. Pricked ears, alarming golden eyes with dark holes to see through, and the black snarl of a wolf licking its chops—right out of a nightmare.

Certain images have a lasting effect and scar the mind. As a child, Annalisse couldn't watch anything on television that featured a wolf. Movies, commercials, anything with wolves or werewolves made her shudder. She occasionally had nightmares of she and the sheep being chased by a yellow-eyed beast with big pointed teeth. Before the wolf caught them, she'd wake up in a heart-thudding, sweaty mess—enough so she'd have to change the sheets. Most of the time, the dreams came when Jeremy noticed coyotes patrolling the fence lines looking for vulnerabilities. Annalisse hated her turn to stand guard with the rifle when predators were nearby.

Annalisse hugged Alec's arm for support. "Why did he have to wear that?" she whispered, trembling.

She checked the hallway from where he came. "Where's Helga? What have you done to her?"

"Who?" Wolfman asked.

"Our housekeeper. Is she all right?" Alec's thumb grazed her hand. "Is that my Glock?"

"Handy you left it on the dresser for me." He waggled the handgun as if it were a toy. "Has a nice feel." His sentences turned more nasally. "Fatso's down the hall. Such a noisy old bitch, but she's quiet now."

"If you hurt her, you're dead," Alec declared.

"What do you mean by quiet? Is she shot? Does she need a doctor?" Annalisse shoved aside the horrifying image of Helga shot, handcuffed, and gagged to focus on their situation. "What do you want?"

"You and me are taking a ride." He let out a guttural laugh, his boots swishing side to side. "More like a long ride. That is, if you still want to see your aunt."

One question answered. He was there because of Kate.

The masked man wiped his free hand on threadbare denim covered in chalky stains. Wet hands and nervous feet for a guy uncomfortable in his role of captor. He must be acting on someone else's orders. Was he someone she'd met before? It was hard to identify a voice smothered by a giant plastic muzzle. Could he also know about her fear of wolves?

"Take me." Alec squeezed her hand and said, "If it's ransom you want. I can pay."

Wolfman raised the pistol at Alec. "I'll take free money. How much?"

"Alec, it's okay." She recalled Drake's reaction when she'd made the same claim to the phantom caller at Walker Farm. Annalisse racked her thoughts for any reason this man would have Kate. If he wasn't the mastermind, who would hatch such a scheme with creature masks, lyrics, and pink rattles? "I'll go." She swiveled to Alec. "Helga needs you. Let me do this."

"You." The cartoon aimed the weapon at her, then where he wanted her to go. "Move to the other end of the couch."

She started to scoot, but his hairy grip stopped her by handling her knee.

"Use this to tie his feet." He handed her a long, braided cord. "Tie it good and tight."

Alec's ankle.

"Why not his hands instead? Tie him to a piece of furniture with his hands behind his back." She licked her lower lip, buying time to think. "I'll tie him and lock him inside one of the bedrooms—or maybe a closet."

"His feet." He bobbed the mask toward the floor.

"Not until I see Helga." Annalisse folded her arms.

"Mouthy with a gun pointed at her. She always like this?" the wolf asked Alec.

"Do I see Helga or not?" Annalisse blurted, not daring to look in Alec's direction.

"Goddamn." The gunman raised a long needle and syringe filled with clear liquid. "We don't have all day."

"No!" She jumped on her knees in front of Alec and fumbled with the cord, flinching against the pistol shoved between her shoulder blades.

"Take a few wraps around the ankles and stretch the cord to his wrists. Do you hear me?" The weapon dug deeper into her back.

"Don't hurt her." Alec grimaced while she worked, looking into her eyes. The sorrow there nearly cracked her heart open. Déjà vu was a real bitch.

"I'll be all right." Annalisse glanced down at her breasts and pinched out her tunic as a reminder of her hidden pistol. She waited a second for a signal that Alec understood.

He blinked slowly.

A hand slapped her shoulder hard. "Now, not Christmas!"

Annalisse went to work, carefully positioning the cord in places that weren't as badly bruised and tied a knot.

"Lay on your side, Alec."

He rotated with his knees high, falling sideways onto the cushions with his hands together. Alec's grunt brought tears to her eyes. She fumbled with the cord, eventually getting his wrists together. Over her shoulder, the hairy hand thrust a needle into Alec's arm muscle, depressing the plunger.

Alec hissed from the piercing.

"You bastard! I did what you asked." She watched Alec slip into unconsciousness. "Stupid." She shook her head. "That wasn't necessary. What did you give him?"

A hard object hit her in the back of the head. "Hey!" She scrunched and swayed. A warmth spread down her neck. The damn guy struck her with the pistol.

White dots jumped all around, and her head stung.

She reached up, pulling away bloody fingers.

"Get off your ass." The gunman wrenched her arm, and she complied.

"Oh, Alec," she whispered, watching his handsome, aristocratic profile slacken. "For the second time, what's in that shot?" Annalisse asked through clenched teeth while holding the cut on her throbbing head.

"Dream juice." The man hacked up a glob of phlegm and swallowed it. "C'mon." He grabbed her upper arm and pushed. "What time is it?" The wolf head rotated a slow one-eighty. "Big M don't take to being late."

"Who's Big M?"

"None of your beeswax." He pinched her arm this time when he held her.

"Ouch. I'm not leaving without seeing Helga."

She bent over and wiped off her knees—just to slap something—and rubbed off the blood. Taking a few calming breaths, she considered her options. Being hasty wasn't one of them. She could shoot him now but never see Kate again. If Wolfie took her, she'd rather be awake and able to plan an escape than knocked out and at someone else's mercy. There couldn't be a repeat of her drugged experience in the Turkish tower if she could help it.

"Go." The gunman pressed the pistol to the middle of her back and stuffed it into the bruise he'd already made. She winced each time he used the gun barrel like a cattle prod as they walked to the master suite.

Standing outside the closed door, he warned, "Make it quick."

Annalisse pushed inside and ran across Alec's steer hides to the bed. "Helga." She patted her arm. "Helga, please be okay." Annalisse swiveled around and narrowed her eyes at the wolf. "Why? If it's me you wanted, you could've called me. It's not hard to get my number. I would've come alone. This is so… unnecessary." She dropped to her knees and watched Helga for signs of breathing.

The housekeeper lay on her side, hands tied behind her in the same black cord she'd used on Alec. A man's handkerchief knotted behind her head gagged her. Saliva drained from one side of Helga's lips. The sight was so nauseating she wanted to yell out. Only sheer will held her together. Other than being tied and gagged, Helga showed no outward signs of being beaten by Wolfie.

"Drugged too, I suppose?" Annalisse didn't turn around.

"Get up." He yanked her by the arm and jabbed the pistol into her side.

She jerked away from his grasp, holding her arms high above her head, then smoothed her top down over a hip. "Don't push it. You touch me again—"

"And what? Say bye-bye to your friend."

Annalisse said a prayer for the housekeeper and Alec as they marched through the bedroom, past Alec, to the big front doors. Her purse rested at the foot of the love seat, apparently of no interest to her captor. Glancing away fast, she pondered how to take the tote along, as large as it was. The cell phone would be useful to call Drake, but Wolfie would insist on pawing through her stuff, surely taking the phone. At least she still had a gun.

What had happened to Alec's security? The same security company whose job it was to watch the estate had somehow missed her aunt's abduction and Wolfman's break-in. Were they partners in Kate's disappearance? Alec should fire the whole bunch of them.

Annalisse turned around for one last look at Alec on the couch, bound tightly into a ball. She was crazy to leave him and Helga, but it was foolish to start a gunfight and risk losing her only chance to see Kate.

"Where are you taking me? Do you have Kate, or did someone else snatch her from the barn?"

He swiftly wrapped her in a choke hold.

She froze.

He forced his pistol to her temple. "You don't get to ask questions or run that smart mouth of yours. I've got an extra shot of dream juice and not afraid to use it. Don't matter how I get you to the M. I just have to get you there. Open the door." He relaxed the hold slightly and pushed her out without letting go of her. "Now lock it, Annalisse."

Him saying her name like they were old friends gave her the creeps. Had he overheard the conversation with Drake and the captain? Did the person who'd sent him tell him her name?

She was so close to his putrid onion odor it was overwhelming. "I can't… move." She nudged him with her elbow and stepped forward. "May I walk on my own, please?" She tugged the door shut. "The door locks automatically." Which was a fib. She pretended to try the door and nodded. She banked on the wolf not checking the lock for himself.

Wolfie shoved her down the gravel path, crunching stones under his leather soles—his hand holding her elbow.

Annalisse scanned the road for the white security van and asked again, "Where am I going?" The security guy wasn't parked in the usual spots. She was so tempted to cry out for Hank or wave her arms but couldn't risk it. Someone—anyone—had to notice the nutty mask. Annalisse had to go, but Alec and Helga needed help inside.

They continued around the pasture and down the winding vinyl fence to a large group of hardwoods with a picnic table in their shade. Alec's estate was so large, it wasn't a surprise she'd never walked this section before. Behind the tree trunks in the shadows, she spotted the grill of a pickup.

Wolfie's gait lengthened the closer they got to the silver truck.

"Do I need to tie or blindfold ya once we get inside? Your call. Truck's automatic, so I'll have a gun on ya all the time. I know how to use it in case ya wanna know."

"You know a lot of things. I get it. I want to go to Kate. Why would I cause trouble? Mess with you, and you drug me and dump me in a hole somewhere. Tie me if you're afraid of a girl." She held her wrists together in front of his Guns N' Roses T-shirt. "Go ahead, if you're worried I'll hurt you."

She added the taunts as a dare to his male ego. Some men got off on feeling superior to a woman, and she'd use it to her advantage if she could. Her submitting would make him the powerful one. Even godlike. She gambled he wouldn't tie her. He would've done it by now. Why get permission when he controlled the situation? As much as she hated this man's horrible smell and beastly disguise, she'd play the part of compliant passenger.

Rounding the hood, the gunman opened the passenger door and pushed her headlong into his eye-watering world of rank excrement and onions. She glanced into the jump seat, expecting to find a makeshift toilet back there.

The smell in the radiating heat sent Helga's pastries and coffee racing to her throat. She rolled down the window once he started the engine.

"This thing's too hot!" He struggled with the mask at his neck. "Don't get any ideas. Run, and you'll never see your aunt again." His anger boiled out of the disguise. He slammed the gearshift into park and jumped outside the truck. "Turn around! Don't look at me," he yelled at her. "Look out your window until I tell you to turn around."

Annalisse twisted and lightly fingered her pistol beneath the fabric. Even if she were able to take his Glock away, she'd risk too much. "Damn," she muttered, staring out her open window. She clutched the edge of her seat, feeling heated vinyl slide under her fingers. As long as they were going to a place only he knew about—and he kept his distance—she had to go along. For Kate.

Something fell on the back seat. Probably the mask.

"Okay to turn around?" she asked.

"Yeah."

Wolfie had disappeared, and in its place, the gunman wore a type of artist's beret and large wraparound glasses. Not a single hair escaped beneath the hat. His perspiring head was shaved as smooth as her legs.

"Why wear the wolf mask on an eighty-degree day? I can't tell who you are with your hat and glasses."

"Put on your belt. I don't want to get stopped because you aren't buckled in." The man's voice had calmed, but it had the same cadence as it had from inside the mask. He wasn't trying to change his voice.

The interior of the cab was surprisingly clear of fast-food containers or cigarette butts. Other than a few gum wrappers and a can of chew, the guy kept trash to a minimum. The pervasive onion stench had to be his own noxious smell. A smell that could've been cured by the use of a little deodorant or even a shower at a rest stop. She opened her mouth to make the suggestion but decided against poking the wolf. He used injectable sedatives like other people took aspirin for headaches.

"Can you at least tell me how long we'll be in the truck? Does Kate know I'm coming?" She shifted to observe him. "How do you know Kate? Who's paying you?" Annalisse watched Brookehaven Stables slide by on her side of the road as the gunman turned onto the highway in front of the estate. "I didn't see a license plate on the front of this rig. I hope you have plates on the back. If you want the cops to steer clear, that is."

"Do you ever shut up?" The man positioned his seat and put the Glock between his legs, picking at his crotch and adjusting his genitals.

She grimaced and inched toward the door, flashing on grungy underwear or, worse yet, no shorts at all. She hoped the air conditioning would kick the temperature down, and she wouldn't have to endure this creature for too long.

"I was told to wear the wolf," he announced. "I thought it was stupid."

"Who told you?" she asked.

"You know."

She stared at him, names darting through her mind. A select few knew about her fear of wolves. Family and a couple of close friends. The man or persons who sent him ordered the costume to frighten her. But why?

Kate might have told someone.

This guy didn't seem capable of kidnapping Kate. Annalisse wanted to laugh at the ridiculousness of it all.

But anything was possible because Wolfie had kidnapped her… and she'd allowed it.

CHAPTER FOURTEEN

When they passed through the Sullivan County line, Annalisse had second thoughts about riding in a Toyota pickup with a bald-headed wolf on a delivery mission—to deliver her to Lord only knew where. They drove southeast on Route 17, the same road she would take if she were returning to Walker Farm. If Kate's abductor had whisked her off to Massachusetts as Drake mentioned or driven through that state, they were traveling in the wrong direction. A straight shot through the Catskills was the more direct path and shorter timewise.

A fierce glare bounced off the hood into her eyes. What she'd give for the pair of sunglasses neatly tucked inside her tote bag miles behind them. She pulled down the visor, which helped somewhat. The traffic was light for a close-to-lunchtime road trip on a work-day Monday. The first day of her "vacation." Browsing antique stores for old books and classic titles from the past with Alec seemed an impossible dream from where she sat at the moment.

Grayish asphalt sloped into the hills, where the double yellow line disappeared into the next winding turn. Shapeless guardrails bent to and fro, leftovers from multiple car accidents. The steel barriers were just high enough to let a nighttime driver know they'd hit something on the way down the hillside. So many roads needed attention, and few received any in this stretch of Orange County.

Annalisse steepled her hands together while her stomach rolled. Her thoughts ricocheted between Alec bunched up on the sofa and poor Helga gagged and hobbled in Alec's bedroom. Would either of them forgive her for going? Every moment since leaving the estate she had to remind herself that she had no choice, but the little voice in her head argued otherwise. She could've slipped the pistol to Alec. While the wolf frisked them, he may not have seen the exchange from inside his huge mask.

She should've risked it.

She might've caused Alec to get shot instead of drugged.

She might've lost her .38.

She'd made the decision she had to live with.

"Are you taking me to the farm?" Annalisse asked the driver, who hadn't uttered a word since they left Brookehaven.

"Nope."

"Are we going to a place in New York?"

"Nope." His eyes never strayed from the road, but he nervously picked at grime under his nails while maneuvering the steering wheel.

"Where then?"

"Let's play twenty questions, only I don't have to answer." His mouth stretched wider.

"Once we cross into another state, the feds will get involved for sure. Kidnapping my aunt and me will bring a whole lot of ugly down on you. Tell me where Kate is and drop me off. I can keep you out of it. Is Kate tied up like Alec and Helga?" His silence brought a tortured sigh from her. "You're enjoying this. Do you have a name? I have a name picked out, but you won't like it."

"Real name or made up?"

"Whatever."

"I like Woody."

"Fine. Like the woodpecker. Woody, who's Big M? You have to tell me who sent you. Is it the gray-haired man who came to the estate on Friday? Does he have Kate?" Annalisse leaned forward as far as the seat belt allowed, searching his face for a reaction. His glasses concealed any expression, like crow's feet at the corners of his eyes if he were smiling or a cold, flinty stare if angry. What she had left as a guide were flaccid cheeks, a drawn mouth, and the twitching muscles in his neck.

"Sit back." He swished his arm at her. "Or I'll hook ya to the headrest."

She did as he ordered and studied the pistol between his legs—Alec's gun, buried in a place she wouldn't dare reach for.

He cupped his zippered fly with a palm and rubbed, facing her. "Like what you see?"

Woody had superior peripheral vision.

Annalisse twisted herself forward and glared through the windshield, sorry she'd spent too much time on his pistol. She stifled a tremor and slumped deeper into the seat. If she planned to stay whole, she had to assume the guy beside her could see through doors.

A whitetail doe with two spotted fawns trailing behind stepped onto the roadway in their lane.

"Deer!" Annalisse gripped the door panel and held her breath. "Slow down. You're gonna hit 'em."

Instead, Woody gunned the throttle and shot around the threesome who'd stopped dead in place, lucky for them.

"If they'd kept coming—I hate drivers like you. Would you have done the same thing for a jogger?" she asked, squeezing the padded molding.

"They're deer, not people."

Annalisse felt like that mama and her babies. Stuck on the road, wanting to get away, knowing she couldn't and too frightened to move. One step in the wrong direction meant Annalisse's life or possibly Aunt Kate's death. Like the deer family, staying in place was the best fallback plan.

"You some animal activist? Save the squirrels and the whales from global warming or somethin'? The way I see it, we were here first—if they walk in front of a truck, they take their chances." Woody squared his shoulders as if he'd espoused the words of a scholar and took pride in them.

"Are you ten?" She forced her lips together to stop her mouth from overtaking her brain before it was too late. Antagonizing him wouldn't get her to Kate any sooner. He'd granted her a big favor by leaving her untied during their trip, but the uneasiness crawling her spine had her wishing she'd never left the estate with him.

They crested the hill that overlooked a major artery to a large body of water. Annalisse recognized the tributaries that fed into Greenwood Lake. The area where they'd recovered her friend's body. She and Chase were part of the search party and had walked across Sam's burial place without realizing it. Almost a year had passed since her death, and Annalisse still couldn't go near the lake. A brutal murder… for a bracelet.

Sam was the only one who knew how many modern art and European painting classes Annalisse skipped and could still graduate or how many guys she'd had sex with and which ones had popped the oh-my-God cork. Her old roommate knew things that Annalisse couldn't and wouldn't confide to Chase.

The last thing her petite friend said to her was, "I hate you, Anna-Poo, you know that?" What an awful phrase to hear from the closest friend she'd ever had. Ever. The Anna-Poo part was Sam's extra zinger. Annalisse despised the nickname given to her long ago by her little sister, Ariel, and regretted ever telling Sam—who'd used it in nearly every argument—because it hurt.

There were five years between the sisters—before the gas main explosion took away eight-year-old Ariel's future and Annalisse's ability to hold on to girlfriends for long. After that day in Kensington when she lost her family, it was easier not to let people in. Having friends only meant disappointment and pain when they left, and Annalisse's friends always left her eventually.

Sam disliked being told what to do. Like Annalisse's insistence she couldn't wear a gold bracelet with pretty horses prancing along her wrist because it was dangerous. A yard sale find from Brooklyn worth millions, and a deadly curse had sealed her friend's fate. Would Sam be alive if Annalisse hadn't harped so often about the bracelet? Left it instead in a jewelry box and not worn it out of spite to prove a point? Part of the blame for Sam's death might be on Annalisse.

"Got the time? Clock died in the truck." Woody tapped on the dashboard.

"Probably noon."

He glanced at her, looking a little like a curious wasp in his glasses.

An unmistakable odor entered the truck.

"P. U." She held her nose from the stench coming in through the air vents. "Skunks are thick up here. Someone must have hit one."

"Never seen eyes that color before."

"Huh?"

"Your eyes. What color is that?"

"It's a mystery," she said, irritated by the way he'd turned the conversation to her.

"Are those fake contacts?"

"I see fine."

"I'd call 'em sea blue. Yeah, like those pictures in the middle of the ocean. Crystal-blue sea."

Now was a good time to change the subject.

"Are we stopping for lunch?" she asked.

His tongue grazed his lower lip. "Maybe."

"I could use a pee break too."

Woody massaged the steering wheel with the heel of his hand as if it were raw bread dough and leaned forward, staring at an imaginary spot on the road.

"Do you see a place?" she asked. "We're between towns. If you'll pull over—I won't take but a minute." She squirmed at the thought of stopping and caught his smile.

"Look, I won't run. I'll stay close to the truck. Unless you'd rather I go on your seat." She patted the armrest impatiently. Talking about relieving herself made the situation worse. "Well?"

Woody picked up the Glock. "Not a bad idea, but not here." He rested the gun on the wheel and did the gross thing over his zipper like before with the other hand. With one noticeable difference. All the talk about her had aroused him.

"I can go without eating, but not—"

"Do you ever shut up? You're pretty, but looks only go so far."

She tried not to think about the extra cup of coffee Helga had poured for her before she met Alec at the graveyard.

The pistol is in his left hand.

Woody was right handed. He'd held the gun on them with his right.

She asked herself what would happen if she drew on him once she got out of the truck. It might be the best opportunity. If she held her .38 on him while they drove, would it get them to Kate any faster or end their trip altogether? Showing her hand too soon was risky.

"Noon ya say?" He slid the gun into his right hand. "Up there might be a good place to camp for a while." Woody pointed the Glock to a wide spot on her side of the road. "I'll slide into that patch of grass. Nobody will see us."

The spot he referred to jutted up a hill into mature pines and scrub brush. Lakes and ponds overflowed the landscape in this part of Bloomingburg. Annalisse couldn't care less about anything but relieving the pressure in her bladder.

"Pull off anywhere." She stuck her arm out the window she'd rolled down. "There's plenty of cover up there." She reached for the door latch as the truck slowed near the first thicket. "I'll be right back."

She sprang from her seat and flew across the grass. Trickling water from somewhere nearby intensified her urgency. She found cover near the base of a tree, checked for poison ivy, lifted her tunic, unzipped her pants, and sighed with relief at the release and the distance from Woody's onion odor.

A twig snapped nearby, and she popped up to investigate.

Woody leaned against a tree a few feet away, a predator eyeballing his prey. He banged Alec's pistol against his thigh methodically. His dark glasses were even more insect-like in the shade.

"Geez. I'm not done." She tugged her jeans up. Stupidly, she hadn't considered he'd follow her, but she was instantly grateful for her choice of a longer top.

"Stop." Woody's voice was icy. He leveled the Glock at her.

She backed a single step, holding her hands up high.

"I told you I wouldn't run. Don't point that at me."

Woody snatched a handful of her tunic cloth and pulled her closer to him.

She slapped his hand away, only to have it replaced by the Glock's muzzle pressed into her stomach. She hissed through her teeth, feeling the metal bite her flesh, and raised both hands again.

"Move." Woody forced her deeper into the brush and closer to the sounds of a rushing stream. "Keep walking until I say stop."

Arms elevated, Annalisse complied, knowing that the deeper she went, the more trouble she was in. She pictured a duel where she faced Woody, her Lady Smith pointed at him and Alec's pistol held on her. Something he'd said earlier floated back. "A good place to camp *for a while*." She was in such a hurry to pee, she hadn't listened. Woody intended something longer than a pit stop.

Native grasses and pine needles gave way to a craggy shore of boulders and the calmest of ponds. In the water's reflection, not a ripple broke the mirror image of glassy treetops and cloudless blue sky. An idyllic place for a picnic. The picture painted on the still pool was incredible and lifted her spirits long enough to clear her mind for an option.

"Big M's not gonna be happy if you're late." She spread her hands outward. "What is all this? I thought you were taking me to Aunt Kate. What's going to happen to *you* if we don't get there on time?"

Woody jerked her by the hair, sending her tumbling to the ground. Rock and debris sliced into her cheeks and arms. Her chin bounced, jarring her teeth painfully.

She flipped over, but before she could get enough leverage to rise, Woody plowed onto her, his weight crushing her lungs.

Her breath caught.

She flailed her arms at anything she could grab and felt her nails sink into his face, ripping off his beret and glasses.

He caught her wrist.

"Dirty bastard, get off!" she screamed. Rolling from side to side, kicking, she tried to break his leech-like hold on her legs. With his thighs pressed hard into hers, she couldn't lift a leg to knee him. His body pinned her, a heavy, stinky burden invading her space and taking her wind.

Gasping, she felt the hot metal of his Glock at her neck, and she stopped struggling—arms at her sides.

Woody narrowed hate-filled eyes at her; his egg-head dripped dirty sweat trails. The welts left by her nails stood to peaks along one cheek.

He pushed the pistol barrel under her chin.

"I don't give a hoot what you want." His breath reminded her of slinging cow dung at Jeremy when he got on her nerves. "Shut the hell up. No one has to get hurt. Namely you." He chuckled and raised himself slightly. "What's that?" He reached toward her breasts where the gun was holstered.

Annalisse scooted backward a little, flat out, using one heel. "Get off me and I'll show you."

Woody clubbed the Glock barrel against her ear.

She screamed and closed her eyes against the pain.

His hand clamped over her mouth. "Shut up," he spat.

Annalisse opened her watering eyes and nodded slowly. Her pulse chugged through every vein. The rotten smell of old garbage brought bile into her mouth.

"When I take my hand away, no yelling. Got it?" he asked.

She nodded again and readied herself—both his hands were full: one held the pistol, the other covered her face.

She had to take Alec's pistol from this guy so that he couldn't use it on her. Before he claimed her hidden weapon or incapacitated her. She calculated his possible moves and waited for a better angle at taking the Glock.

She relaxed her fists and arms enough to signal surrender.

Woody slowly pried his hand from her mouth. "There now." He propped himself on one elbow, easing the weight on her. His expression went blank, and he reached down and touched himself, screwing up his lips. "See what you did? More work for you."

He's not holding the gun.

In the corner of her eye she caught sight of the Glock, not far out of reach if she could flip on her side. Her heart sank to an all-time low since Kate's disappearance. She was about to screw up any chance of seeing her aunt via Woody. Under the best case, she might get his weapon, but he would never drive her to the rendezvous. If there was a rendezvous.

The whole trip could've been a sick joke—and she fell for it.

As Woody reached again for the Glock, Annalisse bucked her hips as high as possible. She rotated on one hip, struggling with him for the weapon.

Unsteady and off-kilter, he jostled the gun.

Through grunts and groans, momentum sent them rolling side over side, but Annalisse snagged the trigger as she tumbled. The hard ground gave way, and intertwined, they slid down an embankment, skidding over pinecones and small branches, to the bottom. Her entire body burned from the friction of their free fall, but she'd managed to hold on to the Glock.

Woody landed beyond her at the pond's edge. On his back.

Annalisse drove herself up on all fours, brushing at the small stones that pierced and bruised her palms. She kept her eyes on the bald man and climbed to her feet, pumped with adrenaline.

"Stay down, Wolfman." She backed up on unsteady legs, inhaling the much-needed air. "Hey." Edging closer, she nudged his shin with the toe of her boot, then walked a wide circle, inching up the hill carefully, her vision trained on him.

Woody's hand moved, and he groaned.

"Don't try to get up," Annalisse barked, pointing the Glock at his head. "Until I say so."

He rolled backward, grinning up at her. "Your aunt's as good as dead." He let out a high-pitched squeal.

She couldn't go to that dark place in her mind.

"You wearing underwear?" she asked.

"What?" At least his laughter stopped.

"Boxers, briefs?"

"Why? Some fetish of yours? Check for yourself."

"Sit up. I won't ask again." She put a few extra feet between them, hoping the filthy man wasn't nude under his jeans, but she'd deal either way.

He bled from one ear and a nostril, which weirdly flooded her with pride. His face was even more crimson than before, thanks to her nails. His T-shirt had ripped in several places.

"What now, bossy?" Woody sneered at her. "Permission to rise, sir?"

"I don't know who sent you to get me or if you know anything at all about my aunt. I'm done with this charade. Do you even know what Kate looks like?"

"I don't have to tell you nothin'. Don't matter what I think. Don't matter what I say. You won't see her again. Not by me anyway."

"You've never seen Kate," she grumbled and took another step back. "Someone's playing me. No more. Get up." Her heartbeat thundered in her ears, and pain whizzed up her neck.

Woody dallied, dusting himself off and making the skeletons on his shirt dance. The entire time, he looked at his feet, which gave her the eerie impression he was about to launch an attack or come for the gun.

She checked Woody's hands for anything he might use as a weapon, backed up a few paces, and changed the hand that held the Glock. She reached underneath her tunic as if she were scratching an itch. The hair on her arms rose, her nerves on hair trigger. Annalisse jerked her .38 quietly from its holster. Within seconds, both hands held firepower on him.

Woody gaped. “Thought I felt a bump.” He shook his head and kicked at a stone.

“Boots off. Pants next.” She bobbed her revolver toward his feet.

He didn’t move. “Why?”

“Get ’em off, and don’t throw the footwear at me. Set the boots by your feet. No bellyaching that your feet hurt.” The dank reeds and rotting flora in the water gave her plan logic as she walked backward.

He glared in a final act of defiance and bent over, slipping off his boots one at a time, then unbuckled his belt.

“That’s good for now. Walk over there.” She motioned him up the bank and closed in on his boots. She glanced at her hands. *One of the guns has to go.* Annalisse tightened her chest and threw Alec’s Glock into the pond as far as she could. She was proficient with her own pistol, which she hoped she wouldn’t have to use.

“Damn crazy bitch.” Woody spat when the Glock made its splash, then started down the rocky bank toward his boots and her.

“Stop. There. I mean it.” She crouched, watching him, then picked up one boot, tossing it into the lake. It slowly took on water and sank into the depths.

“No,” Woody groaned and raised his hands. “I need my boots.”

Annalisse tossed in work boot number two to keep the first one company.

He cradled his neck with both hands and looked into the sky. “How am I going to get back to the truck? Huh? Tell me that one.”

"Who sent you to get me?"

"I already said."

"Give me a name, not an initial."

He shrugged.

"Idiot. I hope you got your money first. I'll pay you a great deal more for a name. Last chance."

Woody's smile spread slowly, unnerving her.

It was late, and she wasted precious time.

She wasn't going to get anything out of him. She wasn't even sure his mind was all there. Nothing he told her now could be deemed trustworthy information. Standing in bright sunshine and burning up, she readjusted the pistol and sloughed a stinging bead of sweat out of her eye. Time to speed things into overdrive and get back to Brookehaven.

"Shuck the jeans." She motioned the barrel at his legs.

"C'mon." He hesitated, then lifted his shirt.

As he unzipped, she thought about closing her eyes but couldn't take the chance he might escape to the highway or rush her. The pants slid downward, revealing a set of black boxers with skull and crossbones. Coordinated with the shirt. How sweet. She sighed in relief.

"Now what?" Woody left his jeans swirled around his ankles.

"Step out and get into the water." Annalisse walked toward him.

"There could be *things* in that lake." His wild eyes looked at the pond, then back at her.

"I hope so. You swim don't you?"

"No." He shook his head repeatedly. "No, never learned. I'll drown." He shifted his feet from what was probably heat burning the socks.

Annalisse bent down, picked up a handful of rocks, and slung them at his bare legs. With her disadvantaged left hand, the group shot made sure of a strike.

He leaned over and rubbed a spot on his knee, laughing a little too much.

She lobbed another round that pelted his shoulders while he was bent lower.

Woody flinched that time. "Fancy girl has her gun, and she throws rocks. Some badass." Message received, he hopped out of his pants and gingerly picked his way to the water, hissing and yipping each time he stepped on something sharp.

"This is stupid." He came to an abrupt stop and crossed his arms, his toes in the water. "I ain't going in there."

"Swim out to the middle." She used the revolver for emphasis.

"But—"

"Do you ever shut up?" she asked with a smirk.

As he waded into the pond that had to be three acres across, she rifled through the pockets for the fob to the truck. He might've left the truck open, but she couldn't count on it. She shook the stiff dungarees upside down. Nothing but a business card tumbled out. There was still a chance he'd left his wallet in the truck and key fob near the ignition. If not, her boots were going to get a good workout hiking the interstate.

Annalisse would love to know Woody's true identity and if he worked for Jeremy.

"This far enough?" Woody yelled out while treading water with a spastic grin.

"Keep going." She glanced at the cream-colored calling card in her hand. A willow tree covered the middle overlaid with WALKER. As she thought. Jeremy had sicced this nut on her.

Wait.

The name was wrong.

She did a double take, sickened by the reality of whose card she actually held. The blue letters popped at her like neon lights blaring their bad news. She lost her balance and slid on her heel down the bank, catching herself from a clumsy fall.

Ethan Fawdray—Farm Manager.

A cold wave washed over her, and she shivered. She retched, wiping spit from her mouth. How had Alec known? Innocent Ethan hatched the diabolical plan to drop a body and kidnap his employer? Why?

Shaking, she scrunched Woody's denim into a ball near her feet and checked the pond. He backstroked as if doing laps in an Olympic pool. Not exactly a person who hadn't had swimming lessons at some point in his life.

"Bastard," she mumbled, standing on top of the jeans. She slipped the card into her own pocket and rubbed beneath her bra band—stretching—feeling lighter without the weight of the gun between her breasts. When she got back, the flashbang would go to the trash heap. That style of holster wasn't for her. Even though it had saved her butt on this trip.

Remembering she'd left a job unfinished before the unexpected wrestling match, Annalisse checked the fly on her jeans and zipped the rest of the way. She picked up Woody's pile, and with a last look at him, she ran up the incline as if she were being chased by a pack of wolves.

CHAPTER FIFTEEN

"Damn." The cute black-and-white-winged dragonfly she'd admired moments ago sank its jaws into Annalisse's arm before she could swat it away. "I didn't know you guys bit people." She rubbed the arm and glanced over a reddened shoulder where she'd left Woody. She stopped, caught her breath, stretched her back, and shook out one leg at a time. Her thighs ached, and the leather boots were chaffing her calves.

The sound of whirring tires along asphalt had intensified in the past several minutes. Almost there. Grass marred by their footprints from the trip to the pond put her on the right path to the parked truck. Hopefully, she could start it and get the heck out of there to check on Alec and Helga. They might be awake by now. She swallowed and wiped her lips in the crook of her arm, tasting salt on her skin. A bottle of cool water would be nice.

As she entered a pollen-heavy area and sneezed, she stopped and peered at the empty trail ahead. Mosquitoes buzzed her ears, and she sharpened her hearing on the cicada competition singing in the trees overhead. Tymbal membranes along the insect's belly expand and contract with the sound of a hundred rattlers to attract a mate. The noise is painful to birds, which keeps cicadas from becoming meals during their daytime chorus.

Pine needles rustled in the hot breeze and leaves crackled.

"Hello? Someone up there?" she asked before taking a few more steps. "Ow," she murmured, bending down to rub the leather over a blistered heel. "Just a little farther, and these boots are history." She wiped grime from her forehead and adjusted her foot to a more comfortable spot in the lining. She must have imagined some other crazy fool wandering the woods during midday. In case Woody followed, she pushed herself to keep walking. By now, he must be on the same trail. She looked behind and shifted the pile of jeans under one arm, with a tighter grip on her pistol.

"You in the trees!" a male voice echoed. "You there."

"I'm here." She waved her gun hand, elated to hear another human. "Help! I'm trying to get back to the road." Annalisse dashed toward his voice. "Where are you?"

"Stop, miss."

She did. Right where she stood. Woody?

Don't be Woody.

Annalisse aimed her .38 at the sound. "I'm being chased. Show yourself. A guy brought me here at gunpoint. Don't try anything. I'm armed." She scanned the woods.

Something popped like a fastener unsnapping.

"Orange County Sheriff! Show me your hands! Do it now!" the man ordered.

Annalisse relaxed. Not Woody.

She glanced around once more. "Yes, sir. Right away." Laying the wadded denim near her feet with the pistol on top, she carefully stepped aside, her hands held high. "I have a license to carry," she added for good measure.

A uniformed officer in the now familiar brown with flat-brimmed hat emerged from the trees, his service-issued Glock trained on her. The tension withered, even with a pistol pointed at her.

"Keep your hands up and walk toward me." The officer met her halfway and frisked her for additional weapons. "Does the vehicle on the interstate belong to you?" His faded denim-colored eyes flickered concern in the shade of his brim.

"No, sir. It belongs to the man who kidnapped me in Monticello. My friends need help. They were both…" She closed her eyes, fighting for composure. "He took me—" Annalisse's body shook, and words caught in her throat. Tears trickled down her cheeks, scaring her because they had a mind of their own, and she needed to stay in control. Kate's overused saying, *Never show a weakness*, ran through her head. "You have to help. He's down there." She started over. "My name's Annalisse Drury. I'm from Manhattan. A good friend of Alec Zavos. I don't have ID on me, but when you run my pistol through the database, it's all there."

The officer's serious expression grew concerned. "Do you need medical attention? Were you—"

"Raped? No." She dropped her gaze. "I fought him for my boyfriend's Glock. Got a little dinged up, but I'm fine."

"Where's the Glock? With the jeans?"

"In the pond. Along with his boots… and him. Those are his jeans." Annalisse smiled, then motioned to the ground with her chin. "My arms are killing me. May I drop them, please?"

He nodded, and she did.

The officer returned his weapon to the creaky belt holster. Baby-faced, the sheriff had the look of a recent academy graduate, unsure what he should say to a traumatized woman with a story like hers.

"There are deep cuts on your face, miss. I can call someone."

The young officer lifted his hat from a tousled, brown mini-mop and recently shaved sidewalls, white above the ears. With a handkerchief, he wiped perspiration from his neck. His button nose and crinkled laugh lines reminded her a little of Chase. *Chase was supposed to bring Boris to the estate today.* She hoped he was there by now helping Alec with Helga.

"Was either weapon fired?" he asked.

"No, sir. You can check my Smith and Wesson."

"Captain! We've got the BOLO," he yelled.

"Captain?" Annalisse asked, massaging and moving her rotator cuff. Her upper body smarted something awful.

Through the scrub and thistle, Captain McDonaugh sauntered into the clearing, all smiles. "Ms. Drury." He looked at her wrist. "I… ah… it's only been a few hours since I left you. Sheer luck Officer

Danvers and I came this way from another call. Who did that to you?"

"I've got this." The twenty-something Danvers chimed in.

McDonaugh gave a disgruntled glance to Danvers. "You're scratched up pretty badly, miss. Bleeding from your forehead. Anything broken? Did he force himself on you?" He turned to his junior. "Eric, call an ambulance."

Her injuries must look as bad as she felt. "I'll mend, Captain. Really. No need to call anyone. Nothing broken but a little pride. The jerk who brought me here was taking me to my aunt. So he says. He's still down there." She nodded over her shoulder. "Get him before he finds another way to his truck. I'm not sure what shape he's in, except shoeless and stripped down to his underwear." She laughed feebly.

McDonaugh cocked a wild brow at her, then turned to his partner. "What are you waiting for? Go. I've already called for backup."

Annalisse imagined Woody in his stockinged feet, searching the water for his boots and giving up—taking to the trail, his tender feet on fire—suffering stickers and bug bites since the critters swarmed in the heat of the day.

"He was supposed to deliver me to a person named Big M. His mind wasn't on that once he got me in the woods on a potty break. Any more information on my aunt? I could use some good news." She smacked her lips. "And a sip of water if you've got it."

***

Sitting in the rear of a squad car that reminded her of the chairs from grammar school English class that made her butt sore, Annalisse slugged down the last swallow of a tepid cola. Tiny bubbles burst on her palate and fizzled down her throat in a last gasp. She minded little that the soda wasn't cold. It was wet, and she was thirsty. Kicking one leg outside the car, she scooted toward the partially open door. She couldn't wait to get on the road.

Annalisse watched Captain McDonaugh's graying head through the iron grate that divided the officers from the bad guys. The captain ignored the crackle of his radio and the dispatcher's monotone voice droning in the background. He had his laptop open, clicking the occasional key while building handwritten notes on paper. An old-school cop. Habits of the predigital age were hard to push aside by the three-channel TV news, vinyl record, and cassette tape generation. Aunt Kate couldn't get the hang of computers until she owned a smartphone—where she discovered the pleasures of online shopping and proceeded to crispy-critter her VISA card limit.

Cruising around in a patrol car giving out tickets in between 7-Eleven robberies appealed to a select few. In Annalisse's estimation, cops weren't paid enough to put themselves out there—every day—with a chance they wouldn't come home. She admired each one of them for their service, grateful the job attracted many who were braver than she could ever be.

"Your junior partner isn't back yet. Is he okay?"

"Officer Danvers has eight years on the force. Sorry to leave your door ajar. Didn't want to lock you up back there in case we had an emergency. Your detective friend should be here soon."

The captain had called Bill Drake once they'd found her and ran Woody's truck plate. Annalisse had so much to tell Drake.

Crack!

A noise reminiscent of a rifle range vibrated the air. Not a car backfire. Sharper than that and farther away than the road.

Knocking his laptop off the tray table, he said, "Get down." McDonaugh dove for the radio and keyed the mic. "Shots fired. Shots fired. Where in the hell is my backup, dammit?"

He went on to jabber something else in chipped speech. She instinctively ducked behind the door, covered her ears, and closed her eyes.

"Who's shooting?" Annalisse couldn't recall if the captain had secured her pistol. "Did we leave my .38 behind? Can you tell what gun was fired?" A vehicle drove up on their position, slowed, then idled behind the patrol car. She twisted her aunt's pearl ring around her finger to remind herself why she was in this stupid place with bullets zinging nearby.

"Miss, stop talking," McDonaugh growled under his breath. "Detective Drake is behind us. I signaled for him to stay put. When I say, I want you to run like hell to the passenger side of his SUV. As soon as you're inside and clear, tell him to punch it and get the hell out of here."

Laying a hand where her heart thudded, her gut lurched up to meet it. She'd managed to land in the line of gunfire again when she thought all of that was solidly behind her.

"I'm ready. Tell me when."

Annalisse rose slightly to secure a solid footing. She pressed a palm against the door panel as a means to push off like a relay runner. Everything else left her mind except getting to Bill Drake's door.

McDonaugh mumbled to someone else on the radio and yelled, "Drury, go!"

Annalisse sprang clear and ran to Drake's car. Her hand slipped on the door latch.

"C'mon. Geez." On the second try, she ripped a fingernail but managed to swing the door wide and jump inside, slamming it in a solid *clunk*.

Bill's round eyes were unable to focus. "What—"

"Go, go, go!" She flapped her hands wildly. "Back to Alec's. I'll explain on the way."

He stomped on the throttle, dust billowing behind them.

"Who clobbered you?" He studied her in a sideways glance and flicked on his turn signal. "I keep a first aid kit in the back."

"As bad as all that? You're the third person to remark on my face." She flipped down the visor and chewed on her lip at her reflection. "Stuff from a meat grinder looks better." Her cheeks were covered in road rash, swollen in blotches, and already scabbing over. Her temple near the hairline was covered in dried blood, and her left eye was blackened all the way to the bridge of her nose. "Good thing I was too pumped to feel all this." She smiled crookedly and stroked her tender cheekbone. "Ugh." She recoiled. Her fingertips pressed the puffy skin gently. "I'm gonna look even prettier in the morning. Feels like a sea of bruises already."

"Ibuprofen in the glove box. I'd take a couple. Tissues on the floor if you need 'em." Bill opened the console slider between their seats. "Picked up a couple of bottles of water. Help yourself. When you come down from your adrenaline high, you're gonna feel like crap. Those cuts need to be cleaned and disinfected when we get to Alec's." He changed lanes and turned to her again. "Feel like telling me what happened after I left?"

"Someone's shooting back there." She snapped the visor back into place. "Got a little intense."

"Maybe you'd better start at the top."

"Did Chase get to Alec's? How are Alec and Helga?"

"Didn't talk to Alec, but your friend is there."

Annalisse leaned back. "That's a relief. If they need medical attention, he'll know what to do."

Bill's jaw twitched, and he brushed hair away from his neck. Burn scars splashed in a starburst shape below his ear to the shirt collar. No wonder he wore his hair in a dated hairstyle.

By the time Annalisse covered the events, with plenty of description about her Woody encounter, her head pounded, and guilt sank in. They were still no closer to finding Aunt Kate. Annalisse blew the only good chance they'd had.

Bill said, "Alec's security man saw your abductor approach the stables. He managed to take down the license number before being taken out of commission himself. Security had a mean bump on the head but kept it together enough to check out the house. He found Alec first."

She glanced at a stack of Bill's business cards in the cup holder. "You aren't going to believe what Woody had in his pocket. McDonaugh doesn't know about it." Digging into her jeans, she extracted the Walker Farm card. She held it up so he could see it and noticed a phone number scrawled on the back. "That's interesting. I didn't see that before."

Bill took the card and pursed his lips. "He had Ethan's card?"

"Flip it over. What area code is 413?"

"Massachusetts." He turned the card over and nodded. "Call the number."

"What do I say?" she asked.

"Ask what town you're calling. Ad lib as you go."

"My phone's at Brookehaven."

"Never mind." He recited the numbers out loud, and the phone rang via the Bluetooth speakers.

"Good afternoon. Stonemaple Cottage Inn," a cheerful voice answered.

Bill shot a quick look at Annalisse and said, "Hello. I'm looking for a guest at your inn. Would you connect me with Katharine Walker? She might have signed in as Kate Walker."

"Just a moment, sir."

"You think Kate's there?" Annalisse whispered.

"A good place to start. It might be Woody's check-in number."

"On Ethan's card?" She rubbed circles on her temples. "He's not in Massachusetts. This doesn't make sense."

The telephone line clicked open. "I'm sorry, sir. We don't have any guests with us by that name. Your friend must be enjoying a stay at another establishment. Is there something else I can do for you?"

"What town am I calling?"

"Lenox."

"Thank you." Bill ended the call. "The Berkshires."

"We still don't know where Kate is. Like someone would put my aunt up at a five star. Yeah, right."

"On the contrary. The connection is there. Our cold trail just turned red hot." Bill grinned and winked. "This is great news. Drink some more water. You aren't yourself yet. Woody never said where he was taking you?"

"Nope."

"As soon as we get to Brookehaven, I'll do a search on that inn. Find out what's around it. My partner isn't far from that area. He can poke around."

Annalisse took a long drink from her bottle. The ibuprofen was smoothing out her aches, and she felt less edgy, but her level of comprehension could be better.

"Why do you think that number was on the back of Ethan's card?" she asked.

"Why not? Is Ethan the only one who has access to Walker Ranch business cards?"

She shrugged. "His name is on them. Why would anyone else use his card?" Annalisse laid her head against the rest and sighed. "Too much to think about right now. I'll be happy to see Alec." She caught a glimpse of Bill's scarred neck and considered prying. "May I ask a personal question?"

"Sure." He steered the next turn. "I'll answer if I can."

"Did you get burned?"

He rubbed the side of his neck as if to soothe a haunting memory. "I used to be a fireman. Got caught in a seven-story roof collapse. Almost bought it." He tapped cruise control and slid his shoe off the accelerator.

An injured fireman with a near-death experience turned private investigator made more sense to her now. Bill didn't fit the cookie-cutter-investigator type.

They hit smooth asphalt in the cross into Sullivan County. Annalisse relished the soothing hum from the roadway. At the county border, they passed a renovated eighteenth-century church refurbished into a modern brick farmhouse. The original belfry and bell sat atop the gable roof at the midpoint, with a new masonry chimney erected on one side near the redwood decking. She hadn't noticed it the first time with Woody.

"What a horrible experience for you, Bill. I'm sorry. Alec didn't mention it."

"We don't talk about it much. For a bunch of reasons." Bill fiddled with a tabloid-size newspaper wedged next to the console. "My hours are better now anyway." He chuckled, rolling the newsprint into a tube and blowing into it.

"A gossip rag? Haven't read any juicy dirt in a while. I could use a laugh." She reached for the paper, expecting him to hand it to her.

"Boring issue." Bill tossed the roll over the headrest, wiping newsprint from his fingers to the seat.

That was strange.

She tried to grab it, but it landed just out of her reach.

Annalisse unbuckled and twisted for a closer look at the huge headline, reading aloud, "THE HOUND CHASES ANOTHER FOX. Please people. Such original journalism. Who this time?" She laughed as she lunged for the paper.

Bill's arm moved in like a slingshot and bumped her sore cheek, blocking her.

"Ow. Watch the road," she exclaimed and bounced backward. "Walking wounded here. Just drive, Bill. Allow me to revel in someone else's grief for a while."

He touched her elbow. "Please don't."

Bill wasn't smiling, and his skin had morphed to ashen of the dead. He had the look of a man who'd just lost his best friend and was about to lose his faithful dog too.

It clicked. "What don't you want me to see what thousands of other people have already seen?"

"Wait till we get to Brookehaven so he can—"

"Who can?" Annalisse hung over the seat and stretched her sore body far enough to snag the tabloid with her fingertips. She braced herself—the photo had to be disturbing.

"The timing is bad. Really bad." Bill stared at the road and in a low voice added, "I'm so sorry."

The pang of the unknown boomeranged through her heart, and she looked down at the front page of *Reveal Reality*.

A couple with their backs to the camera, overlooking an ocean at sunset at some kind of event. She wasn't sure where but expected the piece would say.

The paparazzi photographer had zoomed in on a brunette in a skimpy, backless sundress leaning into a man with his elegant hand cupping her barely covered butt cheek. His chiseled profile and windblown curls were unmistakable.

Say bye-bye to the mysterious, green-eyed Annalisse! Italian starlet Monica Corsetti on Italy's Riviera with Greek magnate, Alec Zavos of the Signorile Corporation. They were…

She covered her mouth.

"Pull over, Bill. I'm gonna throw up."

CHAPTER SIXTEEN

When Alec pushed himself from the sofa, his foot slipped, and he landed on a rug in a hard thump.

"Dammit." He curled into a ball and rubbed his throbbing ankle. Resting his forehead on a grooved surface, he rolled. He let his lids close over dry, gritty eyeballs. Musty fibers with a hint of old-world mildew tickled his nose. He coughed, feeling as if his lungs would explode.

"What the hell hit me?" Drawing a tortured breath, he groaned and whispered, "Focus." His eyes opened to a swirl pattern of blue and cream that scratched his skin and made him dizzy.

Pushing himself on all fours with the help of mushy muscles, Alec crawled from the braided rug back to the couch and plopped clumsily against a pillow. He dropped his head in his hands, squinting through red and pink hazy shapes. Closing his eyes again, he rubbed each one individually, unsure of his location. The room smelled of roses and fireplace soot. Alec ran his hand over the fabric beside him and felt the nubby short pile of velveteen or velvet. *The drawing room.* He squared his shoulders, feeling a little better about finding himself at home.

"Alec?" someone asked. "Did you fall?"

The voice sounded familiar, but Alec couldn't place it with his eyes shut.

"Who's here? Can you give me a hand? The room is spinning." Alec rubbed his sore wrists.

"Lie back, Alec. They said it might take a while. Relax. You refused to go to the hospital, so the paramedics brought you in here."

"Chase?" Alec sat against the cushion and rested his neck. *Why is Chase here?*

Hitting the rug was the last thing he had a hard memory of and little recollection of what had happened before that. He rolled over to find himself stretched out on the green silk fainting couch; his head was propped on a pillow.

"Alec. It's Chase. Don't move too fast, okay. You conked out the last time you did."

"Chase?" Alec tasted copper in his mouth and probed with his tongue, expecting to find pennies lurking behind his molars. "Metal. What am I on?"

"Tranquilizers, they think. Valium or Diazepam. You've been out for a few hours." Chase handed Alec a glass of water. "Take a sip. It'll help with the taste in your mouth."

Alec rubbed a sore spot in his biceps and carefully sat up, taking the glass from a scowling Chase. "Do I look that bad?"

Chase turned away and said something Alec couldn't make out.

"I didn't hear. Talk slower." Alec took a few swallows of water and set the glass down.

"Never mind."

Alec's lids felt heavy, but he fought the drowsiness, opening his eyes wide. He searched the furniture and floral display for Annalisse.

"Kitchen. I was in the kitchen with Annalisse." Alec checked the french doors open to the hall. "Where is she?"

Chase's color rose to a hard pink. He strolled over to the water glass and plucked it from the floor, pausing to view him without regard.

"Are you fully awake?" Chase asked.

"Getting there."

"This will help." Chase flipped the rest of the water at Alec's face.

Alec jumped as the icy stuff froze his neck. "Shit, man." He brushed at the water soaking his shirt.

"I trusted you. You promised to keep Anna safe. How could you let something like this happen to two innocent women? You self-centered ass."

Alec hauled himself to his feet and wobbled. Coming off tranquilizers sucked.

"What did I do? I don't remember. What other woman?" Alec swayed, catching himself at the end of the lounge. "Where's Annalisse?" He heaved for more air and grabbed Chase's forearm. "Tell me."

Chase swatted Alec's hand aside. "Fine. But sit down before I put you down with this." He raised his balled fist and shook it.

Chase rarely came unglued. What had he done that Chase was threatening to punch him out? He shivered and crossed his arms.

While Chase described what Alec's security found, thoughts came clearer and fell into the blank spots. An intruder entered the house, and Annalisse was with him. Alec let her go—couldn't stop her—because she'd tied him.

But go where?

Chase added his firsthand account—how he'd come in with security and found Helga bound and whimpering in the bedroom. He described the scene with ropes and Helga crying with a gag in her mouth.

Alec's throat closed, and his eyes stung. "Has anyone heard from Annalisse? What about Helga? Here or at the hospital?" Alec asked, when the gravity of what had happened settled into his groggy mind. The Victorian clock on the table struck three. Two o'clock Saturday, Kate went missing.

"Helga's okay. She's resting in her room upstairs. And she's as stubborn as you. She wouldn't go to the hospital."

"Helga or Annalisse?"

"The housekeeper. Anna's gone."

"Where? I'll check on Helga in a minute. Where did the wolf freak take my art lady?"

Chase went ridged. "What wolf freak?"

Alec filled Chase in on what he could remember of the gunman and kidnapping.

Chase lost all expression and white-knuckled the glass. "Anna hates wolves."

"Why?" Alec asked. "We might be able to use that to figure this out."

"Use what? Haven't you used Anna long enough? Don't you care what you're doing to her?"

Alec shrank from Chase's tone. "Cool your jets. I know I've been—"

"An asshole." Chase finished his sentence stronger than he would have, but the sentiment was close enough. "Your jet-setting lifestyle is killing her. A little at a time, you're taking away her ambition, her motivation, her soul. On top of everything else, this thing with Kate and some guy dressed like a wolf? Poor Anna must be losing it." A snarl twisted Chase's face; hate flashed in his eyes. "Do you know *why* Anna went to the farm on Saturday? Do ya?" Angry Chase seemed to grow larger. "I do."

Alec cleared more fuzz from his mind. "She goes to the farm most Saturdays to help Kate out. Other than finding a dead guy and—"

"Don't be a jerk. Anna was spending this past weekend at the farm because she wanted advice. Kate's advice. The opinion that means the most to Anna. Next to mine, of course."

Alec had enough of the attitude. "Annalisse isn't your responsibility. It's time she relied on me instead of you."

There was no happiness in Chase's smile. "That's a laugh. You're never around. I am. So is Kate. Hell, your mom spends more time with Anna than you do."

"Make your point. A second opinion for what?"

"She's cutting you loose. Getting away from an egotistical, one-sided… you. She went to the farm to discuss with Kate how sharp an ax to use."

Alec's knees buckled, and he sank to the lounge. He'd noticed how aloof Annalise was when he came home early from Pennsylvania. Had she planned to give him the boot before her aunt had gone missing?

"What advice did Kate give her?" Alec asked, his heart thumping. "I need to know."

Chase shrugged and swept his blond hair back. "I haven't had a chance to talk to her. I do know this: she was devastated when you canceled the antiquing junket. It's all she talked about for weeks. She'd looked forward to it almost as much as her dream vacation to the Callanish Stones in the UK. You can't dangle a trip through history in front of her, then take it away. Brilliant move." His sarcasm coated his words thick as cream. "That's hardcore, man."

Chase verbally kicked him in the nuts, and Chase was enjoying it.

"How much did my security find out about the man who has Annalisse? He saw him, right? Do they have his name yet?" Alec stopped his barrage of questions when the front door clicked.

"Alec. Anyone here?" Drake's voice echoed down the hallway.

Before Alec could answer, Chase darted into the hall. His footsteps came to an abrupt halt.

"Wait up." Alec attempted to follow. He felt along the side table and Chippendale armchair, bracing himself against the wall.

"God, Anna. Let me help you with those."

The grief in Chase's words bothered Alec, but only for a second. *Drake has Annalisse. She's back.* Alec pressed his palm to his chest.

"Babe! Stay there." Alec heard himself yell but wasn't sure how well his voice carried. His ankle turned and he slipped, banging his head on the slide down the paneling. "Son of a—" He got on his knees, and a hand reached for him.

"I got ya. Hang on to me." His detective friend smiled half-heartedly, lifting him from the floor. "Wrap an arm over my shoulder, buddy. You shouldn't be walking. Let's get you to a chair."

Alec allowed Bill to take most of his weight and help him to the love seat. The doctor's warning about leaving the ankle boot on made sense now. He wasn't strong enough to get around without it.

Alec found Annalisse bent over by the door, unzipping her boots. Weeds peppered her dark tresses. She stiffly rose, rolled her shoulders, and stretched her swanlike neck.

Someone had hurt her. Badly. Her battered face and arms touched him in places he wasn't ready to go. Her eyes met his with a raw misery. His gorgeous art lady's bruises and gashes brought unbidden tears.

Alec swallowed the lump in his throat and mustered speech. "Sweetness… you're— I— Jesus." He covered his face with a quivering hand.

Bill turned away from him, his arms folded.

"I take it you're Chase?" Bill asked.

Chase nodded mechanically.

"Annalisse could use a good soak in the tub. Would you mind taking care of that for her?"

Alec watched as Annalisse drew Chase to her breast and gave him a long, shaky hug. The kind Alec hated to witness from the sidelines. He longed to be near her but felt so ashamed and unworthy he couldn't move. He shouldn't have let her go with the gunman. Had the guy raped her? Was he in custody?

She lovingly rubbed Chase's back. "Use the tub in the master suite." The way she looked at Chase, her obvious faith and affection when she spoke made Alec's heart sink. He'd screwed up royally.

"We'll talk later, hon. Don't worry. Be there in a minute." She motioned down the hall.

Chase's chin trembled, he hesitated a moment, then left the room in his slippers without saying another word.

Alec swiped his eyes and chose his words carefully "What can I do?" His voice cracked.

He'd all but verbally consented to the wolfman harming her. Mission completed. He would have to live with that. *Get a grip, Zavos.* Acting like a miserable wimp wouldn't help their situation. Annalisse was beaten up and needed his TLC.

She sniffed but said nothing. From her condition, Annalisse had to be hanging together by a fragile thread.

"How's Helga? At the hospital?" she finally asked coolly.

Alec shook his head. "Upstairs resting."

The sound of paper crinkling drew his attention to a wadded magazine clutched in her hand.

Taking a giant step toward him, she said, "How… Are you okay?" A shaky breath followed. "Woody…

ah, he stuck you with the needle before I could stop him." Her eyes darted to his arm.

Alec rubbed the injection site and bristled from the sensation.

Annalisse opened the paper, smoothing it on one thigh, and wrung it in the opposite direction using both hands. Alec couldn't make out anything but an advertisement.

Bill cleared his throat from the kitchen. "Alec, can I get you something? Help clear the cobwebs." He opened the fridge door and ducked his head to peer inside.

"Annalisse could use some water. Thanks," Alec answered absently while he surveyed her injuries and chilly body language. Her stiffness could mean a bunch of things. None of them good. The kidnapper or someone else had blackened her eye. A squiggly gash already scabbing angled through one brow. She stared right through him—and her cheeks were scratched and stained from crying.

Annalisse's white knuckles clung to the rolled newspaper.

"What is that?" Alec asked, taking a step closer.

"Why don't we let Annalisse get her bearings?" Bill interrupted with a slight headshake that Alec almost missed.

She twisted her mouth so bitterly it shook him. "How could you be so heartless?" She fell on her knees and doubled over, holding her belly. A guttural moan filled the room with so much anguish that it took Alec's breath. She swabbed her reddened nose with a grass-stained shirt. "We don't know where Kate is… and…"

Another groan. "…I believed the business trips. I'm such a sap." She sobbed into her hands.

"What happened?" Alec met her on his knees, face to face, touching her shoulder. "Sweetness, tell me. I want to help."

She sprang at him with her fingernails.

Like a feral cat, she struck, embedding her nails into his chest.

He fell backward, hitting the tile hard. His broken rib flared with paralyzing pain, and he wheezed, clogging his airway.

Standing over him, she said, "We're done. But you already knew that." She dropped the newspaper on his chest as she stomped past him. It unfurled and rolled off onto the tile—a significant piece of the puzzle.

Alec gasped at the ceiling, trying to figure out who'd attacked him. The woman he knew had transformed into some kind of she-devil. He flipped himself over.

"Ugh. I could use some help." His knees were slipping on the tile. Alec couldn't move without Bill's assistance once again. He grabbed him by the elbow. "What the shit just flew by me, Drake? Did I black out and miss the devil in her Pradas?"

Bill's lips tightened into a thin line.

Having made light of Annalisse's pain and regretting it, Alec slumped into the sofa cushion and covered his rib cage with a pillow. "I could use that glass of water." The back of his head pounded where he'd hit the tile. "And something for a headache. Helga keeps it—last drawer on the end." Alec ran a hand through his scalp, leaned back, and closed his eyes. "I flat don't feel good."

"Makes three of us. Here." Bill sloshed the glass of water and handed it to him.

"Easy. I've already had one glass thrown at me today."

"Straight up only. No mixing painkillers." Turning to pick up the newspaper, Bill sat next to Alec. "I should tell you what kind of day Annalisse has had before we get into… what you just witnessed. Let me have the floor."

For what felt like an hour, Alec listened to the story of Annalisse and the man in the wolf disguise. Bill even explained why Annalisse had a fear of the creatures. Something she'd never confided to Alec.

"I was wrong about you," Bill said abruptly.

"Huh?" His friend's comment felt off. Rude and more than matter-of-fact. "What about?"

"You *have* changed. What idiot would two time a woman like Annalisse? That incredible lady loves you. The guy I've been friends with since college would've had the decency to dump her first."

Alec blinked. "She told you she loved me?"

"I'm not blind." Bill tossed the newsprint into Alec's lap. "Front page. Imagine your girlfriend's face when she saw that. Then multiply that look times a hundred."

Spreading out what he recognized as his least favorite tabloid, Alec read the stark headline and gazed over at the edge-to-edge photo cover of *Reveal Reality*. White-hot rage coursed his body when he read about dropping Annalisse.

"Today's Monday, isn't it?" Alec made two-finger circles on his forehead and closed his eyes. "Goddammit, I forgot." He looked earnestly at Bill and lowered his voice. "Brooks. It's him. Don't you see? This is a hoax." Alec studied the top corner of the grainy shot and slapped his leg. "Karl, you lose." Alec tossed the rag at Bill.

"Did I miss something? You've dumped your girlfriend in the toilet, for Christ's sake. How many more do you have in your harem? You're seriously messed up—to the max." Bill shook his head. "I'll never understand you and women."

"Calm down." Alec took another swig of water and pressed the glass to his face, cooling it. "How long have you known me?"

"A while."

"When did you meet Mom and Dad?"

"What are you talking about?"

"As I recall, you flew to Greece with me our first year of college. Stayed the entire spring break. Good times." Alec whistled at the memory of scrawny, lobster-skinned Bill who'd forgotten to use sunscreen, french frying himself on their boat. He was Noxzema white and smelled of menthol for a week. "Man. That was some sunburn, but it won you plenty of sympathetic chicks." Alec suddenly remembered another day with bad sunburns. The images shut down his silliness on the spot. "When Dad died on the yacht last year, I was spared witness to his death. Mom and Annalisse saw it all. I can't imagine how that scene haunts both the women in my life. I wish we hadn't sailed that day. God knows, I wish it."

"Both women?" Bill asked.

"Mom and my art lady."

"But what about—"

"Annalisse *is* my match. I felt it as early as the night of Mom's opening." Alec read the confusion on his friend's face. "Take a look at the top right corner of that picture. Look at the crowd," Alec said gleefully. "Go ahead."

Alec watched eagerly until Bill found it.

"See him? That shot was taken eight years ago." Alec folded his arms. "We were invited to Monica Corsetti's birthday party. I had no idea anyone was behind us taking pictures, but I shouldn't be surprised."

Bill nodded, with more than a hint of shame. "Your dad was there too."

"No mistaking him. You could spot his flirty smile anywhere."

"Who's Karl?"

"A sick son of a bitch who tried to extort money from me. Threatened to go to this rag with a photo and some other info."

"Looks like he did."

"Yeah. Before I had a chance to warn Annalisse." Alec realized his second problem, what this picture might do to the offer to buy Signorile. He'd force a damage-control retraction out of *Reveal Reality* or slap them with the biggest lawsuit in their worthless history. "Karl Brooks married my ex. He might be out of jail." Alec shook his head and explained the rest to Bill.

"Wow. There's a lot to unwrap here. You've got some serious splainin' to do to the lady down the hall. A romantic getaway to an exotic island wouldn't hurt either." Bill looked at a spot behind the couch in daydreaming fashion.

"If I can get her to listen." Alec wanted to laugh off the innocence of it all, but he had to be careful. Annalisse was so badly hurt both mentally and physically, there were no funny anecdotes or easy fixes to her aunt's situation right now. He'd worry about his own wounded ego later. "You didn't tell Annalisse anything about the other case I had you work for me, did you?"

"Not a word, my friend. She'll have to hear about it from you." He flung the tabloid on the coffee table. "There're a few other details we learned today, but they can wait."

Alec sipped his water. "I'm lucky, you know. Now that I've seen the photo, Annalisse handled herself with restraint, considering. She could've exploded."

"She did. On the side of the road," Annalisse cooed from behind the sofa, entering the room in an orchid-colored bathrobe—like a springtime breeze in a place where the air still held the chill of frozen tundra.

"Art lady." Alec wobbled up to greet her with his hand out, a churning gut, and a battered heart. He lingered over her styled, lavender-scented hair—her haunting eyes an emerald green in the dim light.

He drew her essence in with a single breath. "You're ravishing. How did… How are the scratches and bruises?"

Her lower lip trembled, and she caught it in her teeth.

He loved it when she did that. Such a turn on.

"Amazing what soap and water, cold compresses, and a little makeup can do." She pointed to the sofa. "May I?"

Alec moved the sofa pillow so that she had to sit next to him.

"I'll take a walk. Check in with my partner," Bill said quietly.

"No. Please stay. I didn't thank you for what you did. All of it. Even buying the tabloid. We all need a serious *reality* check once in a while. Thank you for your kindness, Bill. I see why Alec thinks so highly of you. I hope Kate gets a chance to thank you too."

Annalisse worked her throat, scrunching the tufts out of her chenille robe.

She would be an emotional wreck until they found Kate. Finding her had to be his top priority, then he'd straighten out his problems with Annalisse.

"I heard what you said to Bill." She laid a trembling palm on Alec's arm.

"How much?" Alec asked.

"Enough to give you a pardon." She offered him a watery smile. "I was ready to strangle your worthless neck—Chase almost beat me to it—but then we overheard you discussing that old picture. Chase is so stressed out. He's in the room next to your suite."

Bill and Alec looked at each other.

"My neck thanks you." Alec dipped in a mock bow.

"Did I hurt you?" Annalisse's gaze softened further. "The splat you made when you hit the tile. I *almost* ran back to check on you." She tugged at his wrists. "They're gouged from the cord. I tied it too tight. What about your ankle?"

Alec caught her by the shoulders as she leaned down. "Shh. I'm fine." He cupped her face in his hands, and her eyes glistened with tears. "We're gonna be fine."

A muffled ring came from inside Annalisse's tote bag.

"Why didn't I check my phone earlier?" She sprang for her tote and drew it out, staring at the screen. She showed the phone to Bill. "Should I answer?"

"Who is it?" Alec asked.

"That thing we haven't discussed yet." Bill turned and nodded at her. "Definitely. Make sure we can all hear. Act normal." He mouthed something undecipherable to Alec.

"Who?" Alec scrunched his nose.

"Ethan." She answered her phone. "What's up?"

Alec's lips soured. *What's up?* Small talk? What about Kate? It didn't sound right. He glanced at Bill, who was in Annalisse's face furiously punching an index finger into his hand.

Annalisse set the phone down on the counter and crept backward as if the phone might be contagious.

"Hadn't heard from you today, that's all." Ethan paused, and all they heard was the sound of his breathing.

"Where's Aunt Kate?" Annalisse slapped a hand over her mouth and glared at Bill, who was holding his head. It was clearly not what he wanted her to say. Stranger yet, she said it like she'd accused Ethan of knowing Kate's whereabouts.

"You sound like you're in a tube. Where are you?" Ethan asked.

"What's the latest from the farm? Maggie feeling better?" She looked at Bill and hunched her shoulders.

"Yeah. Jeremy wants a meeting in the morning. Nine sharp, he said. He thinks you and Miss Walker are playing tricks because he plans to sell this place."

"*Jeremy* called the meeting?"

"You feeling crook today? Yeah, Jeremy."

Bill twirled his hand in a wrap-this-up motion.

"Will you be there?" she asked Ethan demurely.

"If you want me to, I guess." Ethan sounded hollow. "Get a fizzie or go on the turps. You sound like you need it."

"Shit," Alec whispered and stiffened a fist.

"Will do." Annalisse ended the call and looked at Bill. "I screwed that up."

"What did he tell you to do? Fizzies and turps?" Alec was already by her side, noticing her bad case of the shakes.

"A fizzie is a soft drink and the other—he told me to get drunk." She asked Bill, "What about this meeting tomorrow? Should I be worried?"

"You won't be going alone," Bill grumbled.

"We're *all* going. When is someone going to let me in on what just happened?" Alec shoved a fist into his pocket to settle his bubbling anger.

Bill slid a business card across the granite. "Annalisse found that in the kidnapper's pocket. The *only* thing in his pocket. There's a phone number on the back we've already called. My partner's working the lead."

"He took her." Alec clenched his jaw. "I've never liked that guy."

"No kidding. We don't know how deeply he's involved. I did notice how he ignored what I blurted about Aunt Kate though." Annalisse pulled out a barstool and sat. "Ah, my poor feet. Anyone bothered to check on Helga?"

Alec glanced at the kitchen clock. "Chase did a while ago, but it's after five. Time for another peek at her." He turned to Bill. "I'd like you to stay over so we can all go to Walker Farm together. We can get some dinner tonight. Any problem with that?" Alec waited. "As a favor to me?"

"A nice change from hotels. Thanks."

"I'll go up and see Helga. We'll bring her and Chase back something to eat, but I'll let *you* talk to Chase before we go. I don't trust him not to smack me." Alec popped his fist into his hand in jest. "Bill, I have enough questions for you to fill a journal. I hope you can answer them."

CHAPTER SEVENTEEN

For the first time in months, Annalisse stood in Alec's den, floored by the transformation—how his new reality had changed since his father's death. She recognized furniture from the Zavos home in Greece. Alec had placed small objects next to the Georgian Chippendale-style chairs she favored. His dad's Klismos chairs, with their smooth lines and curves, reminded her of the 1960s Danish modern period. Carved pieces with legs that looked like columns, lion's paw feet, and tables with marble tops. All were reminiscent of past Egyptian influence found on Crete. They'd become part of Alec's eclectic collection, along with the aroma of Pearce's beloved Cuban cigars.

The essence of Pearce Zavos engulfed the room. Everywhere. She ran her hand across smooth mahogany and imagined the comfort Alec found in here while he worked. She'd expected to find signs of his father in the stable's office. Now that she thought about it, Alec chose a fitting place for Pearce's shrine inside the estate.

She recalled the first time she ventured into Pearce's tiny study in the villa, holding Alec's hand for moral support. The room spoke volumes about Pearce's need for quiet solitude and his spartan taste in material things. The most impressive articles that took up one entire wall weren't his; they were Gen's. A breathtaking Georgian secretary desk, with a bookcase and equally impressive mahogany kneehole desk, now occupied Alec's office.

Boris meowed from the hallway and squeezed his rusty body through the narrow opening to the den.

Annalisse scooped the fifteen-pound mass into her arms and slung him over a shoulder. "Lardo, I thought we backed off the treats. I can hardly lift you." She scratched behind a warm ear. Boris purred, pushing against her fingertips.

"Is he bothering you?" Chase came in wearing a pale green T-shirt and a bashful grin. "I should've known he'd find you anywhere, even in this English mansion. I still get lost between hallways."

Annalisse plopped Boris to the floor, swiping her hands free of hair. Puffs of it floated through the air. She leaned in for a hug. "Thank you for bringing the cat."

"What about bringing me?"

"Yes, and you too. Silly. That goes without saying. Coming here when you did—helping Alec. My saving-grace guy is always around when I need him."

His gaze sank to the hardwood.

"What's the matter?" She was almost afraid to ask.

"Your other half." Chase shrank into himself. "I said some things..."

The study door creaked and opened wider. "Her other half is an ass. Thank you for reminding me." Alec stretched out his hand and shook Chase's. "What I did yesterday was not only rude, it was wrong. I'm sorry. I'm glad she can count on you."

Annalisse regarded Chase, then Alec, deciding to leave herself out of that particular conversation. She smiled at another of Alec's traits she admired. His old-fashioned upbringing included owning up to bad judgment and apologizing for it. She could see by Chase's body language that whatever had torn between them, Alec had mended.

Alec's entrance brought with it the succulent aroma of hickory smoke.

She gave his crisp poplin shirt a tug and brushed his lips lightly with her own, catching the cedar scent she'd given him. "Helga's breakfast was great, wasn't it? Her renowned egg and sausage dishes *and* bacon and strudel for good measure. She's so amazing. She seemed fine after her ordeal, don't you think?"

Alec reached down to scratch Boris's ear. "She's tough. I left Bill fending for himself back there. I hope he doesn't get a case of the meat sweats. While Helga was piling on the bratwurst, I bussed my plate. I bet Drake has a whole hog on his dish by now." He snorted from deep in his throat.

Boris jumped and scampered away.

Annalisse joined Alec and Chase in a round of feel-good laughter. She wiped her eyes. "I can't remember the last time I laughed like that. Poor Boris. Where'd he go?" She checked under the Louis VIII sideboard.

Helga had mentioned his hiding places, and it was one of the favorites.

"He'll show up when Helga brings his canned food." Alec stepped around his desk and opened his laptop. "I thought I'd get a head start on some research before we leave for the farm."

"We'll get out of your way." Annalisse ushered Chase toward the door.

"Stay, sweetness. We work better as a team." Alec's honest smile comforted her. "I'm making copies for Bill. He wants a list of the hotels and spas in and around Lenox, Massachusetts. Screenshots and printouts. I'm still wondering about the lyrics from that song."

Annalisse waved to Chase as he left and then picked up her tote. Rummaging for her phone, she turned it on. "Here's my take." She found the song online and tapped play, pausing the tune at midpoint. "It doesn't work as a clue for Kate's whereabouts. I'm certain now. It's meant for me. It even mentions Soho where the gallery is. The messages of who are *you*? And I know who *you* are feel like finger pointing, but why drag me into it? Does the kidnapper know me? Is this unrelated to Kate? We don't even know if Kate is being held or… dead." She shook her head. "No, I refuse to believe she's gone. It's only Tuesday. Not quite seventy-two hours."

Someone knocked on the door. Bill walked in, holding his stomach and sweating like he'd eaten too many chili peppers. "You should've warned me your housekeeper was hazardous to detectives who say they're starved. The piggies are at war." He pointed to himself and belched. "Got any antacids in here?"

The room erupted into laughter, and Alec dug into a drawer and threw a packet at Bill. "That should help."

"Thanks." He popped a tablet into his mouth. "Are we about ready to get on the road?" Bill held his stomach and sat carefully in the creaky corner chair. The barley twist made itself known around the middle of the nineteenth century, so the chair had well over a hundred years on it. A larger man would have collapsed it.

Annalisse checked her email and held a breath as a cold shadow crossed the bay window. "Geez. That's creepy. Someone needs anger management." She showed the subject line to Alec without opening the email and waited.

"*Open me, Bitch.* A good morning to you, spammer." Alec gave her an uneasy glance. "No attachment. Do you recognize the sender's email address? Who's at ProtempMail.com? Never heard of them." Alec tapped a few keys on his laptop. "Encrypted private email. Based in Norway."

"Forward it to me, Annalisse." Bill gave her his email address. "Someone's hiding the ISP address. The person could be anywhere in the world. I'll ship it over to Dan. He'll dig into it."

"Have I met Dan?" Alec asked.

"Doubt it. Dan Chappell is my new partner."

"I think I have to open it to forward. Here goes." She clicked on the email. "Huh. There's just a video link." She typed Bill's address. "On the way."

Bill said, "Got it" a few seconds later. "Interesting. Wanna hear this?" He directed the question to her.

"Should I be afraid?"

Bill tapped the phone and set it on the desk.

In less than four orchestral notes, Annalisse recognized the song. Kate loved the haunting, hypnotic ballad by the sexy Welsh singer, one of her favorite performers. Annalisse looked at Alec and grabbed the corner of his desk to steady herself and quickly sank into the nearest chair. Goose pimples came with the trumpets' crescendos, and her throat tightened.

"Heard enough?" Bill reached for the phone.

She held up her hand. "Wait. Let's hear all the words. I don't want to miss anything while I digest this." She knew the disturbing lyrics by heart. The song told of a jilted man who went out of his mind and killed his lover with a knife. When the singer hit the reprise she said, "That's enough."

Alec crouched by her side and touched her thigh. "You've lost all the color in your face."

She dropped her head in her hands. With eyes closed, she remembered Ted waltzing Kate around the kitchen to "Delilah." Back when her uncle spent more time at home. They loved Tom Jones's music.

The lyrics were more than lines in a song, they were a worry.

Annalisse slumped and leaned against the chair back. "That, gentlemen… *is* personal."

"The lyrics or the subject line?" Alec asked.

She patted his arm. "For the record, that's not me in the song. I'm not cheating. I'll tell you myself if you screw up and lose me." Annalisse smiled at the face he made. "Whoever sent that link knows my aunt likes Tom Jones. 'Delilah' in particular." She stood, resting her back against the desk. "When every woman in America swooned over the Beatles and Elvis, Aunt Kate had the hots for the throaty, dreamy-eyed Welshman." She addressed Alec with a softer voice. "You remind me of him. The dark curls, bedroom eyes, the whole bit. I knew there was a reason Auntie always followed you around a room." She winked and continued, "Tom Jones could belt out a ballad. The sweat poured off him on stage. Women peeled off their panties in the hope he'd use them to mop his face and toss them back. Kate would've done it if she were in the audience during one of his performances." Her giddiness must have surprised Alec; his eyes were wide.

"You said personal. In what way?" Bill asked from across the room.

"If someone held Auntie against her will and tried to make her give them the name of her favorite song or performer, or anything at all, she would lie. Out of spite. In protest. Because I know how much she loves this performer, there's a personal connection somewhere."

"What about a secret admirer? She could have told someone in passing in a casual conversation. Who wants to be with your aunt? Did she have any lovers? Anyone who was jealous of her marriage? Angry over or advances she rejected?" Bill asked.

"We've been through this. She didn't and doesn't screw around. Would an admirer call me a bitch?"

"You're sure this is about Kate and not you?" Alec asked her.

"Gut instinct, it's Kate, but I'm no expert."

"The violence in the song should worry you." Bill shook his head. "We have enough evidence to get the FBI involved, but that's up to authorities. I don't like where this is headed. The locals should see the 'Delilah' message. It sounds serious. Do you agree, Alec?"

She thought Alec gave Bill a dirty look, but he turned too quickly to be sure.

"How would Ethan know any of this? How much is he on a computer to go to the trouble to encrypt his email?" Alec's personal dislike of Ethan reared its head.

"You *know* we aren't sure about Ethan." Annalisse remembered something in her purse and extracted a plastic bag from the zippered pocket. "So much has happened, this didn't seem relevant. Now it does. When Bill and I went to the farm on Sunday, I found this." She handed the Ziploc bag to Alec.

Alec wrinkled his nose while he read. "Bungee jumping? I hope you can live with your secrets? Yours or Kate's? Who wrote this?"

"I found it rolled up in my aunt's jewelry box with the gold band around it. My uncle wore that wedding ring. I'd know his dry humor anywhere."

"The dead uncle wrote it?" Bill asked, coming to look at it.

"Hidden under ink pens, written on torn blueprint paper in his handwriting, yeah, it's probably the suicide note he left for Kate. I knew he left one behind, but I never saw it. On Saturday, Kate dismissed the ID card found on the corpse. Do you think the secret he's talking about has something to do with Thomas Taylor? If she'd only told me why that name upset her. We could at least rule it out."

"There must be thousands of Thomas Taylors just on the East Coast. Dan may not have gotten to that yet—I'll remind him." Bill stared at the note again. "I'd like the lyrics to both songs, if you don't mind, Alec, and a copy of this if that's okay with you?" He held up the bag and looked at Annalisse.

"Absolutely."

"You can keep the baby rattle for now. Your uncle's friends or protégés; their names would be handy if you can remember them. Your aunt might have had an admirer from that bunch." A text came in on Bill's phone, and he opened it. "Great. I put a call in to Captain McDonaugh earlier. Asked about Woody the wolf. They caught him after we left." Bill glanced up at her and said, "Still running down his identity. He's not talking. They'll update us later."

"Figures." She huffed out a disgusted breath. "What about my .38? How long do they plan to keep it?"

"I didn't ask."

"I'll replace it if we need to. I have to pick up a new Glock since my girlfriend tossed the old one into a lake." A subtle smile crossed Alec's lips.

Bill went back to handling the gold band through the plastic. "A man who leaves his wedding ring behind is done with the marriage. Most men wouldn't have bothered to take it off. How would you describe their relationship? Happy? Argumentative?"

"He's dead." Her hands went to her hips.

"While they were married, were there any signs of problems in the marriage? Something had to be wrong for him to take his own life."

"Uncle Ted worked a lot. The farm needed constant cash, and bricklaying paid the bills. Aunt Kate never complained, but I know she resented him being AWOL. The farm was a huge burden for her."

Alec plunked heavily into his desk chair and stuck out the ankle boot. "If we plan to make the nine o'clock meeting, we have to leave now. I'll call Brad to bring the Bentley around." He reached for the landline handset.

Annalisse rocked back on her heels and narrowed her eyes. "No."

"No?" Bill asked. Alec had the same questioning look.

"New rules. We change tactics and go on offense. I'm tired of being led in circles with songs and disguises. Jeremy didn't call the meeting last night. *Ethan* did. Calling me names sounds like something Jeremy would say to my face, but he's an attorney and would never put it in an email and leave tracks. Mr. Holier-Than-Thou wouldn't have Ethan call a meeting at the farm. He'd do it personally. Someone's using Ethan."

Alec groaned and lifted his eyes to the beams. "Always sticking up for him."

"Whoever sent Wolfie to fetch me went to a lot of trouble for nothing. They forced me to hurt you and Helga. Someone is playing a high-stakes game with my aunt for their own amusement. How do we know what we're walking into at Walker Farm?

McDonaugh thinks our"—she made air quotes—"*kook* is harmless. He won't be any help. We have to find Kate ourselves—with or without cops. I can't sit around any longer."

"After yesterday, we have McDonaugh's attention." Bill laid the bag with the note on Alec's desk. "Don't forget to copy that."

Alec asked her, "What's your plan?"

"I'd like to send Bill to the meeting, alone. When we're no-shows, the person who truly called the meeting will be pissed. Bill knows the right questions and how to push, and I won't be there to ruin anything with my big mouth. Jeremy brings out the worst in me." She fiddled with the handle on her tote. "Every day that passes without word, I believe that Kate is with someone close to the family or someone she thought was a friend. If they want money or revenge, why haven't there been any demands?"

"What do you think, Bill?" Alec asked him. "Are you okay with that?"

"If that's what you want. What are you two going to do when this is going down?"

"Annalisse is right. I halfway expected wolf guy to ask for a ransom yesterday. It's all too weird. This whole charade is amateurish. But the bastard getting caught might have put Kate in more jeopardy. Someone is stroking us, Bill, and we're no closer to finding her. I'd like to focus on the Stonemaple Cottage Inn. We need to feel like we're doing something to find her."

Annalisse slid her phone into the side pocket. "One other thing. That gray-haired man who came here last week, looking for me. Please talk to Helga about him again. She might remember more details. He could be the person behind Kate's disappearance or knows who is. Ask her about the man's voice. Maybe she'll recognize him as the wolfman who tied her on the bed. That might have been the reason baldy wore the disguise. He knew Helga had seen him here at Brookehaven last week. With hair."

"Fair enough." He looked at Alec from the door and said, "I'll put you in touch with Dan and arrange a meetup near the inn. He's probably already in Lenox by now."

"It might be a good idea for us to follow you in the Bentley. I want to see who's at Walker Farm." Alec beat Annalisse to her protest. "Your heated glare is burning my back. Before you come unglued, I'm not proposing we go into the driveway. We can see a lot from a distance. Then we'll head for the Berkshires."

"What if they see us?" she asked.

"No one knows this Bentley. My new Mulsanne is ready to rip. The drive will give us a chance to christen her."

Bill whistled. "Nice machine." He pulled the door open and nearly smacked into Helga.

"Oh my." Helga hopped backward, one hand on her bun. "I hope I'm not intruding. Miss Annalisse has a caller."

"Who?" she asked.

"An Ethan Fawdray is here to see her."

Annalisse met Alec's eyes, then Bill's. "Ethan's *here*?" Her hackles rose; the first thing that came into her head also came out of her mouth. “No. I can’t talk to him.”

Bill said, “Why don’t I escort him back to the farm and find out what he wants. I’ll make your excuses, unless Alec would rather—”

“You’ve got this, Bill. Go ahead, but don’t let anyone know where we plan to end up today.” Alec closed the door behind the detective, and Annalisse wrapped him in her arms.

CHAPTER EIGHTEEN

"My ears are on fire. By now, the whole crowd at Walker Farm must be talking about us." Annalisse relaxed into the buttery-soft seat and bathed in the aroma of new British leather. The lavish upholstery tenderly cradled her bruised muscles. "Two computers on tables back here." She slid out the chrome holder on her side. "So much wood in the interior." She traced the walnut door panels. "It's like a grand piano in here. Tan and brown—gorgeous, Alec." Fondling the pebbled leather, she added, "Don't tell me what she costs."

"Sixteen cattle gave everything they had for all this." Alec took her hand and gazed longingly at her. "Swelling's almost gone, and I can barely see the bruise under your makeup. You had me pretty shook up yesterday. I hope Bill's not too pissed at us for skipping out on the drive to Goshen. He can tell us what we should know."

"Jeremy will be the one who's livid. Whatever he wants to say to me, he can tell Bill. What I can't get over is Ethan showing up at the estate. What would compel him to do that when he knew we were meeting at the farm?"

"Something must have happened since last night. Or he couldn't pull off what he wanted to with an audience. He knows more than he's saying." Alec's sneer unnerved her.

"Jeremy and Ethan in cahoots. It sounds crazy. Ethan being behind Kate's disappearance is even crazier, but the business card is all we've got at the moment." Annalisse folded her hands and stared out the window.

"We are ten miles out from the destination in Lenox," Bradley announced from the driver's seat, his navy chauffeur's cap dipping toward the console. He wore a curled wire earpiece like a bodyguard. "May I call ahead for you, Mr. Zavos?" The driver from London's Guild Service spoke impeccable, authentic English.

"Please do, Brad." Alec picked up the computer bag near his bare feet and unzipped it. "I don't want to forget this." He held up a thumb drive.

"The *thing* from Bill? Absolutely." She nodded and opened her tote. "Before we go into the inn, I'll help you find a good place to hook the listening device. Keep it running when we're out and about." She fished out a tube of pepper spray and what looked like a small flashlight. "Neither of us has a decent weapon, which kinda sucks. I also carry these." She set both into Alec's hand. "I haven't used the stun gun, which is good because it's illegal in New York. Massachusetts just made them legal. It won't shoot darts like a Taser but delivers billions of volts. Tasers hurt like hell—I know firsthand—but this should bring plenty of pain. Long enough to get away from someone. No more Woody-wolf guys with guns for me."

She activated the device, holding it up away from Alec. Miniature lightning blossomed between the poles.

Alec pulled back and winced.

Annalisse switched it off. "If a person tries to take it away, these metal plates along the edge give a memorable shock. Drops 'em to their knees. That's what the paperwork says. Layers of clothing won't help them. The pepper spray worked well with Peter. You remember Harry's brother-in-law?"

"Who could forget the perv who jumped you? Whatever happened to him?"

"Peter's in jail for embezzlement and selling off art. He lost Westinn Gallery. Not a surprise. The niece had to shutter the doors. Harry worked so hard to keep that gallery afloat. Your mom hated to see the place close. Me too."

Harry Carradine was Annalisse's former boss, and Peter Gregory was his gallery manager. When Harry died at Gen's gallery opening, Peter became the owner in charge. In charge of sending Westinn's beautiful art gallery into Chapter 7 bankruptcy.

Alec dropped the pepper spray into her purse with a click, where it landed on the gun. "Let's hope we don't have to use either of these."

"Now to work on your microphone." She studied the buttonholes on his shirt but couldn't decide where to put the device. Then she saw a small patch of whiskers he'd jumped over while shaving in such a hurry. "Missed a spot. Maybe you'd like me to inspect next time." She nibbled on the salty-sweet area, gliding two fingers over his Adam's apple to the collar. She'd forgotten the driver could hear every word.

"You're on, art lady. Never had a woman shave me before. Care to try it later?" He arched both brows, bumping them twice. "Why not hook it inside the shirt pocket? Like this." He did so and glanced down. "I don't see anything obvious. Do you?"

"Depends on where I look." Her hand brushed his fly and pinched his belly button through the shirt, drawing a mischievous dimpled cheek out of him. "Oh, you meant the microphone… Better turn it on first." She smirked and reached in, flipped a tiny switch, then patted his pocket. "She's on. If we need another one, I'm sure Bill or his protégé has plenty." Leaning into his ear, she added in a whisper, "Think cold shower. I see the inn ahead."

When they parked at Stonemaple Cottage, a shiver tore between her shoulder blades. Noontime's blazing sunshine couldn't melt her trepidation. Boston ferns hung above white wicker chairs and swaying porch swings like pictures in magazines. Cottage quaint wouldn't fool her on this trip. The person responsible for Kate's abduction could be inside the two-story Victorian.

She peered out the Bentley's window and loosened her death hold on the seat. The grounds were anything but scary. In fact, they dazzled the senses. An emerald green lawn and hydrangeas with blooms so large they reminded her of bright blue volleyballs. Candytuft along the path resembled snow mounds piled in the dense, shaded areas. Nothing weird or unusual about the boxwood-lined walkway or the giant antique Gravure hand leading the way. Nineteenth-century engravings made the pointing finger a great tool for the era. In modern settings, they directed guests to restrooms in restaurants and long hallways at bed-and-breakfasts such as this one.

A painted trio of ducks holding each other's wings marched toward a pond on the next sign staked at the top of the hill. The whimsical touches buffered her nervousness. Boy, she could use a long walk beside a duck pond right now.

"I know where we're going once we unpack." She tapped on the window. "Soothing duck pond ahead. My kind of place."

"It's a date. After lunch." Alec looked at his Rolex. "I'm surprised we haven't heard from Drake yet."

After they parked, Bradley opened Annalisse's door. "I'll find out what restaurant fare is available, Mr. Zavos. Unless, of course, there's fine dining inside the inn?" His cool, blue eyes twinkled at her. "Watch your step, miss."

"Let's go to a restaurant away from the inn, Brad. Once we all get settled into our rooms, we'll take a drive. We'd like Italian tonight. My girl has a fondness for seafood pasta." Alec struggled with his right loafer but managed to get it on. "It was a bad idea to take my shoes off."

Annalisse salivated at the thought of shrimp and scallops wrestling in linguini drenched in a cream sauce. She could almost taste the seashore on the wind.

"Very good, sir." The chauffeur in a pressed navy suit closed the door behind Annalisse. "Would you like me to find lodging elsewhere on this trip?" Bradley directed his question to Alec.

Annalisse watched Alec recoil when his puffed foot hit the pavement. His face explained how his ankle smarted without the brace.

"You'll stay in a room near ours. I'd like you close by."

Annalisse leaned her head against his shoulder and sighed. "I'll sleep better knowing that."

"Brad's with me when I'm on the road and out in public. He's much more than my driver. Since taking over the firm, it would be foolish of me not to have a bodyguard."

"You're easily recognizable. I'm glad you finally listened to your mother."

Alec laughed. "Always. Let's see what this place looks like inside."

"If you're fine, Mr. Zavos, I'll bring in your things. Text 9 if you require my assistance." Bradley scanned the perimeter, tipped his hat, and went to the trunk of the Bentley.

Alec pulled a door open for her, and a rush of cold air whooshed her hair back. In the bright and airy main room, she stepped into the late 1800s. Alexander Graham Bell's crank telephones and nostalgic filament light fixtures transported the walls and ceiling to the past. Rustic oak boards stretched across the floor in a straight pattern. Pastoral landscapes in heavy gold frames showered the walls. Street scenes and pink country gardens were reminiscent of Thomas Kincade paintings. Maybe original works. She stood too far away to use her critical instincts. The artwork was a satisfying break to the faded blue posies and ribbon wallpaper that carried plenty of age.

In the next room, burgundy leather club chairs and a white marble fireplace looked somewhat out of place for a Victorian. The design was suited more for a golf course clubhouse. A huge game board sat in the middle of the room on a square glass table. Each player's onyx and ivory game pieces stood several inches tall at opposite sides of the board.

"Welcome. Welcome." A fellow, generously covered in age spots and with at least eighty years of wrinkles, beckoned them over to the reception desk. "Do you have a reservation?" His voice faded on the last syllable.

Alec gave the proprietor his dashing smile. "We called this morning. Alec Zavos."

The man with hairy ears ran a finger down the register and nodded. "Here you are. Staying with us for three days. Two in your party?"

"Would it be possible to get an additional room? Preferably next to us or on the same floor?" Alec put an arm around Annalisse's waist, and with it came instant comfort.

"I have you in the Marquise Suite on the second floor." He clasped his hand together. "A fairy tale. The room has a canopied king-size bed as well as a cozy sitting room and fireplace. The most romantic suite we have for a beautiful young couple." Tapping his pencil into the guest book, he winked. "The Duchess Suite is next to yours and available. A very nice room with a queen bed and a fantastic view of the gardens. Would you like to reserve it for one? For the same amount of time, I presume?"

"Kind of you." Annalisse noted the subtle scent of freesias and glanced around for fresh flowers. "Do you have a Kate or Katharine Walker registered here by chance? She's staying in town, but we aren't sure where."

Alec spun around and mouthed, "Nice."

Humming, the man flipped a couple of pages in the bound register. "No, I'm sorry. I don't see her listed. My granddaughter usually handles reservations, but she plays hooky on Tuesdays." His straight row of teeth dropped, exposing the acrylic gums. Dentures with other ideas had the old man clamp his mouth shut, making a perfect recovery.

Annalisse whirled around to stifle a giggle and walked to the spiral staircase for a quick getaway. "Beautiful workmanship," she said, running her hand over the wood grain, holding back a chuckle. "Authentic." The massive oak handrails and blue carpeted treads zigzagged the stairs to the upper floor.

"Sign here, Mr. Zavos. We'll spiff your room in a jiffy. Our check-in is normally four o'clock, but we can make exceptions if we're able. Allow me to ask when you can go up. It's been unoccupied for a few days. Feel free to wait in the lounge."

He guided them toward the club chairs.

"They are quite comfortable. Not stiff like most leather chairs. Perhaps you'd like to enjoy our first-class restaurants in the area beforehand? I'm happy to recommend Lenox's best cuisine. Our dining hall breakfast service at the Stonemaple Inn starts at seven but ended at eleven. Sorry you missed Cook's legendary french toast Benedict with warm apple-cherry compote. To die for." The talkative innkeeper smacked his lips, rolling his tongue over his dentures as a precautionary measure.

She met Alec next to the chessboard. "I'd like to unpack before we eat. Do you mind if we wait here?" Annalisse peered at the proprietor's name tag. "Mr. Granville, will it be long?"

"One moment." He sped through the door behind him.

"Spry little guy." Annalisse shook her head. "He's as quirky as the inn."

Bradley propped open the main door with his wingtips and rolled two suitcases across the floor. "Would you be good enough to direct me to your room?"

"We're early. The suitcases have to wait. Drop them over by the counter for now. We have a room for you next to ours." Alec motioned Bradley ahead.

"Thank you, sir. Very well then. I'll bring in my things later. I'll be in the car."

Alec opened his mouth, but the chauffeur disappeared through the entrance.

"I thought he stayed with you?" she asked.

"It's his way. He doesn't want to intrude on us."

"That's ridiculous. I'll get him." She got out of the armchair, but Alec pulled her back.

"We'll set the rules during lunch. Brad's used to me traveling stag." In a crooked-finger gesture, he beckoned. "Keep me company, sweetness. I don't want you out of my sight for a minute. No replays of yesterday. We got lucky but made too damn many mistakes."

Annalisse curtsied. "As you wish."

Alec patted the overstuffed leather beside him. "Incorrigible. Park yourself next to me."

No sooner had she landed in the chair than a man in his late fifties emerged from the stairwell. He had thinning gray hair and a close-cropped beard, dressed in a pair of pleated slacks and tweed sport coat. His upturned nose and pointed chin in profile struck a phantom memory she couldn't place.

Annalisse tapped Alec's thigh and spoke in his ear. "There's something familiar about that guy. The beard throws me." She strained forward to see more of him, and so far, they were undetected in the parlor. She wanted a closer look without acting too obvious but couldn't think of a subtle move. "Who would buy such a honkin' gaudy chess game?" she announced in a stage whisper, flinging out her arm.

Her question received the desired effect. The man swiveled in their direction, and Alec gawked at her like she'd learned etiquette in a barn full of jockeys.

"I beg your pardon, sir." Annalisse tapped her ear lobe. "My ears are plugged from the long flight." Annalisse couldn't look at Alec, who must have thought she'd lost it.

The man's face darkened for a brief moment, then he flashed her an overplayed smile. His identity stayed a mystery until he said, "My, my, is that little Ann Drury?"

Charlie Sinclair.

She and Alec rose together, and he clasped her sweaty hand.

The tall carpenter with an osteoporosis stoop came over, too toothy and clown-like for Annalisse to feel at ease once she recognized him.

"I'm hurt, lovey. You don't remember me?" His shoulders slumped theatrically. "What a beauty you've become, Ann!" He reached out to shake Alec's hand. "And you must be the hubby. I'm Charles Sinclair."

The last person to call her Ann had been Peter Gregory, her ex-boss at Westinn. The shortened version of her name sounded oily dripping off his tongue. Enough to make her shudder. Annalisse forced herself to ignore his lovey and hubby remarks since her uncle's best friend played games with women. She wouldn't give him the satisfaction of correcting him in front of Alec. He expected it. He spoke like a child to women for their sympathy—and attention.

Charlie the Letch had a reputation.

"What a surprise," she said.

Charlie pulled her against him in an awkward tug, rubbing her back with way more enthusiasm than necessary.

She withdrew to stand by Alec and added, "How is Sandy? We missed her at my uncle's funeral."

"All right, I guess. We divorced six years ago."

That figures.

"Didn't catch your name." Charlie, ever smooth, dismissed an inconsequential wife. He had such a long string of girlfriends Sandy must have known about.

Annalisse put her arm through Alec's bent elbow. "This is Alec Zavos. Charlie and Uncle Ted built some awesome homes together." She spoke to Alec but addressed Charlie's leer, studying her every movement. *Is he the one who called himself Big M? Did Charlie direct the kidnapping yesterday?*

"Nice to meet you." Alec put a protective arm around her waist.

"Here on business?" She asked as politely as she could muster.

"Naw. Retired now. On R and R with my lady friend. I'm down here guarding the credit cards. Ha." He pulled out the wallet and jiggled it.

"I'd love to meet her sometime." *Not.*

Charlie raised his index finger. "Zavos. The *sports car* Zavos? Well, hell, you must be. Your face is all over the papers." He smirked at Annalisse.

Smugness she could have slapped off his hypocritical face.

"Don't believe everything you read," Alec said.

"Zavos party." Mr. Granville waved to get their attention. "I can show you to your suites now."

"I won't keep you." Charlie said something inaudible to the proprietor, then turned to Annalisse. "Say hello to your aunt for me. Ted had a good woman." He flipped his billfold into a back pocket and vanished beyond the staircase.

Had? Past tense for her uncle or past tense for Kate?

"Mr. Sinclair comes across as one slimy dude. What's your take? How well does he know your aunt?" Alec asked.

"I'd call him a puzzle piece. Why is a friend of my uncle's staying here while Kate's missing? I could fill a book with the antics of Charlie Sinclair. Let's get

Bradley and set up headquarters. I don't want to talk about this here."

***

Bradley rolled the suitcases across a huge, flowered Aubusson rug with blue medallions. Rose ribbon garland swirled around gold musical instruments at the corners. A periwinkle laurel-leaf border matched the wallpaper border in their suite to a tee.

The fireplace hearth and tiny kitchen boasted crystal vases of calla lilies and long stems of purple stock in varied degrees from dark to light. Sweet perfume made their suite fresh and inviting.

"If you'll excuse me, I'll set up in the next room. Reservations are at one thirty." The chauffeur tipped his hat. "We're minutes away. No hurry."

"Go through the adjoining door. Make sure it's open," Alec said.

The door opened into another room in pink décor. She doubted the proper gentleman from Great Britain was thrilled with frilly lace bedspreads and pink velvet headboards.

"We won't be long. Give us about ten minutes."

"Very good, sir."

Alec closed the door with a soft click.

"No peephole on that door. That's comforting. Poor Bradley in a room suitable for a thoroughly naughty night." Annalisse set her tote on the pine-covered cedar chest at the foot of the canopied bed and flopped onto the mattress. "Comfortable." She fell backward onto the pillow. "Mmm. Heavenly."

"Hey." Alec pulled her up. "As much as I'd like to stay here. With you. Right now. Damn." He bent down and opened his lips to hers. "But we have to unpack."

When he kissed her like that, she almost forgot why they were in Massachusetts. She stepped back from his warmth, then noticed a basket out of the corner of her eye. She strolled to the stone fireplace and touched the woven hamper. It held mountains of fruits in season: pears, oranges, and Granny Smith apples. Homemade sugar cookies and chocolate brownies on doily-covered plates flanked it. A small five-by-five box wrapped in pink satin paper and a white ribbon sat next to it on the weathered pine coffee table.

Annalisse picked up the box. "They went to a lot of trouble. Smell that chocolate." The strong cocoa made her mouth water.

Alec swiped a cookie off the plate. "Go ahead. Open it."

Annalisse peeled off the ribbon and shook the carton near her ear. "Hefty. Sounds liquidy." She tore off the paper and lifted the lid. "A snow globe. I used to collect these when we lived in Kensington. They were destroyed in the explosion, and I was crushed. I never felt like starting another collection after that." Her heart lifted along with the globe. She shook it, and the snow specks floated down onto the backs of tiny sheep. "Aw, they're sheep." Annalisse set the globe down hard and jumped away. "Is that a wolf? Alec… Come look at this."

Alec dropped his toiletry bag on the cedar chest and picked up the globe. He turned it over. "China. There's a sticker from a gift shop." He held it up to the light to read the tiny letters. When his phone dinged a text message, he shifted the globe to his other hand to look at the screen. "Drake's fifty miles from Lenox. He has more information on Kate."

"Really?" Annalisse lifted to her toes. "He's found her? Where?"

"I didn't say that. But he did learn plenty from Ethan." Alec set the globe on the table and texted back.

"Tell him where we're having lunch. At this rate, we'll be lucky to make our reservation." Annalisse snatched the glass globe. "I'm taking this thing with us. Someone knows we're here. That's not a generic welcome-to-the-inn gift. Bill should see this." She securely zipped it into the largest pocket. "*Who* was in this room before us? Housekeepers or someone else? I'm asking and don't care how awful it sounds to interrogate the innkeeper. Obviously, the phone number on the back of Ethan's card led us to the right place." She palmed the stun gun. "I can easily hide this in my hand. I'm carrying this today."

"Not a good idea." Alec gently pried it away from her. "I can see it. We can't walk around with a shock weapon unless we want to get arrested."

Three loud knocks hit the door to the hallway.

"Almost ready. Just a minute, Brad," Alec said to the door. "Why are you in the hallway?"

Annalisse looked through the peephole, then whispered, "It's Charlie."

CHAPTER NINETEEN

Annalisse's wide-eyed expression scared the hell out of Alec. When she had that possum-in-the-headlamps look, her sixth sense had kicked in, and trouble waited for them. The day the shooter hid upstairs in her brownstone and later shot Alec, she'd had that look. Alec lifted an index finger to his lips. It was possible if they stayed quiet, Charlie would walk away.

Throat clearing. "Ol' Charlie here. I know you're in there, little missy. I heard you gabbing."

Charlie's insinuating tone grated on Alec's nerves. How much had he heard? Christ, was he peeping at their door for a thrill?

"I'm here with an invitation from Mildred, and I'd rather extend it to you in person, not through a sheet of wood."

Alec looked at her and mouthed, "Who's Mildred?"

She shrugged. "Girlfriend?"

"On second thought, let me open it. Don't trust him." Alec moved toward her.

His determined woman pointed at a spot on the rug. "Quiet. Keep your phone handy. Watch me closely. He wouldn't dare try anything."

Alec tapped a 9 text on his phone, ready to send in case he needed Brad, then picked up the stun gun and slipped it into his back pocket. He had little faith Mr. Sinclair would tell them the truth unless it suited his purpose, but they had to risk his unannounced visit.

She answered, "We're so late for lunch. Can we do this after?"

"I'll just take a minute, lovey. What's the keypad number?"

"No codes." Alec growled. His skin crawled when Charlie used a pet name straight out of an old movie. "Open it a little." Alec tapped his watch. "Get rid of him fast."

Alec swept past her and yanked the door open. "What is it, Mr. Sinclair? You're alone." He poked his head out. "Where's Mildred? Is that her?" Alec gave a pointed look behind Charlie at the empty hall.

As expected, Charlie pivoted for a quick glance. He'd changed his tweed sport coat to a darker jacket over a navy-and-gray-plaid shirt more appropriate for a lumberjack in the woods—on a humid-as-hell day. Why the wardrobe change?

"I'm sorry to say, she's dealing with one of her migraines." Charlie grunted and pushed past Alec with head down, trailing garlic fumes.

Annalisse said drily, "Okay, she's got a migraine. What do you want, *Mr. Sinclair*?"

Alec couldn't believe a man who'd dropped out of the Walkers' lives in 2011 would be so familiar with

Annalisse six years later. Charlie might be closer to Kate than anyone knew. More than she'd admitted to her niece. Unless the Thomas Taylor murder—not Kate's disappearance—implicated Charlie. Annalisse might be too close to learning the truth about the murder, and Charlie was trying to distract her.

"Why, Ann. You wanted to meet my girlfriend, didn't you? What's this *Sinclair* nonsense? I've known your family for…ever." His eyes swept the sitting area. "Nice digs. Beats the hell out of our little slice downstairs." He helped himself to the couch near the fireplace and sat on the far cushion like his bones would break. "Damn sight more comfortable too." He crossed his legs and bounced a foot. "We'd like you both to join us for dinner tonight."

"Her migraine will be gone in a few hours? She must have awesome drugs." Alec baited him again. "I don't believe there *is* a Mildred here with you. Until we see her, we have to decline your invite. Sorry."

"How're you gonna see her if you don't go to dinner? That don't make sense." His face flushed, and he worked his throat. "I see Ann found a good match in you, Mr. Fancy-Ass Car Man. Ted always said she had a mouth on her. So do you. I'm a veteran and don't care for being disrespected."

"Uncle Ted said I was mouthy? Wow." She squeezed Alec's hand.

He felt her tugging at the stun gun in his pocket.

"I actually had another reason for dropping by. A little bird told me about Kate's hard luck with money."

"Who said that? My aunt's quite comfortable, thank you."

"Scuttlebutt says otherwise. Anyway, I borrowed something from your uncle before he died and meant to return it." He fingered his jacket. "I should've given it back to Kate right after the funeral, but it reminds me of the friendship. Thought about selling it more than once because Ted said it was worth big bucks. I felt guilty after I had it appraised."

"So why are you giving it back now?" Alec asked. "What is this valuable thing you carry around, just in case?" Charlie's sudden interest in Kate's welfare and the fact they were expected at the inn had Alec intrigued.

"Do you have it with you?" she asked.

Charlie pulled a tasseled sheath out of his jacket. A stunningly large one, as long as his torso.

Alec clenched his jaw and held out his hand, trying not to shake. "I'll make sure Kate gets it."

Charlie drew a long, sharp blade out in one smooth motion.

"Easy." With hands in front of him, Alec added, "Put it back. We get the idea."

Annalisse gasped softly in Alec's ear. "That's a rare Japanese emperor's blade. Uncle Ted owned it? No way. I never saw it before."

Turning it over in the light, Charlie cooed, "Handmade with real gold inlay. Heavy silver. No cheap wood on this baby. An ornamental ruler owned this I'm told."

Ornamental? Alec feared they had a psychotic in their midst.

"Real old. Fourteenth century. Fine steel from full tang to tip. Goddamn, she's a hunter's beauty, isn't she,

Mr. Zavos?" He pointed the slightly curved blade at Alec and jabbed the air as if in mock battle.

"I'm no expert, but that's not a hunting knife." Alec made more space between him and Charlie, taking Annalisse with him.

"What have you done with Aunt Kate?" Annalisse asked from behind Alec, holding him in an iron grip.

Done with the niceties.

"She's razor sharp. I can tell you that. Cut myself many times. Slices through meat easier than one of them handy electric meat slicers."

Swinging a sword that measured over a foot was risky. The discussion needed to end.

"Are you hard of hearing, Mr. Sinclair? Annalisse asked you a question. Are you holding Mrs. Walker hostage?"

Charlie sheathed the knife. "Fits like a glove. Why didn't you tell me Kate's here? Having some kind of reunion?"

Alec found his demeanor out of character for their conversation. Was he drugged or drunk? Charlie either didn't hear the word "hostage" or ignored it conveniently.

"Please tell us where she is." Annalisse's voice trembled, and she moved to Alec's right. "We won't tell the police you took her. Tell me where Aunt Kate is, and this whole mess is forgotten."

"Took her? Are you cuckoo? Haven't seen your aunt in years. Not my type." Charlie looked puzzled and repeated, "Someone took Kate?" His gray brows knitted together.

Alec watched Charlie's little finger shake.

"Give me Kate's knife." Alec held his hand out. "No one gets hurt today. Better yet, set it down on the table and back off, Sinclair."

"Opened the pink paper, did you? I got a gift too."

"Set the knife down, Mr. Sinclair. I won't ask again." Alec wasn't buying that every guest received a snow globe. Especially one with sheep and wolves.

Charlie's muted glare shifted toward Annalisse. He knew more than he let on.

"Are you on drugs, Charlie?" Annalisse asked.

Charlie swung the sheathed blade up and away from Alec. "Not so fast, fancy pants. I don't give this to just anyone. Don't know you from Pete the Panhandler. This knife is worth, well, it doesn't matter. You don't need to know." He unsheathed it over his head and thrust it at Alec.

Dodging the blade, Alec's bad ankle turned, and he dropped his phone. "Ugh!"

"Stay put, car guy!" Charlie grinned maliciously.

"Nine, Brad!" Alec yelled and twisted, barely ducking another swipe at his neck.

The door between the rooms swung open and Charlie glanced over his shoulder.

While he was distracted, Annalisse charged.

The blade rose over her head.

Alec caught a crackle and buzz as the stun gun pricked the man's jacketed arm.

She'd jabbed it into the fabric long and hard with a growl, then lunged again for another jab.

Alec tried to move, but his ankle wouldn't cooperate, and he crumpled.

"Watch high!"

Charlie screamed, stiffened, and struck the floor. The blade popped out of his hand while he flopped and rolled on the rug like a carp out of water. "Son of a bitch!" He drew his knees up, and his body convulsed.

"Kick the knife away, Alec." She kept the stunner trained on Charlie. "Try that again, you bastard, and I'll bury this in your chest." Her breaths were labored and loud.

She sunk a knee to the sofa at the same moment that Brad swung the Glock at Charlie.

Sinclair shrieked and cowered.

"Are you all right, miss?"

"Help Alec while I catch my wind."

Brad lifted Alec to his feet. "I had removed the earpiece but overheard the conversation escalate and alerted the front desk. I was… engaged." He pursed his lips. "I thought I had time. I used the facilities. I'm—"

"No harm, Brad. I dropped the ball. I should've sent for you sooner. I assumed we had Mr. Sinclair situated until it got out of hand. At least we have it all right here." Alec patted his pocket. "All but Kate's location. I don't think he planned to tell us, but I'm not done with him."

A pounding fist hit the door to their suite. "Mr. Zavos!" More bangs vibrated through the door. "Is everything okay in there?" Mr. Granville let himself into their suite. His eyes widened when he spotted the pistol. "Did someone get shot?"

Charlie lay groaning on the floor, unable to control his twitching legs.

Annalisse slowly made her way to the innkeeper. "No, sir. Our security kept us safe."

Alec rubbed the side of his neck and sent her a glance, letting her know he appreciated leaving out the stun gun. She'd had time to stow it out of sight.

"What about him? Isn't that… Mr. Sinclair?" Granville asked Alec.

"Did he arrive with a woman or come alone?" Alec hoped the proprietor would add some background.

"I… I can check for you. Does it matter?"

Old Mr. Granville shook badly, then hunched over.

Annalisse caught him before he could fall.

"Mr. Granville, sit over here." She led him to the armchair and carefully helped him down.

Alec nodded at her, keeping his eyes on a recovering Charlie. She'd intervened a split second before he'd lost his arm or worse. Waiting to call Brad had been stupid, and he could've paid with his life. And hers.

"God, I hurt." Charlie massaged his legs. "Why'd you do that?" He whined and rolled onto his stomach.

"Maybe because you tried to knife me, asshole."

"Mr. Granville." Annalisse touched his wrist. "Feeling better?"

"Much. Thank you." The man's smile lacked his earlier spunk.

Alec couldn't blame him. The sleepy inn on manicured acres designed for romantic walks in the sunset wasn't accustomed to disturbances like theirs. *Annalisse and Alec, Team Excitement.* His mouth curled in amusement.

"This is important. Did Mr. Sinclair register with a partner? My aunt is missing, and we came here to find her. He or his party may know where she is. Are the police on the way?" she asked.

"My granddaughter." The innkeeper wheezed. "Excuse me. My granddaughter is. She lives close. No need to disturb the other guests. Do you want me to call the police, Mr. Zavos? I'd rather handle this between us since there's no injuries. Cops crawling around would look bad. Unless you want to press charges." He dabbed at his forehead with a handkerchief. "I hope not. I'm not good at this stuff. We run a quiet inn here."

Granville's plea touched Alec. Their arrival *had* disrupted the quiet atmosphere of the Stonemaple Cottage Inn, but it couldn't be helped. Bill was on his way, and Charlie Sinclair probably had knowledge of Kate's disappearance. Like Annalisse, he felt it. Why else would he come to their suite so melodramatically with a weapon?

"Don't you employ premises security?" Alec asked.

"Only for special events and celebrity appearances. We have to book them ahead. May I bother you for a little water, please?" Granville asked Annalisse. "I need to take my leave of you and wait for Rachel." He frowned at the knife. "Do we need that now?"

Alec put the knife he'd taken from Charlie in the cedar chest at the foot of the bed. "Would it be possible to have someone stationed outside Mr. Sinclair's room for a while?"

Charlie got on his knees and crawled to the sofa, pulling himself to the cushion. "Damn you." He fell against the armrest, rubbing the place where he'd been shocked. "No good."

"Brad, check him for more weapons. I'll take his jacket." Alec slowly peeled Charlie's sport coat off. His lifeless arms dropped one at a time while Brad checked all other pockets and his pant legs.

"Clean, sir."

"What are you s-s-saying? What have I…" Charlie slurred and swayed. "Don't feel good. Much drinking too much… much. Feel funny. Nickels in my mouth." He swabbed at his lower lip and tongue.

"Do you know where Kate Walker is?" Alec's voice was sharp.

"Who zat?" He rubbed the back of his balding head. "I hurt. Need nap. Room." Charlie wobbled to his feet.

Annalisse dug around in her purse and studied a leaflet. "He'll be normal in an hour. We can quiz him then."

"I'll take him to his room. Which is it?" Brad asked Granville.

"Allow me to help." The innkeeper came to Charlie's side. "Take my arm, Mr. Sinclair."

"After you finish with him, bring the Bentley around. We'll take our chances at the restaurant."

"Very good." Brad slipped on his dark glasses and adjusted his earpiece. "Come down when you're ready."

"Mr. Granville, before you go, we desperately need to talk with Sinclair today. Please don't allow him to leave the inn. If he placed any calls from a landline, we'd like to know the phone numbers," Annalisse said.

"I'm sorry, that's privileged information. I can't give out guests' personal numbers." The proprietor hobbled with one of Charlie's arms over his shoulder.

Brad took the other and the brunt of Charlie's weight as they walked him out of their suite.

Annalisse dropped to the mattress, covering her eyes. "We're never going to find Kate." She slapped the bed. "We're wasting so much time. He knows a lot, Alec."

"I know." Alec touched her leg and watched her eyes well up. "He could barely string two words together. It's hard, but we have to wait." *Wait for a bunch of things.* He squeezed her knee. "Hey, jumping in when you did saved my sorry ass." He wrapped her in an embrace.

He left a lingering kiss on her temple, and his heart stuttered for more courage. Lucky to have her, he intended to keep it that way—no matter how much he had to change to make it work.

"I'm so ashamed." Annalisse choked on her next breath.

Where'd that come from?

"You were slammed into the most impossible situation when your dad died, and I don't know how you cope. I haven't bothered to ask if there's anything I can do to ease some of your burden. My parents raised me differently, Alec. I've turned into a selfish scatterbrain. Heaven help me. Almost as bad as Jillian." She shoved dark locks behind one ear, and her gaze intensified. "Your schooling, training—future plans upended with little chance of living your dream. That has to be unbearable, and I'm so sorry." She held his hands, and the warmth felt like a campfire against his knuckles. "I want you to find a way to become a practicing vet. Be who you were meant to be. With or without me. I hope you can do that someday." Annalisse pulled her hands away and wiped them on her jeans. "Are you okay, or have I made you bonkers yet?"

"Not by a long shot." He grazed his thumb over her cheek. "Beautiful lady. You are, and you don't realize it. Only a rare woman looks past the facade and the family money. I've always known that you give more than you get. It's time to even the scales." He thought of the room filled with roses back home and the empty velvet bag. "I have big plans, and they involve you and that dream. There's no way I'm moving forward without you, so get that out of your mind. *Amore mio.*"

She had a curious longing in her sparkling eyes, but it vanished as quickly as it had appeared. "I need to feel useful. Where's a note pad or paper in this place? Rachel checked Charlie in, so she has information. Which I'm certain she'll fork over once she finds out she has a *celebrity* hunk in her midst." A tear splashed her cheek.

"Right." Alec's chest tugged as he slowly traced the wet track, and they shared a smile. "There's a pad on the night table." He retrieved it with a pen. "I'm good at dictation. Shoot."

"Ask Rachel if Charlie came alone or with a man or woman. I bet Mildred's made up and he came alone. Did he ever call himself Big M? Did she hear anyone call Charlie that? We can ask if he made any calls from his room phone without violating the privacy policy. When did he book the room? Did he book a second room? When did he arrive? Dropped off or by car? Did he have any visitors? How long did he book the room for?"

He touched her lips with two fingers. "You should've been a detective." When he caught up to her last question, he gave her the go-ahead nod to continue.

"We'll give Rachel a description of the wolfman and disguise. I'd bet he came to the inn and met with Charlie or a partner first, got his instructions, and went to Brookehaven… for me. Speaking of which, I hope Bill knows who Wolfie is by now. His real name might trigger a memory." She clasped her hands and laid them in her lap. "Why me? Why bring me to Kate? Why not tell me what they want and let her go?"

"Don't forget Ethan," Alec added.

"He didn't have time to drive here."

"How do we know where he was last week? He could've taken orders from anywhere. He didn't need to come here."

Annalisse's gaze wandered off. "Good point. Everyone's a suspect until we narrow the list. We start at lunch with Bill. We'll list all possible people who had the opportunity or motive to remove Aunt Kate from the farm. Ethan goes on that list even though he depends on her for a job."

"Of course he gets the benefit of your doubt. Fine. I'd add Jeremy and the sister to it also." Alec wrote their names down. "Anything else?"

"That's good for now. Bill will think of more. Heard from him lately?" She glanced up at the wall clock. "He's going to beat us to the restaurant. Lucky guy. Let him know we've been *detained*." She finished with air quotes.

Alec texted Bill and received an immediate reply. "He wants to know if he should come to the inn instead."

"We're way past the lunch rush. Have him go to the restaurant and wait for us," Annalisse said.

Alec nodded and typed in the message. His screen changed, and the phone rang. He answered, "Zavos."

"Sir, we've had a development."

"Brad? Where are you?" Alec put his phone on speaker. "What kind of development? Don't tell me Charlie escaped."

"Nothing like that. I'm down here at the Bentley. Um… there's been an incident."

Alec ran to the window and looked down at the grounds, but their view didn't include the parking area. He imagined the worst car incidents possible: spray painted, wrecked, or stolen from the lot.

Annalisse jumped off the bed. "What happened?"

"The Bentley needs a tow. Nearest place is Boston. Two hours away," Brad said.

"It won't start?" Alec pulled himself from thinking too negatively and ran through a few new-car quirks. "I'm sure it's something simple."

"The windshield has been bashed in."

"Other than the windshield, is it drivable?" Alec asked.

"I see no other issues with the car, but I can't drive it as it is, sir."

"Please call the nearest dealership, and see if they'll take it in. Dammit to hell. We don't need this right now." Alec swept a hand through his hair. He knew of only one Bentley dealer in Massachusetts.

"I'm sorry, Mr. Zavos."

"Not directed at you, Brad. Did you check to see if anyone left a note or clue as to why?"

"No. As soon as I saw the damage, I checked for dealerships on navigation and called you."

"See what you can do with repairs. And tell them it's for me. I don't know if my name has any pull up here, but it couldn't hurt to hit it hard when you call. I'll pay extra and overtime to expedite. We'll be downstairs shortly. Thanks." Alec ended the call. "Hmm."

"Alec, we're getting close, and stuff's about to happen—already happened. Kate's abductor knows we're here, or Charlie called a goon to leave a calling card. I'm sorry about the Mulsanne. I'm happy to pay the bill since we're here on my account. Aunt Kate's not far. I know it."

"Forget about paying bills."

She sat cross-legged on the floor. "Dangerous to longevity. That's what they should call me. I almost got you killed today. Again."

"Just when I was getting used to *lovey*. Damn. Too bad." He slid down to the floor next to her. "I hated it when the rat called you that, but you aren't dangerous."

"I should never have taken Kate to Brookehaven and dragged you into my troubles." She folded her hands in her lap and stared into space.

"*Our* troubles. Look at me." Alec stroked her collarbone.

"I can't. No wonder you take off so much."

"I don't leave New York because of you." Alec smoothed down her hair. "Your situation at the farm was organic. There was no way to strategize once that guy landed in your aunt's barn. As logical as you are, you want fairy dust to save you from wrong decisions before you make them. Sometimes shit happens, and there's not a thing we can do about it." He grabbed his phone. "I'd better call Bill."

He autodialed him.

"Almost there," Drake said, his voice tinged with annoyance.

"Change of plans. Swing by the inn and pick us up. I'll explain everything when you get here." When Alec ended the call, Annalisse's eyes filled with tears.

"I don't get why Charlie wanted to hurt you. You're a stranger to him. Was he getting at me through you? I've never been called a bitch so many times in one day."

"Yeah, but you *shocked* the hell out of him."

She bumped his shoulder and snorted. "He's had a rotten day too, I guess. I don't know Charlie personally. Only from the rumor mill. I didn't think Kate knew him well. Now I'm not sure. His reputation precedes him, and women in happy marriages stay clear of him. He brought that sword to our room for a reason, but he made up the stuff about my uncle."

"He got my attention."

"The blade can't be authentic. If Charlie owned anything that valuable, he'd sell it, pawn it, you name it. Uncle Ted said he'd lived hand-to-mouth." She leaned into his shoulder. "I need to know Kate's all right."

Alec rearranged a few of her stray hairs. "I'm asking you to stay solid. We're going to know a lot more very soon."

"One way or another. But how many more people are going to be hurt before it's over?"

CHAPTER TWENTY

Understated and elegant best described the small dining room at the bistro. Linen on tables with high-backed chairs, soft accordion in the background. The lunch rush had moved on, clearing the way for them to have a quiet meal. Bill had told them he had news that would break their case free and planned to share updates during lunch. Their conversation with Bill Drake had no danger of being overheard by anyone except the staff, which suited Annalisse fine.

At three in the afternoon, all that lingered in the dining area was the clatter of dishwashers' pans and the aroma of cheesy, marinara sauce with a hint of charcoal grill. Italian food was her favorite, next to a plate full of steamed mussels with chunks of garlic. She was dying for a glass of wine to calm the nerves and clear her mind of Charlie Sinclair.

A pole-thin hostess in a bistro apron, who looked no older than a high school sophomore, greeted them.

"Hi, I'm Haley." The petite redhead bobbed happily in her flats. "Welcome to Serratto's on the Lake.

Would you prefer a booth or table? And will there be two?" She eyed Alec hungrily, like a tempting dessert on someone else's plate. She all but veil danced around Alec so that he'd notice her plunging neckline and voluminous décolletage.

Annalisse wondered how much her daddy had paid for her boob job extraordinaire because breasts like grapefruits on her frame was anything but natural.

"Table for four. A booth in a corner or back room, please. We'll wait here for the rest of our party." Alec ignored the girl's neckline and searched through the glass behind them. He whispered to Annalisse, "Where did Brad and Bill go? They did a sweep of the premises but didn't come back this way."

She shrugged and rolled her earring absentmindedly. "I wouldn't worry. I saw them going out a side door. Maybe Bill forgot something in his blackout rig." Annalisse stood on tiptoe, checking for Bill's car in the lot. "Here they come."

At that moment, the hostess figured out who the wavy-haired Greek was standing in the lobby. Her ridiculous chest seemingly expanded another cup size, puffing over the scoop neckline.

"You're that Alex guy." Her fingertips brushed his sleeve, and she smoothly dove in for a sniff of Alec's cologne.

Alec wrapped an arm around Annalisse, doing his best to be polite but aloof. He gave Haley a swift nod and answered with a joyless, "Hi."

Remembering Kate's glowing face when Alec opened the cologne bottle made Annalisse smile sadly. What if the window to find Kate closed, and she never came back? She would fix what she could and let God take care of the rest. He'd taken her parents, sister, and uncle. *How many more have to go?* A shiver rippled up her spine.

"The scent's called Seductive Jungle," Annalisse declared, shoving the memory of Christmas laughter and Kate's throaty voice back to the recesses of her mind.

Haley popped out of her lovesick Alec-stupor and spun toward Annalisse. She sighed. "You're so lucky."

"I am lucky," she agreed, hoping to end Haley's fixation.

Bill followed Bradley through the entrance, both flushed and sweaty from the blistering heat.

"Thought you'd be drinking a cold one by now." Bill sent an apology to Annalisse with his eyes. "I had a call I needed to take outside. One I think you'll like. I'm waiting for one more confirmation. Today's been full of interesting developments."

"If any of them find Kate, tell us everything so we can help. I'm ready for this to be over." Annalisse smiled at the hostess and took Alec's hand.

"Follow me. This way." Haley directed them to a horseshoe-shaped booth in the back corner.

***

After lunch, Alec moved aside for the pastry chef, dutifully dressed in her double-breasted white jacket and baker's hat. No doubt, the restaurant showpiece—too pretty and perfectly made up for kneading bread loaves and gobs of flour coating her fingertips. There had to be a talented sous-chef behind the scenes.

The chef settled a squeaky-wheeled black dessert cart next to their table. Though tempted, he was too stuffed with veal saltimbocca to add in a helping of ladyfingers and cream.

"May I interest you in one of our scrumptious desserts?" The chef chomped on a wad of pink gum that brought a chuckle to Alec.

"I've hit my limit." Alec leaned back and whispered in Annalisse's ear, "Wait for it."

"Anyone? The tiramisu is light and refreshing. Always room for tiramisu. Or maybe my sinful cannoli? A biscotto with coffee, at least." Her nail made a hollow ting against the glass cover.

The chef's chewing gum floated dangerously close to her lips.

God, this isn't going to end well.

Brad's hand flew up. "I'd like something."

Alec reached for Annalisse's hand under the table and stroked it.

"What can I get you, sir?"

Alec feared that her pleasant visage was about to crack.

"When you got up this morning, did you tell yourself "Today I'm making my restaurant guests ill'?"

The chef released the cart handle and found the edge of her jacket pocket. "No, sir. Are you unwell?"

Annalisse's fingers crawled over her lips, and she turned to Alec with a look of concern.

Bill carefully set his fork on a section of leftover lasagna noodles. “You okay, man? You look gray around the gills.”

Alec stared at the crosshatching in the tablecloth and said, “It’s all right, Brad.”

“What can I get you? An antacid perhaps?” the chef asked, perkier than she should have.

Brad waved the chef over. “I’d like you to do something for me.”

She leaned down and looked at him earnestly. “Yes?”

Raising his napkin, he asked, “See this?”

“Yes, of course.” The chef’s voice wavered.

“Take it.”

She drew the napkin from his hand slowly and raised a manicured brow. “I’ll get you a new one.”

He shook his head.

“You don’t want a new napkin?”

“I want *you* to use it. Spit out that vile, fleshy thing in your mouth, put it in the napkin, and dispose of it.”

The chef whimpered, jerked backward, and dropped Brad’s napkin on the table. “I’ll send the waitress over.” She rushed the cart down the aisle like she was called to extinguish a grease fire in the kitchen.

Alec convulsed with the laughter he’d held back. Annalisse and Bill followed suit, roaring into their own napkins.

“There’s nothing more off-putting at a meal than chewing gum at the table.” Brad’s sincere statement made Alec laugh all the harder.

Finally Alec managed to say, “Hope she didn’t take it personally.”

"I'm surprised they haven't run us off yet." Bill laid his napkin over his plate and dug a spiral book from his pocket.

Annalisse touched her knife against her empty wineglass with a musical ping. "Bradley, thank you for what you did at the inn today. I'm sure Alec already said something to you, but I wanted you to hear it from me. I'm glad you're with us."

"It's what I do, but today, I fell short." Brad grumbled and pushed his spotless dish aside. "I'm sorry to have overstepped with the dessert chef, Ms. Drury." He jerked a little nod. "And Mr. Zavos. It's not my place to criticize the restaurant staff."

Alec started to laugh again.

"I'll leave you in the investigator's capable hands. If you don't mind, I'd like a spot of air. I'll be outside." He slipped on his cap and left.

"He's done that before, I take it?" Bill asked.

"It depends on his mood. With the Bentley down, I wasn't surprised."

Bill consulted his notebook pages. "Ethan and my trip to the farm launched us in the right direction." He addressed Annalisse. "You have great sleuthing instincts. It was a damn good move to stay behind. Worked out better, actually. Jeremy wasn't there."

"What?" Alec asked, and Annalisse's jaw dropped.

"What was the purpose of the meeting?" she asked.

Bill rubbed the side of his nose, then added a sly smile. "Being vague made us believe Ethan. He had his instructions. He was told to be evasive. You wouldn't balk at Ethan's request to come to Walker Farm. But that request didn't come from Jeremy."

Alec said, "Back up. You've lost me."

"Lost us," Annalisse said. "Jeremy *isn't* selling the farm?"

"Still an unknown. That sign with the toll-free number is gone now." Bill flipped a page. "Ethan felt he had to warn you. That's why he showed up at the estate this morning. He counted a half dozen strange cars driving in and out of the farm and overheard conversations that bothered him. Once he found out that Jeremy wasn't coming to the day's meeting, he realized he'd been duped and wanted you to know."

A man in a familiar plaid shirt entered the restaurant and stopped at the hostess station. Tapping the tablecloth to draw attention, Alec directed Bill's gaze to him.

"Drake, are you carrying?" Alec asked.

Bill slapped his waistband. "Always. Why?"

"You're about to meet Mr. Sinclair. Don't let his act fool you. There's no telling what he's capable of. He's a slimy bastard."

Annalisse paled. Her knuckles on the table ledge were as white as her face. "What's he doing here? We left explicit instructions! Damn that screwball inn. I hope he doesn't have another weapon."

"Say again?" Bill asked.

"The hostess pointed us out. He's coming over here. Let me talk." Alec slid out of the booth in case of a second attack.

"At least we took his long knife away," she muttered to Bill.

Sinclair appeared to have fully recovered. Without a sport coat, Sinclair's hunch was obvious. He couldn't hide his age, no matter how much spring he added to his step. He arrived at their table with a toothy grin. As if brandishing a knife in their room hadn't happened at all.

"Well, well. The car man. And you are...?" Charlie stepped near Bill and extended his hand. "Charlie Sinclair."

"Bill Drake," he replied, ignoring the hand.

"Uppity brat. Young people these days. Sheesh. No wonder the country's gone down the tubes." Charlie slipped the hand into his pocket like it was his plan all along. "I left my jacket in your room, Zavos. And you kept something else of mine that I need." He jabbed Alec's arm hard enough to hurt.

Alec frowned. "Touch me again, and you'll regret it. We'll ship your jacket. Leave the address at the desk. I'll handle it personally."

Sinclair's hand fidgeted in his front pocket, and a horrified Alec wondered if he was playing with himself. "About that other item—"

"It goes to Kate Walker. Isn't that what you said? You wanted to return something that belonged to her husband. Something you had no business keeping in the first place. I'll give it to Kate. Don't worry about it. We're still waiting for you to tell us where she is, by the way." Alec crossed his arms over his chest.

"Tell us," Annalisse said, not hiding her disdain, "why are you *really* in Massachusetts? Are you stalking us because your wolf-headed freak never delivered me to Big M? Is that you? Are you the mysterious Big M?"

"Young lady, I don't know the crazy stuff you're saying."

"We're going to report your attack on Alec," Annalisse said matter-of-factly.

"You go right ahead. Using that electric thingamajig ain't legal in this state. I know that much, girly. I still have the marks on my arm." He rubbed his sleeve where she'd hit him with the probes.

Alec caught her attention and tapped the hidden recorder. When it came to anything involving her aunt, Annalisse was fierce but understood when to tame it down. He glanced into the lobby for Brad, expecting that he'd followed Sinclair inside but apparently not.

"If you have nothing of value to tell us, please leave." Alec pointed to the entrance. "We're in the middle of a private discussion."

Sinclair dug deep inside his slash pocket. "There is this one thing."

Bill rested his palm on his pistol. "I'd be careful," he said quietly.

Sinclair raised both hands. One now held a fabric bag. "I was told to give this to Miss Drury. See?" He showed them the pouch and put it onto the table in front of Bill.

"*Who* told you to give her that?" Alec asked, his blood rising.

"Sort of an admirer."

Annalisse reached for the gray bag, but Bill snagged it.

"Wait for Bill to check it out." Alec nodded a thank you to his friend. "Who sent you to find us, Sinclair? We know you're working with someone. I expect it's the same person who has Kate."

"Aren't you going to look, lovey? You aren't pregnant, are you?"

Annalisse's face flushed with pink as she stared Alec's way. "What?"

Bill slid out of the booth, and Sinclair took a hasty step back, bumping a chair.

"I'll be going now. Don't forget my jacket, young man." Sinclair haphazardly shuffled between the dining tables, dodging chairs as fast as he could. He was more frightened of Bill now that he'd shown his true height.

"What about Kate?" Annalisse yelled at Sinclair's back.

"What about her?" His cackle echoed in Alec's ear while he followed the plaid shirt through the restaurant and out the entrance door.

Outside, he scoped out the parking lot for Sinclair's car, drawn to an out-of-place white minivan parked next to a brownish sedan. Alec's money was on the sedan. He considered chasing him, but a full stomach changed his mind. Instead, he walked to where he could see between the two vehicles.

When Charlie reached his driver's side, the door of the van slid open. Before he could climb inside the four-door compact and speed away, three men in white jumpsuits sprang out, and two lunged at Sinclair. Alec was too far away to tell which side the obscenities and insults came from. In a tirade like that, he suspected equal verbal abuse from both sides. Sinclair struggled against the younger, much stronger men. Alec couldn't visualize how they'd restrained him, but he was captured and tossed into the van.

"Huh." Alec couldn't believe what he'd just observed. Sinclair had crossed someone else's radar screen. Maybe he'd pissed off whoever held Kate.

"That issue resolved itself." Brad rounded the corner of the building. "I saw someone checking license plates. I went over to enquire if the chap needed assistance. He asked if I'd seen the driver of that one." He pointed to the brown compact. "After a few more of his questions, I realized he was there to pick up the old con artist from the inn. I thought he was supposed to recuperate in his room."

"He's a mystery, but he left something for Annalisse inside. It would've been nice if the innkeeper or his granddaughter kept their word. Did you find out anything about those guys in white?"

"After I told the gentleman from Midhampton State Hospital what happened—"

"State Hospital? He's a patient there?"

"Was. Someone sprang him about a week ago in an unorthodox manner. They disguised him as a visitor. Perhaps bribed a guard. They filed a report and have been searching for him. When he tried to use a credit card at the inn, they followed him here, I would assume."

"Is he dangerous?" Alec rubbed his twinging rib cage near the break. "Stupid question."

"His wife had him committed after the presidential election—after he came at her with a carving knife." Brad scuffed his sole along the concrete and toed a wad of gum to the edge.

"The man likes knives and didn't like the election results. Not a surprise he'd take it out on his wife."

Alec's stomach turned when he thought how close he'd come to dying at the hands of a mentally ill man.

"A political minefield in that household. She voted one party, and the mister liked another. A little too much, I'd say." Brad sniffed the air. "Smoky."

"Do they have any idea who broke him out of the hospital? Is there anything we can follow up on? The mental hospital must keep a visitors' log. Sinclair's accomplice might lead us to Kate."

"No suspects. Are you finished with your meeting, sir?" Brad asked.

"No, but I'd like it better if you were inside."

"One more sweep outside." His driver nodded and took off down the sidewalk.

Alec recalled the pregnancy remark aimed at Annalisse and the look on Sinclair's face when he said it. He'd better go find out what was in the bag. Whatever it was, the vibes bothered him. He'd spent so little time with Annalisse that pregnancy wasn't in play.

She was all he ever wanted; no one else felt as right. He'd almost gambled his dreams away like a fool. He had no intention of losing Annalisse now.

CHAPTER

TWENTY-ONE

Resting her forearm on the linen cloth, Annalisse couldn't take her eyes from the six-inch pouch beneath Bill's hand. It was as if a hypnotist's watch pulled her into the recesses of the bag, searching for the contents. She'd asked him to slide open the drawstring, but Bill refused until Alec came back from outside the restaurant.

"I don't hear any gunshots. That's special." Bill wasn't smiling, and Annalisse didn't appreciate the humor, having been a victim of gun violence more than once.

"I wonder what's in that bag," she said, tapping the tablecloth.

"I wouldn't want to guess. But since we're waiting, I'll finish telling you about my trip to the farm. Jillian called the meeting. Not Jeremy."

Annalisse considered that. "She knows I don't like her."

"You escaped the last time her highness required your presence." Bill chuckled. "Why give you an opportunity to ignore her again? Easier to lie and use Jeremy's name to get you there. Tell me more about the Walker kids. Living in that house with those two must have been rough." Bill drew his cell phone out and swiped the screen. "Come on, Dan."

Annalisse sighed and twisted her napkin into a bulky pretzel shape.

He continued, "One of them knows more than they're letting on. The daughter is too relaxed. She barely talked about her mother while I was there. I expected a barrage of questions about Mrs. Walker's status. Not one. What kid acts like that with a missing parent?" A hint of a smile passed his lips. "She looked like she'd seen a ghost when I turned up instead of you." He slid his pistol into its squeaky leather holster and snapped it into place. "Then she turned into poor, bewildered Jillian—priceless."

"She'll get over it. What did she want anyway?" Annalisse sniffed the air. "Is it smoky in here? I caught something a minute ago."

"I mostly talked to Ethan. Although I did get back inside the farmhouse to check if Ethan's cards were readily available, which they were. Anyone could've grabbed one and scribbled down a telephone number on the back. There was a stack near the door and in the guest room where Jillian sleeps. I didn't notice any others. Does your aunt have her own calling cards?" Bill opened his notebook and scanned a page.

"Walker promo and PR is Kate's thing, not mine. I'm too busy in the City to help her with that. Yes, she carries her own cards. So, Jillian said nothing? Not even why she wanted me for this big powwow?"

"She wasn't about to talk to an investigator. Made that clear last time."

Annalisse could picture Jillian fuming over her absence but was somewhat surprised that Bill couldn't pull anything out of her. The way Jillian had batted her eyelashes at the handsome investigator should have made her vulnerable to his professional overtures. Private Investigator Drake took his time with interviews, like a cat waiting to pounce on a helpless rodent.

"My visit to Walker Farm was shorter than expected, but Ethan—" His phone chirped, and he picked it up. He spent considerable time on the message, then tapped out a quick text. "OC Sheriff McDonaugh wants to know if you've heard the name Chris Lewis."

Annalisse drew a blank. "No. It's not familiar. Who is it?"

"He's the wolfman from your scenic ride to the woods." Bill pushed the phone aside and leaned back, his crossed arms bulging at the biceps. In that pose, he reminded her of one of those leather-and-armor-clad characters from a gladiator movie. "He did some time for petty theft and a convenience store robbery. According to his last known address, he lives on the West Coast."

"Wolfie came a long way. Do you think Jillian knows him?" Annalisse thought through their conversations in the truck. If Wolfie came from California or the Pacific Northwest, nothing in his speech patterns had tipped her off.

"Jillian made a few phone calls that Ethan overheard. That's how he found out he was being used."

The stainless kitchen traffic door at the back of the restaurant swung out, and their waitress who'd stayed away, probably on purpose, marched through it. She wore a sour expression and carried a fresh stack of cloth napkins. Since they were the only people in the place, which was odd for a restaurant in this area, the napkins had to be a peace offering for Bradley. Annalisse read terror on the girl's freckled, round face. Like she'd rather be tortured in hot fondue cheese than wait on their table.

The waitress set the napkins next to Bill and said softly, "Can I get you anything else?" She eyeballed the empty wine bottle, then picked it up. "Coffee?"

"Just the check. Thank you." Bill smiled rather seductively, which brought a bashful blush from the plain girl.

"Are you smoking meat? Is that charcoal burning?" Annalisse wrinkled her nose.

"It's the first day we've been open since the fire. We weren't supposed to open till next week, but the remodel took so long, the owner had a meltdown. They just finished painting out front. That's why it's kinda empty in here. No one knows we're open yet." She gave a little shrug and brushed at her apron.

"Was anyone hurt?" Bill asked.

"No. I'll come back with your check." She smiled at Bill and left.

"What's taking Alec so long? I should check on him. Would you mind scooting down so I can get out?" She dug her palms into the table.

Bill glided a finger along her wrist and gazed into her eyes longer than he would have if Alec were nearby.

His blue-eyed stare was tender and caring. "Stay, please. He's making sure that Sinclair is gone, or he's talking to Brad. Sit tight."

"What did Ethan overhear?"

"Some of it was personal, but the rest…"

"Is what?"

"He heard arguments between Jillian and who Ethan figured was her husband. The word *divorce* came up a lot. Apparently, she pleaded with him about it, so Ethan's assumption seems reasonable."

Annalisse laughed. "I'm a bad girl for enjoying someone else's misery. Shame on me." She swatted herself in the arm. "For Jillian, I'm making an exception. A divorce is no surprise. I've heard her ridicule her husband's job, complain about her kids, and whine over not having enough money. All while she spent the grocery budget on makeup. I just wonder why it took him so long to see Jillian for who she was? A hateful, spoiled daddy's girl without her *daddy* to rescue her from the mean ol' husband."

"He knew what he was in for. Men aren't as stupid as women think."

"That sounds like experience talking," she said jokingly.

"Ethan also heard *spa* in some of those talks. At first he thought Jillian was making appointments for a back rub." Bill dabbed at his dress shirt with a wet napkin. "Tomato sauce stains, doesn't it?" He tipped his drinking glass and poured more water on the splotch.

Bachelor city. "Can I help you with that?"

Bill raised his hand. "It's under control. I think Ethan meant a massage. Anyway, Jillian's arguments surrounded those spa appointments."

"Her husband didn't want her to spend the money? What else is new? I'm sure Jillian costs him plenty. She loves collecting frivolous garbage. Working in a store is a dangerous place for a shopping addict." Annalisse kept watching the restaurant lobby for Alec, getting more anxious by the minute.

"Ah, but she mentioned her mother being at one of those spas—in one of their little bull sessions."

Annalisse slapped her palm down hard on the table. "How long have you known? Geez, Bill, we've been worried sick. Kate's at a spa? She's never been to a spa before. Are you kidding me?" She sighed, and a lingering weight lifted from her chest. "Which spa? Can we go there now?"

"Ethan didn't know."

"Wait, this can't be. Jeremy doesn't know where Kate is. Last night, Ethan said Jeremy thought Kate and I were playing games. Remember? Jeremy had nothing to do with that meeting this morning. Jillian made up some silly excuse to get me to the farm. It's Jillian who's jerking us around."

"Dan's tracking down facilities. That's what we're waiting for. I wanted absolute proof before I mentioned the spa to you. He'll call me if he finds your aunt. He's searching health spas, day spas, and retreats in the Berkshires. Any place with overnight stays."

"There are tons of places like that up here." Annalisse's heart thumped a happier beat. "But why not tell us Kate checked into a spa? Why snatch her from Alec's stables? It doesn't make sense. What about the empty syringe and turned-over chairs in the tack room? Staged to make it look like a kidnapping?" She clenched her jaw, and her joy evaporated. "If she was just hanging out getting spa treatments, Auntie would've called me."

"If she could. Someone may have taken her phone away to send you messages. If Jillian checked her into a spa, Kate could assume Jillian told you. Isn't that possible?"

Annalisse's nod was frustrated. "That snooty bitch knows where her mother is and didn't tell us. So help me, if that is true—"

"Why have Chris Lewis nab you under the pretense of taking you to Kate? How does Charlie Sinclair fit in? Was he here to watch you or attack you? At first, I thought finding him at the inn was a coincidence. He just happened to show up at the same one." Bill raised the satchel. "What the hell is in this bag? It's substantial but not heavy. Another clue that leads nowhere?"

"Let's find out." Alec slid into the booth next to Annalisse and gave her a quick peck on the cheek. "You didn't start without me, I hope." His smile left a lump of want in her chest.

"Nice you could join us." Bill dropped the pouch on the table, and something inside thudded.

She covered Alec's hand with her hers, wishing they were alone in their suite, Kate was home, and the mystery nightmare was over. "Your skin feels like it's a pizza oven out there." Annalisse caressed him with cooler fingers. "What took so long?"

"Yep. Still as beautiful as the Aegean, and you have your color back."

She offered him a small, shy smile. "That's probably because of you."

"If I can do that, you need more of it." Alec squared his shoulders and lifted the corner of his mouth. "Sorry to keep you waiting, Bill. Sinclair's gone. He won't bother us again."

"How can you be sure?" she asked.

Alec recounted what happened with the white minivan, and Annalisse listened intently. The puzzle pieces still didn't fit at the end of his narrative.

"A mental patient. I have even more questions now." She pushed down the flood of doubts around her uncle's friend. They had enough to worry about without adding Charlie.

"Sinclair's definitely one of the players, but I think he's a small fry. We don't know where he fits yet." Over the next few minutes, Bill attempted to tie in what they knew about Charlie to Jillian's strange attitude and phone conversations.

Alec said nothing during Bill's winding story of deception, divorce, and day spas, but plenty flickered behind his gray eyes.

"Ethan's clean in your estimation?" Alec asked Bill.

"In light of what we now know and my talk with him, I'd say he's completely cleared of dumping Keith Albers in the barn. McDonaugh's holding Chris Lewis, aka Wolfman, in his jail, hoping he'll give them a lead on that murder. The judge denied bail. They think he's a flight risk, and they don't like people who shoot at cops."

"I wondered if he used my gun." Annalisse felt sick that her pistol was used against a police officer. "He'll be in jail for a while. Sicko."

"That sicko could've hurt you, art lady. Don't forget it. If he shot at a cop, he's capable of murder."

"McDonaugh and Detective Trask think so too. As far as that card in Chris's pocket, anyone could have taken one of Ethan's cards and scribbled the Stonemaple Inn's number on the back. Jillian had plenty of opportunity to do it.

"How long before we hear from your partner?" She waited while Bill checked his phone again. "Why can't we look too? We can cover more ground that way. It's hard to sit idle and twiddle our thumbs when we're so close to finding her."

"Let's give Dan a little more time. Be happy Kate probably isn't in any immediate danger. It makes me feel better." Alec reached for the pouch. "Is anyone else interested?"

Annalisse scooted closer. "Be careful."

Bill handed the bag to Alec, who shook it near his ear.

Annalisse slapped Alec playfully on the shoulder. "What is it with you shaking things like that? He did the same thing with the box and rattle."

"I didn't notice any moving parts," Bill said. "Rip off the Band-Aid. Pull it out of there."

Alec drew back the gathers and lifted out a slender wood carving the length of his fingers.

"Let me see that!" She grabbed it from him, mesmerized by the barbaric face. "Super cool. It's smaller than what I've seen before, but it's made like a Maori death mask." *What a unique find.*

Without fanfare, Alec stole the icon from her hand.

"What are you doing?" she asked, indignantly. "I'm not done with it."

"Is it just me, or is a death mask *not* a good omen?" Alec asked with a shake of his head.

"What do you know about these masks, Annalisse?" Bill slid next to her for a look. "Brilliant, Zavos. Fingerprints everywhere. Set it down. It reminds me of Hawaiian totems, like a face on a Tiki pole."

"Similar. A lot of detail for a smaller piece. Bright blue eyes and ornate tattoos." She studied the swirled black lines that extended up the forehead from nose and mouth. "Even small ears and teeth. Incredible." The crevices between the marks were made by an artisan's chisel. "The carving style is Eastern Polynesian. Indigenous people of New Zealand."

Alec hovered his hand over the mask. "Do you think it's good to gawk at this thing? Creepy. I'm putting it away."

"Not yet." Bill turned to Annalisse. "You said death mask. Explain."

"The Maori people are fierce fighters. They've been involved in countless battles over centuries. They came to New Zealand in waves of canoes during the thirteenth century. Isolated from other countries, they developed a unique culture. Part of it included the Maori warrior mask. Much bigger than the one Alec's trying to hide." Annalisse tsked.

Alec moved his hand, and for the first time, she found its eye color was eerily like her own. In a way, the mask called to her, and she stifled a shudder.

"Before warriors went into battle, each man carved a mask. Usually the size of their own face. It's done in case the warrior dies and doesn't return. The mask is said to take on the spirit or soul of the Maori warrior when it enters their carving after death."

"May I? Prints be damned. It's too late anyway." Bill reached for the mask and turned it over in his hand, weighing it. "Not heavy. Like driftwood."

"Museums in New Zealand display actual Maori masks."

"You've seen them?" Alec asked her.

"No. Only in history books. Visiting New Zealand is high on my bucket list. I'd love to spend a few months on a sheep station down there. I hear the landscape is awe-inspiring to photograph, and I could study the culture and sheep management at the same time. Wanna come?" she asked Alec.

"I might be able to fit it in sooner than you think." Alec rewarded her with a larger smile than her own.

"Ha. When the Atlantic freezes over. It's okay. This girl can dream. I'll enjoy my New Zealand souvenir a while longer." Charlie's last words at the table struck a chord, and Annalisse snapped her finger. "That's what he meant."

"Who?" Alec looked at his friend, then her.

"Pregnant women are revered in Maori culture. The Maori post a warning at the entrance of museums with death mask displays. Women who are pregnant or on their period should never enter. They do at their own risk. Charlie must have referred to the warrior mask—this little version carries the same properties as the bigger ones."

"How would he know that?" Alec asked.

Annalisse shrugged off the question and continued, "Some signs warn all women to stay away from Maori artifacts in the exhibit. New Zealanders worry that coming into contact with a mask possessed by an evil spirit can evoke a curse, endangering the woman's life."

"Is that so?" Bill smirked. He scrutinized the back of the carving more closely. "Where's the MADE IN CHINA sticker? They must have left it off this one."

She was disappointed at his attitude. He didn't believe her story and made light of a culture he knew nothing about.

From Alec's jaw clenches, he also caught Bill's slight.

"Curses *do* exist. I wish they didn't. If Annalisse says it's so, Maori carvings aren't pieces we should mess with." Alec tucked his arm around her and gave a gentle squeeze. "Listen to the lady. She knows her stuff."

Annalisse rested her head on his shoulder. Alec's soothing, heady scent relaxed her as much as a bubble bath would. He'd never blamed her for Pearce's death. Although, there were times that she'd wished they had handled the Mushasha curse differently and kept the necklace locked away, in New York. She and Alec's future wouldn't be as complicated as it was now.

"We were disbelievers too. If we had taken Annalisse seriously sooner…" Alec kissed her temple and gave her a reassuring smile that dimpled a cheek.

"After this is over, Bill, I'd like to explain what happened last October because of a rare jewelry collection. It's not a week we revisit often. Painful stuff. But you need to hear about it. Mom would want you to know the whole story."

"When Pearce passed away?" Bill's eyes widened in a way that made her sad.

Alec worked his throat before he could speak. "Dad was murdered."

She patted Alec's hand. "We don't have to go there."

"But what we need to do right now is finish this. I don't understand why Charlie had this mask, and who gave it to him to give to you? What is the significance? I can't imagine it holds any special meaning for Kate." Alec swept her cheek with his thumb. "Ethan's from New Zealand, isn't he?"

Dammit. Annalisse pulled away from his caress. "Please stop. I don't know why this mask is here, but Ethan has nothing to do with it. Can we stop talking about him like he's enemy number one?"

Alec grumbled, worrying his hands and going back to staring at the table.

Bill slipped the mask into its pouch and pulled the strings. "It probably *is* a coincidence that Ethan and the mask have an En Zed background."

"Hey! The Kiwi's refer to their country like that. You've been there?" she asked.

"Yes, but I didn't hear about the warrior masks."

"Ethan could still be involved. He showed up at the farm like a guardian angel sent him there when

Kate needed help the most." Alec wouldn't let go of the idea, and he was giving Annalisse a headache.

"I don't mean to step on your toes, old friend, but I have to agree with Annalisse. I don't think Ethan has anything to do with Kate's disappearance. Let's head to the inn. Since Sinclair is already checked out, it won't hurt to ask the granddaughter that list of questions you two put together in your suite. See what she's willing to tell us once she knows he's an escaped cuckoo bird." His brittle smile softened, and he patted his notebook. "We can add a few more of mine while we're at it. With a little more digging, we might nail down who directed the whole operation."

"So much of this feels wrong. Dump a body, and Kate goes to a spa? Weird tunes and odd presents? I need a notebook myself. Nothing seems connected, but I know it must be. This is as much about me as Kate. And I want to know why. Does Charlie know where Auntie is?"

"He's out of the picture. Jillian is our best bet for finding her. And my partner who's rustling the brush. I've ruled out the parishioners, pastor, and lady friends, including the nice old guy who drove out to see her on Sunday."

"Paul," she added.

"Yeah, that's him. He cares about your aunt and knew something wasn't right when she missed church. I guess you didn't fool him with your okeydokey fib." He laughed. "Paul was very forthcoming. I promised to let him know when we find her. Like you, he can't imagine anyone hurting Kate."

"Health spas aren't hazardous to your health."

He chuckled at Alec. "True, but we didn't have that lead until today. What time is it?" Bill glanced at his phone, and it chirped a text.

Annalisse suppressed the urge to arch over and read it herself. She nervously swept her hair back.

Bill slumped against the back cushion and dropped his head.

Oh no!

A visible burden weighted down or lifted from his shoulders.

Which?

Without looking up, he fist pumped the air.

Annalisse exhaled the breath she'd held.

"That looks promising. What's up?" Alec asked, grabbing Annalisse's hand.

"How would you like to meet my partner?"

"O…kay…" Alec passed her a blank stare.

"I'm sure he's a great guy. Is that it?" she asked, worried again.

Bill's giant smile gleamed like a beacon of hope. "We found Kate."

CHAPTER TWENTY-TWO

It felt like forever and a year riding back to the inn with Bill. He navigated the roads like an old woman on the freeway. Funny, Annalisse hadn't noticed his driving habits when he'd picked her up from her ordeal with Chris Lewis. Then she remembered. The reason for her lapse was the tabloid cover and getting physically ill.

Crowded against the counter in the lobby, they waited impatiently for Rachel, Granville's granddaughter, to check in a new guest at the inn. Annalisse's mouth tasted like old wallpaper paste, and she couldn't help her nervous jitters. She stood by as Alec shifted his weight uncomfortably to his good foot. His ankle needed elevation and rest, and they planned to get plenty at Greylock House where Aunt Kate was staying and Dan Chappell waited for them. Annalisse had so many questions that only her aunt could answer, and she was antsy to leave.

"Alec, why don't you go upstairs and wait for me in the suite," she said, rubbing his back. "Bradley's taking care of the car. I'll stay here with Bill. Lie down and put your ankle up before you fall down." She gave him the sweetest smile she could muster. "We won't be long."

He kissed her temple. "Come up when you're done. Don't leave without me."

"Not a chance." Bill displayed his most professional, investigative face.

Alec limped to the staircase, clutching the room card. The way he barely put weight on his foot told her he'd been on it too long.

"Your room is up the stairs and to the right at the end of the hall. Let me know if you need help with your bag." Rachel handed the key to a man in a three-piece suit and dark glasses who grumbled his thanks and departed.

"Friendly sort," Bill said quietly and moved into the spot where the man once stood.

"May I help you?" The flashy redhead with pretty brown eyes swept one arm in a flourish similar to her grandfather's, but she added a cautious look at Annalisse.

"My name is Bill Drake." He slid a business card across the counter. "And this is Annalisse. She and Mr. Zavos are guests at your inn."

"You're a detective." Rachel laid the card down and stared at Annalisse. "I heard about her. Gran told me what happened in the big suite. Scared the bejesus out of my granddad. Poor old man. I sent him home to rest."

"I'm sorry, miss. Rachel is it?" Annalisse recognized her voice from when Bill called the number on the back of Ethan's card. "I hope Mr. Granville is all right. We were surprised ourselves. Were you the one who checked Mr. Charles Sinclair out of his room?"

"Yes. Gran asked me to watch him. Make sure he didn't leave, but I'm the only one here till six. He wanted to check out early, and I couldn't stop him."

"Of course." Bill tilted his head away from the desk as a signal for Annalisse to stay in the background. "May we ask you some questions about him? It's very important. Did you know he escaped from a state hospital recently?"

Went for the jugular. Annalisse wanted to howl in delight at his tactic. What woman would refuse to answer his questions now?

Rachel covered her mouth and gasped, eyes wide. "What? Is he crazy?"

"I can't answer that. Did he pay with a credit card or cash?" Bill asked.

"He tried to pay with cash, but he didn't have enough."

"How did he pay the bill?" Annalisse added.

"He asked to make a call. I gave him this phone." Rachel picked up the inn phone receiver, then put it down. "The man he called gave me a credit card number, and I finished processing his stay with us."

"Do you have the number Mr. Sinclair called?" he asked.

"I'm sure I can get it for you, but it might take a while."

Bill nodded. "Did you happen to overhear Mr. Sinclair call this person by name? Was the credit card in someone else's name by chance?"

"I only took down the number to run the charge. I'm sorry. It went through with Mr. Sinclair's identification. Are we going to get a charge back? Darn it. That's two this month." She tapped the register.

"Did you also check Mr. Sinclair in?" Bill asked, moving on.

"He came during night shift." Rachel flipped through the ledger and ran her eyes down the pages. "Arrival time 11:20 p.m. on Sunday. Paid cash for a one-night stay, then asked to be extended."

"A room for one person?" Annalisse asked.

Rachel bobbed her head.

"Did he have any visitors or calls while you were on duty?" Bill opened up his notebook. "He mentioned having a girlfriend with him."

"Not that I can remember. Do I need to worry that he's coming back? I hope not." Rachel folded her arms and leaned on the counter.

"No, I can assure you. Mr. Sinclair won't be back. I could use a room though." Bill managed a smile.

Annalisse ushered Bill a few feet into the lobby and whispered, "Bradley isn't using his. He has the room adjoining ours. We can let you in from our side."

"If you're sure." Bill turned to Rachel and waved. "Under control. Thank you for your help. I hope your grandfather feels better."

"When we get upstairs, I'd like to take another look at the blade Charlie brought into our room. Alec stored it in the cedar chest." On a hunch, Annalisse turned back to the counter. "Excuse me. Did you notice a long knife in Mr. Sinclair's possession?"

"You mean the one that went with some costume? I didn't see it, but Gran said he recognized the knife in your suite. Mr. Sinclair showed it to him this morning. Completely fake, don't worry. We don't allow weapons at the inn."

"Thanks." Annalisse motioned for Bill to follow her. "Costume, yeah, right. Fake enough to chop off a person's head."

When Annalisse and Bill went inside the suite, Alec had drawn the curtains and shut down most of the lights. He rested flat on the bed with his ankle on a pillow. His phone played mood music she immediately recognized. A forlorn piano arrangement perfect for deep sleep or as a tranquil backdrop for their rare lovemaking sessions. His hands were crossed over his taut and tempting belly, his eyelids were closed, and she wanted so badly to lie there next to him. It gave her chills listening to the melody and remembering Alec's kisses worshipping her body and the heat of him smoldering her skin, the fire growing in her. A tempest with so much power—she rubbed the gooseflesh on her arm to bring herself back to the present.

"He's wiped out," she whispered, too throaty to hide her thoughts. She felt sexy and lazy at the same time. "Maybe we should let him sleep."

"You heard him. We'll give it a few more minutes. Won't hurt Dan to wait." Bill sank into the sofa.

Annalisse tiptoed to the chest and carefully raised the lid until it clicked and held itself open. She felt between the blankets for the leather sheath.

"Got it."

"Let's have a look."

Annalisse brought it to Bill, and he unsheathed the blade. "Big sucker."

"Check it for markings and a manufacturer."

He rotated the handle and carefully touched the steel. "Not a prop sword. Rachel made this out to be a child's toy. It's a real blade all right." Bill swiped the blade's edge and drew his hand back, sucking on his finger. "Draws blood too. Call me stupid."

"Need a bandage?"

Holding the knife up, Bill smiled and offered the knife to her. "Here's your manufacturer. It's stamped near the hilt."

Annalisse placed a hand on her hip. "Don't keep me in suspense."

"Made in Taiwan."

She closed her eyes and sighed. *So much for the rush of history.* "Thought it might be. It figures Charlie wouldn't have anything of value."

"He was set up, you know. Promised his freedom." Bill sheathed the knife and laid it on the coffee table. "It's safer over there. The person who paid for his room alerted the hospital. Probably the same person who took Sinclair out of the sanitarium last week. It had to be, because the white van made it to the restaurant fast. The state was notified either by way of the credit card payment or by placing a call to them. Once he left the inn— Maybe once you and Alec left, that was the end of Charles Sinclair's part."

"No longer useful." Alec swung himself to the edge of the mattress and yawned. "It would be logical for Chris-slash-wolfman to bring Annalisse here to meet Charlie."

"Might be that simple. How's the ankle?" Bill asked.

"Anti-inflammatories kicked in, and I'm among the living." Alec rubbed his ankle bone. "I'll be glad when it heals."

Annalisse sat down on the bed with Alec. "Someone wanted me and Kate together but not at Walker Farm. For what reason—I have no idea. Stashing Auntie at a spa gave them a little extra time to get me here. This is bigger than Jillian wanting to give her *momma* a few days at a resort."

"What better way to find out than reuniting you two? If you're ready, I'll call Dan and tell him we're on our way."

***

Annalisse and Alec sat hand in hand in Greylock House's posh reception room, a room that would make other spa designers jealous. Surrounded by waves of peach and silver décor, lofty pampas grass in floor vases, and the scrumptious scents of eucalyptus and chamomile, Annalisse finally relaxed. She unwound her muscles against long-stapled, woolen cushions. Actual sheep's wool, she imagined.

In minutes they would see Aunt Kate and finally take her home.

She sipped her glass of chardonnay and said, "I could fall asleep." She snuggled against Alec, warm and comfy. "Soft jazz and soundscapes for the senses. *Up against the sexiest man alive*. Mmm. Perfect."

"That's the point." He twirled her pearl ring with his thumb. "Meditation and relaxation for the stressed out, overworked, and overpaid."

"Said with a straight face too. I didn't know overpaid was a thing." She ran a finger down the lifeline of his palm, and he twitched.

"I never knew I was ticklish there before." He sidled closer, swiping his hand down a pant leg. "But then you're good at dissecting my parts and turning me inside out. Like one of your historical finds you can't wait to dig into."

"I suppose. I do love puzzles, and you're quite a challenge." Annalisse's gaze strayed to the red Reeboks planted near the counter. "What's Dan saying to that cute little receptionist? I can't tell if he's asking her about Kate or asking her out."

Dan Chappell leaned over the stainless counter in a quiet conversation with a platinum blonde in a pixie cut. She wore a silk tunic Annalisse could see herself in. From the girl's bashful smile, she definitely soaked up his charm, happily in his center of the universe.

Dan's skintight jeans left little to the imagination. Neither did the fitted polo pasted on washboard abs. He was far from the typical back-channel investigative guy with an earbud who studied backgrounds on a computer screen. His round, red-framed glasses came off as studious, but Dan's all-male attire was far from stale and geeky.

"I don't know how he did it so fast." Annalisse watched the pair in action.

"He's trying. Not there yet."

"Not that. Usually facilities won't give the names of their guests. How did he find Auntie with so many spas up here? Greylock House is a town over from the inn."

"Maybe someone wanted us to find her. How much of all this was designed to get *you* here? That bugs me. We're here now, so if there're fireworks, we'll be in the middle of the show." Alec looked at his Rolex. "Going on four. Still wanna head back tonight?"

"Absolutely, if it's possible. And a long sleep without interruption."

He raised his brows. "Interruptions can be good. Mind if I come too."

She opened her mouth, and nothing came out. A heated flush rose from her throat and spread to her cheeks.

Alec threw his head back and bellowed, sending every head in the room turning in their direction. She'd missed his infectious baritone laughter that had a way of lifting her spirits.

He squeezed her knee and whispered, "I'll leave the details up to you, sweetness. Thanks for reminding me how good you look in pink afterglow and nothing else."

A delightful shiver of want raced through her, and at that moment, she couldn't care less what anyone else thought.

"Dan, may we see Kate now? What room is she in? We have a long drive back tonight, and we're tired." *Ugh. Whiney niece alert.*

Dan held up one finger, still with his back to them and without missing a word with the pixie girl.

Annalisse slapped the arm of the couch in frustration. “What the hell’s the holdup?”

“We’re about to find out.”

Bill’s partner squatted in front of her with folded hands, a somber report written in his gaze. “I’m sorry for the delay. It seems that Mrs. Walker is having a facial and we have no choice but to wait. It shouldn’t be much longer.” Dan rose and went back to the counter.

“Wow. I can’t get over *Mrs. Walker* and *facial* in the same sentence. I wonder if they have the right woman.” She smiled, remembering the last time they’d talked about places like this. She’d tried to convince Kate a massage would help her relax. Her doctor had recommended it to increase circulation, lower her blood pressure, and improve her osteoporosis. Annalisse tried to make masseuse appointments for her many times, but Kate’s daunting glare and dismissive wave always stopped her. If nothing else, Kate might pick up healthy habits from this trip. Something nice her daughter could finally do for her.

Bill walked through the entrance, preceding a rush of hot air into the lobby. “Haven’t gone in yet?”

“No. She’s having a facial. We wait.” Alec met him near the doorway.

“Anything I can do, boss?” Dan came over, looking ready for a scolding.

“Find a place where we can talk in private.”

“Done.” Dan returned to his favorite place, the front desk.

“Has something happened?” Annalisse asked, joining the men.

“I’ve been running a few leads and found a possible connection.”

The receptionist approached their group. Her diamond piercing on her nostril glinted. “I’m so sorry for the wait. This is a bit unusual since you aren’t guests at Greylock, but Dan explained your… situation. You can use one of our relaxation rooms. Mrs. Walker has another fifteen minutes to go. I’ll come and get you when she’s back in her suite.” The girl’s tunic flowed behind her like a silver cloud.

Dan and the receptionist were on a first-name basis. Good for him. Annalisse couldn’t imagine any room more relaxing than the lobby, but if there were chaises and soft pillows, she was game.

Pixie girl opened a door at the end of a long, pale blue hallway. “If I can be of any further service, use the phone inside. Enjoy the spring water or champagne. I’ll return as soon as I can.”

They entered the inviting room. A sea of chaises and armchairs of overstuffed periwinkle cushions with silver and peach accents. The wall was a seductive mural that Annalisse could almost fall into. Beach at low tide with rippling waves on the sand, starfish, and tiny blue crabs.

Annalisse twirled a three-sixty around the darkened room and smiled at the twinkling tea lights sprinkled among numerous glass tables. Tiny waterfall fountains under banded horsetail ferns diffused the air with restful, falling water droplets. “Take your pick, but try to stay awake. It will be an awesome dusk on the coast.”

Bill chose the longest sofa behind an onyx black table and laid his phone down. "Smells great in here." He sniffed loudly. "What is it?"

"Lavender."

Alec grinned at Annalisse and sat in a boxy armchair made for two. He patted the cushion. "I'd wear it myself if I didn't mind smelling like a chick."

"Speaking as a smelly chick, tell us what you're working on. I'm dying to hear," Annalisse asked Bill as she plunked down next to Alec. Even though they'd found Kate, tons of questions tore at her.

Bill waited for Dan to sit at the opposite end of the sofa. "To satisfy Alec's concerns about Ethan, I ran background checks and went deeper into ancestry. Parentage especially. How or if the Albers body relates to the country of New Zealand. And the warrior mask you have in your purse."

"And?" Alec leaned forward, his eyes bright.

"If it weren't for the carving, I wouldn't have bothered. But Ethan and his home country drew me there as I considered what might be missing. The name that started everything was found on the body of Keith Albers. The one-million-dollar question—why *that* name? That's what I searched for in New Zealand."

"How about Ethan?" Alec asked. "I'd like to know more about him even if Annalisse doesn't."

He missed the dirty look she gave him.

Gritting her teeth, she allowed his question since it was reasonable to check everyone's history. All she knew about Ethan's family was what he'd told her when they were in the hospital waiting room.

"Annalisse, did Ethan tell you his mother's name? First or last?" Bill asked.

"Wouldn't her last name be Fawdray?" Alec looked as confused as she felt.

"Ethan's mom married twice. If my information's correct, Fawdray is the name of her first husband. Ethan's father," Bill said.

"What's that have to do with Thomas Taylor?" Annalisse hated how cryptically Bill approached information sharing.

"Did Kate have any phone calls or correspondence with anyone in New Zealand?"

"Bill, you asked me that before, or somebody did." She sorted through all the interrogations. "No. Ethan is a huge help to Aunt Kate. I'd thank him every day for being there if I could. He..." *His uncle. When they found the ID card on the dead guy, Ethan told her he had an Uncle Tom Taylor. Could that be who was meant to scare Aunt Kate?* "Ethan's uncle is a journalist in Europe."

Alec groaned. "So, what?"

"His name is Tom Taylor."

Dan hummed from the back of his throat. "Interesting."

The room fell silent except for the Zen music and water trickling through the fountains. Everyone exchanged sober glances. The only person who held no readable expression was Alec. *Bless his heart. He's holding his tongue this time.*

"That may be our link. Kate knew the name and probably knew the family. What if your aunt had mentioned to Ethan's family that she needed help at Walker

Farm? It would explain Ethan's sudden appearance." Bill scribbled in his notebook.

"He told me his dad's name is Robert Fawdray." Now Annalisse understood Bill's line of questions.

"*Was* Robert Fawdray. He passed away, and his wife was willed the station. A stepfather raised Ethan, if what I found is correct. His mother's name is Ellen. Ellen Hyde. Is either name familiar?" Bill leveled his gaze at her as if he were cross-examining a witness and she'd better come up with the right answer.

Annalisse pictured letters Kate had written and received and phone calls she'd made over the years. Not one to or from New Zealand. No mention of a Taylor or Hyde family. Her aunt had no friends who went by Ellen and never mentioned that name.

"I'm sorry. Nothing, Bill. Taylor is related to Ethan's mother?"

"He may not be. Kate may know the family, and that's why she trusted Ethan to manage the farm. It could be as simple as Kate's husband having dealings with the Taylor man that Kate knew about. The person who dropped the body in the barn knows why."

"We're so close to seeing Kate. Why not have Annalisse ask her those questions?" Alec asked with a touch of a defeatist attitude.

She took a ragged breath, trying not to think about the migraine skulking behind her eyes. "I'll try asking her, but Kate refused to answer any questions about Taylor. And she won't give us answers until she's ready. She's stubborn like that."

"Don't you want to know?" Alec asked her.

"Honestly… I couldn't care less. All I want is to pack up Auntie and go back to the estate. Take a break from investigators and puzzles. No offense meant." She knew there were no breaks ahead. Jeremy hadn't changed his plans to sell the farm, and someone hounded her—dropped them into a murder and a mystery meant to hurt them. She could feel it. Annalisse kneaded her pounding temples. "I could use a massage. Bad headache coming on."

"I'm sure someone here would oblige." Alec stroked the hair away from her face and kissed her forehead. "You'll feel better after you see Kate. Oh, yeah." He reached into his shirt and pulled off the thumb drive she'd hooked to the fabric. "I've had this running since we got here. Take it off my hands, okay? I think we're done with recordings." He reached across the table, and Dan jumped up, taking the device.

"Thanks, I'll check it out. Beats the hell out of working tower dumps."

"I've recorded the entire knife incident with Sinclair. The hospital may be interested in it."

"I'm sorry about the headache, Annalisse." Bill paused with more on his mind. "I know I was hired to find Mrs. Walker, and I believe we have, but I'd like to stay on this case another day or two." He addressed Alec. "Tie up the ends on the Albers homicide and make sure Annalisse isn't in any danger."

"There's a lot up in the air. Thank you." Alec shook his hand. "You're a good friend. Since you're hanging around, I may as well get a few more USB devices from you."

"Just so happens." Bill handed Alec a couple of flash drives he had hidden away. "I meant to give you backups. Thanks for helping me do my job. You never know what info you might have picked up."

"Auntie's not a well person, and I'll do anything to keep her steady and strong. I'm willing to take a hit if it keeps her safe." She poured half a glass of water and reached into her tote for the painkillers.

"Nobody's taking a hit, sweetness."

The door opened to a blonde in gray spa wear tunic and slacks.

"Are you waiting to see Ms. Walker?"

Annalisse jumped to her feet. "We sure are. May we see her now?"

She beckoned to them. "Follow me."

CHAPTER TWENTY-THREE

As Annalisse got closer to Kate's room, a strange ache washed over her. The white door in the gray wall was so cold and impersonal.

She grasped Alec's hand tighter for reassurance. "This is crazy. I'm afraid to knock. All this way, and part of me wants to turn around and go." Annalisse shuddered and rested her head on Alec's chest.

"I'll knock if you can't." Alec reached toward the door.

She grabbed his wrist midair. "Wait. What if we find the wrong person in there?"

Bill's phone buzzed and broke the silence. He checked the ID. "Orange County. I'd better take this. I'll wait in the lobby with Dan while you talk to your aunt. I'll meet her another time. I could be tied up awhile." He grunted at his phone and turned around.

"Here goes." She knocked, knowing that Auntie always responded to someone knocking in her own unique way. If that didn't happen, she would run for the exit.

"Unless you're Woodrow Wilson, state your business." Kate's voice rumbled through the door.

"It's the right room." Annalisse heaved a sigh of relief into Alec's confused face. "Auntie, it's me… us."

"Lambie!" The door swung open. "Thank the good Lord. Child, I've been so worried." Kate, dressed in an aqua lounge ensemble, pulled her into a hug, strong enough to wind her. "And, Alec. What a nice surprise. Come here." She hugged him as well, leaving a lipstick kiss on his cheek. "When I didn't hear from you, I thought the worst. I knew you had the week off."

Annalisse kissed her aunt, inhaling a mixture of Ivory soap and a spritz of citrus on her neck. She gave Kate another squeeze, then pushed her away. "I'm so mad at you! Why didn't you leave a note when you left Alec's? Why a spa; since when? Did anyone hurt you? Don't you have a phone? Why didn't you call, for Christ's sake?" Annalisse swung her arms wide, her pulse racing.

"I won't have that talk in here. Shut your potty mouth and calm down." Kate wandered near the dresser. "What are you talking about?"

Alec said, "Lady, you look—amazing with your hair down. Wow." He found a chair and sat, but his eyes never left the woman in turquoise.

Annalisse had to admit that Kate glowed like a polished pearl fresh from the oyster. Whatever they put in their facials made such an improvement in her skin. Either that or the makeup she wore had created her magical complexion. The dry spots and wrinkles around her coral mouth and cheeks had all but disappeared. The leggings suited her, and the matching tunic took years from her actual age. Her aunt looked well rested.

Annalisse drew a calming breath. "Alec's right. You are stunning. If Paul could see you now."

"Aw, shush." Kate dimpled. "Think so?" she moved in front of a cheval mirror and lifted her chin. "Maybe."

"Who brought you here?" Annalisse could hardly bear the wait.

"You didn't know where I was?"

Alec answered her. "No, Kate. I came back home unannounced. I was surprised to find Annalisse there. When we looked for you after the storm passed, you were gone. We expected at least a note or a call. A ransom demand—something. We've been working with investigators to find you."

"What? Investigators? Bah. I've been here the whole time." Kate sat on the bed close to Alec. "Lambie." She patted the mattress for Annalisse to sit next to her, and then whipped an arm around her. "Jilli said she called you."

"Nope, she didn't. What an actress." Annalisse scowled. "Why would she lie to me? She knew all the time."

"Jillian said you gave this spa week for me as a gift. She and Jeremy went in on the little vacation. Bought me a few clothes and paid for treatments." She pulled out her tunic, and her locket caught the light. "I thought *you'd* planned this. You're always trying to get me to go to those massage places."

Alec and Annalisse exchanged looks.

"Do they take your phone away at this spa? Why didn't you call me?" Annalisse asked, recalling the fake calls and email spoofs.

"I asked Jillian about that. She took my phone when we got here. The spa wants their guests to stay away from *devices* to relax."

"It conveniently kept you from calling me or anyone." Annalisse shook off the sarcasm and scanned the room, finding no telephone anywhere. "How did Jillian know to pick you up at Alec's?"

Kate dropped her hands into her lap. "When you left me at the stables, the horses weren't in the big barn. By then the wind came up and it was sprinkling. I ducked inside Alec's office but fidgeted something fierce in there. So I went to the tack room. The aroma of oiled leather saddles." She sighed and tilted her head back. "Ah. Much more soothing after the morning we'd had. Those smells back home. Awful." She patted Annalisse's thigh. "It wasn't long, and the outside door opened and in walked Jillian, nice as you please, soaked to the bone. She said she was parked outside the arena, so we left for the spa from there."

"You didn't find that odd? Your daughter knowing you were in my barn? No one took you by force or gave you an injection to put you to sleep?" Alec asked.

"Nonsense. Just me and Jilli. She said you knew we were leaving for Greylock."

Annalisse raised a skeptical eyebrow.

"Before we left, I sent Jilli back to the tack room for my fanny pack. I don't know what happened to the tactical pen you gave me. I hope you can get me another one." Kate gave her the eye. "I was surprised when she showed up there, but after she explained it was all your idea, I didn't worry about it."

Annalisse glanced at Alec and asked, "Yeah, but how did she find you at Brookehaven?"

"That's easy. Jilli told me that she was about to turn in to the farm and saw the cops and crime tape. I haven't seen her in so long, I didn't recognize her following behind us to Alec's place. How's Ethan handling everything without me?"

"Your daughter wasn't worried enough about her mother to find out why the sheriffs were parked at the farm? Did she ask you?"

"I tried to call you from the car, but she told me I worried over nothing. Took my phone right then."

Alec and Annalisse traded glances and explained how they found the tack room and everything else that had transpired since Saturday. They included the findings on the body and the wolfman experience. When they took a break from the narrative, Kate's color had faded to pasty white.

"I don't know what to make of this. Why stage an abduction scene and lie to you about it? And make you tie up Alec and Helga—take you into the woods?" She choked up and rubbed Annalisse's hand. "I'm so sorry. When I get my hands on my kids for this ruse..."

"We think it goes deeper than that." Alec jumped in to finish their story. "When was the last time you saw Mr. Sinclair?"

"Sinclair. You mean Charlie?" Kate soured her lips and closed her eyes. "That ol' horny goat hasn't been around since Ted died. Thanks be to God for watching over me. I heard Sandy divorced him. Finally. The whole town saw him gallivanting around with floozies." Kate obviously shivered. "Vile man."

"Charlie was staying at the inn and tried to come at Alec with a knife."

Kate's mouth gaped before she covered it with her hand. "Is that why you're limping? Did he hurt you?"

Alec shook his head. "Minor fender bender."

"Geez. Don't listen to him, Auntie. He totaled his car trying to get to the farm."

"I'm fine but can't say the same for Sinclair. Annalisse dropped him and not in a good way." He chuckled, then stopped when Annalisse narrowed her eyes at him.

"That crazy nut better not show up anywhere I am." Kate raised her fist and shook it.

"We don't know if it's a coincidence he's up here. He's been institutionalized, so I wouldn't worry." Alec explained to Kate about Charlie's captivity in a state hospital and what they assumed about his unscheduled release.

"I always knew he was a nutcase. My kids went to a lot of trouble to get me here and terrorize you. But why?"

"We don't know for sure who the players are." Annalisse's pounding head needed a break, and she jumped off the bed to pace the sparsely furnished room. "Nice place. White wicker and peach pastels. Very five-star chic."

Someone knocked three times, and all eyes went to the door.

"That's probably Beverly, the owner. Here to pick me up for tea. Come in, Bev."

A heavyset woman in sleek silk pajamas lumbered in. "Oh my. Forgive me, Katharine. I didn't know you had guests. We can do tea another day. It's almost time for your massage with Rafael, isn't it?" Beverly grinned and winked at Kate.

"This is my niece, Annalisse, and her *friend*, Alec." Kate wrinkled her nose just a little at Annalisse.

"Lovely to meet you both. I'm Beverly Case." She lifted on the balls of her feet and gave her hair a sassy shake. "I'm sorry to have interrupted your visit. I should go." Her eyes lit up when she set them on Alec. "You were right. A beautiful couple." Beverly's vóice trailed off.

"Just a minute." Kate hurried to a side table and wrote something on a pad. It took her a while, but she eventually folded the page and handed it to the Case woman. "Read it when you get time. We'll talk later."

"Excuse me, Beverly, I'm curious. Who made Kate's reservation here?" Annalisse asked.

"Why you did, of course. Ta-ta." She wiggled her chunky fingers and left.

Annalisse asked Kate, "Has Jillian been here since she dropped you off on Saturday?"

"She was here yesterday. She comes back tomorrow."

"Jillian was here when that Chris guy came to the estate. She could be heavily involved with everything, including a murder." Annalisse rubbed circles into her forehead. "Too many moving parts. Knowing her, I doubt that she planned this by herself."

Alec might be the better choice to ask Kate about Thomas Taylor. She wished Bill were here to do it instead. *Darn it.* She twisted her pearl ring, hoping the act would speak to her with the right answer. If she made a bad call, Kate would shut her down, and they wouldn't learn anything new.

"Jilli murdered that man? What are you trying so hard not to say?" Kate shot looks between her and Alec.

She smiled. "You're right. Auntie. How many people do you know from New Zealand? Have you heard of Ellen Hyde? Do you know Ethan's uncle?" If her aunt knew any of those people, the truth would come out.

Kate's lips went pencil thin, and her body stiffened. "That's quite a mouthful. I know Ethan's from New Zealand. Case closed."

Alarm bells sounded in Annalisse's head. Her aunt's body language signaled withheld information, and the piercing glare at the end put Annalisse on the defensive. She'd touched a nerve, and her aunt had shut down. Exactly what she'd feared would happen.

"No recollection of Ellen or Ethan's uncle?" Alec asked uneasily. "Mr. Sinclair gave Annalisse a carving that originated there. A Maori warrior mask."

"Why are we talking about a foreign country? Does this have anything to do with solving the murder at the farm or the masked man who went to Brookehaven? Weren't there two men?" Kate evaded the questions with more questions. A tactic Annalisse enjoyed herself because it worked.

Annalisse held up her palm so only Alec could see and traced the letters TT on it.

"Kate." Alec tried again. "Who is Thomas Taylor? It's important. He could be the key to everything."

Her aunt grumbled something and moved to another part of the room. "Times like this I wish I had a pack of smokes." She coughed a syrupy sound from her lungs. "I don't know that poor fellow in the barn if that's what you're asking. Never seen him before." Kate's hand shook, and she tucked it into a pocket under her tunic.

"Auntie, you know that's not what we're after. Now would be a good time to tell us whatever you know about this Tom Taylor. You said you would in the car. I'm ready to hear it."

Kate spun around and pointed at her. "I'm not ready to tell it!"

Her words came out with such intensity, she cringed, and Alec started.

With a sly smile Kate added, "Make you a deal, lambie. I'm here until Friday. When I get home, I promise to tell you everything. I need a few more days to sort things out in my head. Go on home. Walker Farm needs you watching over it. I don't trust anyone else to care for it like you would."

"Uh-uh. You're leaving with us tonight. I'm not letting you out of my sight until we figure out what the hell is going on. People are jerking us around and trying to scare me. I want to know who they are and why. Period. We haven't told you everything. We left out what seems to involve me."

"Like what?" Kate asked.

"Tell us your secret, and we tell you the rest." Annalisse hated bargaining with her like a child, but she'd had enough of the stalling.

Her uncle's suicide note flashed in her mind. His words as clear as if they were in front of her. At this point, Annalisse suspected the man Kate refused to speak about was the secret Uncle Ted couldn't bear.

Kate turned away from her and stared into the backsplash mirror. She'd grabbed the wood ledge with both hands, swaying a little, and hung on as if it were a lifeline.

"Auntie, please."

Two strong knocks hit the door. "Miss Walker… it's Rafael." The voice had a Latin lilt. "Time for your massage. I have a special treat for you, dear." The Spanish flair rolled off his tongue, and without a doubt, the person was a younger man. Kate's favorite.

Kate ran for the door like a schoolgirl waiting for her date. "One moment." She opened it a crack but not enough for Annalisse to see the masseur standing outside. "Come back in five," Kate stage whispered.

"Okay, sweetie."

Kate shut the door. "He's from Brazil." She rolled the *R* and tried to sound Latina while she fanned her blushing cheeks. "That man has a pair of hands on him. Oh. My. Word. I swear I could come just from his sensual fingertips. Mmm." Kate crossed her arms and squeezed herself.

Alec burst out laughing, and all Annalisse could do was go with it. Her aunt was brash and, if she were honest, a mild nympho, but she loved her irresistible spirit.

"Now that we have *too much information* out of the way, you aren't about to leave Rafael and his sexy fingers, are you?"

Kate raised a brow wickedly. "I'd rather not. Can you give an old lady one more thrilling night, lambie? What's the hurry? I'd like to say my goodbyes to the staff and thank Beverly. I hate to rush out of here when they've been so kind to me. I can be packed and ready to go, say… seven thirty in the morning?"

Annalisse waited for Alec's response, even though she thought it was a bad idea. She should grab her aunt and whisk her to Brookehaven. Tonight. Before it got dark. Before anything or anyone could get in their way.

"Brad should have the Bentley back in service tomorrow. I don't see why we can't leave in the morning."

"When do you expect Jillian?" Annalisse asked Kate. "I don't want to see her lying face. It serves her right to find you gone when she gets here."

"With the drive from Goshen and sleeping in—I'd guess noon at the earliest. I don't know why she didn't stay here. It seemed a funny thing to do. Stick me in a place like this and then drive back and forth from the farm." She shrugged. "Her choice."

"Why not let Kate have another whirl with R-r-r-rafael, Giver of Orgasms." Alec tugged Annalisse against him playfully, then addressed her aunt. "Only this time, don't think about it, just do it."

"Alec." Annalisse swatted Alec's hip, trying to get the visual out of her mind.

Kate grinned and opened her arms to Annalisse. "Thinks like I do. You've got a good one. Give me a hug, and I'll see you both in the mornin'." Annalisse relaxed in her warmth long enough for Kate to whisper, "I love you like no one else can."

Alec reached around awkwardly and hugged Kate too, landing a kiss near her ear. "We want a full report."

Annalisse groaned. "Let's go, Alec, before she takes you up on it."

Kate walked them to the door, twisting the locket around her neck. "Get a good night's sleep, kids. I know I will."

When the door clicked, Annalisse said, "I hate leaving her, but it's what she wants. Let's find Bill and go back to the inn. I need a nap before I fall down."

They strolled hand in hand toward the lobby.

"What was that bit about Woodrow Wilson earlier?" Alec stopped in the middle of the carpet. "I don't get the reference."

"Oh, that. Auntie thinks Woodrow Wilson is how this country headed down the road of too much government, leading us away from what the founders outlined in the Constitution. The progressive agenda started with his first presidential term. He introduced the Federal Reserve, federal income taxes, and the Federal Trade Commission, among other niceties." Annalisse started their walk again. "I'm giving you this high school civics lesson so you won't bring him up again. Ever. Everything wrong in this country today, Auntie believes started with our twenty-eighth president. She despises him. The door thing gives her an excuse for discussion. I don't recommend it."

"Not another mention from me." Alec made a slash gesture across his neck.

***

Alec fluffed the pillow behind her head and sat on the bed, holding her hand. Leaving Kate behind had brought out a lot of pent-up emotions from the past few days.

"Kate's going to be fine where she is. It's just one night. I promise you, we're up and out of here first thing in the morning." Alec moved a strand of Annalisse's hair from her tearstained cheek. "I don't know what I can say to assure you. We've been all through this."

Annalisse scooted farther up the pillow and wiped her eyes. "Dammit, Alec. I can't help how I feel. The spa is nice, the people seem wonderful, but I don't like her staying there. Jillian made her go, then lied about it—to me—family. She even used my name to trick her mother. But no, she couldn't do this the normal way. She had to stage an abduction in the tack room. It's mindboggling." She swiped at another tear. "Don't you understand? Gongs are banging, and flags are waving about how wrong this is. Remember how I felt when we were chased from New York all over the Aegean? I knew your mother's necklace would hurt us, and it did. Instincts, Alec. Please trust me."

"How's your headache, sweetness? Can I get you anything?"

Annalisse rubbed her temple, and he caught a whisper of a smile. "It's a dull throb, but I think I can sleep. Maybe after I get a little shut-eye we can go out for a bite? Lunch didn't sit well. It's all knotted up down there."

Alec took the cotton throw from the foot of the bed and spread it over her. "Rest. I'll stay here and watch you sleep. You're beautiful when you sleep." He leaned in and kissed her softly.

"Mmm. Feel better already. Thank you." Annalisse rolled over and scrunched the pillow beneath her face.

"We know where Kate is. Be happy we have that. Relax and stop overthinking things," he whispered.

CHAPTER TWENTY-FOUR

Alec stared through the windshield of Bill Drake's SUV at the pillars outside Greylock House. He'd already second-guessed himself about bothering Kate on her last night at the spa.

"Convince me we're doing the right thing." Alec reached into his pocket and handled the recording devices Bill had given him earlier, clicking them against each other. "Am I a heel for bugging this woman?"

"Look at it this way. When she wakes up, you can tell Annalisse you came here and tried to pry Kate away from her masseur. Earn some brownie points. You could use some." Bill grinned and scratched his two-day beard. "Your girlfriend has a track record for knowing things. Taking Kate home is a good move. Don't screw with the juju. Let's go."

The receptionist standing behind the counter looked even younger than the afternoon model. A big-eyed adolescent girl batted her thick, mascaraed eyelashes at them when they approached her.

"May I help you gentlemen?"

"I was visiting earlier with one of your guests, but my girlfriend left her purse. May we go up for a few minutes? We won't stay long."

Her eyes flashed. "Who's the guest?"

"Kate Walker." Bill answered from behind Alec.

"Nice Mrs. Walker, of course. She's in room 311, but she's entertaining someone right now."

"Entertaining?" Alec alerted to her turn of phrase. "She had a massage scheduled with Rafael, but she should be done by now. Did he give the massage in her room?" Alec glanced over his shoulder at his friend and wrinkled his brow at the thought of Kate actually taking him up on his earlier suggestion.

The brunette's expressive eyes widened if that were possible. "Golly, no." She patted herself in a flutter. "We aren't that kind of place, sir. We have specific massage studios in our facility. I can assure you we are reputable. One of the highest-rated health spas in the area."

Bill stepped up to bail him out. "He meant to say, did Mrs. Walker call someone to her room, or was he or she a surprise visitor?"

"I'm not sure. I've never seen him here before. It could be either."

"Can you describe him?" Alec asked. *Who besides Jillian would visit her here?*

"Medium height, silver-gray hair, blue eyes. Kinda handsome for an old guy." She folded her hands on the counter, ready for more questions.

"As old as Mrs. Walker?" Bill jumped in.

"He stooped a little, but it's hard to say."

Sinclair stooped.

Alec turned away and muttered, "Shit." He had a bad feeling. "May we go up and check on her, please?"

"Is there a problem? Should I call security?" She picked up her phone.

Bill raised his hand in a stop gesture. "Please don't. My friend's being overdramatic." He gave Alec an I'll-handle-this look and leaned on the counter, whispering, "He does that sometimes. May we?"

"She's on the third floor. Please let me know if there's a problem." The girl hurried to a back room.

In the elevator, Bill fumbled with a recording device, applying it to the inside of his breast pocket. He slid his thumb over the switch and verified it was secure. "I don't know who we'll find in there, but it wouldn't hurt for you to use one too, in case we get separated." He spoke toward the recorder. "Bill Drake, Tuesday, on our way to Katharine Walker's room at the Greylock House in Massachusetts. The time"—Bill checked his watch—"is 6:18 p.m."

Alec reached into his pocket and attached the thumb drive near a buttonhole. "I'm overdramatic, huh? Man." He turned the drive on and adjusted his shirt. "Can you see it?"

Bill shook his head.

On the third floor, as they neared Kate's door, Alec heard voices. He stopped Bill and motioned him back against the wall, then leaned out to observe.

"Door's ajar," Alec whispered and raised one finger to his lips.

"Perfect. You get on the other side—I'll stay here. As close as possible to the opening. Do *not* go in or interfere, Zavos, no matter what you hear."

Alec glided swiftly and silently to the other side of the doorjamb. Inside, a man spoke heatedly. There was no response from Kate. Alec twisted his torso so that the device would catch the conversation.

"…miserable, lying whore." Crude words from a man Alec didn't recognize. Not Sinclair.

"You don't have the right to call me that," Kate said in a small voice. "I don't know what possessed you to come back, but I'll thank you to leave. Right now." She whimpered, and Alec wanted to open the door on the spot. The man in there was upsetting her, and he had to think about her weak heart.

Alec nudged the door slightly with his fingertips, and Bill stopped him with a strong headshake and motioned at his recorder.

"I'm still your husband, and you'll listen to me for once, damn you!" His tone was sharper, and he slapped a hard surface.

Alec glared at his friend on the other side of the door. "What the hell?" he mouthed. He wondered if Kate had a husband that Annalisse knew nothing about. No way, not Kate.

"My husband died six years ago, you selfish bastard, and I've moved on. You left me alone to run a farm and raise three kids without an outside income. I don't owe you a plug nickel."

"Did you think I wouldn't find out?"

Alec noted Kate's long pause.

"With that strong resemblance?" he demanded.

Someone moved in front of the door, and Alec jerked away from the opening, but whoever it was had their back to them.

"What do you want?" Kate pleaded.

"Did you enjoy my man-sized present in the big barn last Saturday?"

"*You* put that poor fellow there?"

"He was dying of cancer. Nobody misses a homeless man. Frankly, I was surprised how easy it was to take a life with a bungee cord and my bare hands."

Alec thought he caught Kate gasp.

"It's exhilarating to crush a man's windpipe and watch his eyes go dead. No harm, no foul. The sap wanted to check out." The ugly tale echoed off the walls. "Why not use it to my advantage?"

"God, you didn't," Kate whispered. "I don't know you anymore, Ted."

Ted? The dead husband? Alec's blood froze in every vessel, and he drew a sharp breath. How could that be?

Bill waved to get Alec's attention and pointed to his recording device. He had drifted too close to the jamb and had pressed the device against it.

"I needed him to make my point, and he needed me to off him. What better way to get your attention than a decaying body with your lover's name? Ha. It was brilliant, although messy getting into the ocean for a lungful of water. I have strong helpers even if they are a pain in the ass."

Ted Walker was alive and killing, and he had accomplices. Probably the wolfman and Sinclair. Goose bumps erupted on his arms when he realized how this news would affect Annalisse. Should he go back to the inn and get her? *A showdown like that would be ugly, and we can't upset Kate any more than she must be already.*

"Who else knows about this—about you?" Kate muffled a sob. "We'll be a laughingstock."

"Why did you do it, Kath?" His anguish was palpable. "Didn't I give you enough sack time? You had to go out and find another guy to slap and tickle. Makes me want to puke, you horny bitch."

Alec recoiled at the crude way he addressed her.

"Get out!" she yelled. "You're a fine one to talk, Ted Walker of the walking dead. You're sick!" Kate cleared her throat, and a coughing jag followed. "What about you? Everyone believes you jumped off a goddamn bridge, but here you stand. No wonder all we found in the river were your shoes. Why bother to come back?" A pause. "Oh! You want the farm, don't you? That's it, isn't it? Teddy is out of cash and wants what I've worked hard to keep afloat. Me and Annalisse." Another series of coughs. "Nothing doin', brainless. It's not mine anymore anyway."

"What?" he asked, genuinely surprised. "Jilli said—"

"Jillian? Knows you're alive?" Kate's laughter came out as a wheeze. "Damn girl never did know what's good for her. She's been working with you, huh? No wonder she was so insistent about getting me to this spa. She planned this little reunion, did she?"

That's why Kate was taken from the stables. Ted wanted her on his turf to spring himself on her with no witnesses. Wanted it to look like an abduction to throw everyone off while he planned his meeting with Kate to rock her world. Why such a flamboyant ruse?

"Jilli ain't smart enough to plan this. I couldn't trust that geeky husband to take care of my little girl like he should, so I moved out west and got a masonry job in Seattle. You know, to make sure she was okay. The little twerp hubby spotted me. I didn't know it till she showed on a jobsite."

"God. You two are peas in a pod. Selfish and stupid." A pause. "Hey, stay back. This is a darn good weapon."

Alec wondered what she was holding. He strained to see through the gap but had no line of sight.

Footsteps retreated.

"Where's your precious *Annalisse*?" He mocked her name, and Alec fumed. "I thought she'd be sleeping in the bed next to you?" Ted laughed like he'd cracked the best joke in the world. "Does she know?"

Bill had a strange look on his face, and all Alec could do was shrug.

"That girl's none of your business," she announced flatly.

"I helped raise her, didn't I? Don't you see? I couldn't bear her or you anymore. Taking care of another man's kid under my own roof felt like a boot in the gut every time I looked at either one of ya."

Of course she's someone else's kid. She's Kate's niece. Alec frowned.

"Hell, you weren't around to raise your *own* kids. Never were for that matter. Don't pat yourself on the back. I separated from you those two years because I wanted a divorce. I wasn't looking for your replacement, trust me."

"But you got yourself one, didn't you? Tom Taylor."

"Bah, that's nonsense. I came back to you, didn't I? I'm done talking about ancient history, but know this: I'll fight your murderous hide with everything I have and then some. It was bad enough when I thought you were dead, but this? You abandoned your family, and I hate you for it. And you killed a man to get back at me. Lord forgive you for what you've done."

The elevator door chimed its arrival.

"You owe me—"

Ted swiveled at the noise.

Alec and Bill speed walked down the hall toward the metal doors. Kate's door clicked shut behind them. There was no way to know if anyone had poked their head out first.

"Hello, Alec and friend." Beverly Case smiled at Bill and tottered out of the elevator with a phone in her hand. "Were you visiting Kate? I came by to see how her massage went and to give her back her cell. Her daughter asked that we hold it for her and no incoming calls. A little odd, but we followed her wishes."

"Perfect timing. Would you do me a favor and tell Kate that she has another appointment. Make something up. Just get that man in her room to leave. Insist if you have to. We'll wait to speak with you downstairs. I'd rather not be seen by Kate," Alec said.

Beverly nodded with a bewildered look.

"Good evening, Ms. Case." Alec led the way with his heart pumping like a racehorse down the backstretch. He entered the elevator with Bill on his heels, palming the lobby button twice.

When the doors closed, Alec rested his head against the wall, weighted down and beaten up. An eighteen-wheeler named Ted had run him down and left plenty of rubber behind. "Christ." He pulled out the recorder and switched it off. "Here. Take this damn thing and get them to the authorities."

"I'll download the file and send it to McDonaugh. With what they already have from forensics along with this admission, he'll have what he needs. The recording might be enough to get ol' Wolfie to come clean about Albers's murder. He might even explain how they targeted him." Bill extracted his own device and turned it off. "Annalisse's premonition nailed the case. Aren't you glad we came?"

"The jury's still out on that one." Alec's stomach sloshed against his ribs, and he felt sick.

"We have to move fast and pick up the bastard. Get him off the streets before he disappears underground again. I'll call the authorities up here." Bill faced the elevator door panels and grazed the third-floor button lightly. "Wanna rethink this? Go back and wait for him upstairs? He's committed one murder already."

"My gut says we could make matters worse if he has a weapon. Ted wouldn't risk hurting Kate with the farm in play. What would he gain by killing her? She has secrets, and Ted could be planning to blackmail her. Anyway, if he wanted her dead, he would've taken her out instead of leaving a body." Alec looked at Bill for confirmation.

"Yeah, the spa owner will get him to haul ass out of there. If we went in and tried to apprehend him ourselves, he could bolt and leave town. Let the locals do their job," Bill said.

Back inside Bill's car, Alec scrubbed a hand over his face. He hoped that he'd made the right decision at

Kate's room. The mixture of emotions left him with no good answers. Where should they go next?

Bill downloaded the thumb drive data to his laptop and sent an email to the Orange County Sheriff's Office.

"Done." Bill's laptop snapped shut. "I get Ted's motive, but I have so many questions about Kate and Annalisse."

"So do I, Bill. So do I." Alec sighed back his apprehension. "Ted being alive is going to kill Annalisse. I can't imagine she'll find any comfort knowing that. Who could blame her? And what about Kate? I know how much those two women love Walker Farm. Ted isn't about to lay off now."

"I can't believe that was Ted Walker," Bill mused.

Alec nodded. "I never met him, but it has to be him."

"There was an affair. Motive number one. From what I gathered, Kate had an affair with Tom Taylor what, thirty years ago? She would've been somewhere in her forties."

"Yeah, that sounds right. Walker asked if Annalisse knew. I don't know what he was talking about. Knew he was alive or about the affair?" Alec doubted Annalisse knew about either. She never mentioned any indiscretions.

"Do you know what Walker meant by 'the resemblance'?" Bill asked. When Alec didn't know what to say, he elaborated. "This is going to sound farfetched, but stick with me. Ted's rage built up, he faked his own death, and then years later something popped. He came back and killed an innocent person to punish his wife for the affair. What better way to hurt Kate if you're not able to kill the real Tom Taylor? I understand anger over the infidelity but to kill an innocent in cold blood with your own hands—that takes balls most of us don't have. Look, Ted's angry at his wife for an affair she had roughly thirty years ago. How old is Annalisse?"

"Twenty-nine." Alec groaned when he finally understood Bill's point. "The notes and music—a Tom Jones song about a murder over infidelity. Jesus. It's all there, and Ted was pulling the strings."

"Annalisse is afraid of wolves. The uncle who raised her would know about bad dreams. The wolf costume and the weird snow globe at the inn make sense now, don't they? Ted had so much hatred, he set out to terrorize both women." Bill shifted in his seat and openly glared at Alec. "I think Annalisse is Kate's love child with Thomas Taylor."

"It's all surreal. Her entire life—a sham." Alec dropped his head into his hand. "Man, I can't tell her this. Kate has to."

"Here's the bigger question, my friend. Can you wait for Kate to explain it to her? How will Annalisse feel if she hears the truth from her dearly departed *Uncle* Ted?"

"That can't happen. If she finds out that I knew and didn't tell her, game over. I'll lose her for good. This is a hot, steamy, pile of— She's gonna be devastated."

"An understatement," Bill agreed.

"What if Ted's wrong, and Annalisse isn't Kate's daughter?" Alec considered it a few moments. "Your scenario makes more sense."

"Whether he's right or not, you're neck deep in the steaming pile if you keep what we just overheard from Annalisse. She's been tortured enough."

Dread crept over Alec's earlier bright outlook. "We need to get back to the inn. Start the car. Did you see Ted leave the spa? Damn, I wasn't watching."

Bill tapped the ignition button. "And Jillian was in on the whole twisted plan. But an accomplice to murder? Hard to swallow, unless…"

Alec's phone rang. "Huh, Lenox area code. Maybe it's the inn." His heart sank at another option. *What if it's the spa?*

CHAPTER TWENTY-FIVE

"Why didn't you wake me last night? I can't believe I slept through dinner." Annalisse stuffed an unworn, fiery-red teddy into her overnight bag. She'd purchased it months ago for the bed-and-breakfast outing that kept getting postponed.

"You needed the sleep," Alec replied, his eyes following the lacy scrap.

"It's such a shame you didn't get the chance to see me in it."

"Something to look forward to." Alec's smile was strained.

"Good answer. This is going to be such a fantastic day. Once we pick up Auntie and get her back to the estate, I have big plans." She closed the case and zipped the sides around. "It came to me in my sleep. We have plenty of options to stall Jeremy from selling the farm. Some you might be able to help us with." Annalisse hated the thought of asking Alec for money, but the option was there if they were desperate. "I'm so happy and lucky to have you and Kate."

She spun in circles with her arms outstretched. What a difference a few days made.

"Okay, ballerina girl. By my watch it's 7:20. We're checked out downstairs. Let's head to the spa."

"Bradley's back? Or are we going with Bill?"

"Bill had to take off last night. The Keith Albers case cracked wide open. Seems your wolfman wants a deal."

"That's wonderful news. I hope he doesn't get off completely. That creepy jerk shouldn't be roaming the streets. If they called Bill in, McDonaugh has to believe all of this is connected. Do they know who killed the homeless guy? Was it Woody? I mean that wolfman, Chris Lewis?"

He tightened his lips and shrugged.

"Alec?"

"Brad got here with the Bentley about four this morning. He's waiting for us in the lobby."

"Did something else happen? I've seen your hand-in-the-hair thing a bunch since you got out of the shower. Did I snore and keep you awake?"

"I couldn't sleep. It wasn't you. I'll try to get a nap on the way home if it'll make you stop the inquisition." Alec yanked her suitcase off the bed and rolled his bag next to it. "I wish we'd had a little time to ourselves. I guess I still owe you a bed-and-breakfast trip."

"And the antique shops, don't forget." She grabbed his elbow and turned him around. "I'm worried about you. There's pain in your eyes. Is your ankle bad today?"

"I'm just tired. C'mon. We're burning time." He gave her a weak smile, hardly worth the effort. "Ready, sunshine?"

She couldn't imagine a grumpier guy to dampen her day. He was miles away.

Someone texted Alec, and his face contorted when he read it.

"Who's that? You look like you ate a whole lemon tree." Annalisse laughed, but she did so alone.

"Not important," he muttered. Alec chewed on the corner of his lip as he replied to the message.

His ankle and stiff leg had improved a great deal since yesterday. Other things bothered her though. A preoccupation with something he wasn't sharing ate at him, he'd called her sunshine—which was a first—and her good-natured, easygoing guy had a short fuse today, when he rarely showed any fuse at all. Her happiness faded. *What's up with him?*

***

Alec carefully stayed ahead of Annalisse on the side-walk so he could open the door to Greylock House for her. Whatever happened inside the spa in the next few minutes would frame his future with this amazing yet fragile woman. There was little he or anyone could do to soften the impact of what was about to become Annalisse's new reality.

Alec tugged at the door handle, with his heart bobbing in his throat.

Beverly Case waited patiently at the counter for them.

The humid air outside evaporated in the cold re-ception lobby once they entered. The day was shaping into another sticky one so close to the coast. Zen harps that typically soothed him rubbed a sore spot against his spine with their strings. He felt every injured muscle in his ankle, and he ached all over like a case of the flu. Shitty best described how his body felt.

Annalisse took his hand and literally danced into the room, which made him feel worse.

"Beverly!" Annalisse drew him across the carpet with her. "Is Kate ready? She's expecting us." She grinned at him, then the owner.

Beverly gave him a quick, saddened glance, and he hoped Annalisse wouldn't notice. *Don't be so obvious.*

"Good morning, Annalisse, Alec." She tucked a white envelope out of sight. "I ah… Your aunt left last night after her massage. Something came up, and she had to check out."

"What? She wouldn't do that." Annalisse swiveled to Alec, her eyes filled with disbelief. "Please don't tell me her daughter took her."

"No, nothing like that. Katharine wanted me to give you this." She pulled the catalog envelope back out. Annalisse's name was written on it. "She left strict instructions. She asked that you open it when you get home."

"Why?" Annalisse looked at Alec for his reaction.

"Home, the estate, or Annalisse's brownstone?" Alec didn't care which. Kate had given him three hours in the car to decide how much to tell her. No amount of time would be enough to brace her for what might be inside that envelope.

Annalisse fumbled for words, choking back emotion. "I… I don't understand. It's all set. I pick her up at seven thirty, and she rides back with *us*." She slammed her palm on the stainless counter. "What the hell happened after we left! Who took her? If you know, you'd best tell me right now."

Beverly took a step back, taking the envelope with her. "I didn't change her plans, Annalisse. Please calm yourself." Sweat beads rode her upper lip, and she puckered her wine-colored mouth into the size of a cherry.

Alec wrapped his arm around his girlfriend, and she flinched. "This is a shock, Ms. Case. We don't blame you. Kate's impulsive."

Annalisse heaved an angry sigh. "Do you know what she put in that envelope?" She jabbed a finger at Beverly, and Alec winced.

"No. It's sealed. I'm sure Kate had a good reason for this little mystery. She's such an intriguing—"

"Give me the envelope. Now."

"Shh, art lady. Don't be like this."

"Don't patronize me. Something bad happened." She turned away and glared at Beverly. Annalisse shook violently beneath Alec's fingers. "Did Kate have another attack? Is that it?"

"Your aunt is fine. I swear it. I saw her leave, and she was fine."

Annalisse moaned and leaned into Alex. He had to get her out of the spa before she created a real scene. He reached for the envelope and mouthed a thank-you at the owner.

Beverly handed him the lumpy parcel, and he led Annalisse to the Mulsanne parked near the building. With Brad's help, he buckled her in and closed her door.

Gesturing widely, he said, "Brad, stay within the limit but get us the hell back to the estate as soon as you can." In a view through her window, Annalisse slumped against the seat like a rag doll. "Jesus." He rubbed his forehead, looking for options. *Kate, I hope you're okay and this is the right thing to do for Annalisse.*

For the first thirty minutes, Annalisse wouldn't look at Alec or speak to him. He assumed she'd blamed him for Kate's flight or figured out he knew more than he'd told her. Did he dare tell her who'd been in Kate's room? Alec touched the hard object through the envelope and traced its round shape. When he tipped the envelope back and forth, metal links rustled.

"Are you going to let me see that?" Annalisse asked flatly.

"Welcome back. I wondered if you were napping."

"You weren't surprised Kate left. Were you in on that? Did Bill really go back to New York to see the sheriff?" Her sneer struck him at his core.

"Yes, he did. Everything I told you is the truth." *I just left some truth out.*

"Do you know what's inside that envelope you're stroking like some house cat?"

"No. How could I know that?" he asked.

She shrugged and lifted her nose high, crossing her arms.

"Dammit, Annalisse. You know your aunt. She's as unpredictable as a pop-up thunderstorm." Alec had reached his conclusion. He'd risk making the wrong decision and work on any collateral damage later. If Annalisse found out… Alec shivered. *Finish this—now.*

"Is it cold in here?" she asked rubbing her arms. "Bradley, would you turn the AC off back here?"

Surely Annalisse's attitude had cooled down the interior. Alec could almost see his breath.

"Okay." Alec sighed and picked up the envelope. "Do I know what's in here? No. That's the God's honest truth. Your aunt's the one who wants you miles away when you see what's inside. Not me."

She stared at him intensely and blinked several times.

"While you were napping yesterday afternoon, I went into Bill's room, and we talked about getting Kate out of the spa. You have good instincts, and Bill agreed we should try again."

"*You* tried? Well, it must have worked. Someone convinced her. Why didn't you wake me? We could've gone home yesterday. All of us."

"It wasn't like that." Alec swallowed hard, and his throat tightened. "When we got to her room, we could hear someone inside with her. Their voices were raised, so we stayed in the hall."

"The only one who knew she was there was Jillian. She might have told Jeremy. Was it him?"

Alec wondered if he was strong enough to handle what was coming.

"No, not exactly," Alec mumbled. "We listened for a few minutes before Kate said his name. The door was only open a crack. We couldn't see inside." He wiped his clammy hands down his thighs. "It wasn't anyone you'd expect."

"Charlie?" she asked.

Alec took her hand, and she must have felt his anguish.

"Alec, you're white."

"I thought about going back to get you, but there was no time." He swiped a thumb across her knuckles.

"C'mon, don't agonize. Who was in Kate's room?"

"It was… Ted."

"Ted. I don't know any—No!" Annalisse unbuckled her belt so she could confront him. "You're mistaken."

"We're not."

She covered her mouth and tears filled her eyes. "How? How can you be sure it's him? You've never seen him. It's impossible."

He found a tissue box in the seat pocket and set it beside her. "We overheard their conversation—argument, really—and she referred to him as her husband more than once. I'm so sorry to drop this bomb on you." Alec left out the part about recording them. He'd worry about that later. If at all.

Annalisse rubbed her reddened eyes and blew her nose. "Uncle Ted treated Auntie like crap. I heard him call her disgusting names. Kate made herself scarce when he was home—pretending not to feel well, mostly. He battered her emotionally because he could. It made me sick. I never admitted that to you or anyone because I don't speak ill of the dead." She openly shook. "The son of a bitch wasn't dead." Her tears started again. "All this time he was alive, living— What kind of a sicko fakes suicide, then shows up years later? A dammed selfish one." Annalisse answered herself, then groaned. "Damn. This is freakin' awful. It puts the farm in more limbo." She scooted next to Alec and hugged him. "Could you tell how Auntie was handling the shock?"

Alec laughed uncomfortably. "How does Kate handle anything?"

"Strong. Opinionated. Hardened and entrenched. No wonder she left the spa quickly. Who could blame her?"

Alec slipped the envelope into the pouch in the door panel. Any more truths had to come from Kate herself. He had to stay out of it. From what Annalisse said, Kate had enough reasons to leave her husband. He wondered why she returned to a bad marriage when there were options.

"Rest now. We'll do what she wants. We'll wait to open it." Alec nestled her against him and drifted away from the envelope, and he closed his eyes.

CHAPTER
TWENTY-SIX

Annalisse had picked at the heavy lunch Helga prepared for them. The food aromas alone made her squeamish, but the mixture of lumpy meats and starches staring back at her from the plate was more than she could bear.

"I'm sorry." Annalisse excused herself from the table. "I've lost my appetite. I'll reheat it later." She gave Helga a hug. "Maybe going for a walk might help."

Alec followed her onto the porch, distress shadowing his eyes.

"I have an idea. Why don't we ride out to one of the prettiest places on the estate? One I haven't shown you yet."

"My stomach's so upset. I don't know that riding's a good idea," she said, placing a hand on her midriff as it gurgled.

"Wind in the hair is good for what ails ya. C'mon." Alec wrapped a strong arm around her and walked her to his ATV. "It's only a five-minute ride." His pitiful smile moved her, but then he looked up. A pair of hawks dueled in the sky, shrieking challenges at each other in flight. "Peregrine falcons. Tons of them at the creek. I go there sometimes to think. You'll love it. It's a good place to open Kate's envelope." He pulled it from his back pocket. "I know this is what's churning your stomach."

Riding behind Alec on the ATV, she rehashed the morning's events. She was furious at Kate for leaving without them, but after the initial shock, Annalisse understood why she did it. When Kate was ready, they would talk again. Alec was right.

Alec parked the ATV, and they walked a few yards to the creek. Annalisse sat on the bank, watching pond bugs skitter across the still water. Circle-wakes trailed behind them. Frogs buzzed and hummed to the backdrop of currents spilling over polished rocks. Tranquil sounds. She smiled when she heard a sheep's bleat from a pile of stones.

"Did you hear a sheep frog over there?" She pointed to a marshy area of the bank. "I'd love to see one."

Alec laughed. "He's a little too far north, if you're talking about *Hypopachus.* The one you mentioned is part of a group of narrow-mouthed frogs in the south. How do you know about them?"

"Kate took her trailer on a horse-buying trip one summer and talked about the sheep frogs banding together in chorus to attract a mate. She said when she closed her eyes at night beside the ponds in East Texas, she could swear that she heard a flock of sheep bleating."

"I haven't seen any on Kiamesha Creek. Doesn't mean one didn't hitch a ride." He comforted her with a grin that sent her pulse climbing, and he pulled her closer to his spot on the bank. "No matter what time of year, the creek never goes dry. On horseback, the views are great. Revitalizes the soul—speaking of which..." Alec laid Kate's envelope in front of her. "Now's as good a time as any."

She hesitated.

"We don't have to do this now. Whatever's inside isn't going anywhere." Alec squeezed the muscles at the base of her neck. "You're tight as an arachnid back there. Maybe you should've signed up for Rafael's miracle massage." He lifted one brow.

She sighed wistfully. "Rafael sounded kinda cute." She snapped her fingers. "Darn, missed my chance." Annalisse laid her head on his shoulder and chuckled. She watched ripples gently swirl and dissipate around a fallen log in the water. "Don't you remember? I came close to becoming a zoologist. I learned genus and species of lizards and things around the farm. Drove Auntie crazy."

"See there, we have more in common than we thought. Art lady could've been zoo lady."

"I doubt that we would've met if I had become *zoo lady*. I'll take art lady." She picked up the envelope, running her fingertips over the hard bulge. She tapped it with a nail and gasped. "Alec, I think I know what this is, and it scares the crap out of me."

Alec took the envelope and carefully tore open the short end. "Open your hand."

She did, and Kate's favorite locket she never took off slipped out. Annalisse closed her eyes, but a tear escaped anyway. "Why, Alec? Kate wore this every day.

I don't remember her ever taking this off except when she wore Uncle Ted's pearls." She traced the worn, filigree under her thumb. "This is precious to her."

"Now it's precious to you. Open it. Have you ever seen what's inside? I'd like to."

Annalisse pushed the tiny clasp, and the metal butterflied open easily.

Alec reached for it so that he could see the small pictures, one on each side. "They're pictures of Kate taken a few years apart. There's no mistaking her features, even before she turned gray. Hairdos are different though."

"That one's Kate." Annalisse pointed to the right side. "This one is me before I went to college. We had a professional photographer come to the farm and take a bunch of pictures. Auntie lost it the day I moved to the City. A blubbery mess."

Alec looked at her, then the photos. "Beautiful. You could be sisters." He sat back on his hands, gazing at the stream.

"Funny you should say that. Everyone assumed I was Kate's daughter. Mom looked a lot like Aunt Kate." She put down the locket and picked up the letter. Her hand shook, and that threat of dread returned. "I don't think I can do it. Would you mind reading it out loud?"

Alec opened the two sheets and read, "*Lambie, my situation changed after you left yesterday, and I'm sorry for worrying you. What I'm about to tell you I still can't believe myself. I had a visit from your uncle last night. Now, before you think the old biddy has gone senile and started seeing ghosts, I assure you. I was awake and as sane as that handsome boyfriend of yours.*"

Alec looked up and smiled. *"Ted showed up at my spa room, like the past six years never happened."*

"What you heard was true then. I so hoped you were wrong." Annalisse wrapped her arms around her knees. "Go on." Twining her hands together, she waited for more.

"I won't go into details here, but he admitted to killing that man in our barn. He had helpers. I've written a statement, and Beverly will make sure that the authorities know what I know about the whole dirty mess. Your uncle committed a murder with his bare hands! Over something I did almost thirty years ago."

Annalisse gasped and covered her mouth. "My God. What could be so awful he'd do that? I should be surprised, but knowing how unpredictable he was, is…"

"When I was in my forties, I left Ted. I wanted a divorce, and we separated. No one but my sister knew Ted and I were having problems. I'm not proud of the next part. I had an affair with a younger man that lasted several months. I thought I was in love with this man, but I soon recognized it wouldn't work and decided to go back to Ted. That's when I found out that I was pregnant and couldn't go back. At least not right away. Returning to the farm with a baby wasn't possible, but I couldn't give up a child or have an abortion."

Annalisse froze, afraid to parse Kate's words. Afraid to breathe.

Stunned.

Stupefied.

"You okay for me to keep going?" he asked, scooting even closer and taking her hand.

She nodded and dropped her head into her hands. That earlier dread intensified. Annalisse would never suspect Kate of an affair, but the turmoil at Walker Farm and Ted must have pushed her off the high dive.

"Lambie, please forgive me. I was desperate to save my marriage, and a child by another man would've ended my life. Your parents were having trouble conceiving and wanted children badly. With little convincing, my child had a home with my sister."

She grabbed Alec's arm and choked out, "Is this for real?" She twisted toward him, tears flowing. "What did Kate do? I'm that baby? My parents' miracle—from Kate?" Annalisse sobbed and crumpled to the rocky bank, indifferent to the stones digging into her. She sobbed inconsolably for a time.

"What did you do to me?" She sat up abruptly and wiped her running nose with her shirt. "Thomas Taylor, me, Kate. It's all a terrible lie. My entire life—a fairy tale so *you* could keep your dirty secret. But it wasn't a secret to your husband. How could you?" Annalisse's scream echoed across the stream.

Alec dropped the letter on his thigh and drew her close to him. "Shh. Do you want me to stop?"

She wrapped her arms around his neck and let herself cry until the shakes subsided, and she had nothing left.

"If it weren't for her lover's name planted on that dead guy, I'd still be in the dark. Let's hear the rest." She tucked herself into the crook of his arm.

Alec read, *"So many times I wanted to call you my daughter. I almost got there this past Saturday at the kitchen table. But you have loving memories of the Drurys. I couldn't break those memories, so I held my tongue.*

I was selfish to leave you with Amy, but at the time, I had few options. All I asked from her was to visit the farm often so I could see you grow. When they died, I felt like I was being punished for giving you up. Their lives in exchange for getting you back.

Your father doesn't know. I never told Thomas I was having his child, so before your mind turns to finding him, forget it. He's out of the country, and I have no idea where. I'm sure he has his own family and doesn't need a bastard child hounding him. Looking for him will only hurt you.

Your rightful birth certificate is in a safe deposit box. Not at my regular bank. When I come back, I'll get it for you."

"Where'd she go?" Annalisse seethed over being told not to contact her birth father.

"I have to leave for a while. Lots of dust to let settle. I left my locket for you, and I hope you can wear it close to your heart. It's funny you never asked to see what's inside. My little lambie Annalisse, you've been my truest treasure. Live your life with gusto, and keep that gallant man with his stable full of horses close to you. If you can, remember me without hatred. My decisions were made by my love for you.

Love you always, your mother,

Kate."

She thought she was cried out, but no. Again, tears slid down her cheeks, and she angrily wiped them away. "Dammit. I'm supposed to just accept that I'm some bastard kid not allowed to know who my father is. This time she's gone too far."

"We have time to decide where to go from here." Alec's phone rang, and he answered, "Hey, Bill."

"Did you forget I was coming by today?" Bill asked. "I'm at the house."

"Right. We'll be up there in a few." He ended the call. "I need to meet Bill. You can stay here and collect yourself if you'd like."

She swabbed her face again. "I don't have my purse. Wish I had my compact to touch up my swollen face."

"You look gorgeous. Ride back with me, and I'll give you time for a touch-up. Bill won't notice." He reached his hand out to her.

He pulled her lightly to her feet, and she said, "I have tons of questions for him anyway. What about Jillian and Jeremy? Do they know what Ted did? The bigger question: Were they in on it?"

***

In his estate drawing room, crowded with roses in full bloom, Alec handed Bill a beer and sat down in the chair across from the sofa. He drew in a heady whiff of rose petals and drank from his beer bottle, swirling the cold brew on the back of his tongue. He smiled at the memory of those roses and when they'd read his notes on each vase. The blue velvet bag he'd shown her on Sunday was no longer empty.

Annalisse went to freshen herself, giving Alec time to chat and settle up with Bill. She'd taken the worst news of her life better than he could imagine. Bill's hunches about Tom Taylor and Kate were true, but the real reason Ted Walker had come back was still a mystery. He hoped that Bill had a few more answers for them.

"It smells good in here." Bill sipped his beer. "Are all these flowers for her?" He nodded toward the hall.

Alec gave him a slow smile.

Bill scanned the room. "Women like this stuff?"

"You don't date much, do you?"

"Who has time?"

"So, what do you have? Annalisse got painful news from Kate. You were right. She'd like some closure, as would I."

"After Kate gave her statement to the sheriff's office, we dropped her off at the airport and went back to talk to the detective on the case. Once Chris Lewis, aka Woody, knew he'd better talk or do hard time, he spilled it all. He even had Ted's license plate number, if you can believe that."

"Did they pick Ted up in Lenox?"

Bill nodded. "Ted wasn't far from the inn where you guys were staying. Once I called McDonaugh and told him what we heard in Kate's room, they contacted the locals and picked him up. I hope the recordings are admissible, but with Kate's statement, we should be in good shape to get a murder conviction. They pulled Walker's DNA from Albers's body. Forensics were surprised to find the prints and hair belonged to a dead man."

"Was Chris part of the murder? Who is this Big M Annalisse was supposed to have met? A made-up character?"

"That would be Ted. Chris was his apprentice. M equals mason. Called himself the big mason. Can you believe it? Chris did his grunt work but wouldn't cop to the murder. We aren't sure what Ted offered Sinclair for his help. Possibly just his freedom from the nuthouse." Bill got more serious. "One other thing. The mysterious visitor your housekeeper talked to was none other than Ted Walker himself. If he'd found Annalisse here, the Kate situation might never have happened."

"Wow." Alec shook his head. "I'm not sure Annalisse needs to hear that."

Tapping heels resonated on the hardwood, and Annalisse came through the drawing room doors. Alec couldn't believe the transformation. She wore a pale blue shift and had tied her hair off to one side, looking as flawless as a model in a magazine photo.

"Did I hear you talking about Ted?" She pointed at Alec's beer. "I'd like one of those. I want to hear everything."

"Take my seat. I'll get you a beer or something stronger—like a Manhattan?"

"Thanks, a Manhattan would be perfect."

Bill rose when she entered and sat when she did. "You're stunning in blue. Alec's a lucky guy," he said. "I'm not sure how much you heard, but Kate has given her statement. Your uncle—I mean Ted—is in custody, and so is your Woody character. Orange County also arrested Jillian."

Annalisse gaped, then smiled wickedly. "The bitch gets what she deserves for pulling this awful stunt on her mother. And me. Was she involved in the murder too? Did she know all along that her father wasn't dead?"

"I'm not sure about either. According to Ted, it's only been a few months. He was vague about a lot of things when it came to his daughter."

Annalisse thrummed the wooden arm with her nails. "My bet's on her knowing more than she admits. Of course, Ted would cover for his precious baby girl." She shuddered inside as she recalled the last time she saw Ted Walker fawning over Jillian like someone would a porcelain doll. "Is she still in custody, or did Jeremy bail her out? Is he also part of this?"

"According to McDonaugh, he didn't know anything."

"Why did Ted bother to come back?" Alec came in and handed her the drink.

"We think it was financial. Maybe Jillian's husband put his fist down about Daddy-o living with them."

Annalisse pursed her lips. "That must have sucked. A reason for a divorce if I ever heard one." She raised a finger. "*Ted* was behind selling the farm, not Jeremy? The farm is quitclaimed to Jeremy, but that has to be in limbo now with his father being alive," she said.

"That's not my field of expertise. Jeremy's the real estate attorney. I'd imagine he can't be pleased by Ted's return. Jeremy's loan to his mother might have dropped into a black hole. Are you okay? How do you feel about all this?"

Annalisse sipped her drink and placed the glass on her thigh, pushing the cold deep into her muscles. "I won't be the same for a long time. Maybe never." She glanced at Alec. "I'm blessed in other ways." She bit her lip and stared at the man who kept her from falling apart. Annalisse turned to Bill. "Thank you for making Kate's case your priority. I'm indebted to you and to Alec. But I need to know, did Kate leave the spa with you?"

His voice wavered. "Yes."

"You know where she is. Awesome! Can I see her?"

"Annalisse, neither of us know where she went," Alec said. "She doesn't want to be found right now. She made that clear outside the airport, right Bill?"

"Yeah."

"She flew somewhere? By herself or with someone else?" *Ethan maybe. His job had to be in jeopardy.*

"I have no idea. I dropped her off in the parking lot. I don't even know what airline," Bill said.

"Where could Mom go without a suitcase or money?" Annalisse asked.

Alec smiled. "You called her Mom."

With her eyes brimming tears, she said, "I might as well get used to it." Then she realized. "Ugh. That means the Walker kids are my half... Ewww."

CHAPTER TWENTY-SEVEN

Mature sugar maples and manicured pines hugged the pasture nearest the house, dropping needles and yellow leaves at Annalisse's feet. The promise of an early fall beckoned to her from July foliage. She peered over the tall Kentucky bluegrass in the quiet field and felt… hollow. A moist wind stirred the boughs in a million whispers through the treetops, warning of the impending mountain storm brewing from the north. Aromas reminiscent of Christmas danced in this place for galloping mares and foals—a place of rebirth—a place where aspirations were born. Even though the foals were gone from the pasture, it was her favorite spot on Alec's estate.

She rubbed her hands together, then brought them to her nose. Her fingertips were fragrant and sticky from tying balsam wreaths to the stall doors in the main barn. She felt strangely dire for the rich piney smell and the need to stay busy. How could she reconcile living a fabricated existence for twenty-nine years?

She leaned on the vinyl fence post and tried to imagine how different she might be if her birth parents had raised her. The mystery father and a less secretive mother. Three people—Chase, Alec, and Generosa—she could actually count on to be true to her. Chase was like a brother, and he, most of all, backed her up without questions.

Sighing, she relished the breeze in her hair and the way it cooled her overheated mind. "Kate, I wish you were here. We have so much to talk over." She stared at the gathering clouds thundering in the distance. "I won't think about how selfish you were to shut me out. If I do, I'll get angry, and I don't want to be mad at you—my mom. I owe you everything." She clasped her hands over the top rail, bowed her head, and closed her eyes. Annalisse's breast tightened so much that it threatened to crush her next breath.

The air around her moved. She whirled toward the crunching gravel and Alec.

"You scared me!"

"That was quite a conversation. I thought you were talking to someone." He rested a tender hand on the base of her neck, pulling her into his chest. "I caught some of it. Without saying I understand your feelings, because I could never, Kate did her best with an impossible dilemma. She wanted a good life for you and knew her sister would give you one."

"Why not tell me as soon as I had become an adult?"

"My guess? She couldn't risk how you'd react. You might be mad enough to move away or hate her for it. I don't think she could bear either." Alec rubbed little circles over her shoulders. "Let this sink in for a few days, then reread her letter. Put yourself in her place and try to imagine how frightened she was that Ted might uncover the affair." He pulled back and looked into her eyes with a gleam in his. "Walk with me."

He led her down the steep drive, and they strolled hand in hand. He waved to the security man across the road on the way to the stable. Alec pushed open the squeaky slider and escorted her into his office.

"You always know the right thing to say." She breathed in the scent of fresh shavings and cedar walls. After planting her into a chair across from the desk, Annalisse watched him move to his seat. "Your ankle's improving."

"It's touchy, but I'm tired of wimping out." He folded his hands on the desk. "I'd like your opinion. I haven't talked to Mom yet, but it's my decision. What would you say to my selling the corporation?"

"Signorile?"

"One of the European big-three has wanted Signorile for years. Dad absolutely refused to sell. Mom gave him the look every time he turned them down. She was ready for him to retire."

"That's huge, Alec." She was afraid to hope he'd actually do it.

"What's wrong? Not a good idea?" he asked.

She kept her composure, trying not to come off too gleeful. "It'll free you up, big time. Would your dad approve?"

"He's not here, is he?" Alec grumbled, his brows drawing together. "He doesn't know how I've sacrificed for his dream. What about mine?" He shook his head.

"That sounded lame. And selfish. I haven't said that out loud to anyone else. I have other reasons for selling, but they can wait for another discussion. I'm ready to pursue some personal happiness for a change. A happiness with you, if you'll have me." Alec drew the blue velvet bag from a bottom drawer. The one he'd shown her the day of a thousand roses.

Annalisse's mouth went dry, and she sat back in the chair. She couldn't tell if the bag was still empty or if something was waiting inside this time.

Alec winced. "Big, scared eyes. I wasn't expecting that reaction." Alec walked around his desk and crouched in front of her.

She took the soft pouch from him and felt a box inside. "Alec. I've had so much thrown at me lately." Annalisse handed back the bag without meeting his eyes. "Please. I can't do 'heavy' right now." Tears threatened, but she kept them at bay.

"Okay." With a wounded puppy look, he laid the bag in the drawer, then covering her hands with his own, he said, "We are wasting so much precious time. It took your aunt's disappearance for me to snap out of it. I made you a promise on Crete that I wouldn't go back to my old ways, and it seems… I have." Alec coaxed her up and held her. "Art lady, I don't want to spend another moment without you."

Just a few days ago, she longed to hear him admit he'd spent too much time traveling. She whispered, "I love you, Alec. Have patience."

Voices filtered near the barn. She broke their embrace. "Someone's here. Are you expecting Bill again?"

Three raps tapped on the barn wall. "Knock, knock. Anyone here?"

Annalisse jumped at Jillian's words.

"Damn Jillian. What's she doing here? I thought she was locked up. Shh. Maybe she'll go away," Annalisse said softly, but her heart clambered away in her chest.

"Annalisse. It's Jeremy! Your housekeeper told us you were in the barn. We'd like to talk to you."

Annalisse went to Alec's desk and rustled papers. She motioned for Alec to answer.

"We're in here," Alec said nonchalantly.

"Very busy." Annalisse contributed with a shrug.

"Here you are!" Jeremy's forced enthusiasm and sinister grin made Annalisse ill. He looked pointedly at his sister, as if they'd rehearsed and it was his turn to talk. "Jillian cleared up your misunderstanding about Mom."

"*My misunderstanding?*" Annalisse's pulse ratcheted up. "Jillian has a lot to answer for. How dare you, you sanctimonious—"

"Have a seat." Alec gestured at a couple of straight-backed chairs in front of the bookcase.

Annalisse shot a what-the-hell glance at Alec, who'd stopped her rant.

"Don't take this out on me!" Jeremy shouted.

Jillian planted her wide hips and jingling bracelets into a seat and pointed to the other for her brother. She was quieter than usual, but she'd managed to look down her nose at Annalisse.

"Where did Kate go?" Annalisse blurted.

"I haven't a clue." Jillian's chin went higher. "We've been kinda busy with Daddy." She drew out his name like a child would.

"Shut it, Jillian." Jeremy added a headshake. "She means— As you know, Dad is in a bit of trouble and—"

"Shit, man. Committing murder and faking suicide is more than a 'bit of trouble.' Don't you know what he did?" Alec's question held barbs.

"We haven't officially met. I'm Jeremy Walker." He stood and offered Alec a lawyerly handshake. "This is my sister, Jillian."

"I gathered that. State your business."

"Weren't you arrested?" Annalisse peered past Jeremy to the petulant woman-child in the chair behind him. "Who'd you bribe to get bail? Give out any *special* favors?"

Jillian flung her hair back and snarled, "Take that back."

Jeremy's eyes rolled. "Dad needs high-powered counsel, and I can't pay for that kind of legal defense. Well, I have the money, but I'm not using *my* personal funds. He got himself into this mess." He fell into his chair. "That's what brings me here… us here." His sister pinched his thigh, and he jumped. "Stop it, Jilli."

"Time out." Annalisse held up her hand. "We want the truth."

Jillian's nose shot higher, if that were possible, but offered no snide remarks.

"How long have you known your father was alive?" Annalisse asked Jillian with folded arms. "Did you tell him to fake his death?"

"Of course not." Jillian huffed. "Daddy did his own thing. He didn't tell me or Jeremy. My husband saw him at a jobsite. I wouldn't know he was alive if Brian hadn't seen him there."

"Saw him where?" Alec asked.

"In Seattle. He came to Washington to keep an eye on me." Jillian used her bratty smile. "Brian said the man looked too much like Daddy laying a retaining wall. I had to check. He was surprised."

"Jig-is-up surprised, I bet," Alec added. "Or he was running out of money and *wanted* you to find him."

"You don't know him, so shut up!" Jillian shouted, shaking her finger at him.

"Jilli, be quiet," Jeremy shot back. "She's known for about a year. I was unaware."

"What about the murder of that poor homeless man? Did either of you know about that?" Annalisse leaned on the edge of Alec's desk, holding the corners.

"Absolutely not. Daddy's been staying with me and the kids for a while. He wants his farm back. He told us what Mom did, so who could blame him for what he did. Stupid whore." Jillian's mouth twisted .

Annalisse gasped. "She's your mother, you spoiled brat. She doesn't deserve that."

"You don't know anything."

"Normal people get a divorce when they have marital problems. They don't swan dive off a bridge to make an exit." Alec pointed out. "Jeremy paid your bail?"

Jillian nodded slowly. "Daddy didn't get bail. The judge said he was a flight risk because he disappeared before. He can't leave jail." Her eyes sparkled wetly.

"I'm so worried about him." Jillian swabbed away the first trickle down her cheek.

"Committing a homicide will do that to ya." Annalisse took pleasure in the flip comment that made Jillian curse. "You and your dad worked together to fake her out so that he could make his grand entrance, right?"

"Daddy asked me to set things up for him in Massachusetts, so I did." She rotated one of her bracelets, then smoothed her blouse over her bulging midriff. "Wish I could've been there when he walked in. What a hoot. But I had nothin' to do with that dead man at our farm." She shook her head furiously. "Nothin' to do with murder."

"Why are you here?" Alec asked.

"Dad wants to sell Walker Farm," Jeremy said.

"Yeah, the made-up FOR SALE sign got you going, didn't it?" Jillian gloated. "That was my idea to throw you toward my brother. It bought Daddy time."

"Dad needs good lawyers, and I want my loan repaid. Selling is the only way to cover both. Mom told me long ago she wanted Annalisse to have the farm. That's why we're here. To give you the first option on the homestead."

Annalisse understood. If she couldn't come up with enough to buy the farm, they figured Alec would buy it for her. "You know I don't have that kind of money, Jeremy. The farm has to be worth at least a million."

Jeremy gave her a sly look. "It's worth much more than that to us."

"Where's your mom going to live when she gets back? She'll be homeless, you know." Alec was disgusted.

"We've already thought of that. Mom will come to Washington. She's always nagging me to see the grand-kids. I'll have a built-in babysitter." Jillian clapped her hands a couple of times. "Yay me."

No way. They were milking it hard. Kate would rather be boiled in hot tar and have her skin torn off than move from her friends and live in a strange city. With Jillian. They'd hatched the story to make Alec feel sorry for the Walker's situation and take advantage of his feelings.

"What's your price?" Alec asked.

"Nooo." Annalisse begged him not to get drawn into the ambush. "He's not interested."

"Three million," Jeremy said coolly.

Annalisse coughed. "You're crazier than your father. The farm isn't worth that, and you know it."

"It depends on how badly the buyer wants the property. No one's forcing you, Annalisse. But we thought it was only fair to offer to you first. If you decline… well, it goes to the highest bidder."

"Is Ethan gone? What have you done with the sheep?" Annalisse asked, casting around for something to distract Jeremy. She needed to think.

"We'll send them to slaughter, I suppose." Jillian's contempt for the stock fouled the air.

"Damn you, Jillian. I've never seen anyone so self-absorbed in my life."

"Hey!" Jillian got to her feet.

Alec caught Annalisse's arm and settled it around his waist, then said calmly, "When do you need an answer, Jeremy?"

"By tomorrow morning. Dad's attorney requires a retainer. A big one—and soon."

Annalisse's shakes worsened, and she squeezed Alec tighter. "Leave, please. I need to speak to Alec privately." She turned away from her horrible cousins—*siblings!*—and buried her face in Alec's chest.

"Annalisse has your number. We'll be in touch." Alec took her in his arms.

Behind them, the unwelcome guests shuffled out of the office and disappeared into the evening. The weight of their presence lifted from Annalisse's shoulders.

"Alec, that's too much. Let them find another way," she mumbled into his shirt. "I won't help them. Jeremy has no right to manipulate you like this."

"Shh." He cradled the back of her head in his hand. "We hold the key to everything, and they know it. If Jeremy can't sell the farm fast, his dad will end up with a court-appointed attorney. At least they didn't demand we pay Ted's legal fees in addition to the sale."

Annalisse took his hand and then wrapped his muscular arm around her shoulders as they returned to the house.

***

Annalisse crept with Alec down the long, unfamiliar hallway beyond his comfortable master suite. This end of the hall felt anything but pleasant in its dim mustiness. He kept this end of the house closed off, and she always wondered what was hidden behind the massive carved threshold. The floor creaked, and Annalisse stifled a giggle that came from nowhere.

"Do you ever feel like you're part of a suspense movie about to open a door and come face to face with your fate?" A chill ripped through her, and she reached for his hand. "I've never been in this part of the house."

"Your fingers are blocks of ice. Trust me. Would I lead you to your doom?" Alec gave her the mischievous, killer smile that transformed a handsome man into a pagan deity. "Ready?"

With a push, the wide door swung in, and she was drenched in warm light. Magically, Alec had changed the back corner of the English Tudor home into a huge solarium.

"This is breathtaking! Why haven't we been here before?" A travertine floor, enclosed by brick fascia built to bench height, supported what seemed like acres of windows. Sunlight danced from hanging Boston ferns to glass-topped tables with Oriental lamps. Alec brought decorator touches from his drawing room, but this sunroom was airy, where the antique room was elegant.

He led her around the room. "I was saving it for a special occasion. I wanted a space as welcoming as the drawing room but completely different. Like a photographic negative. Opposites. Instead of vintage luxury centered around a showpiece hearth and mantel, we have light wood and wicker pieces that have *art lady* written all over them." He gloated, proud of knowing her so well. "Relax. We won't be disturbed. I made sure of that."

Annalisse chose the dusty-peach sofa with an assortment of watercolor throw pillows and plunked down, sinking into the cushions. The softness embraced her. "The farm is gone now. I tricked myself into believing in that dream."

"I'll buy the property in a hot minute. It's yours if you want it."

She shook her head sadly. "Kate wouldn't approve, and I can't let you."

"The offer is on the table. Yours and Kate's happiness are all I want."

"Where is she? Dammit, I need to talk to her."

"She won't stay away forever."

"How do you know? All my life, the farm sustained me. My go-to place when I had to fix myself or figure out my life. I don't belong in Goshen anymore. It was all lies and deceit and heartbreak. Kate left, maybe because she's ashamed. I mean… Mom." She rubbed her cheek on his sleeve. "I can't get used to calling her that. Ted told me he'd purchased the farm for himself, not his wife. I believe *it* needed us more than we needed *it*." She forced a ragged breath. "There it is. My honest truth. I can break free of that tether now."

"You sure?"

"Positive. As long as I can visit Brookehaven for an occasional fix to see Harriet?" She laughed, hoping she didn't sound too pathetic.

"I'd like more than the occasional visit, if that's okay with you." He kissed her temple and whispered, "I love you like no one else can."

Annalisse jolted. "What did you say?"

Alec shifted, facing her directly. "You've been holding back from me since you got here on Saturday. I saw it when I walked through the door from the rainstorm. Sweetness, when my mind wanders, it's always to you. It's not the corporation or the horses or the promise of a vet clinic that moves me. I can be the man who takes you on moonlit strolls, horses around, literally, and makes *us* the priority. I knew in Crete we belonged together."

A hot tear rolled down her cheek. "I still feel guilty about that beautiful night in the villa. Gen was still a hostage."

"And you saved her."

"Yeah, we did that, didn't we?" She clutched his hand in hers. "Please tell Jeremy we'll pass on the farm, but I'd like to find a home for the animals."

"I'll have Hank hook up the trailer when you're ready."

"Bring them here? They don't belong on a thoroughbred farm."

"What better excuse to build the brood mares a bigger facility. The Walker Farm gang can have their old barn. Do you think they can manage in the big pasture until I get the new barn built?" Alec smiled reassuringly. "We'll take the livestock off his hands."

"He'll be furious with us for turning him down."

Alec pulled back. "If Jeremy refuses, we'll buy you the flock of your dreams. Any breed you ever wanted—and bring them to Brookehaven. How's that sound?"

"Like a bribe."

"Maybe a little." He bent low and took her mouth in a tender kiss. "If it'll bring you to me more often… since I'll be home more—after I call a board meeting. With their approval, I'm selling the corporation."

A peace enveloped her like a warm embrace.

Alec slid to the end of the couch and pulled out the drawer on a side table, retrieving a familiar blue velvet bag.

"We left that in the office. I saw you put it away."

"It's still there." Alec laid the bag in her lap.

She hesitated, torn by conflicting thoughts. "Kate's on the run, and Ted's going to be tried for murder. Alec, before we make any future plans, I have to talk to my mother." Annalisse handed the small satchel to him.

In the quiet that followed, the twittering birds outside lifted her heart. She could feel his eyes on her, and she knew.

He wanted to be hers.

He *could* be hers.

If he would wait for her.

Her plans no longer included Walker Farm, and like the farm, her Drury name was never destined to be hers. But that was the least of her worries.

"I told you. No pressure." Alec looked away and dropped the bag back into the drawer. "As long as you need." His mouth went tight and grim.

"Will you tell me where Kate went if I promise not to bother her?"

He nabbed the fuzzy throw and draped it over her lap. "I honestly don't know."

"But you helped her?"

He nodded. "I did. I gave her money." Alec held up his palm. "She wouldn't tell me where she was going. Honest. Bill couldn't get anything from her other than she was pretty shook up and so was Ethan. Seeing her dead husband had to be a shock." He snuggled under the throw with her.

"Ethan. He's with her? I hope she didn't travel alone. I miss her so much. When you talk to Jeremy in person, I'd like to go with you."

"I'll set it up for tomorrow." Alec patted her thigh beneath the throw. "Have you thought about paying Ted a visit in jail?"

Annalisse tossed her head. "That's our next stop."

"It won't be pleasant."

"It won't be for him. I'll make sure of it. Kate's a different story. I may need you with me when that showdown comes." Neither meeting promised glad tidings. "Some vacation week. We made it to a bed-and-breakfast but not how we'd planned."

"How about taking a leave of absence from the gallery? I'm calling a meeting in Italy next week. I can get enough directors together on short notice. Can I tempt the historian in you with art, museums, and twelfth-century architecture? Or maybe a carriage tour of Palermo?"

Her heart soared, and speech failed her momentarily. "Oooh, that would be incredible. Do you think Gen will give me the time off?"

"She'll insist. And I'm sure Chase won't mind taking up some of the slack." Alec took her hand under the throw. "I'd like to show you Italy's grand history, but if you'd rather not… I won't beg." He smiled bashfully.

"I'd like to hear you beg." She laughed, happier than she'd been for far too long. "Of course I'll go. If your mom agrees." Annalisse rested against Alec's shoulder. "Have you wondered about the man who pulled Kate away from Ted thirty years ago? I can't believe he wouldn't want to know me. I feel a connection—in New Zealand—and that eerie mask holds answers. It's calling me there." She took a labored breath from another chill. "I don't know who I'll find, or what I'll find out, but I have to learn more about Ethan."

"You may not like what you find."

"We have no future together until I discover the soul within that mask."

"Bill keeps it until we're ready. Let's take the European trip first." Alec kissed her temple.

"And get through tomorrow." Annalisse snuggled closer to him. "Hmm. The Italian experience. Museums, statues, and painted ceilings. Nothing can hurt us there."

THE END

Ewephoric Publishing

Dear Reader,

If you enjoyed *Spent Identity*, please consider leaving a review on your favorite book site. Be sure to sign up for free books, giveaways, and news on future releases in the Annalisse Series as well as other books by Marlene M. Bell. Visit Marlene's website at https://www.marlenembell.com, Twitter: https://www.twitter/ewephoric, and Facebook: https://www.facebook.com/marlenembell.

SPENT IDENTITY
BOOK CLUB QUESTIONS

1. Did the first page draw you into the story? If not, how would you have started the first chapter?
2. Who was your favorite character(s)? Why?
3. Do you have a favorite line from the book?
4. Do you have a favorite scene in *Spent Identity*?
5. Did you like the relationship between Annalisse and Alec? Explain.
6. Was there too much or not enough romance in this second series book?
7. Who was your least favorite character? Why?
8. Did you feel the dialog between characters was realistic? If not, which character needed more work to be believable?
9. Would you have moved the setting in *Spent Identity* to another place? If so, where?
10. If this book were made into a movie, which actors would play these characters?
11. Do you know a person like Aunt Kate? Did you find her character interesting?
12. Do you like the tight writing style, or would you prefer more detail?
13. What was your biggest takeaway from the book? Was there a major theme?
14. Did you like the ending? How did it make you feel?

15. Were all loose ends tied up at the end of *Spent Identity*? If not, what tidbit did the author leave to your imagination for the next books?
16. If you haven't read the first book, *Stolen Obsession*, are you curious enough to read it now that you've read *Spent Identity*? Do you want to read the next installment in the series, *Calico Raven*, book three?

Watch for the Marlene's next book in the Annalisse Series

CONNECT AT:
Marlenembell.com
facebook.com/marlenembell
Follow Marlene on Twitter @ewephoric

For her award winning sheep photography and related gifts, request Marlene's full-color catalog. Please visit:
TexasSheep.com

ACKNOWLEDGMENTS

So many people have contributed to my writing journey with this series. Thank you all.

Elizabeth Kracht of Kimberley Cameron & Associates worked on the early developmental elements of *Spent Identity*. Liz is my go-to Pro for getting the story right. Because her vision is *always* right!

Annie Sarac of The Editing Pen worked her editorial magic on *Spent Identity* and gave the story the sincerity and meaning it needed. I lost track of the passes she made on the manuscript. I couldn't have finished this book without Annie's expertise. Onward to the next series installment!

Ellen Campbell is a marvel with word choice and her ability to crop the narrative succinctly. Ellen looks at novels like no other editor I've ever worked with. My writing says more with less, and I'm eternally grateful to her.

Patti Bulkeley read the all-important early chapters and simmered on them for months. She held her tongue until the final edit and recommended that

I change the blah opening. It's always a good idea to heed Patti's insightful suggestions, and I listened.

In the late 1980s, I quit a lucrative full-time job in the San Francisco Bay Area. *Gregg* knew I wanted to work for myself and encouraged me to do so. Today, I get to create at home—write, take pictures, sell through a catalog, and play with the sheep. My husband's support and love have made this possible. I am so blessed to have you, Gregg! I love you.

A big thank you to my readers and followers online and on social media. I sincerely appreciate each and every one of your emails, comments, and book reviews!

Any and all mistakes are my own.

BOOKS BY MARLENE M. BELL

Among the Sheep (out of print)
Stolen Obsession ~ Annalisse Series Book One
Spent Identity ~ Annalisse Series Book Two
Trading Paint ~ a short story, Volume 5 Texas Authors
Calico Raven ~ Annalisse Series Book Three (coming soon)

ABOUT THE AUTHOR

Marlene M. Bell is an award-winning writer and acclaimed artist as well as a photographer. Her sheep landscapes grace the covers of *Sheep!*, *The Shepherd*, *Ranch & Rural Living*, and *Sheep Industry News*, to name a few.

Her catalog venture, Ewephoric, began in 1985 out of her desire to locate personalized sheep stationery. She rarely found sheep products through catalogs and set out to design them herself. Order Ewephoric gifts online or request a catalog at TexasSheep.com.

Marlene and her husband, Gregg, reside in beautiful East Texas on a wooded ranch with their dreadfully spoiled horned Dorset sheep, a large Maremma guard dog named Tia, along with Hollywood, Leo, and Squeaks, the cats that believe they rule the household—and do.

Made in the USA
Monee, IL
11 March 2023

29672976R00225